Born and raised in rural New Zealand, [...] Melbourne. For the last twelve years he [...] column for *The Roar*, Australia's leading online sports website, [...] has published two non-fiction books: *A World in Conflict: The Global Battle for Rugby Supremacy* and *A Year in the Life and Death of the Melbourne Rebels*. This is his first novel.

GEOFF PARKES

WHEN THE DEEP DARK BUSH SWALLOWS YOU WHOLE

PENGUIN BOOKS

UK | USA | Canada | Ireland | Australia
India | New Zealand | South Africa | China

Penguin Books is part of the Penguin Random House group of companies whose addresses can be found at global.penguinrandomhouse.com

Penguin Random House Australia

First published by Penguin Books in 2025

Copyright © Geoff Parkes, 2025

The moral right of the author has been asserted.

All rights reserved. No part of this publication may be reproduced, published, performed in public or communicated to the public in any form or by any means without prior written permission from Penguin Random House Australia Pty Ltd or its authorised licensees.

Cover photography by John Steele/Alamy
Cover design by Adam Laszczuk © Penguin Random House Australia Pty Ltd
Typeset in 12/17 pt Adobe Garamond Pro by Midland Typesetters, Australia

Printed and bound in Australia by Griffin Press, an accredited ISO AS/NZS 14001 Environmental Management Systems printer

A catalogue record for this book is available from the National Library of Australia

ISBN 978 1 76134 928 7

penguin.com.au

We at Penguin Random House Australia acknowledge that Aboriginal and Torres Strait Islander peoples are the Traditional Custodians and the first storytellers of the lands on which we live and work. We honour Aboriginal and Torres Strait Islander peoples' continuous connection to Country, waters, skies and communities. We celebrate Aboriginal and Torres Strait Islander stories, traditions and living cultures; and we pay our respects to Elders past and present.

New Zealand, January 1983

1
Emilia

New Zealand was greener than Emilia could ever have imagined. The trees, the paddocks, the seemingly endless miles of rolling hills . . . different hues, but all undeniably green. The change in pitch as the train clattered across a wooden bridge had nudged her from her sleep. They were now in what was called the King Country. Emilia found that gently amusing. King of what, exactly? Sheep? They were everywhere, thousands of them dotting the paddocks. Little mobile floor rugs and pullovers, ring-barking the hills with their hooves. No wonder Sanna had so easily found work here as a wool handler in a shearing gang. The supply and demand were untapped. It was like making and selling vodka to the Russians.

The town slowly revealed itself; a scattering of houses at first, then gradually, denser clusters. Emilia, wearing her trademark jeans and black boots, flicked at her neat, shoulder-length black hair and stepped nervously onto the asphalt platform. Placing her pack against the sign, *Nashville, King Country, NZ*, she noticed she was the only person alighting.

'Can I help you, miss?'

The man had appeared from nowhere. He was old, older than her grandfather, a Māori, wearing a dark blue uniform.

'Here, I'll take your pack,' he said.

They shuffled off the platform. 'Postie Plus' said the large red sign atop the shop directly opposite. Emilia's eyes were drawn to the racks of clothing spilling from the doorway, across the footpath. They did things differently here. At home, post offices were for buying stamps and sending parcels and letters.

'Can you direct me to the police station, please?'

'Police? You haven't been here long enough to get into trouble.'

Emilia chose not to respond.

'Down this way, one block, then at the corner, turn right.' He pointed as he spoke, his forefinger gnarled and bent. Arthritic, she assumed. 'It's along there.'

Emilia nodded. 'Thank you.'

He tipped his cap. 'You're welcome, miss. And best not to talk to any strangers, eh?'

Emilia found the counter of the police station unattended. She pressed the buzzer.

A constable presented himself, younger than her. Lance Peterson, his badge read.

'Can I help you?' he asked. He was as green as the landscape outside, but the tone of his voice was warm.

'My name is Emilia Sovernen.'

'I'm sorry,' the constable interrupted. 'Did you say Sovernen?'

'Yes. Emilia Sovernen.'

Peterson raised a finger. 'One minute,' he said, before excusing himself.

Another man appeared, this one with a large barrel chest, deeper voice and a presence that spilled over the counter. 'Ms Sovernen, I'm Detective Inspector Tom Harten.'

They each took a moment to eye the other.

'Ms Sovernen, you've travelled a long way. May I ask how long you're planning to stay in Nashville?'

Emilia tolerated the question. Wasn't it obvious? 'For as long as it takes to find out what happened to my sister.'

DI Tom Harten pushed a mug of tea across the table. White enamel, its blue rim looked as chipped and worn as he did. 'I'm sorry I don't have a proper cup and saucer,' he said. 'Sugar?'

'No, thank you.'

'Sweet enough, eh?'

She hadn't come here for small talk.

'Right, then . . . where would you like me to start?' he said.

'It's more about where we finish.'

'Listen,' he fidgeted uncomfortably. 'I'm sure you understand how allowing you this meeting is highly irregular. The investigation was very thorough. The interdepartmental investigator said so in his report. As honest as we sit here today, I promise you we did everything we could. I'm very sorry for Sanna, and for your family. But the fact is, there are times, not very often, but rare occasions, when we don't get a result.'

Emilia sipped her tea. 'A result? Like a football game?'

He sighed. 'You have a copy of that report, you already know the evidence. Out of respect for you travelling halfway around the world, I'm happy to give you some of my time. But I need to be honest with you. I'm not going to assist you to run another investigation.'

'So, this is like, how you say . . . a cold case?'

'That's not a term I'd use, no. But –'

'But you stopped looking for her. Right?'

'As you know, it's been almost a year. If more evidence came to light, and it stood up, then of course we'd intensify the investigation.'

Emilia pondered his comment. 'So, what do you need from me? For you to reopen the case.'

'Are you sure you want to go down this path?'

'Why else did I travel all this way? To be patronised?'

Tom drew breath. 'A body. If we had a body, the case would be escalated.'

Emilia barely flinched. She could see she'd impressed him. She was made of sturdy stock. 'Or the person responsible?'

'Of course. But trust me, we're not getting to him without a body first.'

'Him? Or them?'

'Well yes, either. We have an open mind on that.'

'I have an open mind too. Don't you think that is helpful? An outsider's perspective?'

'Potentially, yes. But don't forget that we brought in detectives from outside. No assumptions were made about potential local suspects. We stripped everything right back.'

'From outside? Different town or city maybe, but still people thinking the same as you. Not Finnish thinking.'

'No, not Finnish thinking,' he said, clearly fishing around for a way to move things along. 'Ms Sovernen, dress this up however you like, dance around the edges about different cultures and so on, but the bottom line is that your sister Sanna, she disappeared without a trace. Until we find some hard evidence, something that links her to a person of interest or a location, then I'm sorry to say, she is still a missing person, and –'

She caught his eye and stopped him in his tracks. She knew his words were intended as a conclusion. A full stop. But her determination told him she was interpreting them as a challenge.

All of a sudden, his cold case didn't seem so cold anymore.

2
Ryan

Ryan Bradley strolled into the offices of Jack Nash Real Estate and found Jack sitting at his desk, waiting for him.

'Bang on time!' said the older man. Jack's shirt was an exact match for the paint on the office walls. Too much blue. He indicated for Ryan to sit.

'So, here we are again. I still can't believe it didn't sell last year. It's such a great house. Your mother looked after it tremendously well.'

'You know why it didn't sell, Jack. You never sold a house for months after Sanna went missing.'

'Well . . . buyer demand dropped off for a while, that's true. But the town's over that now. Stock is moving again. In fact, last month saw record sales for the agency. An all-time record!'

A tick under six foot tall and muscular in all the right places, Ryan shifted uncomfortably in the chair. It was built for a midget.

'I'm sorry,' said Jack. 'Please excuse my thoughtlessness. People have moved on, but obviously you worked closely with Sanna in the shearing gang. It must have been a tough year for you.'

'It helped going back to Dunedin to university. But yeah, this summer, it was hard coming back and getting through the shearing run.'

'Well, anything I can do to help . . . you know that.'

Ryan nodded.

'The good news is that while prices definitely came off a bit in the . . . you know . . . in the aftermath, they seem to have recovered. We should be able to get what you were hoping for last time.'

'I don't care about the money. This is my final year at university. To be honest, I just want to sell, and move on.'

Jack pushed a 'Terms and Conditions of Engagement' form across the desk. 'Are you sure about cutting ties? Nashville is your home, Ryan.'

Ryan sighed and signed the form. 'Home's still home, right? But the things I want to achieve – don't take this the wrong way, or do take it the wrong way, whatever . . . this isn't the place to do it.'

Jack took the form back. 'Sounds like you've made a few decisions.'

'A friend of mine, well, not a friend, but he told me . . . you have to stand for something. I'm going on twenty-three. I've done a lot of thinking over this last year. It used to bug me what other people think, but now, with Sanna going missing, the best thing I can do is to stop feeling sorry for myself and get on with life.'

Jack nodded. 'Just don't forget Nashville. This is where your true friends are.'

'You mean Philip? It's not like it was, Jack. He thinks I think I'm too good for him and all that. And I'm over trying to prove that I'm not. I honestly don't know what happened there.'

'If it's any consolation, I don't think he thinks any better of us. Me and Lois, we hardly get a word out of him these days.'

Ryan stood up. 'You're family. You'll sort it out.'

'I'll put the For Sale sign back up tomorrow,' said Jack. 'As soon as there's a decent offer on the table, I'll let you know.'

Ryan shook Jack's hand, another task ticked off his list.

3
Emilia

Emilia suffered the detective and his watery, lukewarm tea out of necessity. Courtesy too; he was, after all, polite and clearly not a buffoon. He was just as her father had described him, after his trip to Nashville in the days immediately after Sanna's disappearance.

Emilia felt shame for not having travelled to New Zealand with her father. He'd insisted that she remain home and try to focus on her business clients. With her mother's aversion to air travel, and the hysterical state she was in, it felt like a sound decision to stay and keep watch. As it turned out, Emilia was all over the place at work; emotional, unproductive and testy. She should have been with her father.

But that was then. A year later, she was determined to do everything she could, either to find out what happened, or to help the police find out. Then she'd be able to return home, face her parents, and tell them honestly that everything that could have been done for Sanna, they had done.

There was a detachment and smugness to Detective Harten that didn't sit well. She sensed his casual indifference to incoming matters and the glacial pace at which the wheels of justice turned. If he was the man leading the investigation into Sanna's disappearance, it was no surprise that they were no closer to finding her today than they were a year ago.

No closer? Who was she kidding; at least back then they were looking for her. Now, it was: 'Show me a body and then I'll try harder to find out who did it.' This was her sister they were talking about. Bright, sparkling, precious Sanna. Who deserved so much more than a missing persons file at some country police station, in the middle of nowhere, in the middle of a country on the other side of the world.

At least he'd been good enough to step her through the main details of the case. She knew them anyway, by now better than him she was certain, but it was still important to hear things from the police's perspective. Even if she disapproved of their handling.

'I don't know what people have told you about Nashville,' he said, 'but we made a profile for every male between fifteen and eighty years of age. If the person responsible was included in that lot, I'm fairly certain I'd know about it.'

'Where I come from, Detective Harten, fairly certain means not certain. You understand what I am saying?'

'As I said, we've kept an open mind throughout, and we still are. But we are as certain as we can be that Sanna did not leave Nashville of her own accord. The most plausible theory is that she was picked up on the side of the road, by someone not from this town, and taken to somewhere else.'

'You use the word theory. Is it really theory, or is it guesswork?'

'I've been transparent with you, Ms Sovernen, please don't push me. It is exactly what I told your father. We are guided by evidence. And in this case, we simply don't have the evidence to say with any certainty what happened.'

'But . . .?' He had to have a view. They always had a view.

'If you're asking for my personal opinion . . . off the record, my belief is that we are dealing with a serial killer.'

Serial killer. She had been waiting for the cue. 'Roisin McCarthy, twenty-three years old, a visitor from Ireland, seen hitchhiking north of Gisborne on the 23rd September 1970, reported missing: despite a widespread investigation, no trace was ever found. Ruled by the coroner to have died at the hand of a person or persons unknown.'

Emilia spoke with mechanical precision, as matter-of-factly as a headmaster calling the school roll. 'Stella Herbert, a native Māori New Zealander, twenty-nine years old, seen getting into a white station wagon or similar vehicle, on the night of 17th February 1973, on the outskirts of Kaikohe. Excuse me if I don't have that pronunciation perfect. Again, no further trace was ever found. And Stigi Hofsteder, a West German tourist, recently turned twenty, separated from her travelling companion after arriving off the inter-island ferry in Picton, on the 4th November 1977, seemingly vanishing into thin air, save for her scarf being discovered in a roadside ditch, two weeks later, seventy-five kilometres from where she disappeared.'

'Very impressive,' he conceded.

'Then there was Mary Atkins, last seen hitchhiking on the outskirts of National Park, heading north, on the 3rd March 1980. Not more than forty kilometres from this very police station. She never arrived in Auckland as planned, no further trace ever found. And finally, 20th February 1982, Sanna Sovernen. Somewhere in this King Country of yours, she disappears without trace.'

'Five girls in twelve years.'

'Yes. And of course your news media ties all of that together. Because there are similarities, and because of the timing, the gap between each incident makes this plausible. And because a serial killer is a big story.'

'You already know, we made sure Sanna's story got national prominence. If there was someone out there who had any inkling about who did this, if it was their boyfriend or husband or someone in their family, they would know about this and have every opportunity to come forward.'

'Let me run something by you, Detective. In the overwhelming majority of cases, serial killers work within a geographic boundary they are familiar with. These five cases . . . mostly they are spread far and wide. Hours of driving in between. Where would the killer go without risking being caught or making himself known? Where would he sleep? Eat? Where would he hide a body? Where there is no risk of the body being found, or him being seen? In a place he doesn't know?'

The DI sat silently.

'In one area, then yes, perhaps this is possible. And your countryside, your native bush, it is perfect for swallowing secrets. But in all of these different areas, spread across New Zealand?' She drew breath then continued. 'Stella Herbert: criminal convictions for burglary, wilful damage, assault on a minor, a known drug user, sexual history longer than your arm, Detective. There are a hundred reasons and ways for her to have died. Stigi Hofsteder: known to have argued violently with her boyfriend on the ferry crossing from Wellington before she disappeared. He was the prime suspect but with no witnesses and no body, he was never charged. Eventually, he was allowed to return home to West Germany.'

'Yes,' he nodded. 'And your point is?'

'Mary Atkins: credible reports link her disappearance to the release on the same day of a prisoner from the Waikune prison facility, located only a few kilometres from where she was last sighted. A man who six weeks later committed suicide, said by an acquaintance to be because of his guilt.'

'I repeat, your point is?'

'My point is . . . there is no mysterious serial killer, is there, Detective?'

'That's Detective Inspector. Ms Sovernen, I don't wish to be rude, but I have other duties to attend to. If you don't mind, I think we'll leave things there for today.'

'This is a small town. I understand how desirable it is for police to be protective of their community. You have to live with the people.

I get how you want to move on. But this list you made of your local people, this profiling you speak of, you need to revisit this.'

Tom wasn't listening anymore – he was already up out of his seat, on his way out of the interview room.

Emilia followed him to the door, raising her voice across the top of the young Constable Peterson, who was sitting at his desk, doing nothing in particular. 'You may not like to admit it, Detective, but you and I both know something happened to Sanna, right here in this town. Nashville. And if you won't find out who was responsible, I will find someone who will!'

She fixed a glare on Peterson. It was evident that in his time on the job he hadn't seen anybody challenge his DI like she had just done.

He quivered. 'Would you like some more tea?'

Emilia needed more than weak tea. 'Where do I find this shearing gang?'

4
Ryan

Outside, blue gave way to yellow. Jack's real estate office was located next door to the cinema, the tall glass doors covered, head to tail, with posters showing off New Zealand's most famous yellow Mini. The movie *Goodbye Pork Pie* had been a smash hit last year in all the main centres, and was still going strong on a victory lap around the regional towns. Like everyone, Ryan had laughed at its irreverent Kiwi humour. Sanna would have enjoyed it too, he was sure of that. Explaining all of the locations and in-jokes to her would have been fun.

He peered through the glass into the foyer, the carpet a kaleidoscope of competing colours and patterns. Nothing inside had changed since he remembered his mother taking him to see *The Sound of Music* when he couldn't have been more than five or six. And later on, when he was old enough to go unchaperoned, him and Philip watching *Battle of Britain*, open-mouthed, the cinema screen filling with bloodied goggles, as a Spitfire pilot made the ultimate sacrifice.

There was another time, when they were thirteen, when Philip challenged him to a bike race, into the cinema foyer, then up opposite sides of the theatre, in a mad dash to the top of the stairs, before racing back down again to the footpath outside. All while a film was playing in front of the Saturday matinee crowd. Their hi-jinks earned gasps and cheers, but saw them banned from the cinema for a month; a small price for the plaudits they had thrown their way for having the guts to pull off such a stunt. Ryan won the race, after Philip fell off his bike near the top.

Ryan realised it was another thing Philip never really got over. Things had been a bit off between him and Philip since he'd started university. In the three years Ryan had been working as a wool presser over the Christmas holidays, those catch-ups had become fewer, and more forced. Imagine that: the two of them close friends all their lives, now butting heads, the start of it traced back to a silly pushbike race inside a cinema.

Ryan noted the advertised session start time: 7.30pm. Even though he'd seen it twice already, he was momentarily tempted. But that risked running into people who would ask him about Sanna's disappearance. Or enduring them whispering behind his back. Nearly a year had passed. Why couldn't people just move on?

There had been days, long dry afternoons in the woolshed, when Ryan ached for Sanna. What hurt the most wasn't his grief, but the dread of what might have happened to her. That she'd had terrible pain inflicted upon her. Died a horrible death. That she'd been sexually assaulted. He hadn't talked to anyone about it; who was there to talk to, anyway? At the beginning of this new season, Carl had addressed the gang as they sat around the dinner table, and they paid their respects to Sanna there and then. Carl's message was clear. They needed to stay staunch, honour her spirit out of love and respect, but then move on, not keep revisiting things in a sad or maudlin way. In her time with the gang, Sanna had been strong. Now, they all needed to be strong for her.

Carl always talked sense, and his words helped Ryan realise that it was the same for Sanna's death as it was for his mother's. You never stopped loving and you never stopped remembering. But the grieving process was finite.

He was clear now. There would be no hiding in a car-chase movie. He would drive back down to the shearers' quarters at Neville Hanigan's farm, in time for dinner, fill his stomach with Ronnie's roast mutton, sleep it off, and then tomorrow at 5am sharp, he would knuckle down into his job, and leave Sanna behind him.

'Hello, Ryan.'

The detective inspector's voice snapped him back into the present. 'Mr Harten.'

'Tom.'

'Yes. Tom.'

'I was driving past and saw you standing there.'

'I'm putting the house back up for sale,' Ryan said, nodding towards Jack's office.

'Good luck with it. Probably better you move on.'

'What do you mean by that?'

'Listen, son, don't be sensitive. You're growing up, just find somewhere to go and do it. Get on with your life.'

Ryan could make his own decisions. He didn't need any help, even if it was well intended.

'I'll warn you now,' Tom continued, 'I don't want any silly business happening, but I've just met with someone. She's staying at the Riverside Motel.'

Ryan wasn't sure what he was getting at.

'She's from Finland. Emilia. Emilia Sovernen. I expect she'll want to speak with you.'

Ryan shuddered, his feet fixed to the spot. He searched for a response, a question, anything . . . but no words came. He wanted to tell Tom that he'd just put Sanna behind him, but there was an electric charge coursing through his body. Evidently, he hadn't.

'Like I said, no silly business. It's time for everyone in Nashville to move on.'

Ryan never heard Tom's words. His head felt like it contained a swarm of locusts. *Move on?* That's what everyone wanted to do. But had everyone done enough for her? Her sister Emilia obviously didn't think so. And Ryan, in that moment, standing at the entrance to the movie theatre, knew it too. The bush didn't devour people like Sanna. Not on its own. Somebody had put her there. The time for glib acceptance and running from the truth was over. It was time to do the right thing by Sanna.

Fourteen months earlier, November 1981

5
Ryan

Ryan wasn't a morning person. He cursed the new day and the throng of intemperate, bleating sheep; 4.55am was no hour to be swathed in their piss, shit and snot. Ammonia permeated the darkness, stabbing at his eyes as he pushed on, wading further into the tightly packed pen, thinking only of the girl, the new backpacker Carl had hired.

He had just a few minutes to fill the catching pen for each shearer before the hum of the electric motors and the buzz of the handpieces kicked in for the day. Woe betide the crackly transistor radio heralding the 5am news with a shearer walking into an empty pen.

Ryan made eye contact with a likely target, willing the sheep to move along. Bull had bragged about picking up sheep and tossing them over the rails, like bags of cement. There were times when the sheep got the better of Ryan, and he hated them for it. But never enough to overstep that line. Finally, the sheep responded, and he flicked at the next one, then another; that usually led the rest to fall in behind. He held the gate steady, and a run of Merinos slipped past. Ryan dropped his shoulder, pushing and squeezing the last few in, until his feet slipped out from underneath him and he fell onto the slimy, shitty floor. That was all he needed. His new Adidas Roms – three blue stripes set against sparkling white leather barely a fortnight ago – had already turned a weary shade of brown. He lay flat on his stomach, cursing and hoping there was no-one watching.

But she was there, looking down at him from over the railing. He closed the gate and caught his breath. He now had just three minutes to fill the other two pens.

'Don't you have anything better to do?' he said.

'This is more fun.'

Sanna Sovernen. She could laugh all she liked. She was too pretty and her hands too soft for this kind of work. He would put money on her not seeing out the season.

When he got back onto the main floor, Ryan found the farmer waiting next to the wool press.

'127 kegs is ideal,' the farmer said. 'Definitely no heavier than 130.'

Ryan knew the drill. A good operator could pump out bale after bale with little or no variation in weight. Some wool pressers counted fleeces as they went into the press, others developed a touch for it: how the wool felt in their hands and under their feet when they jumped into the press to tramp it down. Ryan desperately wanted to be *that* presser.

'How's it outside?' said Ryan. There was nothing farmers enjoyed more than being asked about the weather.

'There's a shower sweeping up the next valley, from Hanigan's farm, where your quarters are, but it'll miss us,' said the lantern-jawed farmer. 'I'll bring the rest of them down from the top paddock after lunch. You'll be working straight through the week.'

Ryan nodded. *Working straight through.* That was the job. With covered yards to protect flocks from wet weather, and the precision with which Carl organised the schedule, days off were rare.

'I drove into town yesterday,' said the farmer. 'That chap at the bank, Jack Nash's boy, Philip . . . he was asking after you.'

'Was he?'

'Wanted to know if you could handle this work.'

'Did he? And what did you tell him?'

'I said, a good chef is only as good as his next meal, not his last one.'

'Gee, thanks for nothing!'

The farmer winked at Ryan.

Ryan fitted a new wool pack into the bottom box of the press.

'I remember watching you boys play for the school first XV,' the farmer continued. 'My nephew Craig was in the same side.'

'That's right.'

'Philip Nash was a battler. One of those guys you need to make up the numbers. But you – you can play rugby.'

'I'm hoping to make the Varsity A team, when I get back down there.'

'Good luck with that,' the farmer said. 'Not that you'll get much mileage from your mate.'

'What do you mean?' asked Ryan.

'Bit of envy there, I reckon.'

Ryan laughed. 'Well, I'm not jealous of his job. He can have the bank!'

The farmer stroked his chin. 'Don't forget, one-twenty-seven kegs. Or else I'll be straight in there to tell him how shithouse you are.'

Ryan couldn't have his reputation being slagged off around town. 'Piece of piss. Leave it with me.'

He quickly scanned the floor. The girl, Sanna, was still there, watching him. Watching him with a cheeky smile on her face.

The shearers observed a strict hierarchy. Carl's was always the number-one stand; Pete, number two; then Bull took the third stand. Each shearer was assigned a rousey to pick out the belly and crutch wool with their brooms, keep the stands tidy and free of stray wool, and – when each sheep was fully shorn and dispatched through the porthole, down the race to a counting pen – to collect the fleece and transfer it to the main sorting table. They had a few seconds to trim the fleece of any discoloured wool, after which it was Ryan's job to press it into bales.

Lacey was Carl's younger sister; their combination was a given. Their brother Pete's rousey was the uncomplaining, easy-going Crystal. Sanna, the newbie, drew the short straw, working with Bull. She didn't get things right every time, but she was a hard worker. Ryan liked that about her.

The team worked silently; the pre-breakfast shift no place for chatter. Later, with a mug of tea and a hot breakfast in their bellies, and shards of natural sunlight beginning to leak into the shed, there would be time for banter. Ryan's mother had always impressed upon him, 'A job isn't worth doing if you don't do it properly.' Grateful to her for passing down her work ethic, he valued the hard, physical aspects of the job. It guaranteed he would arrive at the first rugby practice fitter and stronger than any of his teammates, whose summers favoured cruising the beaches of the Bay of Plenty and Coromandel. Each night, when dusk barely turned to dark, after he crawled into his tiny wire-sprung bed, in the shearers' quarters at Neville Hanigan's farm, Ryan thought wistfully of beaches and bikinis. But it was always only for as long as he could keep his eyes open. A minute or two, never more.

'Hurry up or you'll miss out!' yelled Ronnie, from her makeshift kitchen in the far corner of the woolshed. She was a Matenga. They were a big local family, her father a railway worker, her mother a Māori warden who, for years, had walked the streets nipping trouble in the bud. His mother would have said that Ronnie liked more of her own food than was good for her, but Ryan loved that she was a good cook. He appreciated his three square meals a day.

Ryan finished washing his arms and dried himself off with a thin, miserable towel that bore the consistency of sandpaper. He was always last to eat, choosing to refill the catching pens while the handpieces and motors were shut off, and the sheep were less edgy and more willing to run. Besides, he preferred to eat alone, able to quietly gather his thoughts, even if it risked people branding him as aloof. Growing up in Nashville was one thing. Constantly having to prove you belonged was another thing altogether. 'Coming,' he replied.

He plucked three Flintstone-sized loin chops from one of the electric frypans, scooped two fried eggs from the other, then ladled tinned spaghetti onto the remaining space on his plate. Two slices of buttered white toast went on top, cold by now, but that was how he liked them, then he took his tea and found a seat on the floor, leaning back against a timber post.

Sanna scraped her plate clean and sat down near him, flicking her two tightly bound pigtails over her shoulders.

'So, would you like me to tell you about Finland?' Her tone was musical and playful.

'How do you know I don't know all about it already?'

'Away you go then,' she said.

'You don't eat sheep for breakfast, like this, you eat reindeer.'

'Not for breakfast,' she giggled. 'And . . . anything else?'

He shrugged, maxed out on Finland already.

'It's okay,' she said. 'I didn't know much about New Zealand either before I came here.'

'So why here? Why not Australia? Or America?'

'All the cliches. Because your country is beautiful. And different to mine. And the people are so friendly.' They both looked at Bull.

Ryan laughed. 'Right.'

'It was really my girlfriend, Lise. She wanted to come here. My mother begged me not to go: too far away, too different, too dangerous. But we planned it for months, all of the places we'd visit together. Then, as soon as we arrived, she hooked up with an Austrian guy, and now I'm on my own.'

Ryan nodded.

'It's okay for me, this way,' she continued. 'I like this job: good money and it's off the normal tourist trail. You know, an authentic experience.'

'Authentic?' Ryan scanned the rest of the gang, dotted around the woolshed. 'That's one way of putting it.' He laughed, this time a little uneasily, aware that Bull was staring at them.

'I'm going to meet up with Lise again when it finishes. Before our visas expire.'

Carl's voice cut across their conversation. 'Ryan? Sorry, mate, but do you mind giving the farmer a quick hand in the yard?' He gestured towards the door. It was an instruction, not a request.

'It's okay,' Sanna said, standing up. The shearers were finishing their turn on the grinding wheel, sharpening their cutting combs; it was almost time.

Bull yelled out, 'Hey, lawyer boy! You heard him, shift your arse.'

'Can you promise me one thing?' he whispered.

'Yes?'

'On your last day here, you'll take that broom of yours and shove it right up his you know where.'

She laughed. 'I promise.'

'I mean it,' said Ryan. 'Don't let me down, okay?'

'Don't worry,' she smiled. 'I'm not going anywhere.'

6

Sanna

'Here, get some of this piss into you!'

Carl lifted bottles of beer from the crate and placed them on the red Formica top of the pub's leaner. Sanna didn't have many other bosses to compare him with, but Carl was a solid family man, friendly and fair, who prided himself on always paying his bills on time. And now, with them having cut out early, and a rare spare day tomorrow, before the start of the next shed, he had driven the gang the hour it took to get into town, and was doling out beer like he was Kris Kringle.

The Mountain View Hotel was Nashville's only pub, although Sanna had learned it was far from being the town's only drinking establishment. The business types, and most of the farmers, drank at the Workingmen's Club nearby, and you could always get a beer at the squash club, while the rugby club did a roaring trade whenever there was a match on. She'd even heard that the police station had its own bar, although she hadn't yet had the pleasure of visiting.

Naming the hotel 'The Mountain View' had been someone's idea of a joke. Standing outside on the street, you could no more see the mountain than you could the Hanging Gardens of Babylon. But she supposed it didn't matter. The locals simply referred to the main bar as the 'Gorilla Pit'.

It was DB for everyone except Bull, who insisted upon Waikato Green.

'I don't know how you drink that swamp water,' said Carl.

'Mother's milk,' said Bull.

The light reflecting off Bull's cracked glasses lens made his comment sound more sinister than it probably was. Carl had once told the gang that there was nothing wrong with Bull's eyesight, he simply chose to wear spectacles with the left side cracked, because it made him look more menacing. Between that, his brother being a patched member of the local Mongrel Mob, the spider-web tattoo that circled his neck, and his perpetual sneer, he was doing a fair job of it. Sanna found it hard to believe that Bull was in the throes of becoming a preacher. But they'd all learned not to engage him on religion.

The gang stood in a circle around the leaner and drank: to their health, to good weather, to compliant sheep, and the fact that in the morning, for the first time in four weeks, they wouldn't need to drag themselves out of bed at 4am to go to work.

It was beer for the rousies too. Perhaps the bourbon would come out later; truth serum, as Carl described it. For her size, Crystal could put the beer away. She'd grown up in a drinking household, telling stories of her and her brothers, not even at high school yet, finishing off the leftovers after the adults had flaked out, the strains of popular local artist Prince Tui Teka fading into the night sky. Aping their parents and their friends, stumbling around acting drunk. Until they actually were.

Sanna had a soft spot for Crystal. She appreciated her warm nature, and how she was trustworthy and authentic. Crystal was a quiet, happy drunk, unlike Lacey. A stroppy, pocket-rocket blonde, Lacey and her billowing sponge of hair ruled the woolshed floor through a heady combination of bitchiness and nepotism. Her tongue was as sharp as her fingernails, which she worked on with annoying regularity. Probably because it was her way of deflecting; not able to hold her own in meaningful conversation. Being in a family gang afforded Lacey a status that, on merit, she didn't deserve. Sanna found her hard to avoid and harder to like.

Suzie was part of the gang and she wasn't; a spare rousey, always around to fill in when someone was sick or needed time off. She proudly proclaimed that she was built like a brick shithouse, and could sink half-a-dozen bottles in a heartbeat, one for one with Bull and Pete, go for a slash and be back in no time, thirsty, looking for the next. Sanna had heard Pete describing Suzie to Bull as being 'one-and-a-half axe handles across the backside'. She doubted he'd have the nerve to say that to her face, lest she snap his skinny frame in half. She laughed to herself: imagine trying the local slang on her friends back home.

Sanna stood amongst them, increasingly accepted as part of the gang. She wasn't built for drinking, but she always made an effort to join in. She'd taught them a traditional Finnish card game, Paskahousu, which had gone down well; even more so when she revealed that the literal English translation was 'shit pants'.

She caught Ryan looking at her. Momentarily, he was embarrassed, then she allowed herself a coy smile to let him know she was flattered. She felt a tiny jolt inside of her, now she knew for sure there was interest. Tonight they would all be drunk. Soon, when they were back at the quarters, when they weren't too hungover, it would be time for them to get to know each other better.

7
Ryan

Bob Marley's 'One Love' kicked out of the jukebox, snapping Ryan's thought pattern. That was Ronnie's doing – Marley was never far from anything she did. Getting together and feeling alright was the motto of her life. She'd mourned for six weeks after Marley's passing earlier that year: full black veil, curtains drawn in her house, the whole works. It was unhealthy and obsessive, but at least his music was soothing. Imagine if it had been Leo Sayer she worshipped. Ryan couldn't stand that awful song. It never made him feel like dancing.

'Here he is. About fucking time!' Lacey called out.

Her fiancé, Owen Franklin, leaned over and gave her a peck on the cheek. 'Got any money?'

'I'm not your fucking bank manager,' she squawked. 'At least you've had a shower and smell nice. You wouldn't be getting a blowie later if you hadn't.'

'There's a tab,' said Carl. 'Grab whatever you want.'

'Thanks,' Owen said.

Ryan wouldn't want to live his life being bossed around by Lacey, but Owen was old enough to make his own decisions. He had a good job driving a stock truck – he didn't need her. He chose her.

'Hey, did you hear what's going down at the club?' said Carl, to no-one in particular. 'Snorkel Titmus got caught tickling the till.

Apparently, he's been making up fake invoices and paying himself. Been going on for years, they reckon.'

'Always thought he was a shifty bastard,' said Pete.

Ryan did a double take. That was a bit rich coming from Pete. He'd always hidden his true personality behind his guitar.

The Nashville Workingmen's Club was two blocks away from the pub. Ryan didn't mind it there – it was where Philip drank too – but there was always friction over one thing or another, often about how the club wouldn't allow women to be members. Ryan thought it was archaic and unnecessary, but there was a vote on it every year, and attitudes were slowly starting to shift. Women could now sign in as guests on certain nights when there was a band or DJ on, although there was gaffer tape stretched across the floor, near the snooker tables; a line the women weren't allowed to cross. For their own benefit, it was said, so they weren't subjected to any unseemly language.

Ryan looked across at Lacey and Suzie, riffing about one of their old school friends.

'It's her fourth sprog. Different fella, each one.'

'She was always a mad rooter, even at school.'

'She needs to get it sewn up.'

'She needs to get what sewn up?' asked Sanna.

Maybe the club had their rules right after all, thought Ryan. For everybody's benefit.

'A little birdie told me I'd find you lot in here.' Detective Inspector Tom Harten had pushed his way into the circle.

'What can we do you for, occifer?' slurred Lacey.

'Don't mind her,' said Carl, embarrassed. 'What can I get you?'

'Bit early for me just yet, still working. But thanks, anyway.'

'Never stopped you before,' laughed Carl.

'Times are changing, Carl. We're hearing they're gonna phase out the traffic cops. Make us all the same. Start bringing in squads from out of town. Whanganui, Hamilton . . . they're gonna go from place to place doing blitzes. The days of driving around pissed are finished.'

'Won't worry me,' said Bull, grinning. 'Sow the seed, get on the weed.'

Lacey belly laughed so violently she half-choked herself.

'I'm doing a run through town,' said Tom. 'There's been a spate of thefts from motor vehicles this week. We're advising everyone not to leave valuables in their cars and keep them locked up.'

'Who is it?' Carl asked.

'Out of towners. They know what they're doing too.'

'Put Suzie onto them. She won't fuck about!' Lacey hooked her arm around Suzie's neck as she spoke.

'If they touch my wheels, they'll be dog tucker,' said Bull. 'They can fuck off out of it.'

For a pastor-in-waiting, it looked like Bull's church wasn't going to be as inclusive as he'd made out, thought Ryan.

'We'll get it sorted,' said Tom. 'But in the meantime, don't make things any easier for them.'

Sanna smiled across the leaner at Ryan. She had no car, and no concerns.

'So . . . this a demotion, is it?' Lacey was at it again. 'It's a long way down from missing girls to petty car thieves.'

'Jesus, Lacey!' said Carl.

'It's okay,' said Tom. 'She's not the first.'

The disappearance of Mary Atkins, a hitchhiker in her early twenties, was the biggest thing that had happened in town for years. She'd been making her way from Wellington to Auckland in early 1980, and was last seen thumbing a ride on the main highway south of town, before failing to meet up with family. No trace of her had been found. Hordes of visitors flooded the town for weeks on end, although eventually, after the police investigation came up empty and the TV news crews and journalists had interviewed every local who wanted their fifteen minutes of fame, the story fizzled out and things returned to normal.

'So why didn't you find her?' said Lacey. 'Or, more to the point, the bastard that did it?'

'It wasn't for the lack of trying,' Tom insisted.

'Well . . . the fact is, because of you not doing your job, there's a killer still out there and none of us girls are safe.'

'This is rugged country. If someone really wants to hide something, that makes it very hard for us.'

'Well . . .' Lacey slurred again. 'That's just . . . weak as piss. If you want my opinion.'

'Which he doesn't.' Carl pushed his sister away from the leaner.

There was an awkward silence. Ryan wished he was sharp enough to find words to break it.

'I hear you're finally putting your mum's place up for sale,' said Tom, doing the honours.

'Yeah.'

They stepped away to the side.

'Good luck with that.'

'Jack reckons it should sell okay,' said Ryan.

'Well, as much as he thinks he does, Jack Nash doesn't know everything. If it doesn't sell, you'll just have to hang around here; set up a legal practice in town.'

Ryan's beer suddenly tasted flat. 'That's not what I had in mind.'

'Let's face it,' said Tom. 'Isaacs has had it good for too long. Town could do with the competition.'

Ryan didn't bite.

'What's the matter? Don't want to get your hands dirty defending the local riff-raff?'

Tom was challenging him. 'I wouldn't have the experience to start off here on my own. You know that.'

'I thought you were a Nashville boy. Through and through?'

'I am.'

Tom frowned. 'If you want to leave Nashville . . . go and be a city lawyer . . . that's fine. Do it. You don't have to pretend you fit in.'

'I'm not pretending. This is my home. I'm just like everyone else who lives here.'

'Oh, right.'

'It's just that I've got reasons to move.'

'Reasons? Or excuses? Don't be making excuses, Ryan.'

'Excuses? You mean, like you just were?'

'Really? So, you're a detective now, are you?' Tom snapped. 'Reckon anyone off the street can just waltz around solving cases like this?'

That wasn't what Ryan meant, but now Tom had put it that way, the notion did seem ridiculous.

'There's an old saying around here,' said Tom. 'I'm sure you know it. "When the deep, dark bush swallows you whole." It means your time on this earth is done and there's nothing anyone can do about it. I'm a detective, Ryan, not a miracle worker. If someone wants to hide a girl in the bush, this is the perfect place to do it.'

8
Ryan

Jack Nash was the closest thing to a father Ryan had ever known. When he was growing up, Ryan had never wanted for a firm, male presence; his mother raised him perfectly well. But Jack always seemed to be around whenever they needed an extra pair of hands, and that was fine. And because he was Philip's dad, that made them almost like family.

Ryan watched Jack drive a metal stake into the forgiving pumice soil. 'For Sale', the sign read, in bold blue. 'All enquiries to Jack Nash Real Estate, Ph 8393.' Jack wasn't just anybody. Nothing happened in Nashville without his hand being all over it. He saw it as taking on the responsibility passed down through generations of the Nash family. 'It's a fine balance,' Jack would say. 'It's not for me to meddle in other people's business, or tell them how to live their lives. But once you're born a Nash, it's your job to ensure that when you eventually pass on, you leave the town in good shape.'

Jack dropped his sledgehammer and stepped back to check the sign for level.

'When do you think we'll get some interest?' Ryan asked.

'Hard to tell, to be honest. But it's a solid house and, look at this garden . . . Edith always did such a great job keeping it in order.'

Ryan's mother's pride and joy, a large rhododendron, 'Hardgrove's Royal Star', commanded the centre of the lawn. In full bloom, it blushed and beamed bright red, resplendent in the warm afternoon sun.

'You're doing the right thing selling, Ryan. Yes, we could have rented it out, but with you away at law school, and . . . some of the people we get as tenants these days, they just don't have any respect. For eighty bucks a week it's not worth risking the place being trashed.'

'It's okay, Jack. It's just a house.'

Jack gathered his tools and placed them in the boot of his tan Kingswood sedan. 'Don't worry. When you come back I'll find you another place. No commission.'

Ryan didn't want any special treatment, but that was Jack's way. He was always doing someone a favour, or calling one in. 'I doubt I'll be back. Not to live, anyway.'

'Oh, mark my words, you'll be back. Nashville's in your blood.' The Kingswood revved into life. 'I'm sure Philip would like to catch up and hear how you're doing. You haven't seen him since you've been back.'

Ryan wasn't aware anyone had been counting.

'You're a good sort, Ryan, but going away to university like that, then coming home . . . just be careful, that's all.'

'Careful? About what?'

'You know how it is. People around town . . . you don't want to let people think that you might be better than them now.'

'That's just club talk,' said Ryan.

'I'm just saying. Okay?'

'I don't think like that, Jack. I'm a local. I'm just like everyone else.'

Jack jagged the column shift out of neutral and rode the clutch. 'Anyway, you know where to find him,' he said, pulling away from the kerb.

The pebbles on the driveway crunched underneath Ryan's feet as if he were stepping across bags of potato chips. He walked under the carport, where green paint was giving way to rust, to the rear of the house. The back door beckoned but he wasn't tempted to go back inside. Sleeping over, following their session at the pub, had only reminded him of how much work he still had to do to empty the house of his mother's things. He'd become expert at making excuses not to get the place cleaned up properly. His mother had lived all of her life in Nashville, most of it in this house. He needed to be sure he wasn't erasing her legacy too soon.

It was here that she'd given him three rules for life, which for all of his twenty-two years, he'd so far managed to observe. 'Don't rely on the government for a living'; 'Don't be a schoolteacher'; and 'Don't do drugs or you'll be kicked out of the family'. That last one always made him smile. He had no brothers or sisters, and had never met his father. It would be some achievement to be kicked out of a family containing only two members.

He saw that the woodpile he'd stacked as a teenager, too many times to remember, was now nothing more than sawdust and a few stray pieces of totara, the neighbours having helped themselves at a suitably respectful time after the funeral. He'd scored many a try for the All Blacks on the back lawn, dodging and weaving past hulking Springboks, sprinting away from Wallabies, and outsmarting the French, chip-kicking over the clothesline, regathering the ball on the bounce, and diving over in the corner, near where the compost burner still stood.

Philip Nash had been there too, Tommy Hazelwood from number 22, and Billy Pokere, taking turns to pick sides, then battling it out, two on two, on the lawn after school. Rugby, league, soccer, cricket, running races, big-time wrestling – whatever took their fancy. Or else they would take to their bikes, lording over every last inch of the town.

Then there was their 'Dare Club' – at least before it came to its inglorious end, when they were fifteen. Ryan couldn't remember exactly whose idea it was, but he, Philip, Tommy and Billy wrote down four dares and drew one each, the performing of which would bind them together as blood brothers. Ryan was tasked with buying a packet of condoms off busty Phyllis Huston, over her counter at Richardson's Pharmacy, while his mates lurked in the background, revelling in his embarrassment.

'You want *what*?' shrieked Phyllis.

Ryan had agonised over what to ask for. 'French letters' sounded too formal. 'Prophylactics' was worse. 'Rubbers' too familiar. Phyllis wasn't much older than he was, and she had a boyfriend. She would understand. He whispered again, 'A pack of joes, thanks.'

Phyllis's laugh was loud and cruel and cut through the whole shop. 'You hear that, girls? Ryan here wants a pack of joes!'

Ryan shrank into his sandshoes. 'C'mon, just help me out, will you?' he pleaded.

'They're called condoms. Large, medium or small?' she bellowed.

It was all Ryan could do not to bolt, never to show his face in town again.

She leaned over the top of the counter and peered downwards. 'I'll give you the regular – how's that?'

A few years on, Ryan noted how Phyllis now had three kids and a fourth on the way. Perhaps she should have kept them for herself.

Ryan's dare turned out to be the least traumatic of the four. Required to lick all over the box of straws on the counter at the milk bar, Tommy got busted in the act and received a decent clip over the ears from the owner, while Billy's mission to take a dump in the town's public pool landed him a twelve-month suspension.

It was the evening after Philip had shoplifted two bath plugs and a carpenter's chisel from Bailey's hardware store that Ryan's mother opened the door to find Jack and Philip outside, along with a constable, calling time on the hi-jinks. They were good boys, Jack and Edith assured the constable, they would see to it that the lads kept on the straight and narrow. Which, ever since then, they'd done.

Tommy hadn't been so lucky. He'd always been fascinated by the local rivers and streams. The popular swimming holes were never enough for him – he was obsessed with finding new places, like he was some daredevil explorer. Until their school certificate year, when it cost him his life.

His parents raised the alarm when he didn't return home one night, and his drowned body was found two days later, submerged, wedged between river rocks. Ryan's mum kept him home from school for four days, before and after the funeral. He thought it was overkill at the time, but later he understood it was her way of dealing with the shock and realisation that he could have been the one not coming home for dinner.

Billy's father was a train controller who, just before they were due to finish school, was transferred to Wellington. There'd been talk that those types of jobs were going to be phased out, so he was being smart, getting in ahead of things. 'Downsizing' was what the local paper described it as. Others called it 'centralisation'. Ryan hadn't heard anything of Billy since the day they left, during their sixth form year.

Which meant, of their original crew, just two remained. Ryan was surprised when Philip showed no inclination to go to university, starting as a teller at the bank. Ryan didn't look down on the bank. Well, not really. It was a respectable job, but . . . the town would always be there to come back to later; it wasn't something to bind yourself to at the first opportunity. Ryan might have seen things differently if he had a father of his own, but there were a lot of things going on in the world, more than drinking in the same club, week after week with your old man. Why lock yourself into one path, when it was possible to keep a foot in both camps?

Ryan scanned his mother's lawn one more time and glanced again at the back door. There was nothing left for him to see. What he thought was the presence of his mother wasn't actually her at all. He was making something up out of nothing.

Walking to his car, his mind drifted back to the look Sanna had flashed him in the pub. He had a good feeling about her. There was a connection there and he was excited about where it might lead. But it was also past time to catch up with Philip, and if it made Jack happier, all the better. After all, Ryan Bradley and Philip Nash were blood brothers. Nashville was their town.

9
Philip

In the year since Philip Nash had moved out of home, he'd never missed a Sunday night family dinner. Jack sat as he always did, at the head of the timber dining table. Lois elegantly bent down in front of her trusty oven and, from the warming tray at the bottom, removed a juicy, perfectly browned, rolled rib roast of beef. She transferred it to a wooden carving board and delivered it to the table.

'Smells delicious,' said Jack, honing his prized carving knife. He set about shearing off neat slices, each of them a uniform third of an inch, while Lois served up the vegetables.

'Thanks. Mum, it's not like I don't get well fed at my place,' Philip said, winking across the table at his fiancée, Becky. Truth be told, he was tiring of the ritual, and having to suffer his father's incessant intrusions, but a free, hearty meal every Sunday was too good to turn down.

'I know you get very well looked after,' said Lois, tapping Becky on the arm, before placing a jug of rich, thick brown gravy on the table.

'Ah, the crowning glory,' said Jack. For nearly thirty years, Lois's cooking had been the constant in their marriage. They ate voraciously, not out of hunger, but because the food demanded their attention. It wasn't until his plate was half empty that Jack spoke again. 'Everything okay with the house?'

'Yes,' said Philip. 'No problem.'

'Becky?'

'Yes, Mr Nash. It's lovely. We're very grateful for your assistance.'

'You'll need to modernise it at some point. The weatherboards need a paint. I've been looking at colours. And the kitchen and bathroom need doing up before any little ones come along. But it's got good, sturdy bones.'

Lois sighed. 'Jack, don't keep pressuring them like that. They might not want children just yet. It's up to them to decide.'

Jack harrumphed, dismissively.

'Besides,' Lois continued, 'I'm sure Becky's father will insist on them being married first. Isn't that the case, dear?'

'Yes, I'm sure,' she replied, very politely for someone who was being spoken about rather than spoken to.

'Then just get on and let us know the date,' said Jack. 'I've already had a word with Keith Thomasen from the golf club. It's a nominal amount to hire for the reception, and they'll organise all the catering.' Jack sat back in his chair and began chortling. 'I'm sorry, Lois, I know I shouldn't laugh, but I never thought we'd ever be sitting here with our son, talking about him marrying the vicar's daughter.'

Lois raised her eyebrows towards Becky, in half-apology.

'Don't take that the wrong way,' said Jack. 'We're very proud to have you in our family. But, I mean . . . it wasn't an obvious fit.'

'It's fine, Mr Nash. I'm not your typical vicar's daughter.' Becky blushed. Her words hadn't quite come out the right way.

'C'mon, Dad, that's enough,' said Philip. 'When the time comes for a wedding, you'll be the first to know, like you always are.'

Dessert was Lois's famous bread-and-butter pudding. Another hit.

'Listen, son,' said Jack, 'we need to talk about the Rotary Club project. The children's playground upgrade.'

'What about it?'

'We're short. Around eighteen hundred dollars. If you'd attended the last meeting, like you were supposed to, you'd know that already.'

'I'm not really sure I'm cut out for Rotary.'

'Oh, but you are. When a Nash makes a commitment, that's the end of it. We don't let people down.'

'I never made any commitment. That was you, on my behalf.'

'You're going to end up managing that bank, son. It's not about being cut out for it; it's part of your job.'

'You said it yourself about Rotary. There's some dead fish in there. That pommy bloke from the council. Swanning around in sandals and long socks. What's that about?'

'So, are you saying the bank should only lend money to people who wear proper footwear? I only sell houses to people I like? We'd be out of business in a flash, both of us. That's not how it works, son. Not to mention the damage to our legacy.'

'Jesus! Dad, don't start that bullshit again.'

'*Philip! Language.*' Becky was keen to keep the peace.

'Just because your great-grandfather was the first white settler in the area, you think every descendant has an entitlement to be the town guardian.'

'Not entitlement. Responsibility. Thomas Nash had this town named after him. There's not a day goes by when I don't feel proud of that. And you shouldn't wear it like it's a burden.'

Philip sighed. It was pointless arguing with him, and it wasn't fair on his mum. 'What do you need?'

'I know the bank is already a major sponsor. But do you think you could squeeze another two thousand out of them? Just to finish it off properly?'

Philip winced. 'Christ, Dad, that won't be easy. That amount is outside of the local manager's authority.'

'Philip! Don't be so negative,' scolded Becky.

'Nothing worthwhile is ever easy, son. But I'll make sure everyone around town knows it was you who got it over the line.'

'Two thousand?'

'Two thousand,' said Jack. 'And for that, the bank can have a plaque on the side of the sky rocket.'

'Gee, that'll be the clincher,' Philip sighed.

'Philip!' said Becky, through her teeth, once again.

Lois stood up. 'Now, who's ready for a nice cup of tea?'

Philip didn't feel like talking on the drive home, and Becky never needed an invitation to fill the silence: 'Your dad does a lot for this town . . . It's people like him who keep things ticking over . . . He was a rock when everything went crazy over that missing hitchhiker . . . I don't like how people take him for granted.'

'Enough!' Philip jerked the car over to the side of the road and pulled up suddenly. 'There's two things my dad wants,' he said, gripping the steering wheel so tightly his veins bulged out of the back of his hand. 'He thinks one day he's going to pick up the paper, on Queen's Birthday Weekend, or at New Year, and he's going to see his name on the honours list. A medal for services to the community or something like that.'

'And what's so bad about that?' queried Becky, gently.

Philip rolled his eyes. Becky could be so naive at times.

'And the other one?' she probed.

'You know that already. He wants me to be him. So that I continue the Nash family lineage.'

'Is that so bad?'

'But don't you see? It's all on his terms. It's not about the family name, it's not about me making my own life, it's about him. Is that what you want? My dad controlling our lives? I sure as hell don't.'

'You know he means well. We wouldn't have our nice house if it wasn't for him.'

'Fuck him! Fuck the house!' Philip slammed the steering wheel so hard the car shook. 'You know what the worst is? He thinks I'm stuck here forever, under his thumb. Thinks I'm too gutless to do anything about it. Well. Fuck. Him!'

Becky reached across and placed her hand on his. 'I don't understand why you're so angry.'

'I'm not angry. I'm pissed off!'

'I think we have a wonderful life,' said Becky. 'We have plans. I can't imagine what could get in the way.'

Philip slammed the gearstick into place and sped home, without once looking her in the eye, or saying another word.

10
Ryan

'They feed you like this at the university? Or are you too busy at the library?' It was Bull, gnawing and sucking at a bone, full of his usual, mocking nonsense. Ryan hated the way he dominated the gang's common dining table. Wanting to enjoy his dinner, he ignored him.

'Too good to talk to us now, eh? Mister big-shot lawyer-man.'

'I never said I was a lawyer.' Instantly, Ryan regretted biting back. Bull had him on the hook now, his head tilting, as if to gain a better line to Ryan through his right eye, his good one.

'There's only one law,' said Bull. 'God's law. True God, the Holy Spirit. Not that mumbo-jumbo they teach you.'

'God's law?' Carl laughed heartily as he stood up. 'We went to Sunday School as kids, didn't we, Pete? Wasn't anything like the shit you talk!'

'I've made my pact with the truth, brother,' Bull replied. 'When the day comes, you will understand. And there'll be a place for you too. I will see to it.'

'There you go, Ronnie,' said Carl, winking and wiping his hands on her cook's apron. 'Bull's going to see to it personally that we're all saved. It's not what you know, it's who you know!'

Carl excused himself. Every night after dinner he would attend to business; tracking down farmers in the district to coordinate future jobs, or burying his head in his ledger.

His brother Pete had no such interest. Ryan noted how his lack of personality perfectly matched his physique. Physique was the wrong word; he was impossibly thin, skinnier than the guitar he carried everywhere. It was no surprise he'd taken his school nickname with him into adulthood: 'xylophone ribs'.

Bull would always have his Bible close at hand – a tatty, sorry-looking tome that had suffered years of abuse, and occasional bouts of anger. Pages were torn where his frustration and temper had got the better of him, usually on the back end of a booze bender. Ryan had seen pages covered in scribbled notes, some of them transferred into Bull's own hardcover notebook, into which Bull was essentially rewriting the Bible.

The Bible according to Bull.

It had taken less than a day, Ryan's first on the job, for Bull to corner him and proclaim that it was God's will that in the near future he would lead his own congregation and that Ryan was welcome to join. He wasn't ready to start just yet; he needed a little more money from shearing to buy a plot of land on the edge of town, where he'd build his church. That would give him time to hone his message and to learn all that came with being a pastor.

Ryan dismissed it as utter rubbish. Bull just cherry-picked quotes from the Bible, selecting phrases that would sound convincing if repeated enough times, or an ambiguous passage that would allow him, with some poetic licence and the stroke of a pen, to keep multiple sex partners, and abuse and swear at anyone he didn't like the look of.

Church? Cult, more like.

It was just Bull and Pete at the table now, drinking beer and talking shit, in between Pete strumming Jim Reeves tunes. According to Bull, humanity had just fifty years left to prepare for Armageddon. Or was it insurrection? Ryan wasn't sure, but whichever, Bull and his followers would be spared. Or something like that.

*

Ryan pushed open the door of Neville Hanigan's woolshed, and peered inside. It creaked but, as he anticipated, there was no-one there to notice. The shed was sited a good three hundred metres from their quarters and, because of the way the track skirted around the edge of a hillock, it wasn't visible from there. In the fading half-light he could see that the shed was swept clean, in readiness for when shearing for Hanigan's flock would begin in a couple of months' time. There were no wool bales to sit on – they'd long been sent to market – but in one corner there was a pile of jute fadges; wool packs. Not exactly a triple-sprung mattress, but better than the dusty, timber floor. They would do.

He sat in the quiet and waited. The shed felt warm; native timber softened by age and infused with lanolin and sheep shit. It smelled comfortably familiar, although Ryan wondered if Sanna would agree. Suddenly, he was acutely aware of his own scent – a heady blend of Swarfega and Old Spice. The best he could hope for was that everything would cancel itself out. Or she had a blocked nose and the beginnings of a cold.

Ryan recognised the same creak. The door slowly opened and there she was. He already thought her pretty, but Sanna's silhouette heightened her cheekbones: and his anticipation.

'Hello?' she said, tentatively.

'Over here,' said Ryan. He extended his hand and she found it in the semi-darkness, sitting down next to him on the wool packs. 'I wasn't sure you'd come.'

She shrugged. 'I couldn't let you miss your lesson on Finland, could I?'

Glad for her having unbraided her hair, he gently brushed the loose strands away from her face, tucking them behind her ear. He smiled and sensed her smile in return.

'So, what's tonight's lesson?' he asked.

She whispered back, 'Finnish girls.'

He'd been expecting to talk, both of them to uncover more about each other's past, but her assertiveness put paid to that. Everything felt so comfortable and natural. Conversation would only have fouled things up. Ryan placed his arm across her shoulder and pulled her down, until they were lying alongside each other. Their kiss was tense and awkward at first, then gradually more natural and familiar. Comfortable, pleasurable, then suddenly more urgent.

He slid his arm down her back, cupping her shoulder blade at first, to protect her from the ground, but then it was her responding to his kiss, her lips pressing against his. She pulled back and he allowed his hand to slide across her breasts, back and forth, each in turn, as if his hand and her breasts were made for each other. She was in control now, climbing high on top of him, arching backwards, then dropping her head down, merging their breaths, her breasts accessible through the veil of her hair. He grabbed at the bottom of her skirt and lifted it up so that it rode around her waist. She squeezed tightly around his legs and pressed her crotch into him, rubbing and sliding, gently at first, then faster and firmer as she found her cadence. Ryan could feel her wetness on his thigh, and sense her intensity; catching her grimace, transitioning between pleasure and pain. Then, after what seemed like another minute, but it could have been half or double that, he couldn't tell, she bit hard into his earlobe, and her whole body trembled and shook, like a flimsy, balsa-wood house trying to withstand an earthquake.

When it was over, Ryan lay alongside her, still and silent, acutely aware he had no idea what to do next. He'd never had a girl orgasm before with him; if that's what it was that had happened. How long was he supposed to lie there and hold her? She trembled in his arms again, smaller this time, just for a few moments. An aftershock, he figured. He searched for something to say, something that wouldn't sound trite, that might add to the moment. Better to say nought, he decided, just in case he got in the way of more tremors.

She nuzzled her face into his, and kissed him softly on the lips. 'Sorry. I think I bit your ear.'

'It's okay,' said Ryan, glad she had broken the ice. He felt her reach down with her hand, and slip it into his shorts. He was harder than a shearer's metal handpiece. 'Your turn now,' she whispered.

11

Neville

Neville Hanigan pushed his plate to the centre of the dining table, stood up and gazed out through the large plate-glass window. Despite the arriving dark, he could make out the wire fence running along the driveway from the house, and beyond that, the outline of his woolshed. Down the incline to the left, the silhouette of his pride and joy, a stand of native kahikatea, imposed itself. Comprising seven acres of natural bush, straddling the creek that ran through his farm, its value to Neville was immeasurable. Late to the conservation debate, he now recognised those trees for what they were: a vital part of the heritage of the local area and – the tallest of New Zealand's native tree species – the nation itself. As saw logs they were probably worth more than treble the value of his wool clip, but that calculation was moot.

It was some miracle the trees were there at all, the King Country having been stripped of much of its natural bush earlier in the century. Between the wars, timber mills popped up everywhere, elbow to elbow, feeding a nation's insatiable thirst for native timber, clearing the way for the land to transition to grazing country. It was as if for every tree felled, its place was taken by a shovel full of super phosphate and ten sheep. Neville didn't know why this small pocket had been spared, but he was glad these trees were going nowhere.

Shifting his gaze beyond the woolshed, the lights of the shearers' quarters were now prominent. Theirs was a useful arrangement. It allowed the shearers to stay in the district and not have to travel each morning from town, and for him, it meant some easy cash for buildings that would otherwise have stood vacant. Carl's gang were heavy drinkers but they were never any trouble. The lights would be off within the half-hour.

There had been times in the past when Neville felt guilty, silently peering out of the window while Janet remained at the table, picking away at her meal, staring at the chair he had just vacated. Guilt, he now concluded, was a wasted emotion. During the day, this was her window – he would set her up in her favourite chair, with a blanket in winter or a cool drink in summer, and leave her to her own company while he went about his farm work. Because she never left the house, her condition had consumed her and she it. In the process, Neville felt crowded out. Something simple, like gazing out of what had become her window, was a way of reclaiming at least part of his own house.

It was well known around the district that the accident had been his fault. Almost three years ago now, something innocuous – inattention while trying to flick a wasp out of the car window, instead of focusing on negotiating the narrow gorge road safely. They had both paid a heavy price for it. Janet had lost her liberty and her capacity to speak; Neville his conscience, for wishing she had died rather than drawing him into her misery.

At least she was able to attend to basic functions independently. Bathe herself, dress, eat and shit. Thank heaven for small mercies. If he'd been required to nurse her to that extent . . . well, he just wouldn't have. Before the accident, he'd felt that her being an only child, orphaned before she turned five, was a blessing. No in-laws to pretend he liked, no pesky nieces and nephews running amok during school-holiday visits. But lately, the way she was, it was problematic.

What he wouldn't now give for a mother-in-law to take Janet under her wing, so he could be left in peace.

Did that make him a bad person? Not if feeding Janet three times a day, shopping for supplies, ferrying her two or three hours each way, to and from specialist appointments, without receiving anything back in return except a blank stare, counted for anything. The specialists said she should be able to communicate via writing or drawing, but she was incapable even of that. Or she refused. Selective mutism, they said, emphasising the first word. There was no emotion, no acknowledgement, no expression of appreciation; not even any anger. If only she would abuse him, throw the kitchen sink at him for her state and her suffering, or rage with him over something. Anything.

Neville peered out through Janet's window. He couldn't be certain – his eyes weren't what they once were – but he thought he noticed movement down at the woolshed. It was probably nothing, but if it was a door swinging open and shut, he would need to fix it closed. He grabbed a torch and, at his back door, slipped on a pair of tired, dirty working boots he'd long given up lacing. Instantly they moulded to his feet, as familiar as his mother's hot Milo in winter. His porch was lined with an array of footwear – gumboots of various shapes and colours, work boots, tramping boots, sandshoes, slip-ons and jandals. It was something his brother Barry teased him about, although Neville thought it no different to all the coloured highlighters and marker pens Barry, an accountant, kept on his desk.

Neville carried the torch only for insurance, able to walk the path to the woolshed eyes closed. Besides, if there was anyone or anything up to no good, better for him not to announce his arrival. Rather than use the main door, he approached from the low side, near the counting pens. He quietly stepped up and inside, the internal shape of the building providing him with cover, the main floor slowly revealing itself as he inched forward. He heard them first. A low, soft groaning. Unmistakably female. Rhythmic and repetitive, his heart skipped a beat, then another two, then he was intoxicated by it. They were tucked around the corner, where he kept the wool fadges. He could make them out now, locked together, the girl on top, in control, the lad underneath – the wool presser from Carl's gang, passive and obedient, seemingly a junior partner in the union.

It came as no surprise to Neville that of all the thoughts racing through his mind at that moment, none were to turn and run, to leave an amorous couple to their moment of pleasure. Neither was he tempted to announce himself. A polite, gentle cough, or the light of his torch, was all that would be required to let them know they were trespassing.

Instead, Neville did the only thing he could do in the circumstances. He swallowed, slowly and deliberately, ensuring that the sides of his throat were moist, to ward off any unexpected cough-inducing tickle. He made certain his feet were stable and steady on the spot where he was standing. And through the cover of dark, and a silky spiderweb, he watched.

12
Ryan

The long, narrow entrance to the Nashville Army Disposal Store was lined with second-hand furniture. It had been that way for as long as Ryan could remember. Dressers, chests of drawers, filing cabinets . . . the usual array of trash studded with an occasional treasure. The place smelled the same as it always had; Ryan never could put his finger on what it was. Mustiness, ancient history perhaps, linseed oil leaching out of decades-old timber tables and chairs. Or was it the racks of heavyweight, khaki army uniforms and slouch caps? He couldn't tell if the army gear had seen action or not, but those racks had a distinct odour: the stench of war, no matter real or imagined.

Working at the store had been Ryan's second-ever job, after his paper round; he and Philip, hired by the owner, Mr Colin Trescothick, in the school holidays. They ran his errands, brought his morning tea – usually a scone, but occasionally a custard square or a sausage roll – swept the floor clean, and sorted through all of the comics, magazines and books dropped in by locals. The boys were tasked with setting aside any duplicates or damaged items and pricing the rest for sale – some single, some bundled together in a package. It was their dream job, complete with the perk of being able to take home whatever comics they chose to read for themselves, as long as they returned them for resale. Philip favoured war comics, the good and true men of the RAF dealing to 'Jerry' in their Spitfires, whereas Ryan was more a *Beano* and *Tiger* guy, with a soft spot for *Roy of the Rovers*.

Their downfall was Mr Trescothick detecting a drop-off in productivity, coinciding with their discovery of a stash of *Playboy* magazines under an old counter at the rear of the building. Ryan remembered the occasion of their sacking like it was yesterday, Mr Trescothick springing them under the counter, in the throes of comparing Miss December's assets with those of her counterparts from June and July, tut-tutting while tugging away at his wire-brush beard, considering his words carefully before bringing down judgement. 'I can't tell you how disappointed I am with you lads. But I won't mention anything to your parents. I'll leave it up to each of you to explain to them why your services are no longer required.'

The shop was empty, and Ryan saw that Colin was nestled into his office recliner. He hadn't aged a day. For all Ryan knew, he was still wearing the same trousers and jacket he'd worn the day of the dismissal.

'Hello, Ryan. Good to see you.'

Ryan found his handshake reassuring. 'You too, Mr Trescothick.'

'It's Colin.'

'Yes, sir, of course.'

'Edith was a fine woman, Ryan. It's been a big loss for this town.'

'Thank you, sir. Colin.'

There was something in his tone that gave Ryan reason to pause. Colin had been a widower for all the years he'd known him. The way he spoke . . . had there been something between him and his mother?

'But now it's time to move on, right?' said Colin. 'It happens to everyone.'

'Yes. I mean, obviously I need to go through the house and do a run to the tip. But I thought I'd come in here first, to see if there was anything of value that you wanted.'

Ryan watched Colin tug at his beard, in his trademark manner. No, it was settled. Not only was he a loner, his mother disliked facial hair. A hardy collection of bristly whiskers like that? He would never have done.

'It's really up to you,' he said. 'You can decide for yourself, deliver what you want to sell down here, or else I can have a trailer sent to the house. There'll be a small fee, of course.'

Ryan wasn't equipped to make so many decisions.

'I'll be honest with you,' Colin went on, 'we've had a bit of a run recently. Bruce Hopkins, up near the school, the Armstrongs, both of them went within a month of each other, plus the Garrett estate from down the river. And with talk of the meat works shutting down, there aren't the buyers around either. Put it this way, I'm not short of stock.'

Ryan wasn't exactly sure what that meant. There'd always been way too much stuff crammed into his store.

'If you like,' said Colin, 'I'm happy to go to the house, take a closer look, and pick out the items that are worth selling. And you can deal with what's left over. How does that sound?'

Ryan pondered for a moment. 'How much is that flak jacket there?' He stepped out of the office, picked it off the rack and tried it on. It fitted perfectly. 'One of the shearers in our gang reckons Armageddon is coming. You can never be too prepared.'

Ryan pulled his Mark II Cortina into a vacant car space across from the bank. He would have preferred a more anonymous colour than its bold British racing green, but since picking it up for a song in his final school year it had never missed a beat. Tearing at a white paper bag, he set about finishing off his steak pie and ham sandwich. The sandwich was an exercise in precision engineering; it was as if tea-rooms were in competition with each other to fit their sandwiches with the thinnest possible sliver of ham. Ryan picked out the sorry slice, held it to the light and waved his other hand behind it. The ham was translucent. He could have read the newspaper through it. Reuniting it with the bread, complete with its equally miserable smear of mustard, he took it all down in a single gulp.

Momentarily, he'd thought about sitting at a table inside. But for the cost of a few flakes of pastry on the floor, there was refuge in his car. Nobody to ask why he'd left his mother's house sitting vacant for so long, nobody to press him on his university study or ask when he'd be returning to town to open a legal practice. That didn't mean what Jack had said was right; that he wasn't one of them anymore. He'd had a taste of city life, was getting himself an education, but so what? He loved Nashville, and it wasn't a crime to want to move beyond conversation about weather and livestock prices. What Jack said was bullshit. He still got his hands dirty. People would still respect him. Eating alone in the car didn't prove anything.

Through a large window, Ryan saw two tellers, no-one he recognised. Alongside was the desk where Philip sat. If you weren't fleeing to the city, or taking an apprenticeship or a farm job, this was as close to career progression as it got. Straight out of school into a job as a junior bank teller, graduation to intermediate clerk, where Philip was now stationed, then accountant – which wasn't actually a proper, qualified accountant, more just a fancy name for 2IC. All with an eye towards the manager's office, waiting for the day he packed up his golf clubs and vacated to a bigger town, with a bigger manager's office.

It had been nine months since he and Philip had spoken, near the end of last summer's shearing season. It hadn't ended well; an argument that Ryan assumed was just the beer talking between mates, but which Philip seemed to take more seriously. About something he . . . well . . . it wasn't that Ryan couldn't remember. In the absence of any phone calls or other communication, he actually had no idea.

Ryan brushed his mouth clear of crumbs, wiped his nose on his sleeve, crossed the road and walked into the belly of the bank, straight up to where Philip sat. No offer of a handshake was forthcoming.

'Phil.'

'If you want money, you'll have to see a teller.'

'I don't need money.'

'No. I suppose you don't.'

Ryan hadn't come looking for a fight. 'What does that mean?'

'Nothing,' said Philip. 'I'm sure Carl is paying you well.'

'Listen, I'm in town for the day, I was just seeing if you're interested in having a drink after work.'

'Has my dad been talking to you?' Philip snapped back.

'No. Well, yes . . . about my mum's house.'

'If he says anything about me, tell him to mind his own business. Okay?'

'Why would he say something?'

'Because . . .' Philip waved his hand, dismissively. 'Doesn't matter.'

'He doesn't mean any harm. I think he just wants everything to be how it used to be.'

'Yeah, well, we're not kids anymore.'

'I'm sorry,' said Ryan. 'If I've come in on the wrong day, I can come back another time.'

'No need for that,' said Philip. 'It's just . . . you know what he's like. He gives me the irrits.'

'I get it,' said Ryan, not really getting it. 'Anyway, are we gonna have a drink or not?'

'Sure. I'll be at the club later. With Slurps.'

'Slurps? Gerry Darlow? Like . . . he's your mate?' Ryan was aghast.

'Yeah. Don't look like that. Why not?'

'Why not? Like he's a sneaky, slimy little weasel who used to steal stuff from everyone's schoolbags. We hated his guts. What happened there?'

'Not everyone goes to university, Ryan. Slurps might never be a lawyer but he *contributes* to the town. We've just joined the fire brigade.'

Ryan had heard about how people not quite right in the head volunteered for fire brigades so they could win favour by putting out fires they'd started themselves. Or did despicable things to hitchhikers.

'Listen,' said Philip. 'You're welcome to drop by. But if you do come, don't carry on like a dick, that's all.'

'I just want to catch up for a drink. Be a part of it. You know, like mates.'

'Good, then.'

Ryan was glad for the accord. 'So, I'll see you at the club?'

'You remember where it is?'

'Yes,' said Ryan, only half-smiling.

13

Ryan

'Thank you, gentlemen. It's now time to conduct the weekly members' draw. The jackpot currently stands at a tidy 310 dollars. Stand by.'

As the intercom crackled to life, the gathering of members at the Nashville Workingmen's Club suspended their conversations, drew breath and waited in eager anticipation for their number to be called.

'I reckon I'm the most relaxed person in here,' said Ryan, downing his beer.

'That's nothing to boast about,' said Philip. 'You could always sign up and pay your membership fee, like everyone else.'

'I'm a bloody student! At the other end of the country!'

'I heard you've got a bit of cash coming from your mum's house,' said Slurps.

Ryan didn't care much for Slurps and he didn't care for the implication. A big bruiser of a man, carrying a beer belly of someone fifteen years older, Slurps also had one of those ridiculous porn-star moustaches; what the locals called a 'flavour-saver'. In his case, without a love interest, nor any prospects, that description was wildly off target. Before Ryan could tell him to mind his own business, the PA sparked to life again.

'And tonight's lucky number is three-seven-three. Let's see . . . that's

Kev Hutchison . . . Kev, if you're here you have ninety seconds to present yourself at the bar to claim the jackpot.'

Shouts of 'Redraw' echoed around the room.

'If you're looking for Kev, try that new district nurse's house,' came a voice from an adjacent group. There were loud guffaws all round. 'Tells his missus it's draw night at the club, then he sneaks off there to get his leg over.'

Slurps low-whistled. 'Expensive root,' he said, to a circle of knowing nods.

'Thank you, gentlemen. Unfortunately, it seems that Kev isn't here to claim the prize, so next week's cash jackpot will increase to 320 dollars. Also, don't forget that tickets are now on sale for next month's cabaret special, the duo Brenda and Charlie, they're up from Wellington. By all accounts they're very entertaining, so make sure you get in and book, partners as well, should be a great event. In the meantime, enjoy the rest of your evening.'

Ryan's eyes did a lap of the bar. Most of the faces were familiar, even if fewer of the names were. In a town this size, there was only ever one degree of separation.

'My old man reckons you might get seventy-five grand for your mother's house,' said Philip. 'Not bad.'

Slurps snorted in his beer. 'Jesus. Why am I paying for my own drinks?'

'You know I pay my own way through university. And before my mum died, we spoke about things she'd like me to do with some of the money.'

'I can get you 6.25 per cent on a six-month term deposit,' said Philip. 'You won't do better than that.'

'We'll see,' said Ryan.

'We'll see? A country bank not good enough for you now?'

'That's not what I meant,' said Ryan, trying to keep his growing frustration in check.

Philip laughed. 'I mean, look at this fancy fucking shirt. You're not at some lawyers' cocktail party.'

'What do you mean? I bought this shirt in town!'

'Bullshit, you did. Slurps? What do you reckon?'

Slurps gave Ryan's shirt the once-over. 'Too fancy,' he concurred.

'And what about when they came around with the meat tray?' Philip continued. 'The only person – the *only person* – in this whole club who didn't buy a raffle ticket was you.'

'I'm working in a bloody shearing gang. We've got meat coming out of our ears!'

'There you go, totally missing the point. You buy a ticket to support the club. Support the town. It doesn't matter whether you need it or not.'

Ryan knew he'd lost the battle. 'What are you guys drinking?' he sighed, heading off to the bar. 'Anyone else need a beer?' he shouted out across the room.

'Hello, Ryan, you're looking well.'

The man's handshake was warm, if a little on the soft and flabby side.

'Hello, sir. Nice to see you.' It was one of his old high-school teachers, Mr Pihama, waiting in line at the bar.

'We're at the club. It's Terrence.'

'Of course. Sorry . . . old habits.'

'So, you're back again for the summer?'

'Yes. I'm working for Carl Stensness. Pressing.'

'Yes, I know. You're looking toned and fit.'

It was probably an innocent comment, but Ryan winced. Fit? No problem. Toned? Mr Pihama had always been single. There had been speculation at school about his sexual orientation; that was the price paid by thirty-something-year-old men living alone. Ryan didn't care for the gossip; it wasn't any of his business. Still, 'toned' didn't sit right.

'So, you're not a regular in here. Are you on a break?'

'Not really,' said Ryan. 'We cut out this morning. Start again tomorrow.'

Terrence gestured towards a vacant leaner, and they parked themselves at one end. 'Nice,' he said. 'And law school? How's that working out?'

'Pretty well, I think. I don't have my exam results yet but I'm not expecting any unpleasant surprises. This is my final year, then I'd like to get started on making an honest living.'

'As a lawyer?'

They laughed together. 'And how do you enjoy the lifestyle down there?' asked Terrence. 'I know a few Otago graduates myself.'

'It's great. Most people are from somewhere else. Everyone's there to have a good time.'

'I always picked you as having the potential to go on to bigger and better things.'

'Bigger and better than what?'

'Well, don't get me wrong. I've lived and worked here most of my life, and I don't see myself going elsewhere, not now. But you . . . I guess what I'm saying is that it's horses for courses.'

'Other than graduate, I don't really know what I want to do long term. Not yet.'

'And that's perfectly fine. You're young.'

'Twenty-two.'

'They don't call this phase "the key to the door" for nothing, you know. Embrace it all. What do they say? Let the cards fall where they may.'

Ryan nodded, unconvincingly. 'I get what you're saying –'

'But why don't I practise what I preach?'

'Yes.'

'I was watching you and Philip earlier. I went through exactly the same thing as him. Resentful of my friends who travelled overseas, or obtained university degrees and did something with them. But then –'

'Attention please, gentlemen.' The club's intercom waited for no man. *Just a courtesy announcement that the bar will be closing in an hour's time. And I've also just had confirmation that there are no out-of-town cops, just one constable on tonight, who I've just been informed is at the station, so please drive sensibly and you should be fine. Thank you.'*

'Have to say,' Terrence resumed, 'there's something to be said for living in a town where it's okay to drive home with a skinful of beer. Carefully, of course.'

Ryan hadn't really thought of it like that before.

'Do you know George Willard, Ryan?'

'Don't think so. He's not from school?'

'He's a character of the author Sherwood Anderson. I think you should check him out. There's a lot of you in George. And that's no bad thing. Don't ever apologise for getting ahead and leaving Nashville behind.'

'But I still don't understand why you didn't leave, after you got your teaching certificate.'

'Nashville is changing, Ryan. The railways, the freezing works, the hospital . . . they're all getting squeezed. The school roll is dropping. People are either losing their jobs or they're in fear of losing them. And fewer people means that our little society has become more insular. People look sideways at each other, you know what it's like. But towns like this take a grip on people. People establish strong roots – they're not leaving, whatever happens. I'm one of those people. So is Philip. You're not. Don't feel any worse for moving on. Just because others of us can't.'

Ryan took it all in. 'But I haven't moved on. I'm here, aren't I?'

'Are you? Really?'

Ryan frowned. 'Better get back.'

'Next time you get a day off and want to drop round for a coffee, you're very welcome,' said Terrence.

'Um . . . I . . . I don't drink coffee,' stammered Ryan. It was the truth, but even if he did drink coffee, he would have said it anyway.

Ryan found Philip and Slurps at one of the large snooker tables.

'What were you talking to that arse bandit about?' said Slurps.

'I'm not exactly sure,' said Ryan. 'I know what you're thinking. But I say he means well. And he was one of our best teachers.'

'Did fuck all for me,' said Philip, expertly potting a black.

'If you ask me, there's something creepy about him,' said Slurps. 'There were a lot of people around town pointing the finger at him after that hitchhiker went missing.'

'Still are,' said Philip.

That business again. It really had left its mark. Nobody in town seemed capable of letting it go.

'But why would he kidnap and murder a female hitchhiker?' asked Ryan. 'You just said it yourself.'

'What?' said Slurps. 'Because he's a poofter? Doesn't matter. People like that, they're all fucked up. You never know what's going on in their mind.'

Ryan certainly had no idea what went on in Slurps' mind.

Philip followed up with an easy red and got back into position on the black. 'There was all that talk about a serial killer, but that was just arse-covering. I heard the coppers know for sure it was him. They just didn't get enough evidence.'

'It could have been anyone,' said Ryan.

'Yeah, but it wasn't just anyone, was it?' Philip dropped the black again, in the same corner pocket. 'It was someone. Someone walking around scot-free. Like it was the perfect crime.' The next red lay on an acute angle.

'I've shot a few stags in my time,' said Slurps. 'But I often wonder what it would be like to kill, you know . . . a real person. Not just that, but the perfect crime. So nobody knew it was you that did it. What do you reckon?'

'What do I reckon?' said Ryan, taken aback. 'How do I know? I'm not planning on killing anyone.'

Slurps winked at him.

'The perfect crime? I hope you're joking,' said Ryan.

The cue ball sliced into the red on a forty-degree angle. The red dropped, without touching the sides. 'Perfect,' said Philip.

'In fact, I reckon I might ask our friend Mr Pihama about it, next time he's in here,' said Slurps. 'He's one of those people who likes to know too much about other people's business. You know what I mean? Always pops up when you least expect it, without good reason. In my book, that's D-A-F.'

'D-A-F?' Ryan wasn't familiar with the term.

'Dodgy as fuck.'

'Maybe it is,' said Ryan. 'But come on, it's not really fair to judge people like that, is it? At university I've met a few –'

'You know what you're sounding like?' said Philip, peering up from the table. 'Someone who thinks that just because they've gone off to university, they know everything. Or they suddenly have to save the world on behalf of whales. Or starving Biafrans. Totally out of touch with real people.'

'That's bullshit,' said Ryan. 'Not everyone has to conform to the way you guys see things.'

Philip laid his cue down on the table. 'You used to be one of us. But you've turned into a chook feeder.'

Ryan considered letting things go. Only for a moment. 'Mate, why are you so angry?'

'Oh, I get it.' Philip stood up straight. *'I'm the one with the problem . . . is that it?'*

'Maybe you are, yes.'

'Maybe *you've* forgotten that it's never a good idea to have a crack at someone who's holding a pool cue.'

'Whoa, fellas,' said Slurps, sliding in between. 'Time for a chill pill.'

'Don't worry, we're good,' said Philip, reluctantly backing off.

Ryan nodded. 'Yeah. We're good.' He gathered his thoughts for a few seconds. 'Same again?'

He didn't know if things were good or not. But it was best to leave it for now. There'd be time enough for things to work themselves out for him and Philip; one way or the other.

14
Bull

Bull placed his handpiece on the floor, pushed the newly shorn ewe down the chute, straightened his back, and glanced at the grease-infused watch hanging on his stand. It was a gift passed on to him by his uncle Hohepa, on the day he stopped shearing. Bull had already decided he'd hang it on his pulpit, so that every time he delivered a sermon, he'd reflect on all of the toil that had earned him his church, and instil in his followers the value of hard work.

He slapped at the tide of sweat that swathed his neck, took a quick swig of water, and backed into his catching pen. The first ewe slipped out of his grasp. No matter, he took the next one, hooking his arm securely under its neck, dragging himself and the sheep out onto his stand.

The process was the same every time. There was no short cut to shearing a sheep. Everybody did it the same way because it was the only way. From behind, he leaned over the top of the sheep's head, tightened its belly with his left hand, stretching the skin, then made the first strokes, north to south, with his right hand. The sheep stirred, he paused, then tried again. This time it kicked and squirmed. Once more he stopped, repositioned them both, and tried for a third time.

Bull hated it when sheep didn't sit for him. They were all stupid, the lot of them. There wasn't a dumber creature in the whole animal kingdom. But the really stupid ones, the ones who wanted to fight the handpiece and wriggle like white worms, they made him piss blood. If they were resisting, he wasn't shearing, and that was costing him money. And for what purpose? They were going to be fleeced regardless – why make a scene? All the dumb fucks were doing was increasing their chances of being cut. Accidentally or deliberately.

Bull made two neat, clean blows, exposing the pink belly skin, but on the third the sheep kicked out again, this time with conviction.

'Fucking mongrel!' he shouted, a flash of white heat filling his glasses. At once, he pulled on the back of the sheep's head, exposing its face, and, with his right hand, smashed the whole weight of his handpiece into the sheep's jaw.

Sanna recoiled in horror.

'I fucking warned you!' shouted Bull at the sheep, repositioning it and reactivating his handpiece.

'What are you doing?' cried Sanna.

He ignored her. But still the sheep wouldn't do as Bull wanted. *'Fucking sit straight!'* His rage incandescent, he needed to teach this ewe a lesson. Bull dropped his handpiece, clenched his fist, and drove two sharp punches into the side of its face.

'No! No!' Sanna was shrieking now. She struck out at Bull with her broom, but he handled it easily, grabbing it cleanly in one hand. He jerked on it, pulling her towards him, then shoved his face into hers.

'Don't you ever tell me what to do,' he spat. *'Ever!* Do you understand?' He held his pose, to ensure she took in his threat.

Sanna seized the opportunity, launching a fierce kick into his balls.

Carl yelled out, over the top of the commotion, *'Bull! What the fuck are you doing?'*

'What do you think I'm doing?' he said, crumpled on the floor.

'Doing me out of a contract, that's what you're doing,' shouted Carl. 'Pull your fucking head in.'

'You fucking animal,' Sanna spat at Bull, through a sudden release of tears.

'That's enough from you too,' said Carl. 'You've made your point.'

Bull slowly got to his feet. The lawyer-boy had poked his nose in and now had his arm around Sanna. Lacey had seized the opportunity to light a cigarette and fluff her hair. Skinny Pete was the only sensible one, still shearing, minding his own business. The ewe, meanwhile, blood streaming from its right eye, jaw shattered, was wandering around by the press. It could fuck off – he never wanted to see it again.

'Bull, listen to me!' Carl had taken control. 'Take five minutes, get some fresh air, and calm down. You can't do this shit.'

Bull snorted. The day was coming, sooner than any of these people realised, when he would be able to do whatever he damn well wanted. Because it would be his church. His god. His teachings. His word.

'Do you understand me?' Carl repeated.

Bull nodded. The moment had passed. Thinking of his church had calmed him. His day would arrive, but for now, Carl was boss. 'Yes.'

'Good. Now let me sort this shit out.' Carl called out, 'Ryan, grab that ewe. Let's have a look at it.'

Bull brushed past Ryan on his way out. 'If you want to make yourself useful, lawyer-boy, tell that girl to be ready when I get back. With her mouth shut. And tell her, if she ever does anything like that again, I'll fucking kill her.'

15
Ryan

On the drive back to the quarters, Ryan gazed out the window at lichen-covered fence posts and wire, unsure which was holding up which, willing the van around every bend. Tourists came from all over the world to marvel at rugged, beautiful landscapes like this. Right now, he would have given his right arm to be anywhere else.

Part of it was down to fatigue. The job ran in a predictable cycle: the beginning an ordeal as his body adjusted to the long days and physical work, then a plateau as his muscles transitioned out of soreness into the training zone, where he could feel himself getting fitter with every day's work. But now, after weeks without a decent break, he was starting to slide down the other side. Wake-up calls at 4am and the accumulated lack of sleep were taking a toll.

None of which excused Bull. Banished to the back seat, he was still too close for comfort. Carl was smart, keeping Sanna up front, as far away from Bull as he could. It was his way of letting her know that he had her back, to shore her up for work again tomorrow.

Ryan wished he could reach out and rub her shoulders – nothing sexual, just enough to let her know that even if there were bad people and dark acts, the world was still a good place. In any case, Sanna had shown that she didn't need him or anyone to mother her. The way she had stood her ground, berating Bull, calling out his brutality, sitting him on his arse . . . that was impressive.

Even so, he could see she was upset by how the sheep had been treated. The slow ride home gave him time to prepare his lie. He didn't have it down pat, but he would stumble his way through it. He and Carl had taken the ewe to the rear of the covered yards, made it comfortable, and from there, the farmer and his children would nurse it back to full health as a pet. That was all she needed to know.

Ryan gave Ronnie a heads-up on the way into their common area, and she scrambled through her cassettes for something to lighten the mood, settling on The Commodores. Ronnie never travelled with the rest of the gang. She used her own car, leaving after the lunch dishes were cleaned up, to drive into town to catch up with whānau, or return loaded up with supplies, in time to make a start on dinner. When the gang returned to quarters, they'd pile out of the van, shower, then grab a cold beer before dinner was served at the communal table, on the dot at 6.30pm. The deal Carl had with Neville Hanigan provided them with meat as they needed it, and they would invariably eat roast mutton, with roasted vegetables and something green; cabbage usually, or watercress or puha if Ronnie gathered some from the roadside. Ronnie always made a rich, thick gravy: proper gravy, whisking flour into the pan juices. Occasionally she'd surprise them – a corned brisket, which Ryan didn't mind, or maybe sausages with fried onion. But never chicken. For some reason, Carl had decreed it off limits.

It never bothered Ryan that they ate the same thing, day after day. As well as the dinner roast, there were thick loin chops for breakfast, and cold sliced meat in sandwiches for lunch, with lettuce. Ryan liked to smear the bread with a delicious slurry of mint and tomato sauce. The meals didn't just come with the job, Ryan considered them one of the perks. He watched Sanna poke at her plate like she'd suddenly turned vegan. They made eye contact across the table. It was a signal for them to meet at the woolshed.

He always arrived at the woolshed before her. At first, he thought it was coincidence, but she eventually confessed that she watched for him to slip out of his room and around the back of his building, then counted to one hundred, before doing the same. Knowing she was so calculated about it pleased him.

They had been meeting for nights on end now. In such a close working and living environment, where there was little space for secrets, this was theirs. There was a moment in the middle of a busy run, when he'd pondered whether he was drawn to their woolshed meetings by the sex, or by his desire to get to know Sanna better. When he realised it was both, that also pleased him.

Tonight wasn't the night for sex. He heard the familiar creak of the door, she joined him on the fadges, and they snuggled in tight. Not once did either of them mention Bull. He asked about her childhood, and they compared their favourite toys, and discoveries made on adventures while growing up. Nuzzling his face into her hair as she spoke softly to him, he realised it was what he needed too. So lost were they in the moment, neither of them realised they had company.

16

Neville

The elderly lady wore butterfly-rimmed glasses, and a mauve, hand-knitted cardigan: out of habit, not because the air temperature demanded.

'How are you today, Mr Hanigan?'

'Fine thank you, Betty.' It was said by others that she was nosy, but Neville always deemed her intrusions polite and well intentioned. She ran an efficient library; quick to shoo away any noisy children, and she always reserved for him the nice table by the window, where he would take his notes.

'Anything I can help you with today?' she queried.

'No, but thank you for asking.' He knew every inch of every shelf.

As it was most mornings, the Nashville town library was empty. He sat at his favourite table with a book he had read before – he was there to double check a few details. He cross-referenced his notes, then, satisfied with his work, closed the book and returned it to the space from where he had picked it. He allowed himself a moment of self-congratulation. He had finally made it through all of the books on geography, travel, Asian history and sociology: there wasn't a title remaining that could add to his knowledge. From a short list of three, including Thailand and Vietnam, he made his decision. Subic Bay, in the Philippines, was to be his new home.

'Bye, Betty, have a nice day,' he said on the way out.

She smiled in return. 'You too. See you next time.'

There wouldn't be a next time. His business here was done.

On the road north, Neville played things out in his mind. Subic Bay was an old US naval base, which had been on the verge of falling into disrepair in the years following the war, but seemingly had stabilised, with a population of around 250,000. Not too small, not too large, it had enough western-style infrastructure to keep an expat like him happy, with beaches and forests aplenty. Also, it was within striking distance of Manila should he ever need to travel there. There were girls, plenty of them by all accounts, which he'd read about in *The Truth* newspaper. By New Zealand standards the paid girls were a bargain. And there were others who were looking for a handsome foreigner to wine and dine them, and provide companionship, for something agreeable in return. A veritable smorgasbord. Best of all, it was private. Nobody would know he was there, and nobody would care enough to try to find out.

He was done with the farm, as it was done with him. And the town too. People in Nashville were well meaning, but they were cosy. Too cosy. Everything happened the same way, day after day, year after year. He understood it was the surety and comfort that appealed to folk, but that very thing had sucked all the life out of him. *'A great place to live, work and play'* proclaimed the large billboard on the highway entrance. He'd often thought about scrawling underneath, 'Yes, but it can also mess with a man.'

There were things that he'd miss. His trees, and the rugged, physical nature of the King Country. The landscape opened out a little in the north, the countryside more rolling than the jagged edges of his farm, dominated by large limestone formations that appeared to randomly pop out of the earth, resembling a teenager's pimple-ravaged face. And while large swathes had been conquered and converted to farmland, there remained huge pockets of native bush. Some of it formed part of the national park system, some was protected nature reserve, and the rest of it the most inhospitable and inaccessible ridges and gullies the sawmillers never got to. North or south, this was God's country. Even if it was no longer his own country.

Of course, this wasn't the only place where natural beauty was to be found. New Zealanders had a parochial view of their country that sometimes tipped over into smugness, and a blinkered outlook of what the rest of the world offered. He would find beauty in Subic Bay, and soon forget what he had left behind. Beauty in the landscape, beauty in the flesh.

Best of all, he would finally be free of Janet. She would be free of him too, he reminded himself, albeit in feeble justification. He had expected to feel a twinge of guilt, but instead he drew strength from feeling none. The farm's cash reserves were low, the amounts he'd been secreting away over the last months had seen to that. Janet would be left with the farm, and after the bank sold it up, as they inevitably would, taking whatever they needed to pay out the loan, there would be a little bit of money left over. Enough to find her a place in a care home.

Arriving at his destination, he strode into the travel agency.

'You're not from around here, are you?' said the agent, after introductions had been completed. In her mid-forties, with a swirl of tightly knotted hair a cyclone wouldn't shift, she looked like she knew her stuff.

'No. I live south of Nashville. Down the river.' Neville could see that the agent was confused. 'I didn't go local because . . . let's just say, I feel more comfortable dealing with someone from out of town.'

'Of course,' chirped the agent. 'We always act with the utmost discretion and professionalism.'

So you should, thought Neville.

'Now, where exactly is it that you'd like to travel to?'

'Manila, please. In the Philippines.'

'Excellent. Is this for a couple?'

'No. Just myself.'

'And would this be for business or pleasure?'

He glared at her. Too many questions.

'I'm sorry,' she said. 'And when would this be for?'

'Around two months' time. After the wool clip is sent away and I've banked the cheque.'

'And the return?'

'No return. One way.'

Neville arrived home in the mid-afternoon. Janet was standing at the window, enjoying the afternoon sun, exactly where he knew she'd be. He made her a cup of weak tea and left her to her thoughts, whatever they were. There were farm jobs to attend to and maintenance work on the shearers' quarters outstanding. On second thought, he'd put that job off for the morning, after they'd all gone to work – there was a more important task to complete. On the return drive from the travel agency, Neville had thought of some more questions for the agent. There was nothing wrong with Janet's hearing so he couldn't use the phone in the house. He'd have to use the one in the woolshed.

Inside the shed, with the shear a few weeks away, the floor was clean and bare. Next to a support column sat a small pile of fadges, the place where the young backpacker and the wool presser met for sex. That had been a pleasant diversion, watching them grow in confidence together, expanding their repertoire. There was something about her – he couldn't say precisely what, but something primal – that drew him to her. This last week, however, his titillation had begun to give way to frustration. It was their sex, not his. And then last night, the two of them just sat and talked. The buzz he got was diminishing. It was time to stop watching and start doing.

The phone, along with the one in the shearers' kitchen, was on a party-line with the house. It was just a matter of lifting the handset and making a call, like he normally would.

'Hello, Harkness Travel, Cynthia speaking.'

'Hello, Cynthia, it's Neville Hanigan. I was in this morning.'

'Yes, of course. How can I help?'

'I was thinking about things more after I left. As you know, you've offered to help arrange my tourist visa. After I arrive in Manila, I will attend the immigration bureau to apply for conversion to a resident visa. I wonder, would you be happy to write a letter of reference to support my application?'

Cynthia stammered. 'But . . . I only just met you today, for the first time.'

'And?'

'Well, you're a gentleman, but isn't there someone near you, someone who knows you better, who can write a reference for you?'

'Yes,' said Neville, the greasy woolshed phone slippery in his hands. 'But as I explained . . . discretion and all that.'

There was a short silence. 'Well, I do appreciate you giving us your business. I suppose I could draw up something formal and professional.'

'Thank you, Cynthia. I appreciate it.'

'I must say, you do seem hell-bent on living there.'

'Yes,' he snapped, cutting the conversation short.

Hanging up, he never heard the click when Janet replaced the handset on the house phone.

17
Sanna

Sanna craned her neck and took in the sheer rock face that rose straight up from the road. Peering the other way, over the vertical drop, she saw where the horseshoe of the river matched the curve of the road.

'Wow, this is spectacular,' she said.

'It's called Blind Man's Bluff,' said Ronnie, in tour-guide mode.

The road cut right through the middle of the face; the brittle, layered honeycomb form of the papa, more clay than rock, soft and grey, making a spectacular visage. Dotted around were large chunks that had sheared off the face and tumbled down onto the road. Perhaps that explained the name – apprehensive drivers rolling the dice and crossing the bluff with their eyes closed? On the other hand, she supposed it kept the local panelbeater in steady work.

'It really is very kind of you to do this,' said Sanna.

'Honestly, love, it's no problem. I was coming into town, anyway, to pick up supplies. Is everything okay?'

'Yes,' said Sanna. The doctor had been warm and friendly, like a favourite uncle. He didn't pry, just asked her some basic questions about her medical history, then prescribed what she wanted: the contraceptive pill. With Suzie covering her shift, her only discomfort was feeling foolish for not having arranged it sooner.

'I hope you don't think I'm just saying this,' said Ronnie, 'but I really like having you in the gang. You're bright, you work hard and you never complain. Not even about my cooking.'

'That's nice of you to say,' said Sanna.

'If there's one thing I can't abide, it's princesses.'

'Thank you. I understand you meaning that as a compliment.'

Sanna relaxed in her seat and enjoyed the scenery. Looking at the pockets of bush reserve, she imagined how inhospitable this country would have been before deforestation. Finland was heavily forested too, but differently: not as dense. Now that much of this bush had been cleared, the landscape felt as warm as its people. Well, most of the people. Bull was a reminder of how evil never strayed far from the surface. She was young but not so naive that she would allow herself to drop her guard.

'I'm glad you're happy here,' said Ronnie, snapping her thought pattern. 'After the British arrived in New Zealand, they fought wars with the Māori in the Waikato province, and the Māori retreated to Ngāti Maniapoto territory, an hour or so north of here. Because the land wasn't as flat or as fertile, the British didn't value it as much and didn't chase the Māori over where the battleline had been drawn. After that, a Māori chief took refuge here – his name was King Tāwhiao. It is said that he wore a large white bowler hat, and one day he placed that hat down on a map and proclaimed that all of the land under the hat would form his country: the King Country.'

'How interesting,' said Sanna.

'You didn't know that, did you? We're actually living under a hat!'

'No,' Sanna laughed.

'Eventually an accord was reached, a road was built and then the train line was cut through from north to south, which in turn brought the sawmillers, then the farmers. I'm not from one of these original tribes. My great-grandfather was a rail worker, descendant from Ngāpuhi, up north. But I'm proud to have my roots here.'

Turning off the tar-sealed river road onto loose metal was a test for Sanna. Potholes the size of hula hoops rattled her teeth and, in other places, too much loose metal on the road sent the rear end fish-tailing. Ronnie's car was a beast, a huge, bright orange Valiant Charger. It was far too big for her, but Sanna liked how it franked Ronnie's personality.

'I bought it for the stereo system,' Ronnie admitted. 'Six speakers. Surround sound.'

Sanna thought about what her friends would say if she returned home with a vehicle like this. She would be laughed out of Helsinki.

'Have I converted you to Bob Marley yet?' asked Ronnie.

The bass reverberated right through the springs in Sanna's seat.

'What do you listen to back home?'

'My parents were very particular about music,' said Sanna. 'We grew up listening to Sibelius.'

Ronnie pondered for a moment. 'Hmmm . . . I don't suppose they're a reggae band.'

By now, Sanna had travelled this road many times without concern, but she could feel a queasiness building.

'I've never been to Finland,' said Ronnie. 'Never been overseas, come to think of it. It's a big thing for us Kiwis, to head off for some OE, then come back and settle down. Silly me, I stayed at home, chasing a fella. Look where that got me. Pretty dumb, eh?'

Sanna didn't reply, focusing only on the road through the front windscreen.

'You got a fella? A boyfriend?'

Sanna felt a growing discomfort from the sweat on her face and neck, and a strange, unpleasant taste in the back of her throat.

Ronnie realised she was talking to herself. 'Not too far to go now, love. Just another fifteen or twenty minutes.'

Without warning, the salty saliva welling in Sanna's mouth gave way to a rush from the pit of her stomach. She lurched to her left – as she did, grabbing the door handle with her right hand and flinging the door open with her left. Projectile vomit launched into the still country air, in a rainbow's arc. Such was her out-of-body experience, she was only vaguely aware of Ronnie's shriek of horror and the Charger sliding to a halt.

Sanna sat strapped into her seat, caked in sweat, head slung low and to the side, spitting out the last remnants. She was in shock; at how rapid the onset of the episode had been, and how violently her body had reacted. Through a watery haze she could make out Ronnie, who had walked around to her side of the car.

'I see diced carrot is popular in Finland too!' Ronnie laughed, stepping carefully. 'You got a bit on the door handle, and some on the outside panels. Far better than all over yourself, or in the car.'

'I'm sorry,' Sanna mumbled, reaching for some green foliage to wipe her mouth with.

'Careful,' snapped Ronnie. 'Watch out for the cutty grass.' She opened the back door. 'Don't worry, bit of a spew, happens to all of us, eh? Sit tight and I'll find you a rag to wipe yourself up with.'

By the time Sanna saw and heard the van arrive, she had rediscovered her land legs and settled into her role as chef's assistant. Peeling potatoes and chopping cabbage, along with a mug of hot chocolate, had her back on an even keel. She liked Ronnie and was happy to take her instruction. Car sickness and a bit of work was no price to pay for being given the afternoon off.

She watched the gang pile out of the van and head to their rooms. Carl made his way directly towards them.

'Hi, Ronnie. Did you pick up my mail?'

'Nothing in the box, sorry.'

'Really? Not even any bills? Guess I can't complain about that, eh?' He took a purple plum from the fridge and noticed Sanna. 'Oh, hello. Looks like you've found a new job.'

'She's not bad at it too,' said Ronnie.

'Well, don't get used to it,' said Carl. 'You're back on the floor tomorrow.'

'No problem,' said Sanna, winking back at him. She liked Carl. It was nice to have a boss who cared so much about her.

18
Carl

Carl Stensness stood naked in front of the bathroom mirror, pausing momentarily to reflect in the glory of, at thirty-three, carrying the body of a wiry, buck-jumping twenty-year-old. He lifted his left arm, and angled around until the mirror image trapped the best of the light. The red lump under his armpit had grown since yesterday, now the size of a twenty-cent piece, with an angry head forming on the top. Grease boils were a regular hazard of the job. Most took care of themselves and came to nothing. Others took on a life of their own, and needed to be nipped before infection had a chance to take hold.

From his bathroom bag, Carl took a fold of tissue paper, which he unwrapped to reveal a needle and cigarette lighter. With the dexterity of a sober, experienced surgeon, he carefully held the base of the needle with his left hand, and torched the tip with his right. Sterilisation achieved, he found the sweet spot in the mirror again, zeroed in on a point a whisker below the tip of the boil, and pierced the skin. Immediately, milky coloured pus began to escape – a trickle at first – until Carl gritted his teeth, pinched the boil between his fore and middle fingers, and forced them together. The pain was excruciating, piercing into his brain like an ice-cream headache on steroids. Then it was over, the stinging gone as quickly as it had arrived. He mopped up the pus with toilet paper and put the needle away for another day.

Over the last season, aches and pains in Carl's back had become more persistent. It was typical, he'd been warned, an occupational hazard, yet the discomfort was always present, a nagging reminder of how his body was being asked to perform tasks it wasn't actually designed for. Shearing was a slog, hard enough without annoyances like grease boils thrown into the mix. With this pressure valve released, he would sleep more comfortably and tomorrow would be an easier day. Until the next one came along.

Carl prided himself on never having taken a day off work. They were a tough breed, the Stensness clan, their father a chiselled, tough-as-teak saw logger, who never got sick, because he couldn't afford to, and because it wasn't their way. Technically, Carl did leave a job once, the year he tried shearing in Australia, before he set up his own business, but that was different. Lured by the promise of better money and a juicy exchange rate, he landed a stand in a gang working in western New South Wales. However, the grass didn't prove to be greener at all. In fact, it was a dusty, drought-ravaged hellhole, where he never came to terms with unbearably hot woolsheds, and persistent, annoying pests, like Australia's national bird, the blowfly, and interfering union delegates, intent on taking a chunk of his pay for some reason he was never able to fathom.

He'd been on the verge of throwing it all in, to spend a week on the piss on the Gold Coast before flying home, when it was all taken out of his hands after he took a dislike to some locals at a pub. They were nothing more than a bunch of hayseeds with too much to say for themselves, but, crucially, they held a numerical advantage. Two black eyes and a broken jaw later, that was his Australian shearing experience done – not something he'd ever felt like reprising. Setting up his own contract run was a godsend. It was financially rewarding and suited his organisational skills. And he'd proved to be a good boss: he liked his staff and they respected him.

As he knew he would, Carl heard the shower next door turn on. The bathrooms had separate entrances, men and women, in a small outbuilding attached to the back of the kitchen. Partitioned into two, each held a separate toilet, vanity and shower, mirror images of each other, with space for dressing and undressing. No money had been wasted on the thin sliver of jib-board partition; it was as if Carl had custom designed the bathroom facilities himself, so perfect was the set-up. His modification was the icing on the cake. It had been a fast, simple job to arrive early one day, slide away the plastic soap and shampoo holder that hung down against the side of the shower, and drill a small hole through the plasterboard, into the adjoining shower. On the other side, the tiny peephole would be visible only to someone who knew it was there. To make it doubly safe, he stuck to the sides of the cubicle and near the hole, a series of colourful, waterproof transfers, the kind used by children, so as to confuse any potential wandering eyes.

In the years since, Carl had enjoyed many moments with the rousies who had come through the gang. Not that he considered himself a deviant or some kind of grubby voyeur. He had standards, he insisted to himself. For one, he no longer dwelt on his sister Lacey, usually taking it upon himself to coincide his shower with one of the other girls instead. Two seasons ago there had been an Asian girl working with the gang for a month – Angel, she called herself. He didn't know what had happened to her. She ended up getting a ride back into town after work one day with Ronnie, never to return. But for the time she was with the gang, he devoured the tone of her skin, her slender belly, and breasts which seemed perfectly proportioned for her body. Angel was by some distance the worst rousey Carl had ever employed, but he had only fond memories of someone who was the prettiest rousey he'd laid eyes on.

Until now. With the soap holder in his left hand, and his penis in the right, Carl pressed up against the hole, suspended his breathing, and watched Sanna. She was facing him, completely lathered in a soapy foam. Slowly, she massaged the soap into her body, then arched her back, letting the water cascade over the front of her shoulders and chest, between her legs to the ground.

When they were both finished, Carl dried himself off and quickly threw on a shirt and pair of shorts. He was halfway through a beer by the time Sanna emerged.

Watching her make small talk sitting alongside Crystal, Carl stared right through her sweat top, the image of what was underneath still fresh in his mind. He felt no shame. He was a good boss and what he was doing was harmless and victimless. Debbie would never know; with the money his contract run brought in, she wanted for nothing. They had a bach at Lake Taupo, she enjoyed French champagne and she rarely wore the same clothes twice.

There were phone calls to make, but Carl fixed his eyes on Sanna one more time, laughing with Crystal, her semi-dry hair hanging in waves over her shoulder. He didn't want her to be like Angel. If she was going to disappear on them too, best it wait until the end of the season.

January 1983

19
Emilia

'You're a bit early, love. Pub doesn't open for another hour yet.' The woman's voice was friendly, matching her face.

'No, I'm not here to drink,' Emilia said. They were standing on the footpath, outside the Mountain View Hotel.

'Most tourists, they usually go up the mountain. Or take a jetboat ride down the river. Not hang around here, eh?'

Emilia was intrigued by the woman's uniform. Her badge read 'Māori Warden'. Not police, but obviously some kind of authority figure.

'Honey Matenga,' the woman said, extending her hand. 'I usually patrol around here at night-time, but lately we've been having a few truancy issues. The school appreciates it whenever I pick up any strays who might be wandering around town.'

Emilia shook the woman's hand. It felt learned and kind. 'Emilia Sovernen.'

'Sovernen? Not many people pass through here with that surname, eh? I'm picking that's no coincidence.'

'The constable told me this was the last place my sister was seen, in the carpark opposite this pub.'

'I'm very sorry for your loss, dear. Terrible business. I met your father when he was here last year. It must have been very difficult for your family to deal with.'

'Thank you,' said Emilia. 'I'd just like to know what happened.'

'Of course.'

Emilia could see behind the woman's eyes. Was there the glimmer of an opening?

'How long are you here for, love?' Honey asked.

'I don't know. Until I find some answers. Better answers than what the police have.'

'There were a lot of them here, eh? Town was swarming with cops for weeks. Newspaper reporters and TV too. Everyone did their best to find her, love.'

They crossed the street. There was no-one else around; nobody running errands, no kids playing hookey from school.

'Over here,' said Honey. 'This is the carpark. I told the police, of course, it's on the record. But this is where I saw her. Around 11pm. She was standing on her own. Your sister, next to her backpack.'

'You were here?' Emilia's heart skipped a beat. 'You were working that night?'

'Why don't we go and sit down and have a cup of tea?' Honey suggested.

Despite Emilia's perfect English, half of the cafe menu she didn't understand. The remaining half held little appeal.

'The house special is toasted sandwiches,' said the young waiter, drawing out the carpenter's pencil he had wedged behind his ear and hovering it above his small notebook. 'Ham, cheese and tomato is popular.'

Emilia nodded.

'I can do you some hot chips on the side, too, if you like.'

'Thank you. And some water too, please.'

'Just a nice, hot cup of tea for me, please,' said Honey.

Emilia thought the waiter looked barely fifteen, fluff swirling around his cheeks where stubble might have been. School seemed to be optional around these parts. From where she sat, she could see behind the counter into the kitchen. He appeared to be doubling as chef, arranging the ingredients onto two slices of white bread, and dropping a scoop of chips into the deep fryer.

'Here you go,' he said, returning with the water.

'I'm sorry,' said Emilia. 'This glass is dirty.'

The waiter was unmoved.

'Here.' Emilia held the glass up to the light, for Honey to add her assent. No question, it had been AWOL at the time of the last dishwashing cycle.

He took the glass and gave it a couple of vigorous swishes with the bottom of his tee-shirt. 'There you go,' he said, replacing it on the table.

Honey shrugged her shoulders, as if to apologise.

The sandwich, when it arrived, seemed benign, but there was a problem with the chips.

'What?' the young man snapped, sensing Emilia's disquiet.

She nodded down towards the bowl. A couple of the chips had turned black in the frying. Highly unattractive, they weren't for eating.

The young waiter leaned forward. 'Oh, sorry. Not sure how they snuck in there.' He slid his fingers into the stack and removed the offending pair of chips with such dexterity he touched fewer than half of the others.

Honey offered a polite, embarrassed smile. All of a sudden, Emilia didn't feel so hungry.

'So, tell me,' she said, 'when you saw my sister, that night in the carpark, did you know who she was?'

'I'm sure you're aware, love, Nashville isn't a big town. Five thousand or so. People get to know people. Even when they don't know them.'

'So . . .?'

'I never met your sister, or spoke with her, if that's what you're asking. But I knew who she was. I'd seen her at the pub, with the shearing gang.'

Emilia gestured for her to go on.

'I've been doing this patrol for a long time now. Most nights, it's routine. I'm just a presence, eh? Being around, that helps nip trouble in the bud. It can stop someone going too far and giving their missus a clip around the ears if they know I'll go to court and testify against them. And if it happens anyway, then at least there's someone there to help, calm things down, or in some cases, take them to the hospital.'

Emilia frowned.

'Don't get me wrong, love. There's a lot of good people in this town. Wonderful people. And most of them know how to go out and have a good time without belting the tripe out of each other. But some nights when I put my uniform on, I say to my husband, "It's a full-moon night tonight." You just get a sense that it's going to be one of those nights, when the grog kicks in, the violence boils over the top, and regular people do crazy things.'

'And that night? Was it one of those nights?'

'Yes. Unfortunately, yes it was.'

Emilia checked with Honey to see that she wasn't taking up too much of her time. Honey wasn't in any hurry to be somewhere else.

'I'm very sorry, love. I wish it were different, but I never saw your sister leave the carpark. Not walking, nor in a car. There was a fight inside the bar, then it spilled outside – a bad one. I got involved with sorting that out and calling the police in. There was a lot of shouting, and pushing and shoving. It was chaos, really.'

'A perfect distraction for Sanna to disappear without anyone watching.'

'If you put it like that, yes.'

Emilia knew about the fight already. But it was something else to hear about it first-hand, from someone who was there. It chilled her to know that an argument, a fight, about nothing much, probably . . . fuelled by alcohol, she said . . . the fact that it happened right at that moment was all it took to wipe her sister from the face of the earth. Was that really how tenuous our grip on life was? She needed to speak to people in the shearing gang, as soon as she could.

'You're very kind, talking to me like this.'

'You're welcome, love. I just wish I was more help, eh?'

'And this gang, the people she was working for, what are they like?'

'They were good to her. In fact, I know she was popular, and she was happy amongst them.'

'That's the impression I got too, from her letters.'

'One of the shearers is half-mad, but if you're asking me, there's no killers in that lot.'

'Um . . . I don't mean to be rude, but how can you be so certain?'

'Because one of them is my daughter, that's how. Ronnie, their cook. If one of the gang had taken your sister, she'd know. And if she knew, I'd know.'

Emilia paused.

'Like I said, love. Around here, you get to know people.'

Something in the older woman's body language triggered a response in Emilia. As warm as Honey was, at the end of the day she was just like the detective. Biased in favour of their town and its people. A crime as bad as this one couldn't be committed by a local, because that would reflect poorly on their community. And themselves. On their own judgement of their neighbours. Instead, it was easier to blame an outsider. Someone who just happened to be driving through town at precisely the moment a huge fight started in the pub and spilled outside. Or some mysterious serial killer.

How coincidental.

How convenient.

20
Ryan

Carl pushed his last sheep for the morning down the chute and gingerly straightened his back.

'Good run?' asked Ryan.

'Not really. They're a bit sticky. Be patient, don't force it.'

Carl brushed his comb, dabbed a spot of oil onto it and passed the handpiece over to Ryan.

Ryan recoupled the handpiece, then peered over the top of the gate. The pen still held a dozen ewes. He charged in, hooked his arm underneath the neck of his unlucky victim, and dragged it out.

Pressing was mostly a stepping stone for young would-be shearers. A way to learn the ropes, to pay one's dues. A season on the press provided opportunities to jump on a stand in the meal breaks or when a shed was about to cut out, to be taught the correct technique, and to practise by repetition. But Ryan had never pretended that this was his career path. Carl didn't care. He didn't need another shearer to be developing underneath him, and even if he did, there were enough skilled men around the district who would eagerly accept a regular stand.

Even so, it was unthinkable in a shearing gang that anyone would continue to work as a presser without learning how to shear. Ryan was fit, able and young. And now, in his final year before graduation, even if this was his last season with the gang, career or no career, it was a matter of pride. The first time he'd tried, two seasons ago, he'd taken fifteen minutes, and made all of the usual rookie mistakes. Not stretching out the skin enough with his left hand, and too timid with his right, fearful of cutting the sheep's skin. That only made nicking it and leaving it covered in blotches of red all the more inevitable.

He'd watched thousands of sheep being shorn. Getting things done in the right order was the easy part. But that was like watching a professional hit a golf ball, then expecting to flush it out of the centre of the clubface when it was your turn. The variables – the heat of the handpiece, the wriggly sheep who wouldn't sit how he wanted it to, how the atmosphere affected the stickiness of the wool – all added up to a task far more difficult in practice than it appeared.

With the rest of the gang nose-deep in lunch, Ryan set to work. He surprised himself with a smooth, trouble-free start. Then, dropping into position for the 'long blow', he reeled off four impressive, full sweeps in succession. What he now realised – it was a shame he had taken so long to figure it out – was that shearing was three parts bluff. Sheep could sniff a bumbling novice a mile off. If your body language was confident, they were happy to oblige. 'Fake it till you make it' was the way of the woolshed.

Finishing up, Ryan thought it a good shear: a couple of tiny nicks, but a nice, even fleecing. He was still slow, but upon inspection, nobody would be able to tell if it had been done by him or one of the shearers. It was a job to feel proud of.

Except for one thing. The ewe had a mop of hair on top that was straight out of Spandau Ballet.

Bull lifted his gaze from his lunch plate. 'Huckery job,' he laughed loudly.

Ryan could see that he hadn't cleaned the head – the 'top knot' – off properly. Just a couple of quick strokes would be enough to tidy it up, but instead of sitting the ewe back down into the correct position, he let overconfidence get the better of him, allowing it to stand on its four legs. It didn't need a second invitation, bounding off the stand onto the main floor.

'Look out, sheep on the loose!' yelled Carl.

'Oh my God, watch out!' screamed Ronnie.

Startled and disoriented, the sheep darted to all corners of the shed, its half-mop flopping from side to side with each change of direction. Ronnie took refuge behind a bale. Everyone else was belly laughing – everyone except Ryan, who was desperate to catch the ewe before it found the door, leaped outside and did some real damage to itself. Finally, it got bogged in the pile of fleeces in the centre of the floor, allowing Ryan to pounce and take it down, with a rugby tackle any All Black would have been proud of.

The gang applauded and hollered in unison.

'Alright, you've all had your fun. Get on with your lunch,' said Ryan, by now beyond embarrassed.

'I'm sorry for laughing at you.'

The voice stopped Ryan in his tracks. For a fleeting, wonderful moment, Sanna was back in the shed, back in his life. Until she wasn't.

He knew who this woman was. Emilia Sovernen.

Ronnie had driven her down to the farm the afternoon before and the two women had obviously struck up a connection. He'd excused himself early from dinner last night, not because he was trying to avoid her, but because it all felt so awkward. And now it was his turn.

Meeting Sanna's sister for the first time had triggered an emotion. He knew what it was. Guilt. He'd spent the last year feeling sorry for himself. Accepting the police line that it was all too hard. That, no matter how tenacious their investigation was, sometimes nature had the final say. How Sanna wasn't the first and she wouldn't be the last;

swallowed into the deep, dark recesses of the King Country bush, never to be seen again.

'It's okay, everyone else laughs at me too,' he said.

'Do you mind if I join you?' She jumped up next to him on a finished bale.

The question was moot. 'So, what do you think of shearing work?' he asked. 'Think you're cut out for this kind of thing?'

'I'm an architect. I could design you a more efficient shed. But to work inside it? No, I will leave that to you and your colleagues.'

Ryan nibbled at Ronnie's freshly made Madeira cake, ready for his interrogation.

'Did you get to know Sanna well?'

What could he say? Tell her the truth? Did she want him to make her family's grief even more intolerable?

'I've been watching you. You work hard. You treat the girls with respect. Treat the animals with respect. I know Sanna would have liked those qualities. You would have been a good friend for her.'

Ryan gulped. 'I was the one who reported her missing from outside the pub. We got along, yes. She was a good worker too. Quick to learn. She fitted in really well.'

'With everybody? Did everybody like her?'

'Yes, everybody.'

'So, you don't think that anyone from –'

'Do I think anyone from the gang had something to do with her disappearance?' He nodded towards Pete. 'All he cares about is his new guitar.'

'And . . .' Emilia gestured towards Bull.

'Well, look, you never know what goes on in someone's head. He's crazy, that's for sure. But I'm not a psychologist. I really have no idea.'

Emilia wasn't put off. 'So you are saying it is possible? That it could have been someone from the shearing gang?'

'That's not what I said, no. What I said was that I don't know.' He needed to use the final few minutes of the tea break to refill the catching pens. 'Excuse me, I don't mean to be rude but I need to push on.'

She thrust out an arm. 'One more thing, please. Last night, the girls mentioned the owner of the farm where we are staying. Neville Hanigan. What can you tell me about him?'

'He's a sick fuck.' Ryan felt better for telling it straight.

'So, do you think . . .?'

'Absolutely. He's the type of person, yes. But do I think he *actually* did it? Followed us all into town and hung around outside the pub, without being seen? I'm not so sure about that.'

She seemed let down. He could see Sanna in her eyes.

'Let's talk more,' he said. 'Later, after dinner.'

21
Emilia

Later came around quickly. There was chit-chat around the dinner table, superficial but good-natured; she could sense the girls were beginning to warm to her. When the eating was over, Ryan grabbed a couple of beers and gestured for her to accompany him down to his room. They sat on the verandah, side by side.

'Sanna never really took to New Zealand beer. Let's see how you go.'

'Thank you. I will do my best,' she giggled.

'I know Sanna wrote to you sometimes. Was there anything she said . . .?'

'Said? About you? Or about the gang?'

'Any of us.'

'Nothing really, not anything specific. We were close, like sisters should be. But she was also private.'

He seemed relieved. Was he hiding something?

'We gave her letters to the police,' Emilia continued. 'She wrote about making decisions to change her life, but it was mostly what you'd expect from anyone discovering themself on the other side of the world. There was nothing that provided any clue.'

'I think she changed, that's fair to say,' said Ryan. 'This job does that to you. You get into a rhythm, things become automatic, so you get a lot of space and time to think things over, decide what you might do next.'

'Did she have a boyfriend? Or talk about having a boyfriend?'

'I went through all that with the police.'

'Sorry.'

'Carl is married. To his wife and the job. Pete, he just plays his guitar – I doubt Jim Reeves was going to sweep Sanna off her feet. And Bull . . . it was all she could do to work in the same shed as him, let alone start a relationship.'

'Which leaves just one man?'

She'd backed Ryan into a corner.

'We got along, just like I said. And we talked about Finland. She told me about your family holidays on the frozen lake.'

'And . . .?'

'And, what?'

'You know what I'm asking. Was there anything more between you?'

Ryan looked Emilia in the eye. 'No, nothing more.'

There it was again, the same look of relief she'd seen in him a few minutes earlier. Was he lying to her? Even if he was, why lie about it? They were both young, single and attractive. What reason would they have not to hook up together? And what reason would there be to keep it secret?

'So then, tell me about that night,' she continued. 'Was Sanna inside the pub when the fight started, or had she already left?'

She listened intently as Ryan slowly filled in the blanks, until eventually she could no longer ignore his yawning.

'I'm sorry. You're tired.'

'No, I'm sorry,' he said. 'I don't mean to be impolite. It's not you, I promise.' He sprang to his feet. 'How long are you planning to stay here with us?'

'One more night, maybe two, then I will go back into town.'

'And you're staying at the Riverside Motel?'

She recognised all the prerequisites to making a good barrister: never ask a question you didn't already know the answer to.

'They are good people, but for me to stay in town for longer, I'm going to have to find alternative accommodation.'

Ryan gestured for her to stay put while he darted inside his room. He re-emerged, handing her a piece of scrap paper. On it he'd written 'Jack Nash, 8393'.

'Give this man a call. Tell him you've been staying down here at the quarters with me, and it's okay for him to give you the key to the house. He'll show you where things are. As soon as we get a day off, I'll come up and see that you're settled in.'

'You have a house?'

'It's a long story. But yes. It's for sale, although don't worry, you can stay for free. There's stuff all over the place and it's a bit dusty, but you'll be safe and comfortable there.'

'Thank you,' she said, smiling. She liked this man, Ryan Bradley. He was helping her, and as long as he was helping her, he was helping Sanna.

December 1981

22
Ryan

The coffin was a modest, radiata pine affair, topped by a wreath of fresh flowers and a large, framed photograph of the deceased. It sat front and centre of the modern, A-framed, Presbyterian church, defiantly alone, a metaphor for how Colin Trescothick had lived his last thirty-seven years. Ryan filed in amongst a group of older townsfolk he didn't know. At an opportune moment, he slid into a vacant pew, halfway up.

By his best count, this was his fourth time inside a church: two other funerals, and a wedding, that of his old babysitter, Raewyn Lang, who had lived two doors along from his house. He never really understood why she'd invited him. There were times he'd been a real pest to her – insolent, not going to bed on time, demanding ice cream and, as soon as he'd learned a new swear word at school, not hesitating to use it on her. But despite having every reason to do so, she never once complained to his mother. Supposedly asleep in bed, he would hear his mum arrive home from her weekly 'housie' session, ask Raewyn how he'd been, and she would reply the same way every time, 'He's a sweet boy, never any trouble.'

Raewyn and her husband had driven from Auckland to attend his mother's funeral, and it provided him with the opportunity to offer an apology, of sorts, for being so obnoxious, all those years before.

'Yes, you were horrible.' She smiled back at him, clasping his hand in hers. 'But we're here for your mother, that's all that matters.'

Ryan sensed the church filling around him. It was a respectful turnout, bigger than his mother's; hardly surprising since Colin Trescothick, although a loner, had been a prominent retailer in town who involved himself in community affairs. It was only a week since Ryan had spoken with him, arranging the collection of a wardrobe, sofa and the kitchen table and chairs, to be transferred from the house to his shop. One week conducting business, the next week, sitting inside a church, with the same man lying just a few metres away, stiff and white, inside a pine box. Such was life.

Someone else sidled in alongside, taking him by surprise. 'Ryan,' he said, inoffensively.

'Philip,' nodded Ryan in return.

Philip gestured towards the coffin, and Colin's photograph sitting atop. 'Look at that beard. Not a whisker out of place.'

Ryan could only imagine the hours that Colin had spent tending to it over his lifetime.

'What was it?' asked Philip. 'A heartie?'

Ryan nodded. 'Dead before he hit the ground. Wouldn't have known a thing.'

'Probably all those custard squares we used to buy for the old bugger,' laughed Philip.

Another person pushed into their row – a woman.

'Hello, Ryan.'

'Becky,' he acknowledged. 'How are you?'

'Fine, thank you,' she said, taking hold of Philip's arm.

There was history between Becky and Ryan. She had pursued him determinedly, to attend the school formal as her partner. In the end he'd relented, not because he'd fallen for her, but because of the dearth of suitable alternatives. The night was a disaster, Becky introducing them to all and sundry as a couple, and constantly whispering into his ear, begging him to sneak off to the seventh-form common room and deflower her. It was to his eternal regret that he had obliged.

It was a touch awkward, but her now being an item with Philip was probably a good thing. Philip hadn't been at the ball, having already left school to start at the bank, and unless she'd been silly enough to tell him about their dalliance, which he was pretty sure she hadn't, then sleeping dogs could lie just where they were.

Mercifully, the service was short, the minister delivering the requisite amount of religious spiel, the price paid for holding the funeral in his church. Then followed an appropriately bland account of Colin's life. Widowed early, Colin never remarried, and there were no children. There was a younger brother, Arthur, a dairy farmer from Stratford, who provided a nice eulogy, if lacking in humour. That was fine. Anyone who knew Colin Trescothick knew he was no Billy T. James.

The trio hung back as the coffin was carried from the church and the mourners fell in behind.

'You going to the cemetery?' asked Philip.

'No. If I leave now, I can be back down the river in time for the afternoon run.'

Philip nodded.

'And you?' asked Ryan.

'I'd rather not,' said Philip.

'Yes, we are,' said Becky. 'It's his job. You know, being with the bank and all that.'

'Don't you start,' Philip scowled. 'You're as bad as my father.'

'Your dad means well,' said Ryan.

'He does indeed!' said Jack, taking them by surprise. 'I'll see you at the cemetery. There's someone I'd like you to meet, son.'

With that, Jack was off as quickly as he'd appeared, shaking hands in every direction, like a too-eager-to-please politician on the hustings.

'Looks like that's sorted, then,' said Ryan, grinning.

Philip scowled again.

'Listen, I'm sorry if I gave the wrong impression the other night,' Ryan offered.

'Water under the bridge,' said Philip.

'Are you sure?'

'Put it this way. People change, I understand. We're not schoolkids anymore, right? You've gone away, it's a different kind of lifestyle down there, and . . . well, if that means you're moving on, or turned into a bit of a dick, then so be it. I was wrong to challenge you on it. We should just accept each other for what we are.'

Philip offered his hand which, without thinking, Ryan shook. Over his shoulder, Becky shrugged back at him. So that was it then. It was all decided. Ryan simply needed to acknowledge that he had become a bit of a dick, and all would be okay between him and Philip. No problem.

Ryan turned the key in the ignition and crunched his car into gear. No problem? Like hell it was no problem.

23

Ryan

However functional, the wool press wanted for aesthetic elegance. It was a hulking, imposing conglomeration of steel and timber. If it was a car, it was no popular, new Japanese model. It was Ryan's mum's old blue Hillman Super Minx, the one she dropped him off to school in as a kid. An armoured tank thinly disguised as a car.

Ryan leaned up and over the side of the boxes and jammed fleeces into each corner. Sweat spilled off the end of his nose, into the greasy, lanolin-infused wool. He called out to the girls on the floor, 'Four more!', and between them they added the rolled-up fleeces. With both boxes full, the process of marrying the two together – the grunt work – could now begin. Ryan grabbed a fadge lid and laid it flat across the top of the box farthest from the centre pole. Tensing the muscles in his back, he deadlifted the metal lid, grunting as he placed it on top. Solid cast iron, it was heavy enough to cause serious damage if it wasn't handled properly. Carl had told of how his previous presser, the one before Ryan started, had wound the box up too high, so that when he pushed it around for it to sit above the bottom box, the lid fouled on a rafter and slid right off the top, crashing down onto the presser's head.

'Knocked him out cold,' Carl had said.

'The lid went right through the floorboards,' added Pete.

'Spent three days in hospital, then we never saw him again,' said Lacey.

'I heard he got brain damage,' said Bull, enthusiastically.

Like a grinder on a racing yacht, Ryan swung purposefully and rhythmically on the handle. It was heavy work, but he'd developed strength on the job, technique too, and steadily the box rose above the ground. With the two boxes now vertically aligned and the lid attached, Ryan removed the steel rods that were speared through the bottom of the top box, from one side to the other. He was like an illusionist pretending to unskewer his assistant.

Now began the race against time. Fleeces were building up alongside the sorting table. The shearers' catching pens were thinning out. Bales needed to be pressed. So many competing priorities. Ryan launched into his work, grabbing hold of the large metal handle and pumping it up and down, like an oversized car jack. Gradually the lid lowered, inside the margins of the box, and the wool from two boxes was compressed into one. This was the part of the job Ryan really enjoyed, feeling, with each swing of the handle, his deltoids and pectorals tighten. Whatever the law had in store for him – and at this stage he wasn't quite sure – he couldn't imagine it offering rewards like this. Quite the opposite, if the stories about portly barristers and lawyers lunching daily on steak and chips and scotch whiskey were true.

He paused to catch breath, then swung the top box out of the way and set about sewing the lid and fadge together. Ryan's sewing skills were rudimentary, but he hustled around each side, the sharp point of his large needle piercing the material cleanly, at regular intervals. Satisfied, he sliced through the twine with his pocketknife and tied off the final knot. It was now a matter of releasing the pressure on the two rods that were holding the lid down, and watching the wool inside expand into the tightly sewn fadge, the top rising a couple of inches, just like his mother's best soufflé.

But something was drastically wrong. Ryan watched on in disbelief as, pressure released, the top of the bale billowed upwards – not inches, but a couple of feet. Then more. It climbed up towards the ceiling, like crazy Spakfilla, taking the lid with it, until, inevitably, it crashed onto the floor with a fearful thud. The whole shed stopped in unison. Shearers and rousies together, every eye was trained on him, watching him frantically try to figure out what had happened.

Then it started. Bull laughed, low and scornfully, joined in harmony by Lacey in the upper octave. They were laughing at all of the wool that had spewed out over the top and sides of the box; laughing at Ryan's naivety and misfortune. Laughing because it was their handiwork.

Ryan soon figured what had happened. He'd been busy out the back, penning up, and someone – Bull – had switched the fadge he'd placed inside the box, with four lids, one for each side. To anyone looking, it gave the impression that it was a regular, whole fadge. After the two boxes were filled, despite Ryan expertly sewing everything together at the top, once the pressure came off there was nothing to stop the wool billowing out in all directions.

'Fuck it!' Ryan cursed softly to himself, trying not to let his annoyance show. Now hopelessly behind, the bale would need to be redone from scratch. He was weary and tiring. But he was more pissed off that it was Bull.

'Hey, lawyer-boy,' Bull yelled from his stand. 'I need a refill.'

'My pen too,' said Pete, in on the joke.

Ryan looked towards Sanna, who shrugged her shoulders. At least she wasn't party to it, and even if she had realised what was going on, she was too far down the pecking order to make a difference.

There was nothing for it. He pushed all of the wool clear of the press, and fixed a new fadge into the box. Grabbing hold of the fleeces, he tossed them back into the press, then rushed out to the pens, to resume mind games with the sheep.

*

The ride back to the quarters didn't improve Ryan's mood. Pete was strumming away, on another Jim Reeves bender. Carl, from the driver's seat, was sharing vocals.

'Nashville's favourite son,' Pete would say. Ryan wasn't convinced Pete understood that Jim Reeves' Nashville was not the same Nashville they'd grown up in, but it made no difference. Soon after starting the job, Ryan had complained to his mother that the music drove him spare. Instead of sympathising, she scolded him.

'It's good, honest music.' Gentleman Jim, she called him.

Out of the corner of his eye Ryan caught Sanna laughing. She knew how much he hated it when Carl sang along. She was unflappable. The stuff with Bull, his temper snaps and cruelty, it had upset her, but she hadn't let him shake her. It annoyed Ryan that he could let himself get riled about some ancient country singer, yet when she had something genuine to be upset about, she handled things so coolly. He'd heard about European directness. People made jokes about it, mostly against Germans and the French, but it seemed the Finns were in on it too. Now he knew there was a good side to it. He could learn a lot from her.

Ryan allowed his mind to wander. He loved this countryside and how he was inexorably connected to it, physically and spiritually. He loved the spotted palette of autumn, after the tall poplars turned yellow. In spring, he treasured the familiar whiff of freshly cut grass that would waft across the newly shaved hay paddocks and settle upon the town. In winter he welcomed the icy frosts and soupy fogs that would slowly escape out of the valleys, except on the days they didn't, when the white mist would press in close around his body and the chill would take hold right inside his joints and not let go.

Carl's question came out of nowhere. 'Ryan, you had Terrence Pihama teach you at school, didn't you?'

'Yes. For a couple of years. He was okay.'

'I heard the police were looking at him. For the Atkins murder.'

'About fucking time,' chimed Lacey.

'Technically, without a body, it's not really a murder,' offered Pete.

'What do you say, Ryan? Do you reckon he did it?' Carl was insistent.

Why do people keep asking me? 'Um . . . I have no idea' was the best Ryan could muster. It was also the truth.

'This town really does seem obsessed about women disappearing into the bush,' said Sanna.

'For good reason,' said Bull, nodding. 'For good reason.'

24

Sanna

In all her life, Sanna had never felt so tired. After days without a break, she had become zombie-like, mechanically but barely performing her duties, her broom now a crutch to prevent her from keeling over. She'd never been afraid of hard work – indeed, she embraced it – but the exhaustion, mental and physical, was on another level. She had come to loathe Carl rapping on her bedroom door every morning, sometimes only an instant after she'd put her head down to sleep. But as fatigued as she was, she wasn't someone who backed away from a commitment. She would see things through to the end of the season.

Having Ryan in the gang helped. He was the closest to her in age, and wasn't like the rest of them. Shearing wasn't his life, that lay elsewhere. Even though this was his home region, he was more like her, someone passing through, the job a means to an end. She looked forward to their evening dalliances. He had been shy and awkward at first, and the setting wasn't exactly perfect. She would have enjoyed sleeping with him; actually sleeping side by side, waking to feel the warmth of his body on hers, before flirting playfully over breakfast. But she was grateful for the woolshed. It was better than nothing.

Ryan had become an increasingly assured lover – he had learned more about what made her tick. It helped that she liked him too, as a person. His work ethic, his values, his affability . . . all things to admire and enjoy in a man. One day in the future, when it would be time to settle down with someone and raise a family, these would be qualities she would seek in a husband and father of her children. She would not accept anything less. By the time that came around, Ryan would be a distant memory. She was under no illusions that this was anything more than a passing fling for both of them: a holiday romance. And that was just fine.

Approaching the woolshed, Sanna's gaze was drawn up towards the farmhouse by a light shining in a large window. With darkness advancing, she was confident that she couldn't be seen herself. The figure standing in the window intrigued her. The gang had talked about the farmer's wife, Janet, one night over dinner.

'She's a cabbage,' Lacey had said, with apparent authority. 'Ever since the accident, she just sits there all day doing nothing. I feel sorry for Neville. One little thing goes wrong in the car and you get saddled with that for the rest of your life.'

Sanna wondered if some little sympathy might have been reserved for Janet. After all, Neville had all of his faculties, and his liberty. She had met him once or twice, when he had come down to the shearers' quarters. It wasn't much to go on, but there was something discomforting about him. Not at all somebody worthy of her sympathy. If he was a victim, it was hard to understand how he had suffered more than Janet.

Sanna paused at the entry into the woolshed, and looked again towards the window. Her eyes were tired, and it was hard to be certain, but the figure didn't look female. Maybe staring out the window ran in the family? Husband *and* wife? She held her gaze for a moment longer, until she felt her spine shudder. He was a creep, everyone had said so, but her reaction told her it was more than that. What if he was capable of evil? She would need to be on guard whenever he was around.

*

After the sex was over, Sanna kissed Ryan softly on his forehead and rushed back to her room. Her routine was the same each time: sneak quietly in through the door, undress in the dark and slip into her bunk, taking care not to disturb her sleeping roommate.

'Did you have a nice time?' Crystal's voice startled her.

'I'm sorry, I thought you were asleep.'

'I never sleep until after you're back.'

Sanna didn't know what to say. So much for her affair with Ryan being private.

'He's a good guy,' said Crystal. 'Kind and strong. I'm happy you're together.'

'I didn't think anybody knew.'

'The others are too preoccupied with themselves to notice,' said Crystal. 'But I've seen the way he looks out for you when we're working in the shed.'

'It's nothing serious.'

'Sure.'

Sanna was too exhausted to tell if Crystal was agreeing with her or being sarcastic. 'When we finish the season, I will meet up with my friend again, and then my visa will expire. So it can never be for the long term.'

'But let's say you forget about the visa situation for a minute. If you had the choice, would you want it to be something more?'

Sanna paused momentarily before answering. 'Nothing is forever. Whatever we have, whoever we share it with. We are here, a moment in time, then we are gone. To another moment, in another time.'

'Sounds to me like you've been listening too much to Bull.'

They giggled together.

'Goodnight,' said Crystal.

'Goodnight,' said Sanna. She rolled onto her side, knowing that as soon as she fell asleep, Carl would be hammering at their door again.

25
Tom

Detective Inspector Tom Harten hooked his arm out of the driver's side window and slapped a magnetic blue flashing light to the roof of his 'detective issue' Holden Belmont. He led the posse out of the police station carpark, right, then right again onto the main highway. They travelled south, out of town, Harten in the lead car, alongside Andy Harris, a detective from the Whanganui drug squad. Two constables followed behind in a marked car; then another two marked police vehicles, each carrying a pair of out-of-town members on loan for the day. Bringing up the rear were two rented three-tonne trucks, each with a high, sealable cab.

Strung out on the long straight before the highway rejoined the river, the convoy made for an impressive show of strength. Oncoming vehicles pulled over to the verges, as if they were paying respect to a funeral cortege. That always gave Tom a buzz, knowing, at that moment, his work was the most important thing in this small corner of the universe.

The drugs bust had been a while in the making. Cannabis was a scourge in the local community. Tom never cared about the odd joint being passed around at a party; he knew eradication was impossible. But increasingly, people had woken up to the commercial possibilities of growing and dealing, and had adopted that as a career option.

And there were too many people in Nashville who thought that drawing the dole and sitting around permanently stoned was a valid lifestyle choice. Not on his watch, it wasn't.

Twenty kilometres south the group split into two; Tom and his constables taking a sealed side road, while the others took the next turn-off, not much more than a narrow, metal track that snaked deeper into a river valley.

Ten minutes later, Tom and Andy wended their way up a gently curving driveway to a modest, timber farmhouse.

'Watch out for the kids,' said Andy, pointing to two little ones playing in the front yard.

'It's always more fun when the whole family's home,' said Tom, with a grin.

A man appeared on the front porch, in shorts and a singlet that barely concealed his paunch.

'Mario,' said Tom, tipping an imaginary cap.

'Detective,' the man replied.

'I expect you know why we're here.'

'Yeah. The warrant of fitness on the trailer expired. I was just telling Rose I needed to pick up a new one, wasn't I, darling?'

'That's right, he was.' His wife, Sharon, had joined him on the porch. 'Ashleigh. Be a good girl, take your sister inside. Go on!' She shooed them into the house and flashed a mocking smile back at the policemen. 'Can't have them exposed to police brutality – they're too young for that.'

'We're not here to make trouble, Sharon.'

'Trust me, you lot are always trouble.'

'Didn't hear you say that the night I held your mother's hand for two hours while she was trapped inside her car,' said Tom.

Sharon struggled for a comeback. 'You're due in for a haircut.'

That much was true, but Tom wasn't here to talk about that.

'There's real criminals out there, you know,' continued Sharon. 'Snatching hitchhikers off the side of the road. Why don't you do something about that?'

Tom stood, unmoved.

'Go on then, do your worst. What's he done?'

Constable Peterson stepped forward. 'Mario Mason, I'm arresting you on suspicion of cultivation, possession and supply of a class C drug, namely cannabis.'

Tom watched on as his young constable finished reading Mario his rights. Peterson's delivery was improving.

Mario already had his wrists presented for handcuffing. 'Yes.' He gestured to Sharon. 'You better run inside and get me a proper shirt, love.'

'You'll be home by lunchtime, don't worry,' she said. 'They've got fuck all. It's just a fishing expedition.'

'We've got a squad and two large trucks around at the plantation as we speak. I wouldn't be waiting on lunch if I was you.'

Within half an hour, Tom, Andy and Peterson were at the plantation site. It was well hidden, but Mario hadn't counted on an injection to the police budget providing for increased helicopter surveillance in the region.

The size of the plantation took Tom by surprise. 'It's always the greed that gets them in the end.'

Andy nodded in agreement. 'Good result, this.'

'Beats the hell out of being stuck in the middle of a domestic,' said Tom, ruefully. Domestic violence, much of it fuelled by alcohol, was becoming increasingly prevalent. 'Beats looking for missing hitchhikers too, just quietly.'

'Yeah. Mary Atkins. Sorry about all that business. Nobody wants a serial-killer case hanging over their patch.'

'You know what it's like, mate. Just when you think it's all over, red rover, you get a phone call from some brass, insisting you follow up on what some kooky clairvoyant has told the women's mags.'

'Don't envy you any of that, mate. Any cop who says he wants to head a high-profile, needle-in-a-haystack case, like that one, is either an egomaniac or a bullshit artist.'

'Well, as we know, no shortage of both of those in the job,' said Tom. They laughed together. The best jokes were always grounded in truth.

'C'mon, Billy, get it down your gullet!'

'Don't be a girl's blouse!'

The gathering of off-duty policemen was growing increasingly impatient.

'Get fucked. I'll do it when I'm good and ready.'

'*Down! Down! Down! Down! Down! Down! Down! Down!*' The chant grew to a deafening crescendo. The young constable with his lips perched on the edge of a full jug of beer had no choice. He craned his neck backwards and deposited the lot down his throat, in one hit.

'Good work, Billy!' hollered one.

'About fucking time,' said another.

'Good to see your boys letting their hair down,' said Tom to Andy, both of them perched on stools at the bar.

'Well, I reckon we all deserve a night on the piss,' Andy replied. 'The hospitality here is first class and, let's face it, it would be a crime to let this beautiful bar go to waste.'

The pair nodded in unison and drained their pint glasses. The bar was a project Tom had overseen two years ago: conversion of one of the old padded cells attached to the rear of the station into a drinking hole for their own use. Small and cosy, it was a tasteful feat of joinery, the envy of other police stations around the North Island. Andy was right – if it couldn't be enjoyed on a day when they'd nicked Mario for growing and dealing, then when could it be used?

Tom ducked around to the other side of the bar, to refill their glasses, just as Peterson, the only person at the station still sober and in uniform, stepped in.

'Very sorry to interrupt, sir, but she's here.'

'What? My wife?'

'Mrs Graves, sir.'

'Please tell her, Peterson – and you can quote me on this – that she can't fucking drop in here on a fucking whim, whenever it might fucking suit her. Got that?'

'Sir.'

Peterson was back within seconds.

'Yes?' said Tom, irritated.

'She says, sir, that she's not fucking dropping in here on a fucking whim. She says she has important information she would like to discuss.'

Tom rolled his eyes at Andy. 'You pour 'em, mate. Won't be a minute.'

The detective's illicit affair with Wanda Graves was an open secret around the station. Probably around town too, but he was beyond caring.

'Wanda. I'm not sure if the constable explained to you, but it isn't exactly a good time.'

'Is it ever a good time for you, Tom?'

Tom frowned. Was that an attempt at humour or an insult? 'Sorry about tonight. But it's been a big day with the Whanganui boys. And we got a nice result.'

'I'm happy for you. For all of you. But . . .' she leaned forward and whispered, 'as I told you, Henry will be back on the weekend. And, you know, a woman's got needs.'

Tom whispered back, 'And without blowing my own trumpet too loudly, I reckon I do a pretty fair job of catering for those needs.'

'Put it this way,' she said, 'you're good, but it's like what you told me about your job. You're only as good as your last result.'

That one was an insult. Or a challenge. 'Give us half an hour,' he said.

As he spoke, Peterson presented himself again.

'Sorry, sir, but I've just taken a phone call. I think you'd like to know.'

'Yes, what is it?' said Tom, even more irritated.

'Skeletal remains, sir. There's been a body found in a shallow grave, in bushland, up near the National Park.'

Tom and Wanda locked eyes. 'Forget what I just said.'

Wanda's excitement was palpable. 'Let me sit in the back. I'll keep out of the way.'

'Not a chance,' he snapped.

Tom rushed back into the bar. 'Sorry to break up the party, but we've got a job. Skeletal remains. National Park.'

'Jesus,' said Andy. 'What do you reckon? Atkins, the missing hitchhiker?' The location tied in.

'No fucking idea, mate. But we'd better go in separate cars. Dunno how long this might take.'

They scrambled their things together and rushed to the carpark. The night air hit Andy with a rush, and he belched up a mouthful of beer.

'Probably shouldn't be driving,' he said.

Tom kept walking. 'How many fingers am I holding up?' he shouted back.

Andy looked puzzled. 'You aren't. None?'

'Exactly. You're all sweet, mate. Follow me!'

26
Neville

Neville Hanigan hated having his time wasted. Something wasn't right with the backpacker and the presser. Where had the passion and excitement gone; her arms stretched aloft revealing youthful breasts, while straddling his body and riding him for all she was worth? Instead, there was a lot of talk. Silly talk about their childhoods. All of that bored him. This wasn't what he'd come to the shed for.

He eased backwards, careful not to force any squeaky floorboard. Out of sight, he found the side door. The dark was no impediment, he knew the shed backwards, but as he reached for the handle, a sharp, sudden sound from above took him by surprise. He let out an exclamation. It wasn't much, but it was audible.

'Hey! Who's there?' he heard the presser cry out.

Neville pushed open the door. Adrenaline charged, he bounded down the steps, but eying the open paddock, he knew it would be futile to run. He spun around, ducked down low, and crouched under the steps, tucked into a tight ball.

Seconds later the door reopened. The wool presser was standing right on top of him.

'Is there anyone there?' The girl had joined him.

'Nothing I can see,' said the presser.

Neville was shocked to notice his hat had fallen off his head and was protruding slightly, out from under the steps. Heart pounding, he held his breath, inched out his right hand, and slid the hat back in.

'Must have been a possum,' the presser said. 'They crawl along the rafters. Usually, you can see where they've been by the droppings on the floor.'

'It's a little bit creepy,' she said.

'Yeah. Let's call it a night. I think we're done talking, anyway.'

Neville listened for the door to close again. He sat, knees pressed against his chest, and counted to himself. Only when he reached one thousand did his heart rate return to normal, and he felt safe enough to come out from his hiding place.

Neville went straight to the oak glass cabinet, found Johnnie Walker, and set him free. His close shave had frightened him, but now that he'd gone undetected, he revelled in it. The slug of whiskey took the thrill to another level, sharpening his anxiety, then just at the point where it became uncomfortable, lowering him, calmly and surely. Disappointment from the evening's proceedings was forgiven and forgotten. This was unexpected, but in a strange way, it was better.

He got up to check on Janet. It was earlier than her regular bedtime, but not unprecedented that she should retire early. It wasn't as if there was any point in her waiting up for some evening conversation – to chew over the farm's finances, or discuss the Springbok rugby tour of New Zealand. A pivotal, divisive event, full of protests and violent confrontations, every adult in the country was still arguing about it. Everyone, it seemed, except Janet.

He tapped on her door. In the early days of their marriage, this had been the matrimonial bedroom. Before the accident, before he'd taken up residence in the second bedroom. The bedside lamp was still on; she usually took her time before turning it off, and some nights, for whatever reason, it would stay on right through. She was lying flat on her back, her default position, staring up at the ceiling.

He walked over to the bed, took her hand and squeezed it gently. 'Goodnight,' he said, before straightening the bedcover and walking out. Not long now and he wouldn't have to bother with this pretence anymore. He poured himself another double shot, and from the filing cabinet that stood in the corner of the kitchen, he pulled out a handful of maps that were folded into tight, neat rectangles. The one he was after was dog-eared and worn, pocked with holes where the folded corners had been. His forefinger circled around it, a detailed topographical map of the region. It was predominantly green, with vein-like blue rivers and streams cutting across it, and whorls of black lines circling at intervals; tight and narrow where the peaks were, like giant-sized fingerprints stamped onto the page.

He opened a second map and sat it on top of the first. Smaller, it lacked the detail of the other map; instead, it contained all of the roads of the region, and names where all the farms were situated. His own name was there, exactly where it should have been, NJ Hanigan, along with his closest neighbours, on the town side, the Tuckwells, and, a few kilometres further up the road, heading south along the river, JP Pearson and Sons.

Neville worked the two maps in tandem. The smaller one provided him with familiarity. Knowing exactly where the farmhouses were and who owned them was useful. The larger map provided a detailed picture. How the tight metal roads twisted up and around hills, and where the farmed paddocks gave way to pockets of natural bush. Together, they told the story of the region. They also told which locations were the most remote. Which dead-end roads were unlikely to have much – or any – passing traffic on a given day. Which spots contained the little nooks and crannies that might serve him well.

His eye came back to a place north-west of his own farm, a forty-five-minute drive away. That road continued on past a couple of farms, the names both unfamiliar to him, and ended at a forest reserve; rugged, inhospitable country that spread for miles to the west. That area was sometimes frequented by hunters, wild pigs mostly, although he'd heard of deer hunters trying their luck in there as well. If he chose his time carefully, the chance of crossing paths with anybody, on their way in or out, was slim.

Happy with his work, he put the kettle on. In the morning he would finish a small job, replacing a faulty water pump. Then, if there was time, he would drive up there and take a closer look.

As was his custom, Neville turned on the late TV news and relaxed into his black, faux-leather recliner-rocker, extending the footrest. Behind him was the dining table, other maps still unfolded across the top of it, with his hat sitting on top. Like King Tāwhiao's white bowler hat, it marked out his country. Neville Hanigan's King Country.

27
Tom

Tom and Andy drove as far as they could along the rutted, pumice track before stopping and continuing on foot. The path extended down a gentle slope from what was an old, now-abandoned sawmill. Tom's powerful torch afforded them smooth passage; twisting his ankle in one of the many water channels was the last thing he needed.

A couple of hundred metres into the scrub they came across two men, standing alongside a mound of dirt, just to the side of the track. Tom recognised the taller man, Morrie Yates, as the owner of the petrol station, up on the highway.

'Morrie. How are you doing?'

'You fellas took your time.' Morrie wasn't in the mood for pleasantries.

'What's the story?' asked Tom.

'My young fella rides his trail bike through here. He stopped to adjust something, noticed this mound . . . Something didn't sit right, so he had a look. Then we called you fellas in to suss it out. There's bones in there. Human I reckon.'

'Have you . . .?'

'Neither me or my boy touched a thing,' insisted Morrie.

'I'm going to have to speak with him directly – you know that?'

'I sent him home to get ready for bed. It's a school night.'

Tom sighed. He'd worry about that later. He nodded to Andy and, together, they stooped over the mound. Morrie had it right, there was a skeleton partially visible in the dirt. Human not animal. They'd need to get a forensics team in from Hamilton, but they wouldn't be here until late morning, at the earliest. Tom leaned in closer and gently brushed some of the dirt away.

The skeleton was more visible now. A right foot, ankle, and, extending lengthwise along the makeshift grave, a tibia and fibula. Tom paused before scraping away some more. Something wasn't right. For one, this wasn't the remains of a petite young woman. Mary Atkins was slight and tiny; barely over five foot tall. This wasn't her.

There was something else. The condition of the skeleton. It was too clean. Where were any clothing fragments? Any tissue residue? Any discolouration? This shallow grave and mound: it was too fresh. Tom shook his head and stood up.

'Morrie. You or your son . . . you wouldn't be taking the piss, would you?'

'What? You think I've got nothing better to do than stand out here all night?' came the curt response.

'What's the matter?' asked Andy.

'Take a closer look, mate. That's no body. Someone's having a lend. It's one of those fake, medical skeletons. You'll probably find a price tag on the other foot.'

28
Philip

Never once had Philip questioned his choice to skip university to leave school and start with the bank. Until now. Not that he suddenly coveted a degree; there wasn't a subject that caught his eye enough for him to commit three or four years of his life to it. Nor was he desperate to leave Nashville. The King Country was in his blood – if he pulled up stumps, where else would he move to?

Things, however, had changed. He was sick of his dad and his intrusions; sick of the straitjacket that was banking; sick of waiting for an opportunity to climb the ladder into a slightly less mundane position; sick of the well-meaning but tiresome Becky, to whom, in a moment of self-doubt where he panicked himself into thinking there wouldn't be any other options down the track, he had agreed to commit the rest of his life.

He'd caught note of his moodiness. Sharp and snappy with the bank staff, dismissive of Becky, snapping at his mother for no good reason. Hunting offered some respite, although, because of their respective prowess, he was mostly at the mercy of Slurps as to where and when. He hadn't lost his mind, he wasn't going to go crazy and do anything silly, but still, he needed a circuit-breaker. Some kind of escape. Not alcohol – that was already an everyday part of the lifestyle, albeit there would no doubt be another day soon, when his father or the local doctor, probably both, would impress upon him that he drank too much and, for the sake of his liver and the people around him, he would need to lay off the grog for a bit. And, just like the other times, he would tell them to mind their own business.

Philip did the honours with the pint handles, and he and Slurps claimed their favourite snooker table. The club was abuzz with chatter around the police being called last night to where a skeleton had been found, supposedly of the missing hitchhiker. Only it wasn't her at all. Or anybody. It was raising a few laughs around the club, although the word was that DI Harten was spitting chips.

On the hour, the intercom crackled to life, announcing this month's new member induction. A tradition as old as the club itself, prospective new members were nominated by an existing club member, their intent to join posted on the noticeboard in the foyer, before a formal vote was held amongst the members present on induction night. This time there were two nominations: the first, a newly transferred teacher from South Africa who Philip thought harmless enough and who would fly through the process without any trouble. He also supposed the second nominee, Ryan, would do the same.

The voting process was identical every time. The prospective members waited in the committee room, along with their proposers, out of view and earshot of the main bar. One by one, members used a small wooden barrel containing red marbles on one side and black marbles on the other, to draw out, hidden from view behind a screen, the marble of their choice, and place it in the boxes representing each nominee. The equation was simple. Two black marbles and a candidate would be denied membership.

Inevitably there were jokes about filling the boxes with black marbles, but even so, nobody could remember the last time anyone was blocked. People who weren't suitable never got nominated in the first place.

'Remember, the club needs all the members it can get,' announced Abe Lewis, in charge of proceedings. 'Let's get this done quickly so we can bring them in for a celebratory beer.'

Slurps took his shot, laid down his cue and cast his vote. 'Your go, mate,' he said on his return.

Philip wandered over. Ryan hadn't been himself this summer, and it seemed like he was developing a bit of an attitude. Probably not deliberate, Philip conceded, but it was there, every time he mentioned something he'd learned or somebody he knew from university. Fair play to him, though – they'd argued last time they were together at the club, about Ryan not buying a raffle ticket, just breezing in and taking everything for granted. Becoming a paid-up member, instead of relying on him to sign him in, was the least Ryan could do.

Philip stood over the barrel, fumbling around in the pile of marbles. There was nothing wrong with Ryan wanting to join the club. What was wrong was his dad nominating him and the two of them sitting inside the committee room right now, thick as thieves, probably having a gossip or a whinge about him while they waited. It was so typical of his father – organising everyone's life for them. Now he thought about it, it probably wasn't even Ryan's idea to join the club, but his dad's. So that Ryan would owe him something back later on, and his dad would once again have his fingers in everything that happened in the town.

He'd overheard his dad talking to his mum last week, about how they should invite Ryan for Sunday dinner, because his own mum had passed on and, anyway, 'He's as good as family.' That always pissed him off. Ryan wasn't family. They were just kids growing up together, who happened to live in the same little town. Friends, not family. And now, he wasn't even sure if they were that. Friends hung out and did stuff together. Naturally, without having to force anything. They understood each other. Since he'd gone to university, Ryan had become a different type of person. And the worst thing was, he didn't even realise it.

Philip grabbed a marble and checked the colour. Red. That was the other thing. It was almost like his dad was using Ryan for insurance. In case his own son didn't measure up enough to be entrusted with the Nash lineage, or went off the rails. Ryan wasn't a Nash – he could never be that – he was an orphan being brought into the family fold. Well, fuck that, fuck the both of them. Philip didn't need any insurance or plan B to cover for him. He saw things differently to his dad, but he was capable, he had things under control. He sure as hell didn't need Ryan to step in for him.

Philip dropped the red marble, squinted into the barrel opening, and pulled out a black one. He scanned around quickly, saw there was no-one watching, slipped his hand back in, and took out a second marble. A second black one. He dropped both into the box with Ryan's name on it, returned to the table and took his next shot.

29
Ryan

It took all of Ryan's energy for him to lift his plate off the communal table, return it to the kitchen and grab another beer. He was glad that Sanna could see it in him, the same exhaustion he saw in her. Tonight they would give the woolshed a miss and recharge their batteries. He was so tired he'd even stopped caring about getting laughed at for being blackballed at the club and being denied membership. It was embarrassing, to be sure, a big shock when it happened, but when Abe Lewis came into the committee room to break the news, it was Jack who was more upset about it than he was.

Pete put his guitar down, giving Bull space to start on one of his practice sermons. Usually that was a cue to get as far away as possible, but with his legs unwilling and his eyes drooped almost to a close, Ryan was stuck fast.

Bull commanded the head of the table. 'Here is the truth, people. It is why we are all gathered today at the Church of the Oracle. Christianity, conventional Christianity, has failed you, it has failed all of us. Its truth is not truth at all – it is a mere house of cards, built on a falsehood. Built on the lie that Jesus Christ is God the son. Jesus Christ is in fact not God the son, he is the son of God. The son of the Holy Spirit. Jesus Christ was a man conceived by the Holy Spirit – God – whose life was without blemish and without spot, a lamb from the flock, thereby being the perfect sacrifice. Thus he became our redeemer.

'I know this to be true, because this very Bible knows it to be true. And my friends, if we band together, if we all stay true to our beliefs, if we learn the truth together, and together we reject evil, and the teachings of evil, then together we will grow stronger. And that, people, is what will deliver us unto salvation when the day arrives. The truth.'

Ryan had to admit that Bull's delivery was improving. It was already good enough to win over anyone with a weakness, who might be looking to be won over. Bull's own day of truth would come when people who knew more about religion than he did – real theologians, real religion – would hold him and his utterings up to the light. Even then, Bull was such a master manipulator he would no doubt turn the scrutiny and criticism to his advantage, to play the oppressed victim. Which in turn he would leverage into bigger and bigger followings.

'Tonight, I talk about the truth that is death. We do not fear death, because we know death. We know the truth of the thorn in the flesh.' Bull was on a roll now. Crystal raised her eyes at Ryan – she was too sensible to be drawn in by his nonsense – while Sanna didn't bother to disguise a monster yawn. Ryan noticed how Ronnie had pulled herself away from the dishes and was now sitting at the end of the table, listening attentively.

'The thorn in the flesh is not some undefined illness. Corinthians 12:7 tells us of individuals sent by Satan to disrupt the apostle Paul and his ministry, hellbent on causing death. But we do not fear this . . . no, we do not. And why not? Because death is not the believers going to Heaven in the presence of the lord, or the unbelievers going to Hell . . . no, it is not. Death is a continuing state, a continuing state that ends only when Jesus Christ returns for his saints. Thessalonians 4:13–18, Corinthians 15:51–54 tells us this. It tells us that our souls are not immortal, thus we do not – as some religions teach, incorrectly – remain dead until the final resurrection . . . soul sleep, they call it. No, in death we continue, if we believe in the truth, we continue, until Jesus Christ returns.'

'But what about the unbelievers?' Ronnie asked. 'Is it the same for them?'

'The unsaved do not go to Hell. We are all continuing in death. The difference is, upon the return of Jesus Christ for his saints, they die again.'

'Sounds better than Hell, Ronnie,' said Carl. 'But still, not a great option.'

Bull continued. 'Should you choose to be born again, to be baptised in the Holy Spirit, then you shall be saved. And not only shall you be saved, you can never lose that Holy Spirit through the committing of sinful acts.'

'Whoa, hang on a minute!' Now Carl was interested. 'So, let me get this right. In this church of yours, the Church of the Oracle, if I agree to be baptised, to be born again . . . I can steal money, I can covet thy neighbour's wife, I can –'

'Bend her over and pound away to your heart's content,' laughed Pete, his ribs rippling through the thin material of his tee-shirt.

'I can commit all of these sins, and there are no consequences for that?' said Carl, completing his sentence.

Pete slapped his thigh. 'Now that's *my* kind of church!'

Bull was insistent. 'Confessing your sins and saying ten Hail Marys? Is that really consequence? Once you submit to the core truth, the acknowledgement of the Holy Spirit as the true God, then your faith and your belief can never be taken away. Everything is forgiven.'

'But you can't just pretend there are people who don't have problems, who can't abide by clean living,' said Ronnie. 'What about them?'

'Ah . . . there is no Hell, but I didn't say there is no devil. Alcoholism, violence, homosexuality, depravity. It is possible for the devil spirit to exist in any believer. And we have the power, any of us, to cast out those devil spirits where we seek to do so.'

'Even in yourself, Bull?' Carl had just about heard enough. 'Not saying you're a homo, but I reckon you've got form with the others.'

'What is important as a pastor is not so much the embodiment of the church, but the teachings of the church. I do not seek to hide the truth, not for myself or anybody. My role is to teach the truth.'

'Well, I'm glad we got that sorted out,' said Carl, leaving the table. 'Wouldn't have been able to sleep, otherwise.'

'Ignore him. Bull, I'm grateful, and thank you for sharing with us,' said Ronnie.

That was Ronnie all over, noted Ryan. Polite to a fault. He leaned in close to Sanna and Crystal.

'So, what do you reckon? We all get baptised tomorrow?'

Crystal laughed it away.

'I'll admit,' said Lacey, overhearing, 'I struggled with the lamb from the flock stuff. A bit rich.'

'The Church of the Hypocrite Oracle,' said Sanna.

'That has a nice ring to it,' said Ryan.

'Today, I show my people the way of the light. Tomorrow I rape, pillage and murder,' said Sanna, mimicking Bull.

'If you want my advice, don't be underestimating him,' said Pete, picking up his guitar again.

Ryan caught a glimpse of Bull, eyes shut tight, clasping his Bible to his chest. His whole act was transparent and laughable. But in that very moment of Sanna mocking him – his figure captured under the halo of the outside lamp, looking for all the world like some mutant Jesus – he didn't find it funny in the slightest. No question. Bull was capable of anything.

30

Sanna

Winding slowly along the gravel road, the headlights of Carl's van pierced the blackness of the pre-dawn. 'Looks like we'll cut out this shed around noon,' Carl advised. 'Quick lunch, come back and shower, then that should give us all a couple of hours in town to get any jobs done.'

'I can go and check on my wedding dress,' said Lacey.

'Yeah! Get them to take it out a size,' said Pete, reaching over and grabbing a fistful of his sister's midriff. 'Too much of Ronnie's cooking!'

'Fuck off!' she snapped, batting him away.

The ruckus shook the sleep out of Sanna. She had an older brother too, Kare, as well as her sister Emilia, and had been close to both of them at various times. Kare had graduated from university in Helsinki, and had a nice job at a telecommunications company with his own office and an expense account. He was fun and caring, and she missed him. They ribbed each other, like all kids did, but he would never have tried to humiliate her in front of other people, as Pete had just done with Lacey.

There were six years between her and Emilia. Few enough for them to have been thick as thieves in her younger days, when Emilia would dote on her and dress her up for the amusement of her school friends. Emilia was sisterly and kind, helping her prepare for the rigours of high school and puberty. But while their bond was still there, now it felt like it was buried deeper. Emilia had got serious about her career as an architect, while she chose to travel the world. Their paths, quite naturally she supposed, had diverged. It would be important for them to reconnect when she returned home. Sometimes during the middle of a long shift, Sanna would think of Emilia. It helped pass the hours but, deeper down, it was more about imagining a time when circumstances would allow them to be together more. For now, each of them was finding their way in the world. But Sanna was certain their unspoken bond would draw them closer together, and they would end up shaping each other's lives.

It was 3pm on the dot when the van pulled up outside the library, and the gang spilled out onto the footpath.

'Righto,' said Carl. 'Do what you need to do and I'll be outside the pub at eight sharp. Don't be late.'

Sanna and Ryan separated themselves from the others. 'I'm going to visit the police station,' he told her. 'I have a project coming up in the first semester, and I'm hoping to get some help with it.'

'I have to go to the bank,' she said.

'Will you come with me afterwards? To the house?'

She smiled. 'Would I be intruding?'

'Not at all,' he laughed.

She smiled again. 'I'll wait for you, after I've finished at the bank.'

Despite it being the second week of January, there were still Christmas decorations dotted along the counters and lining the walls of the bank. Sanna waited in line, behind a wide-haired blonde woman, overladen with gold jewellery.

'Really?' said the woman to the young female teller.

'I'm sorry, but it hasn't arrived.'

'Really?' Louder this time, just to make sure that everyone

heard her. 'That's simply not good enough. You tell me, how long should it take for a new chequebook to arrive? Go on, how long?'

The teller, not even Sanna's age, didn't shirk. 'Usually, after ordering, they arrive within a week.'

'But not always, evidently.'

'I'm sorry. We can do up a temporary option for you now, if you prefer.'

'But I don't want a temporary option. I want *my* chequebook. Do you not understand?'

'I do, madam. But I'm sorry, I can't give you something that isn't here to give.'

The woman spun around in frustration, corralling Sanna. 'Have you ever heard of anything so ridiculous and incompetent? How hard can it be to supply a new chequebook?'

Sanna shrugged her shoulders. What was she supposed to do about it?

The woman turned again to the teller. 'Do you have any idea who I am?'

'Yes, Mrs Harten,' said the teller.

A man, seemingly more senior in rank, but not much older than Sanna, emerged from behind a desk. The woman locked him in a fierce stare.

'I warned my husband. I told him, don't accept a transfer to these cowboy towns. Half the town are crooks and the other half won't appreciate the policework you do. People have no idea what constitutes proper service. And here we are.'

Before the man could say anything, she backed away, towards the exit. 'I'll be back tomorrow. And if that chequebook isn't here, you can expect a visit from my husband!'

The young man rolled his eyes at Sanna. 'Debbie,' he said to the teller. 'Why don't you grab some water and take a few minutes? I'll take care of this,' he added, inviting Sanna to sit at his desk.

'Sorry about that,' he said. 'My name's Philip. How can I help?'

This must be *Philip*, the friend Ryan had mentioned once or twice. Momentarily, she thought of acknowledging the connection, but decided against.

'I'm here to collect my chequebook. Is it ready?'

She'd kept such a straight face, it was a few seconds before he realised he'd been had. 'Ah, right. Very funny.'

'She was extremely rude,' said Sanna.

'Thing is, people that come to live here from the cities, they expect things to happen automatically for them. Or else they think that local people band together just to make their life a misery. We don't. It's them who don't know how to pull their heads in.'

She smiled. 'I have some cash to deposit, but also, I wish to make an international transfer.'

'Of course. Where to?'

'Finland.'

'Interesting. I was wondering about that accent.'

'It's Finnish.'

'Yes. Thank you.' He rapped his pen on the desk. 'I think this is a first for the bank. But no problem, of course,' he said. 'Just excuse me for a moment, I'll go and grab the correct form.'

He returned quickly with the paperwork. 'There's usually a ten-dollar transaction fee for overseas transfers, but in this case I'll be happy to waive that,' he said, holding his gaze.

Sanna hadn't been expecting special treatment.

'Would you like anything to drink?' he asked. 'Tea? Water?'

'No, thank you,' she replied.

Together they completed the form. Philip was efficient and helpful. Too helpful really; there was no way this was how regular customers were treated.

'What about a real drink? After I finish work?'

So *that* was it! She'd come to the bank to send a transfer, not be propositioned. 'I'm sorry?'

'You know, a drink? After I finish work.' He looked her up and down again, then winked. 'I can sign you into the club. I think we'd get along just fine.'

'Really? And what makes you think that?'

Philip gestured down at the transaction form.

'Oh, I get it,' she said. 'What did you say the fee was again?'

'Ten dollars.'

Sanna fumbled in her purse, stood up, walked over to one of the tellers, and pushed a ten-dollar note across the counter. 'Apparently, this is what your boss thinks I'm worth,' she said, before striding out of the bank.

She found the police station easily; Nashville wasn't the sort of place you got lost in. Enjoying the sunshine on the footpath outside, unburdened by passing car and foot traffic, her mood levelled off.

A few minutes later, Ryan emerged. 'All okay?' he asked.

'Yes,' she lied. 'And you?'

'All good. Are you happy to walk to my mum's place? Ten minutes, tops.'

'Sure,' she said, suddenly wanting to hold his hand, but resisting the urge to embarrass him in public.

Immediately, she liked the house, not just because this was where he'd grown up, but because it exuded warmth. She circled the impressive garden, then stood for a moment on the front lawn, pleased about her decision not to go to the pub with the rest of the gang, failing to notice the car that glided past them. They were inside the house by the time the car drove past again, this time in the other direction.

31
Philip

Philip skedaddled out of the bank as quickly as he could. The Finnish girl had embarrassed him, and hearing the staff giggle behind his back made him seethe even more.

His mood was already dark, Slurps having phoned at lunchtime, wanting his chainsaw back. Instead of going straight to the club, he had to duck home after work and grab it from the garage. If he was quick – in and out – he'd miss Becky and be spared the usual ticking-off about how much time he spent drinking with his mates, and how little he spent at home. A small mercy.

Nashville had gone batshit crazy after news broke about the skeleton that wasn't. It didn't take much to stoke up the serial-killer story again. Then Slurps confided over a beer how he'd got the idea to wind the cops up, ordering one by post from a supply company in Auckland, then burying it in a shallow grave, somewhere he knew it would be discovered.

That was the thing with Slurps; he was a loose cannon. It wasn't enough for him to bury the skeleton and be done with it. He got more of a buzz from boasting to blokes at the club and basking in the notoriety. Mad bastard. Yesterday Philip had seen a TV news crew driving around town; like they'd done at the height of the original story. Someone in Auckland had obviously got a sniff of it. It was all just mind games, he concluded. The cops were using the media to try to put pressure on the person responsible. Shake whoever it was out of their comfort zone, to see if they could rustle up something out of the ordinary. He kind of understood it, but it was amateurish. They would need to do a whole lot better than that.

Swinging off the main street, onto the road heading up towards the golf course, he suddenly, impulsively swung the car hard left. In the throes of wondering why, his eyes were drawn to the large rhododendron, Ryan's house and the couple standing outside. His eyes zeroed in, not on Ryan, but the girl with him. The Finnish girl from the bank.

Philip drove by without being seen. There was something about her – attractive, in a foreign kind of way, worth more than a second or third look. Her features, the high lines of her cheekbones, the way she wore her hair . . . nothing like any local girl he'd ever known. Definitely worth having a crack at. But here she was mixed up with Ryan. The way he'd been acting lately, perhaps that explained where she got her attitude from?

A couple of hundred metres later, he turned onto the hill road. Another hard turn carried him back in the direction of town, directly past the Bradley house. On approach he slowed, but this time they were nowhere to be seen, obviously, now inside.

His mind ticked over. She owed him. His dad was right about one thing. Nashville was their fucking town. *His* town. She needed reminding of that. And it wouldn't do any harm for Ryan to be reminded as well.

32
Ryan

Ryan invited Sanna to sit at the kitchen table. 'I know exactly what my mum would have said.'

Sanna was curious.

'What's your name again, dear?' He mimicked his mother's voice.

'Sanna,' he replied to himself, play-acting all three roles.

'Sanna? What kind of a name is that?'

'It's Finnish.'

'Oh. As in, from Finland?'

'Yes, Mum.'

'Oh, how interesting. I've never been to Finland.'

'Not many New Zealanders have, Mum.'

'Bit too close to Russia for my liking.'

'As if she would have gone otherwise,' said Ryan, breaking the fourth wall.

'That's a bit cruel,' said Sanna.

'Sorry, I forgot one,' said Ryan. 'When are you two going to get married?' He cringed, just as he would have done if his mother had said it.

Sanna saw through his act. 'I know you act tough, like a boy should. But you were obviously very fond of her.'

He smiled. 'Things were different when she grew up. In towns like this, Mum and girls like her, they were taught to serve their men. And their families. So, without a father around, she kind of had to do two roles. I can laugh at it now, but she was just being protective.'

She allowed him a moment to reflect.

'Let's see if there's anything to eat,' he said, jumping up, scouting the kitchen. There were slim pickings. 'Looks like we're on the fish-paste sandwiches,' he said. 'Gourmet version. Toasted!'

'What about all of this?' Sanna asked, opening a cupboard.

Ryan looked inside and shook his head. The cupboard was full of tinned food of every description. Beans, corn, creamed and kernelled, beetroot, asparagus, peas, spaghetti, baked beans, tomatoes, soup, sardines . . . Anything that came in a can, it was there, by the dozen.

'Looks like your mum was preparing for a nuclear holocaust.'

Ryan laughed. 'That's just her way. If the local supermarket had a special on, she couldn't resist it, even if she didn't need it. Supporting the local community and all that.'

Sanna held up a tin of briny, mushy asparagus and screwed her face. 'A toasted cheese sandwich will be perfect.'

After they ate, Ryan quickly tidied the kitchen. It wasn't yet 7pm. They still had time to kill before Carl would be at the pub to collect them.

'What's all this?' Sanna had taken a manilla folder from a sideboard and was thumbing through the contents: a bunch of newspaper clippings.

Ryan took a closer look. 'This is weird. It's all stuff from the missing hitchhiker case.'

'Why would she have kept all these?'

'Good question.' Ryan was nonplussed.

The folder was comprehensive; it was as if every single newspaper article concerning the crime was in there. What on earth could have driven his mother to do such a thing?

'Maybe she thought one day they'd catch the person responsible and you'd end up working on the case?' said Sanna.

'As silly as it sounds, you're probably right,' he conceded.

'If I ever go missing, I hope someone cares enough about me to make a folder like this,' she said.

'Sanna, don't joke about that sort of stuff!'

'Okay, no folder,' she smiled. 'But promise me you'll keep looking. Okay?'

'Yes, I'll keep looking. I promise.'

'Show me your room,' she said, recognising the need to change the subject.

'It's just a bedroom.'

'Does it have your things from childhood?'

He nodded.

'Show me,' she insisted.

They sat on the floor, looking through old photos that he took from the bedside drawer. And more newspaper clippings; like the one where his mother had circled Ryan passing his grade one pianoforte exam, and another which listed his third-place ribbon at a local swimming carnival, for backstroke.

Sanna noticed that, of all the photographs, there wasn't a single one of Ryan's father. 'Maybe we can't change things that are already done,' she said, 'but there must be times when you have regrets about the situation with your father. Does it ever make you angry?'

'No, not now,' he explained. 'Once I got a bit older, and my mother made it clear that she was never going to give me information about him, or even talk about it, then I just found it easier to respect her wishes.'

She gently stroked his arm.

'The thing is, it really didn't make any difference in the long run. I still had my friends, like Philip. We had a normal life, like normal kids, you know? It was a lot of fun. And his dad, Jack, he was always looking out for me. Still is, really.'

'What do you mean?'

'Oh, you know . . . stuff like getting to this age, where you have to make decisions about what you're going to do. He's a lifer, a local through and through. I never want to lose that, but . . . there's also something pulling me away. I want a career.'

'So why is that a problem?' she asked.

'It's not. At least, it shouldn't be. Some things have to happen in their own time. That's why I haven't been in a hurry to clean up all my mother's stuff and sell the house. Because once I do, it will be like my time here is done. I mean, I've accepted that she's gone. But she's still my connection to Nashville.'

Sanna smiled softly and nestled her head onto his shoulder. 'If someone in my family passed away, I'd be devastated.'

A few moments later, she stirred. 'You know something?'

'What?'

'In all of the times we have been together, we've never made love on a bed. A proper bed.'

'This is still the same bed I had when I was five,' said Ryan. 'The springs are shot. They stretch right down to the floor.'

'I don't care about that.' She was unbuttoning her blouse.

It wasn't how either of them had imagined their first time in a bed, with the sense of Ryan's mother having lain in the next room, stricken with cancer. But Sanna took the lead, and the ease with which his body relented, and synched into hers, soon took care of any objection.

Minutes later, they were done. Ryan lay on top of her, breathing hard into the pillow, trying to catch his breath. Suddenly, Sanna started giggling and laughing, so hard he placed his palm across her mouth to settle her.

'What's the matter?' he said.

'I just saw it,' she shrieked. 'What on earth is that?'

Ryan rolled off her so he too was facing upwards. Stuck to the ceiling was a poster of Charlie's Angel Farrah Fawcett-Majors; all teeth, hair and cleavage, staring back down at them.

Ryan laughed. 'Maybe that should be your new look? What do you think?'

'Seriously,' she gasped, 'I'd rather die!'

33

Slurps

It never bothered Slurps knowing he wasn't the sharpest tool in the shed. There was a place in the world for everyone; it had been his choice to give school a wide berth, just as it was other people's business if they chose to be brain surgeons or rocket scientists. School wasn't going to make him a better shot, or teach him how to navigate his way through thick bush. He suffered the teachers as they suffered him. They knew their time was better invested elsewhere, which suited him just fine.

The teachers were as bad as each other really, although one in particular annoyed him: Terrence Pihama. Slurps saw straight through his schtick. He was always too interested in other people's business, always available for a 'chat'. What they called being a 'trusted advisor'. Which was just a fancy name for sleazebag. A dishonest sleazebag. Someone who went out of his way to win the trust of the female students, but was as bent as his dog's hind leg.

Slurps never understood why the school employed teachers like him, the ones who wanked on about great novelists or balance sheets or the chemical compound of atoms, whatever that was. Or worse, insisted that everyone was equally worthy and what was important was to be the best individual you could be. For fuck's sake.

Thankfully, the school years passed quickly enough, helped by him getting an after-school job with Max 'Corn' Cobb, at his mower and chainsaw repair shop. Corn was no great shakes as a teacher, but none of that bothered Slurps – he was happy to tinker and teach himself on the job. He soon learned how to make a stricken chainsaw hum. Figuring out how to do it himself doubled the satisfaction.

Corn wasn't much of a businessman either as it turned out, owing a bit of money around town before doing a runner when the people from Inland Revenue came looking for him. There followed a meeting of creditors, which confirmed that the business wasn't worth anything, and with nothing left for anyone to lose or gain, it was decreed that Slurps could take over what was left of the operation, to see if he could make a go of it. Which, as far as he could tell, because nobody ever came around to cause any trouble, he figured he had. Some people might have said the stuff with the skeleton was causing trouble, but they didn't know what they were talking about. Winding the cops up for a laugh, that wasn't criminal or illegal, it was just a bit of sport.

And, as much as he despised teachers, the thing that Slurps hated most about school was the girls. He just didn't understand them, never had. An only child, his mum having passed away early and his dad a chronic alcoholic, he supposed some people – a counsellor or a mentor like Terrence Pihama – would describe his upbringing as 'lacking suitable female role models'. As if it was some kind of excuse, which it wasn't. Slurps knew he wasn't cut out for women, and women weren't cut out for him. He'd never had a girlfriend, he was never going to marry, and that was that.

None of which meant, like any other red-blooded male, that he didn't have sexual urges. Strong urges. He'd noticed the stirring inside his body growing more pronounced in recent weeks. He had no idea what to do about it; finding a woman and starting a conversation with her was out of the question. If he was being honest, it was beginning to bother him, sometimes keeping him awake at night. It would be nice to find some release.

34

Ryan

Ryan didn't exactly know why he felt uneasy around Neville Hanigan. Not that he knew much about him, other than they ate his sheep for breakfast, lunch and dinner every day. But he seemed awkward, more than a bit creepy, and he wore his pants too high.

'Wool prices holding up?' asked Carl, across the communal table.

'Could be worse,' grunted Neville.

Nobody quite knew what to say to him, and he was no smooth conversationalist himself.

'More mint sauce?' offered Ronnie. 'Or cabbage?'

Ryan liked the way Ronnie did her cabbage. Sliced thinly, steamed rather than boiled, with knobs of butter melted in and salt and pepper sprinkled over the top.

'No,' said Neville. 'But thanks for inviting me.'

'It's your bloody sheep we're eating,' piped up Pete, in a rare moment of animation. 'I think that entitles you to a feed!'

Neville nodded and kept eating.

'Do you like Jim Reeves?' Pete was on a roll. '"Mexican Joe"?'

Here we bloody go, cringed Ryan.

'Not particularly,' said Neville.

Ryan took a swig of beer. That was a relief.

Wool prices and the menu ticked off, there was another lull in conversation.

'Looks like a full moon tonight,' offered Carl, tamely.

Ryan noticed how everybody was avoiding making eye contact with Neville, hoping for dinner to pass quickly. He also noticed Carl. Leering. At Sanna. That was weird; he'd never seen that before.

'My mum used to play netball with your wife,' said Crystal.

'Well . . . Janet hasn't played for a while now,' Neville replied.

'Why didn't you bring her down for dinner?' asked Sanna.

Neville glared at her like he'd just been asked the most ridiculous question. 'Janet doesn't go out. Not anymore.'

'But why not?' Sanna pressed. 'Maybe that's what she needs? To socialise with other people? Can't do any harm.'

'I'm sorry, which university did you get your medical degree from, again?'

Sanna brushed it off as nonchalantly as if flicking a fly away from the table. 'You don't need to be a doctor to know it isn't healthy to be sitting around inside a house all day long. Like it's a prison.'

'You go, girl!' whooped Lacey.

Ryan noticed Neville's cheeks redden.

'Righto, let's leave that one there, shall we?' said Carl. 'Neville, I'll show you those damaged weatherboards I mentioned. In the kitchen, where the rats have eaten through.'

Ryan waited by the door inside the woolshed. When Sanna arrived, he took her hand and led her over to the fadges.

'I've been looking forward to seeing you . . . I've been thinking about a few things,' he started off. 'About how things are between us. Say, if you want to slow –'

She held her forefinger up to his lips to stop him. Gently, she pushed him backwards, until he was laid flat. She then went to work unclasping his belt. He lifted his buttocks slightly to make it easier for her to pull his jeans and underpants down. He was at her mercy now, and she knew exactly how it went from here; using her hand at first, then her mouth. It was intense, personal and exhilarating.

Afterwards, Ryan held Sanna tightly in his arms, and they allowed the moment to wash over them. When the glow began to fade, and Ryan felt the first signs of discomfort from the floor, he wondered where exactly he should restart the conversation.

'About before. Sorry if I was out of line. But I was just wondering if we needed to talk about things?'

'There's something I didn't tell you,' she said.

'Yes?' Ryan replied, nervously.

'When I went to the bank, the guy there . . . the one you told me about . . . your friend, Philip.'

'Yes?'

'He hit on me.'

'He what?'

'He asked me to go for a drink with him.'

'A drink?' Ryan was taken aback. 'Who does he think he is?'

'Listen, I don't want you to do anything. I was angry at first, but I realise I overreacted. He's your friend. And it's not like he knows about us.'

'That's not the point. He's engaged to be married, for a start.'

'Oh.'

'And you're taken.'

'Am I?'

'I'm sorry,' said Ryan, 'I didn't mean it like that.'

'So, what do you mean?'

Ryan's head was spinning like a post-hole borer. He needed to stop digging.

'Ryan?'

'Yes?'

She wasn't letting go without an answer.

'I mean . . . we've never properly spoken about it, and I guess it's obvious that we have feelings for each other.'

'Yes.'

'And I don't mean that I can tell you what to do, or who to talk to, or anything like that. And I'm not saying anything for the long term either. But . . . I think this is something more than just casual. Is that what you think?'

'Sure,' she said, in a straightforward way that contrasted with his nervousness.

'So, that's it? Just "sure"?'

'Yes. I agree with you. Not just casual. Boyfriend and girlfriend.'

It all seemed so formal, so matter-of-fact. Was he supposed to shake hands on the arrangement?

'Okay, then,' he said. 'That's good. I think. Is there anything else we need to talk about?'

'Actually, yes there is,' said Sanna, pulling herself away from him.

Her withdrawal took Ryan by surprise. 'What is it?'

'I think I'm pregnant.'

35

Neville

By the time Neville returned to the house, Janet had put herself to bed. Not yet asleep, she lay flat on her back staring up at the ceiling. Through the ceiling – for all he knew – to the outer reaches of space, so far removed was she from reality.

He was still seething at the backpacker for having the temerity to challenge him about Janet. Not just because she was hopelessly wrong – he wished he could drag her up here right now, so she could see for herself what a basket-case Janet was – but for doing it so publicly.

He'd been brought up to show respect: for elders, for people in positions of authority, for hosts whenever you were a guest in their house. This was his farm, and the shearing gang, which she was part of, were his guests. For that insolence alone, she deserved being put back in her place.

He put the kettle on. Maybe it was a foreign thing? She was Scandinavian. He'd heard they could be a bit cold and direct. That sounded like code for downright rude. She was also young. That wasn't cultural. On his trips to town he'd noticed how the younger generation would cut ahead of him in the supermarket. And, just a couple of weeks ago when he admonished a young man for dropping litter on the footpath, the scraggy youth turned around and gave him the fingers. What he'd learned about Filipinos was that they were friendly and polite. That would be a pleasant change.

Neville sipped his tea. Briefly, he contemplated talking to Carl, to let him know to pull his staff into line, to tell them to mind their own business. On second thoughts, he would deal with her himself. Find the right moment where he could tell her a few home truths. Scare her a little. Yes, that would do nicely. She'd had a good run at things, using his woolshed for her own pleasure. It was all a little too easy for her. It was time she was dragged down a peg or two.

36

Ryan

Ryan attacked the drive into town with more aggression and less respect than the winding road demanded. Awash with emotion, he'd hardly slept, the day passing by in a blur. Sanna was pregnant, it was his – obviously – and he now had to decide what to do about it. Things were complicated. They lived in different countries, but he'd heard there might be some regulation that allowed couples in their situation to stay together. Or perhaps, for Sanna to remain in the country, they would need to be married. It was his responsibility, he'd have to find out for certain.

There was also the business with Philip. His first instinct was to go straight to the club, to call him out to the carpark, to warn him off. But a dalliance with a patch of loose gravel on the shoulder of a bend, and a near miss with a road marker, tempered him. After a few moments' introspection, he edged back onto the road, this time a full thirty kilometres per hour slower.

What would he achieve by making a huge scene in front of other people? He would embarrass Philip, hurt him too if it came to that, because he was fitter and stronger, and fancied himself in a one-on-one. But it would come at a cost. Philip was a Nash: that counted for something. And now, apparently there were people in town looking sideways at him, thinking that because he was a law student, he was too big for them. This would hardly help things. Word would invariably get back to Becky, and that wouldn't be fair on her. And would Sanna even want him to defend her honour? There were now three of them to consider. Done. He'd call Philip instead, handle it quietly. That would be better. For everyone.

Ryan drove straight to the house and set to work in his mother's room, stripping the bed for the first time since she'd been taken into care to live out her final moments. Jack had insisted there was more likelihood of attracting a buyer if the place was less cluttered. When he stood the bed and mattress on their sides, up against the wall, he felt a strong sense of satisfaction. Finally, things were changing.

Next was his mother's linen press; chock-full of sheets, blankets, pillowcases and towels. There would be a good home somewhere for these. He packed them all neatly into the boxes he'd had delivered months ago, which had been sitting in the spare room, unused. A half-mad intensity had taken hold of him, and he attacked the kitchen: crockery, cutlery, cookware . . . old-fashioned, but in good enough nick to be distributed around needier households. He packed the tinned food as well – no matter the expiry dates, someone would be grateful.

Pausing over a beer at the dinner table, Ryan was sparked to life by the shrill ring of the phone. He let it ring out, annoyed at himself for not having got around to having it disconnected. Whoever was calling, it could only be a distraction. Or trigger another memory, like the time Carl interrupted him one night after work, when he was towelling down after his shower.

'Ryan. Sorry to bust in, but it's the phone. For you.'

'For me? Nobody rings me.'

Except for his mother. After she had just received a cancer diagnosis.

'Pancreatic . . . One of the bad ones . . . Riddled with it, the doctor said . . . Three months, tops.'

'Fuck, Mum,' was all he remembered saying.

'Put the kettle on, will you, dear?'

What Ryan recalled most vividly were the endless cups of tea. He never discovered if it was out of boredom or some physiological change in her body that induced a craving for Choysa. At the end of the day, he supposed it didn't matter.

He remembered the cancer taking root; the change in her physical appearance rapid and profound. Three months proved wildly optimistic. Her puffy, friendly cheeks withered away in front of his eyes, until bone was the prominent feature. And skin. Skin and bone. Whoever coined that old cliche knew what they were on about.

They argued – him telling her she'd put on a bit of condition; her snapping back, 'Don't patronise me, Ryan. I might be dying but I haven't turned into an idiot.'

Whenever he wiped his nose on his singlet, she grizzled, 'You're going to be a lawyer, Ryan, you're better than that.' He could only sigh in return. Philip was leading the charge around town to criticise him because he didn't fit in, and here she was, trying to prove his point.

There had been jobs to do around the house, but Ryan procrastinated. She would be shifted to respite, then to palliative care. Replacing the faulty burner on the stove-top was hardly going to make a dent in her quality of life. Ryan would help her with the crossword, filling time until the next cup of tea. Then, during the afternoon, he would allow her to drift off to sleep, despite her imploring him not to let her. Her hours on earth were numbered, she said, she didn't want to let them slide by and miss out on anything. Perhaps it was the medication messing with her. Her pain was manageable – at least, that was what she told him – although she was such a tough, stubborn woman, he wasn't sure if that was true or not.

He recalled her being stirred by a gentle thud on the front porch, the local newspaper airmailed across the lawn by a paperboy on a bike.

'Remember when you used to do that?' she said.

'Yes, Mum. Of course.'

When Ryan brought it inside and handed it to her, she brushed it away.

'We used to call it the "two minutes silence".' Now look at it. Even that's too generous. Not fit for wiping your arse with.'

She was right. It was so thin, it was a close relative of the ham from the local cafe.

'Just read me the death notices, will you? I like to know who it is I've outlasted.'

With her time running out, he knew it would be his last chance to ask the burning question.

'It's never a good time to talk about your father, Ryan,' she had told him on another occasion when he'd raised the subject, insisting that she would go to her grave without inflicting Ryan's father upon him. Ryan had seen his birth certificate when it was needed in the university application process. 'Father, *John Smith*. Address, *No fixed abode*.' What on earth did that mean? He was a travelling salesman? A wrangler for a circus? Or someone who never wanted to be found? She eventually conceded – the only detail she ever let slip – that he'd lived in Auckland at one point. If that was true, and he had his doubts, it was of no help; the smallest of needles in the biggest of haystacks.

'I've never let you down, not once in your life,' she said, in a short burst of energy. 'You'll just have to trust me on this one, Ryan. You haven't needed him in your life so far and you won't need him in the future.'

He remembered making her dinner that same night – a poached egg on toast. Her selection. Soft and runny, just how she liked it, with salt and a light dusting of white pepper across the top. He'd watched her savour every mouthful, imagining himself on death row, awaiting the chair, permitted a final meal of his choosing. Crayfish tails fresh out of the sea, dipped in malt vinegar, pork with crackling, apple sauce, crispy roast potatoes, bread and butter pudding with sultanas. Poached egg on toast? Hardly.

After she was done, Ryan helped his mother to her bed, her shuffling steps noticeably shorter. He placed a fresh glass of water next to her, on the bedside table.

'Anything else you need?' he asked.

'Don't just be a lawyer, Ryan. A paper shuffler. Be a good lawyer. Help people who need helping.'

'Sure.'

'And marry well. Leave me some grandchildren to be proud of. You've already let a good one go.'

That was out of left field. 'What? Who do you mean? Not Becky Armstrong?'

'Lovely girl. You were perfect for each other.'

'No, not perfect at all, Mum.'

'I've seen them downtown together. Her and Philip Nash. Not like you to let Philip get the better of you.'

It was pointless arguing with her.

'You'll make a good father, Ryan. I know you will. Just don't leave it too late.'

Ryan smiled to himself now. She would have been happy to know that – for once – he'd done as she asked. His smile faded, though, as quickly as it had come. Since Sanna had told him about her pregnancy, he'd had a hundred questions spring to mind about parenting. Things that he would have asked his mother for advice on. He felt sad she wasn't here to provide it. But mostly, he was sad because she would never know the joy of being a grandmother.

His work at the house done, Ryan cruised into Nashville's main street. For most people, even non-shearers, 11pm was past bedtime. The lights of the local takeaway shop sparkled, an oasis for peckish stragglers.

Parked outside was a police car. Ryan could see at the counter a constable, still in uniform. They'd never met, but he'd been pointed out to him before. Peterson. Instinctively, he hit the brakes and pulled over.

'How are you, mate?' Ryan asked, upon entering.

'Good, thanks.'

'Just knocked off?'

'My shift finishes at midnight, but it's dead. They don't mind us clocking off a wee bit early if that's the case.' Peterson nodded towards the counter. 'In time to get a feed on the way home.'

'I'm sure they get it back off you on other days,' said Ryan.

'Yeah, tell me about it.'

'Last order,' the lass behind the counter called out. 'We're closing up.'

Ryan realised he'd been so engrossed in his mother's things, he hadn't eaten. 'Um, yeah, good idea. Give us a piece of gurnard . . . and a sausage, thanks. And just a few chips. That'll do.'

Ryan could sense that Peterson was sizing him up. 'Do you know who I am?' he asked.

'People usually say that to coppers when they want something for nothing, or when they're trying to get out of trouble.'

It hadn't come out how Ryan intended. 'No, that's not –'

Peterson smiled. 'You work with one of the shearing gangs. For Carl Stensness.'

'Yes,' said Ryan, moderately impressed. Then again, that was the police's job. To know everybody and their business. 'It's not my real job, though.'

'Nup?'

'I'm studying to be a lawyer. At Otago.'

'That sounds impressive.'

'No, I . . .' stumbled Ryan. There he was again, showing people he had tickets on himself. 'I came in the other day, but your boss wasn't around. I'm supposed to go back the first semester with information for a criminal law project. Maybe you could help me out with that?'

'Maybe. I guess it depends,' said Peterson. 'I'm not exactly a mover and shaker down at the station.'

The server appeared with a large, puffy parcel of butcher's paper. 'A dozen fried oysters, one tarakihi, one sausage and chips. Here you go.'

Peterson took his dinner. 'Wanna chat?'

After a few minutes, Ryan joined him in the police car with his own dinner.

'Oyster?' offered Peterson.

Ryan liked fried oysters, but it was poor form to hijack another man's meal. He pecked at his own chips instead.

'So, what's this project?' Peterson asked.

'Well, we have guidelines, but basically we're free to choose the topic. I'm doing "Constructing a prosecution case for murder in a rural community".'

'Sounds interesting,' said Peterson, 'although we don't get a lot of murders around here.'

'Sure. But that's kind of the point,' Ryan answered. 'I'm interested in highlighting the differences between city and country. Large populations versus small towns. How that feeds into putting a case together. As you say, because it doesn't happen often, and because usually either the victim or the perpetrator, or both, are known in the community. And whether that feeds into prejudices, or how people choose to co-operate or not, that sort of thing. And, one more . . . because the police are local, members of the same community, what that means in terms of objectivity, as opposed to letting preconceptions take over.'

'Hmmm.' Peterson didn't look sure.

'So, I was thinking ... I know files are classified and all that, but maybe if I came in to speak with the detective inspector, do you think he'd be able to go through a few things with me? You know, with the Atkins case?'

'Well, I don't know what he'd say,' said Peterson. 'He's away on a course, down at the college. And then he's got a week's leave. He's still getting over racing up to the National Park, thinking someone had found her remains.'

'I heard about that,' said Ryan. 'That wouldn't have gone down well.'

'No,' laughed Peterson. 'That's an understatement.'

Ryan nodded.

'Want any more?' he asked.

Ryan shook his head.

Peterson took the paper, wrapped it into a ball, and wiped his mouth on the outside of it. 'Hang on,' he said, slipping out of the car to place the rubbish into a bin, then jumping back in.

'So, you went to school here, as well?' asked Peterson, returning.

'Yes. Primary and high school. Kindergarten too.'

'But finally you've escaped. Made it into law school!'

'I wouldn't say *escaped*.'

'That's ironic, isn't it?' said Peterson. 'We're a similar age and it's forwards and upwards for you. And me ... I could have ended up anywhere — Auckland, Tauranga, or Napier, that's quite nice — and I get posted here.'

'You make it sound like a prison sentence,' said Ryan.

'Isn't it?'

'Only if you let it be. People actually choose to move here, because they like the fishing, or the tramping, or skiing in winter.'

'I don't do any of those things,' said Peterson, ruefully.

'Listen,' continued Ryan, 'there are heaps of sport and recreational choices here. Or if you just want to get on the piss, it's a good town for that too. There's no reason to sit around feeling sorry for yourself.' They'd been sitting in the car for nearly forty minutes. 'I need to push on. Got an early start in the morning.'

'Sure.' Peterson sounded disappointed. They shook hands. 'Hey, listen,' the constable said, 'if you're around on Thursday night, I've got another late shift.'

'Right . . .'

'If you wanna drop in to the station . . . you know, late when it's not busy. I'll have a look around and see what I can find.'

'Cheers.' Ryan waved goodbye, hopped back into his own car, and started off down the river road. In just a few hours Carl would be banging on doors. He'd surprised himself: for one, he'd never thought of himself as a mentor, and certainly not to a cop. And if sticking up for the town he was in the process of leaving behind tested the bounds of logic, it felt like the right thing to do. Peterson made it sound like the worst thing on earth, being transferred here, but for anyone with an ounce of get up and go, a sense of adventure, Nashville was paradise.

All of which made his own decision to leave more difficult to reconcile. Getting a degree meant he had to leave – there was no choice. Later, when he was older, when he'd seen a bit of the world and made his fortune, that would be a good time to return. It would be like he never left. Wherever he stopped on the way, he would never lose Nashville.

37

Sanna

Sanna pushed her bedroom door open and shielded her eyes from the morning sun. It was nearly 9.30am, more than five hours since the gang had left in the van. It was unlike her, but when Carl's reminder knock rattled their door, she couldn't will herself out of her bunk. She'd managed to avoid morning sickness so far, but the headaches were next level. She'd never suffered them before, certainly nothing acute like this, and she appreciated how Crystal came back in to give her tablets and check in with her. She appreciated even more not being checked on a second time.

With Suzie in camp for a few days, Sanna knew she wouldn't be making trouble for the others. Suzie wasn't really Sanna's cup of tea, but right now, having her around to cover for her was a blessing.

She took her time dressing, letting the medicine do its work. She figured the pain was probably linked to her pregnancy; nothing physiological, more the stress from everything being so unexpected.

Slowly, her eyes adjusted to the solitude the pleasant valley offered. With hills pinched tight on both sides, there was no grand, sweeping vista. Instead, she embraced the intimacy. One valley, one farm. On the other side of the hills, left and right, more valleys and farmhouses, with woolsheds in all of them. And somewhere nearby, a community hall where, once or twice a year, farming families would descend in their Sunday best, for a local fete, or to formulate an angry response to the regional council's plan to increase rates.

To clear her head, Sanna meandered along the path leading up to Hanigan's woolshed. The pens outside were empty; in a few weeks' time, the noise and activity that would accompany the shear would be a stark contrast. Expecting the shed to be empty, she entered cautiously. Without Ryan there, it was just an ordinary, dusty, smelly space.

It might have been her imagination racing ahead of itself, but Sanna could feel Emilia inside the woolshed. Her letters home were infrequent, and mostly they were generic – one update for the whole family. She resolved to write to Emilia when she got back to the quarters. For her eyes only.

Sanna sat for a minute, on the fadges. Life in a shearing gang was intense; they were in close contact all day at work, in the van, over drinks and dinner, and sleeping. In the middle of a run, she could let her mind drift off. But she was never truly alone. Not unlike, she imagined, crew on a submarine. If you weren't able to cope with that, it was the wrong job.

She turned a full circle, making a mental note of the cues she would draw upon to describe the shed to Emilia. The blackened stencil hanging over a nail on the wall; the large sorting table, lacquered with the grease of thousands of fleeces; the battered hot-water heater, it too attached to a wall, once gleaming white but now flaked with rust – like everything else in this shed, a dusty shade of ochre. And the smell, the same smell that every woolshed had. Sheep and their shit.

Shit. It was everywhere. Like the saying she'd heard many times. Pete, in particular, was fond of using it. 'You're in deep shit now,' he would say, if she hadn't cleared Bull's stand quickly enough. In New Zealand language, she was in deep shit. Pregnant. Up the duff was the way they described it here, and to top it off, the child would be without a proper father. Thousands of kilometres away from home. She closed her eyes for a moment, and thought again of Emilia. As comfortable as she now felt in the gang, and as much as she liked Crystal, there was nobody Sanna could confide in. She wondered what would Emilia do in the same situation. And then she wondered if she was ready to tell her. Soon, perhaps.

Outside, she'd found herself drawn to the nearby bush. She had lived all her life in Helsinki, but like most Finns she experienced and enjoyed life in the countryside through school excursions and weekend trips with family and friends. She valued nature, and was fiercely proud of Finland's countryside. There weren't the dramatic mountains of Switzerland or New Zealand, but it was unspoiled and natural. It was also accessible and welcoming. By comparison, the New Zealand bush felt inhospitable: dense and impenetrable. Deep, dark bush. Finnish forests invited people to wander in for a stroll, or, in winter, to breeze along tracks formed by cross-country skiing or snowmobiles. New Zealand's bush invited people to bury things where they would never be found.

Sanna wondered what this reserve might be hiding. The largest trees towered magnificently over the rest of the canopy. The undergrowth she was less convinced about. She walked to the edge, searching for a track to present itself, but no easy access was offered. She was struck by how dense it was and how dark it all looked. There was earth between these plants that had never seen the sun. It hadn't rained for days, yet there was moisture leaching from the edge of the bush, as if inside, somebody had left a hose on slow drip. Perhaps if she climbed over the wire fence and pushed apart the fronds of the ferns, there would be a way in. But her shoes weren't made for this kind of exploration, and besides, too far in and there was no guarantee she'd find her way out. She hadn't come all this way to be swallowed whole.

She followed the fence line up the gully and emerged at the top, above the farmhouse. From there it was a straightforward walk back down to the quarters, following the track that the farm vehicles had worn. Passing in front of the farmhouse, Sanna felt the woman's presence. She craned her neck and there she was, standing at the large, plate-glass window; slim with long, straight blonde hair which framed eyes that felt distant and hollow. Not only was the woman expressionless, any semblance of life had been embalmed from her face. She was a figurine.

A figurine with moving parts. The woman waved, mechanically, her arm hinging at the elbow. Sanna stopped and waved back, hoping to get a reaction. The woman waved again. Encouraged, Sanna smiled, as broadly as she could manage, impossible for the woman to miss. She was rewarded with a smile in return. The woman was rooted to the spot, but underneath her bleached-white skin it was good to see there was blood circulating.

Sanna made her way to the door. Raising her arm to knock, she realised it was already open. She gently pushed the door and peered inside. The woman turned to face her.

'Hello. My name is Sanna,' she offered.

The woman smiled back at her.

'Are you Janet?'

Janet nodded and gestured for Sanna to come further inside, and to sit at the dining table. The room was sparingly furnished, a central lightbulb unadorned by a lightshade. Soft cushions and other homely touches were conspicuously absent. The only warmth came from outside, from the sun. The house felt like a spartan, eastern-European hospital room, not the home of a happily married couple.

Janet relaxed in her chair. Sanna wondered what she was supposed to say to someone who couldn't communicate in return. Anything that wouldn't sound trite or condescending. A solution came to her. She wouldn't try to maintain a conversation. What was the point? Instead, she would talk. About who she was and where she came from. And if that went well, she would talk some more – stories from Finland, about her family, her sister and brother, anything that Janet might find interesting or stimulating, even if she was unable to talk back.

'As I mentioned, my name is Sanna Sovernen, I am twenty-one years old. I am visiting New Zealand from Finland. I am here to stay and work with this shearing gang. I love the New Zealand countryside, and I have found the people are very welcoming. I have made many friends since I've been here.' She paused. 'Would you like to be my friend?'

Sanna watched Janet intently for a reaction. She wasn't a hundred per cent certain, but she could swear that Janet's facial complexion changed, right at the moment she asked about being friends. Did Janet understand her? Was that a kind of message? A sign perhaps that she was frightened of her husband? Sanna surveyed the drab living-room again. Janet's life must have been terribly oppressive. Of course she wanted to be friends.

Sanna looked around for a pen and piece of paper. She found what she needed on the desk near the kitchen, where it seemed her husband did the farm accounts.

'Here. This is my name. Sanna.' She passed Janet the piece of paper on which she'd written her first name. 'So you know, for next time.'

Now Sanna was torn. She wanted to stay here, to see if she could encourage Janet to come out of her shell. At the same time, she couldn't wait to get back to her room, so she could write to Emilia and tell her all about this encounter.

38

Slurps

Slurps sat on his doorstep, sliding down a couple of beers in the sun, watching Philip's car sweep around the horseshoe bend in the paddock leading to his house. The property, his uncle Alfred's old place, resembled a junk dealer's yard in the aftermath of a hurricane. Rusted car bodies mingled with what remained of old sofas that hadn't yet been eaten away by rats. S-bends and guttering sat amongst random bundles of rotting timber, rolls of carpet, the shells of chainsaws and lawnmowers, and a wheelchair with just one wheel. Nothing that was useful or desirable.

Slurps held his beer aloft as Philip parked his car amongst the detritus. 'Want one?'

'Nah, mate. I haven't got long. Becky wants me to help her father with a job at the church.'

'No worries.'

'Let's just do it,' said Philip. 'Got some targets?'

'A few. We can put the rest of them together in there,' he said, nodding towards the garage.

Slurps wriggled his body into the grass mound, ensured his stability, then popped his head and his bolt-action .22 rifle over the top. He checked his breathing and, squinting into the sight, saw his first target come into focus. He figured she was taller than average, with long, flowing black hair, set back off her face by a chequered headband. She wore a matching cloth band around her wrist, presumably to wipe away sweat, or perhaps the fake grease that the make-up artists had daubed on her, some of which had been smeared across her ballooning breasts. On her feet she wore heavy working boots, and in her right hand she held a spanner, oversize, as if to rubber-stamp the fantasy that she was a mechanic. For the avoidance of doubt, she straddled a tyre that lay flat on the ground, the car it belonged to raised on a hoist behind her.

Slurps had cut the picture from one of his stash of men's magazines he'd collected, and mounted it onto a wooden cross. He liked her, and liked the idea that she was, like him, a mechanic of sorts. Hers was the first cross in a line of twelve, speared into the earth in the paddock behind his house, side by side at one-metre intervals. The black-haired mechanic sat alongside a voluptuous Amazonian woman with ochre skin, and a leggy blonde, who was more your stereotypical Hugh Hefner type. And so it went, along the line. All different, all the same.

Overdue a hunt, Slurps and Philip were scheduled to go out next weekend. The best shot in the district, with a burgeoning tally of competition trophies and sashes to back that up, Slurps never liked going out cold. Practice made perfect. And even though Slurps rated him a respectable shot, Philip too always needed the target practice.

Satisfied his left elbow was solidly planted, Slurps found his target and cocked his right finger over the trigger. Without him having to ask, he heard Philip, snuggled alongside, suspend his breathing. The female mechanic had a healthy triangle of pubes, black to match up top. Even from forty metres away, through his scope, he could make out the curls of hair: the promised land.

Calm and controlled, with just the barest hint of heart-rate elevation; that was Slurps' go-zone. How he loved that sound, the bullet zinging out of the barrel, matched only, an instant later, by the sound of it thudding into the target. He laid down his rifle and grabbed his binoculars. The bullet had pierced the girl's pubic area, leaving her legs and stomach untarnished. *Bullseye.*

Slurps repeated the process for the next two. Same result. Three home runs. He was in perfect nick. 'Your go, mate,' he said, passing over the gun.

Philip took out the next three, although not as clinically. If the third one had been a stag, she would have been wounded in the hind quarter, and he would have had to finish the job off.

Slurps set aside his trusty .22 and picked up his other weapon – a 12-gauge shotgun, the one that had been handed down to him by his uncle during Slurps' final year of school. The shottie was a different beast altogether. It never felt as certain in his hands as his .22 did, but nor was it supposed to. He loved how it was a true test of his shooting prowess. If he could handle this like he could a .22, he'd consider himself a true marksman.

He swung his aim back towards the first cross. The girl – the mechanic – was fixed stock-still, albeit now more airy in the nether regions. For all she knew, she was staring back into a camera lens, listening for the click of the shutter, and for the instruction of the cameraman, exhorting her to change pose, to broaden her smile, to push her chest out for the punters to savour. Only this time, the clicking sound was no harmless camera. In one instant she was pouting innocently back at Slurps. In the next, shotgun pellets rained towards her, blowing her head right off the cross.

'Yeah, baby! Fucking awesome!' shouted Slurps. 'That's how you fucking do it!'

'Jesus,' said Philip. 'Give us a go with that fucker.'

Slurps slipped two fresh slugs into the breech and handed over the shottie, as Philip got himself into position. 'Take your time, mate,' he said. 'It's not a race.'

Philip raised his trigger arm and took careful aim.

'Which target are you going for?' Slurps asked, fumbling for his binoculars.

'The one on the end, far right.'

Slurps found Philip's target. Only this one was no busty centrefold. He put the binoculars down. 'What the fuck is that?'

'Not bad, eh? Just a little something I knocked up earlier,' laughed Philip.

Fixed to the top of the cross was a photo of Ryan, full head and shoulders, torn from the pages of their school magazine.

'I always hated that photo,' said Philip. 'Outstanding achievement, my arse.' He repositioned the shotgun, resting for only a couple of seconds, before Ryan met the same fate as the busty mechanic, obliterated into a thousand fragments, floating away in the breeze, into the next paddock.

'Bye-bye, Ryan,' he whispered.

39
Ryan

Ryan slowed his car to a crawl as he came onto Blind Man's Bluff. He made out Philip's car at the other end. They were both on time.

It was Ryan's suggestion to meet here – roughly half the distance from town to the shearers' quarters. Neutral territory. Their cars met in the centre, both pulling onto the verge between the road and the cliff face.

'Thanks for coming.' Ryan took up a position on the bonnet of his car.

'No problem,' replied Philip, doing the same. 'If I'm not home, Becky thinks I'm at the club, whatever I'm doing, so it makes no difference.'

'How's the bank?' asked Ryan, searching for an ice-breaker.

Philip laughed. 'C'mon, Ryan! Since when did you give a toss about the bank? You've got no idea what I do.'

'How's your mum and dad?' he tried again.

'I'd rather not talk about them.'

'Your parents are good people.'

'My mum would bake you a cake before she baked one for me. And don't get me started on my dad. You don't know the half of it.'

'What do you mean by that?'

'My dad's a fraud, Ryan. Don't tell me you can't see that. Thinks we're some kind of entitled royalty. Thomas Nash, the first European settler ... Did you know Nashville is named after a horse thief? That's what the real Nash family history is. Stealing horses. We're common fucking criminals!' Philip laughed sarcastically. 'The best he can do is spend half my life telling me I should be like him, and the other half telling me I should be like you. Do you know what that feels like?'

'No.'

'You know what's ironic? Now I realise there is something I envy you for. You never had a father.'

'You don't mean that.'

'Don't tell me what I know, Ryan.'

Ryan didn't know what else to add. Gentle lilt of the river aside, the silence took hold.

Philip broke the ice with a low laugh. 'Haven't seen you down the club.'

'What's that supposed to mean?'

He laughed louder. 'I wouldn't take it personally. I reckon the vote was a reflection on my old man more than you. You should have vetted your proposer more thoroughly; that's where you went wrong!'

Ryan let Philip's laugh run out. 'You really think that's what happened?'

'C'mon, man! Why do you think this place is called Blind Man's Bluff? Open your eyes!'

Ryan let it go. He hadn't come here to talk about Jack.

'So why are we here, if you don't mind me asking? I assume it's not to take in the scenery?'

Ryan swallowed hard. 'I know you offer favours at the bank. To proposition girls.'

Philip laughed again, before it dawned on him that Ryan was serious.

'Really? Is that what this is about? You think I'm hitting on your girlfriend?'

'She's a friend. From the shearing gang.'

'Oh, just a friend?' Philip pondered for a few seconds. 'So . . . in that case, if she's not your girlfriend, you shouldn't have any objection to me having a crack at her. Right?'

'Sanna's a good girl, a long way from home. She doesn't need you bothering her.'

'I must say, she struck me as someone quite capable of looking after herself. But then again, that's always been your way, hasn't it? Make it all about you.'

'C'mon, mate. That's bullshit.'

'Is it?'

Ryan rolled his eyes.

'You think something bad might happen to her? Is that the problem?'

Before Ryan could reply they were disturbed by a rockfall, over his shoulder. They watched a few small rocks chase each other down the bluff face, leaving a small vapour trail of dust in their wake, before coming to rest on the verge.

'Listen,' said Philip, 'why don't we settle this once and for all?' He went to the boot of his car and emerged with his rifle.

Ryan's heart stopped beating.

'We'll both be better off if we don't pretend we're mates.'

'Whoa!' exclaimed Ryan, raising his hands and arching backwards. 'It's not –'

'Shut up!' barked Philip. He walked straight past Ryan, stopped, peered upwards and pointed. 'See that? There's your rockfall.'

Ryan looked towards the top of the bluff, but he couldn't make anything out.

Philip lifted his rifle and took steady aim. Seconds later the shot came, and with it, another fall, this one larger than the one before.

'Fucking goats. Nothing but pests.' Philip puffed out his chest, impressed by his own show of marksmanship.

Ryan walked over to look at the goat. If it hadn't died from the gunshot, its neck had been broken in the fall. 'So, what are you going to do with this?' he asked.

'What do you think?' said Philip, returning his gun to the car. 'Why don't you take it back to your friend, and give it a proper burial. Tell her what an arsehole I am while you're at it.'

'You *are* turning into an arsehole, you know that? Becky deserves better.'

'Becky? Becky is my business, you stay out of it.' Philip grabbed a firm hold of his car door. 'Ryan, I don't know why you wasted my time – and yours – asking me here. Thing is, you don't belong anymore. The sooner you accept that, the better.'

'I didn't realise that was for you to decide.'

'I'm not deciding anything. Figure it out for yourself. I'm just giving you some friendly advice.'

'Not so friendly.'

'Yeah, well . . . that's the first thing you've said for a while that's true. Keep working on that.' Philip hopped into his car, did a sharp U-turn and sped away.

Ryan walked over to the goat. It didn't feel right leaving it there like that. He gathered some rocks and swept a pile of loose papa over the carcass with his boot. If it didn't rain – and there was none forecast – the makeshift grave would hold, and keep the falcons at bay for a few days.

Later that evening, Ryan parked outside the front of the police station and waltzed straight in. It was empty; the only people likely to be troubling the constabulary would be too drunk to find their way to the station. Nor would the police be rushing to collect them, unless absolutely necessary. Nobody liked doing paperwork late on a weeknight.

Constable Peterson greeted him cheerily. 'I was wondering if you'd come in or whether that chat was . . . you know . . .'

'Just talk?'

'Yes.'

'No, this is for real,' said Ryan.

'No worries. My partner clocked off half an hour ago. Town's dead. I could do with the company, quite honestly.'

'That sounds like an offer for a cup of tea,' said Ryan.

Peterson jumped into action. Ryan figured that wasn't his default mode, but the tea was hot, and the pair of Milk Arrowroot biscuits welcome.

'You know I can't invite you onto this side. Not when I'm one-up,' Peterson apologised. 'Regulations.'

'All good. I don't want to get you into trouble.'

Peterson returned to the counter carrying a couple of bulging archive boxes, held together by industrial-strength rubber bands.

'So, what did you come up with?' Ryan asked.

'Well, as I mentioned, there aren't actually many murder files. A domestic violence one from last year, and there was that bloke shot in a dispute over a dope plantation. So you're right, the only one that really fits what you described is that hitchhiker case. Mary Atkins. As you know, there was nobody charged so . . . the difficulties of prosecuting a murder case and so on.'

'Well, it depends,' said Ryan. 'Was there nobody charged because there were no suspects and no evidence, or did they have someone in the frame but couldn't make a case?'

'Oh, there were plenty of suspects, don't worry about that,' said Peterson, nodding at the boxes. 'I wasn't here then, but there was profiling done on all sorts of people.'

'And?'

'It's not as simple as ranking suspects. It's more about putting people into different groups: locals, travelling salesmen, truck drivers, gang members, people known to the victim . . . that sort of thing.'

'Like a shearing gang, for example?'

'Yes, I suppose. I don't think you're in there, if that's what you're asking.'

'I was down at university when it happened,' said Ryan.

'Of course. And you only need what's relevant for your study, right?'

'Yes.'

'Because –'

'Don't worry, I'm not here to cause trouble.'

Peterson nodded.

'So . . . if you were able to spare me a pen and some paper, how long do you think I could stand here with these files?'

Peterson checked the clock on the wall. 'I'd say forty minutes, forty-five tops.'

'Perfect,' said Ryan.

Ryan read and wrote like a man possessed. His mum's newspaper clippings were one thing, but this treasure trove was the real deal. The Mary Atkins case was fascinating. It was almost as if it had been split into two separate investigations: one for out-of-towners, one for locals. The detectives had expended a huge amount of energy and effort. There were copious, exhaustive notes; a number of travelling sales reps had undergone multiple interviews and had their private lives laid bare. There'd also been a lot of attention placed on a man who'd been released from prison on the same day Mary had last been seen. He'd literally been dumped out onto the same highway, just hours before she had been, a few kilometres away. The prison was minimum security, more a farm than a place of incarceration, and the man's crime was white collar embezzlement from a local council. Nothing about him screamed opportunist murderer, other than opportunity. The detectives had followed him up, tracking him down in Auckland and interviewing him three times. Then things took a turn for the worse, the man dying by his own hand, found hanging from a beam in his garage.

That outcome divided the police, according to the notes. One view was that he was Mary's killer and knew that the game was up. The other was that he was despondent at his wife leaving him, health issues, nil job prospects, and by the police hounding him. Without physical evidence, the police couldn't know for sure which version was true. What Ryan thought undeniable was that nothing had been left unturned in an effort to squeeze out the truth.

The same couldn't be said for the second pile, the one containing all of the locals. Names jumped out at him: it was a 'who's who' of Nashville. But compared to the other box, the individual dossiers were thin and rudimentary. Bull was described as a contract shearer, working for Carl Stensness, address at the date of the disappearance, 'uncertain'. That was all, save for a handwritten note attached to a standard form: 'Religious fanatic, brother and sometime associate of local Mongrel Mob member.' Where was the rigour, the notes that spoke to Bull's personality traits, his predilection to violent outbursts and animal cruelty? *'Religious fanatic'*: two words jotted down in an offhand way, by a policeman simply looking to tick a box and cover his backside. What if Bull was a deranged individual who, under the cloak of twisted theology, might sacrifice a girl's life at the drop of a hat? His theory about police treating locals differently was beginning to add up. How would they know what Bull was capable of if they didn't investigate thoroughly?

Another folder piqued his interest. Here, the police had cross-referenced a list of men known to have been in town the evening Mary had last been sighted, who potentially could have been driving around while she was still in the area. Those interview transcripts followed a consistent pattern: 'In what direction did you drive home? Did you observe anything out of the ordinary? Any cars or trucks you'd never seen before? Did you see her on the highway? Near the hotel or on the main street?' All were blanks, the lot of them. They were useless as witnesses. Which, in Ryan's book, made them all suspects.

The list from the Workingmen's Club jumped off the page. There had been eleven men still in attendance at closing time: barman Abe Lewis, Alby Charlton, Don 'Macca' McHendry, Terrence Pihama, Manny Waikete, Sonny Turinui, David Soames, Chris Eaton, Jack Nash, Philip Nash and Gerry 'Slurps' Darlow. Quite the regular crew. Soames and Eaton were said to have left together, in Eaton's utility. Jack Nash told police that he walked home, which seemed reasonable, given his house was on the town grid, a few hundred metres away. The rest of them drove off on their own.

Ryan could see why there'd been such a focus on his old teacher, Mr Pihama. Once he'd left the club, there was no-one to vouch for his whereabouts. But where to start with the others? Alby Charlton was in his late seventies and frail. Sonny Turinui was apparently so pissed his mate Manny had to put his keys in the ignition and start the car for him. Slurps was a degenerate, but was he capable of pulling off the perfect crime? Philip, he'd known since primary school. He'd developed an attitude, but so what?

If he was being honest, they were a motley, unlikely bunch of killers. But what if the real perpetrator was among them? A local, still walking around town, potentially emboldened enough to strike again?

Detective Inspector Harten had led the investigation. Usually, it was problematic for a lead detective to be familiar with potential suspects, because of the dangers of creeping assumption and bias. A small piece of evidence that might draw attention to an unknown person might be dismissed when it concerned a local, because it didn't fit the prevailing view. Which was why reinforcements had been brought in from outside the region.

On the other hand, that detailed, intimate knowledge was invaluable. Why waste precious time chasing down rabbit holes when the local detective drank beer shoulder to shoulder with these men and already knew what made them tick? These were authentic relationships: knowing what position a man's kids played on the school rugby team, knowing which hand he held his cock with when he had a piss. That was worth more than a hundred academy profiling sessions.

Peterson sidled up to the counter. 'I'm ready to close up. Are you done?'

'Yeah, thanks,' said Ryan, looking down at his scribbled notes. Whatever the outcome, Ryan felt sure he would impress his lecturers and classmates; even if it meant another night of little sleep.

'Thanks, mate. Really appreciate it,' he said, shaking Peterson's hand.

'Glad I could help. Good luck with your assignment.'

Ten minutes down the river road, Ryan's crammed head began to clear. Harten had been too protective of the people he knew and lived alongside. It wasn't fair on Mary Atkins; her remains lay somewhere in the local bush. She had not been served justice. And because of that, somebody was enjoying a freedom they weren't entitled to.

But there was something else nagging him. There was something missing. Despite purporting to be an exhaustive list, nowhere in all of the files, the records of interview, the scribbled notes . . . *nowhere* . . . was there any mention of Neville Hanigan.

40
Ryan

If this was what being a lawyer was all about, Ryan would need to rethink his choice of profession. The drab, lifeless office of Isaac Isaacs, Barrister, Solicitor and Notary Public, hardly screamed inspiration and thrills. It was, however, conveniently sited, directly opposite the funeral home. Isaacs would read his mother's will, Ryan would collect whatever savings she had ferreted away, and he would walk straight across the road and write a cheque to settle the account for the funeral expenses. Simple and quick; just what he needed. After all, he'd had a busy few days, dealing with Philip about his behaviour to Sanna, then trying to process all of the information about the Mary Atkins case. And the job. Always the job. Fleece after fleece, bale after bale.

He stood in the waiting-room, absorbing its mustiness. Isaacs' assistant, his frumpy, thirty-something daughter Madeleine, not only still lived at home with her parents, she had quite possibly never spent a night apart from them. Her desk contained nothing but rudimentary stationery supplies, except for at one end, where an old-style cash register sat, complete with push buttons and tabs signifying pounds and pence; what he'd once heard his mother describe as a 'Jewish piano'. It was too big for the desk and looked hopelessly out of place. A family heirloom, Ryan presumed.

The only solicitor in town, Isaacs had a monopoly on legal work. Conveyancing, business, criminal, family ... Isaacs was an all-rounder, by necessity, to ensure he had enough regular work coming in. Without another lawyer around, Ryan wondered how he managed conflicts, and how he decided which side of a matter to take. If he remembered, he would ask him after the reading of the will was complete.

The phone on the desk rang, snapping him back to the present.

'You can go in now,' said Madeleine, flashing a toothy smile.

Ryan had never met Isaacs before, although he knew him by sight. North of sixty, short and balding, his gesture for Ryan to take a seat betrayed a slight stoop.

'Thank you for coming in today, Ryan.'

'No problem. Thanks for seeing me so late, so I didn't have to miss much work.'

'I understand you're studying to become a lawyer.'

'Yes.'

'Whatever you might hear, it's a noble profession. Enjoy it.'

'Thank you, I will.'

'And whatever the big-city firms promise you, I can tell you, there's something gratifying about serving a community like this.'

Ryan smiled. The crafty old codger was feeling him out as a buyer for his practice.

'Right,' said Isaacs, shuffling a couple of sheets of paper. 'Let's get down to business.'

Isaacs began by apologising for the whole process taking months longer than it should have.

'Please ... that's my fault,' said Ryan. 'Truth is, with my mum, I just needed time to let things run their course. That's why I never pushed you.'

Isaacs read the will from start to finish. It wasn't long, two pages including the preamble, which seemed to be nothing more than a device to ensure that it was only he who had any claim to her estate. There were no surprises, no unexpected mentions of his father, no previously unknown siblings appearing out of the woodwork, no safety deposit boxes full of pearls salvaged from an old shipwreck. There was the property, of course – freehold – and a cheque account at the local bank, which Isaacs confirmed had a current balance of a tick over nine thousand dollars, and a term deposit, maturing next October, of five thousand dollars. Save for the usual utilities bills, there were no creditors accounts or liabilities of any note. It would be a straightforward matter to settle her estate, leaving Ryan with the house, plus a modest amount of cash, at the end of it.

'I should have arrangements completed within the fortnight, and have a cheque drawn up for you then. If you'd like to liaise with Madeleine, you can come in and collect it.' Isaacs seemed happy with his work, if you could call it that. Ryan thought it typical of his mother to keep things simple.

'Thank you,' he said, shaking Isaacs by the hand.

Ryan considered his options. It had just gone 5pm. He could stop in at the pub for a couple of beers before driving to the quarters, go up to the house and mope around for no good reason, or drive straight back to the quarters, to be there in time for dinner.

It was no contest. He needed to rejoin the gang, to show appreciation to Carl for letting him cut and run early to attend the will reading; even if it meant there was now a mountain of wool on the floor, and he would need, in the morning, to press like a man possessed.

At the end of the main street, Ryan spied a vacant car space outside the dairy, and swung in. He went straight for his favourite ice-cream flavour. 'Orange chocolate chip, thanks. Double scoop.'

'Do you want chocolate dip?' asked the owner.

'Sure, why not?' Ryan was as lean as a whippet, rib cage protruding from his abdomen. One extra dip of chocolate wasn't going to tip him into obesity.

Unable to wait until he was in the car, Ryan bit into the top as he made his way out the door. Attention diverted, he crashed shoulders with a woman entering the shop.

'Hello, Ryan!' she said, gathering her composure.

'Jesus! Sorry, I almost got this all over you.' It was Becky, his old flame, of sorts.

'That's okay, no damage done. How are you?' He noticed how her smile was as broad as it was overeager, just like it was the night of their dalliance at the school formal.

'Good thanks. Yes, all good,' Ryan stammered.

'We've never had the opportunity to talk privately, but I just want to say I'm sorry about your mother. I came to the service, was stuck at the back of the church.'

'Thank you. Yes, I saw,' he lied, unsure if she was lying too.

'So, how are things with the shearing gang?'

'Yeah, pretty good. Actually, I'm on my way back down the river now. Just stopped in for the essentials first,' he said, holding up his cone. The orange ice-cream had started to run in streaks, like lava escaping the crater of a volcano, from the gap between the bottom of the hardened chocolate covering and the top of the cone. It was all Ryan could do to lick it away and keep up with the conversation. 'What about you? Still in town, haven't made a dash for it yet?'

'What do you mean by that?'

Her snappy tone told Ryan he'd messed up. 'No, no, I didn't mean anything by it. It's just a figure of speech. You know, how everyone at school used to joke about escaping town.'

'Not all of us have the opportunity to travel away to university, Ryan. My mother has been ill as well. I didn't feel comfortable leaving her and Dad alone. That's why I took a desk job at the primary school.'

'Good for you,' said Ryan, trying to recover the situation. Too late, he was sure; more evidence of his snooty attitude was now bound to get around. 'Anyway . . . I see you're all hooked up with Philip now?'

'Engaged, yes. My father quite likes him.'

'Well, that's always a bonus.'

'I'm sorry about that business at Mr Trescothick's funeral. Philip hasn't quite been himself lately.'

'That's okay. I'm sure it's nothing.'

'It's . . . let's just say there's a lot of responsibility that comes with being a Nash in Nashville. And a lot of expectation.'

'Of course.'

'Tell you what, why don't I talk to Philip and we have you over for dinner?'

'Well . . .' Ryan searched for the right words, to let her down gently.

She leaned in to whisper, 'Don't worry. He doesn't know anything about our little secret.' With the look of a wanton seductress, Becky clasped her hand over his, the one holding the ice-cream, and slowly bit into the top of it. Chocolate and orange smeared over and around her lips, which she removed expertly with her tongue, without ever losing eye contact.

Ryan couldn't get into his car quickly enough. He sat for a few seconds, trying to compose himself, wondering what on earth had just happened. It was only after he was ready to move on that he noticed streams of orange flowing over his hand and wrist, dripping onto the seat and floor of his car.

41

Sanna

The late-afternoon run passed quickly. Sanna was grateful for those days when they came, because they were rarer than the ones that dragged. Those were the times when Bull was invisible to her, and she was more aware of the other rousies and Ryan. Together they were keeping good time; they were turning into a solid, efficient team. Even Lacey, whose usual trick was to blame her moods and general unco-operativeness on her period, was pulling her weight for once. She'd laughed out loud when Ryan told her that, while he was no expert, even he knew that no woman had five or six menstrual cycles a month.

She looked to the centre of the floor. With another bale securely stitched, Ryan released the pressure, popped off the lid, and opened the side door of the box. She was sure this was his favourite part of the job, snapping his steel baling hook into the top of the bale, yanking it from the box and manoeuvring the 127 kilogram mass across the floor. From the back wall, he took a spray can of black paint and a well-worn stencil, and marked the sides and top of the bale: 'PWS' being the farmer's initials, and '22' for the number of bales pressed so far in this shed. Satisfied with his artwork, he ripped the hook into the bottom of the bale and, with an almighty heave, hoisted it up so the bale sat on top of another one. He jumped up and, one big breath later, repeated the action, shouldering the finished bale onto the top layer of what was now a three-high stack.

'Nice job,' said Sanna. The electric motors had switched off; she and the others were finished for the day.

'Nice job to you too,' he said, jumping back down. He glanced across at Carl. The shearers were washing down and packing away their gear. 'Wanna give me a hand for a minute?' he asked.

He placed a new fadge inside the box and together they quickly loaded fleeces into it. Clearing the floor would not only impress the farmer when he dropped in later to check, it would give Ryan a flying start for the morning. It felt satisfying, helping him. Doing something together that wasn't just sex on Neville Hanigan's woolshed floor.

Sanna got up from the communal table and grabbed a beer from the fridge. 'While I'm up?' she asked the table.

'Whaddya reckon? Is the Pope a Catholic?' laughed Carl.

She ferried half-a-dozen bottles over to the table, where they were claimed within seconds. She then reached across for the metal fish slice and, holding the bottle in her left hand, tapped it twice on the side with the slice, before, in one swift motion, like a virtuoso conductor flourishing a baton, swooshing the blade upwards, scything the cap clean off, sending it cartwheeling through the air.

A round of applause rang out. She took a triumphant bow, happy she'd added another skill to her repertoire.

'How's things going with your house?' Carl asked Ryan.

'No nibbles yet,' said Ryan. 'I finally pulled my finger out, tidying the place up. That should help.'

'People are funny, aren't they? It's a perfectly good house but . . . they don't want . . .'

She could see that Carl had inadvertently started down an awkward path. 'It's okay,' said Ryan. 'I know what you mean. Dead people. They don't want to be associated with dead people.'

'She didn't cark it there, anyway,' snapped Lacey. 'She died at the hospital.'

'Thank you, Lacey,' said Ronnie. 'Very helpful.'

'Alright, don't get sarky! Just telling it how it is,' Lacey huffed.

'You still mates with Ray's son?' said Carl.

'Yeah,' said Ryan. 'Well . . . yes, I think so.'

'I meant to tell you, I ran into him the other day, when we were in town. He was asking about you. He wanted to know what sort of presser you were.'

'A ratshit one!' Bull's voice cut across the table.

'Why would he do that?' said Crystal.

'Well, whatever he might think, we think you're wonderful,' added Ronnie.

Ryan shrugged his shoulders. 'You're not the first person he's asked.'

'I didn't give him anything,' said Carl. 'Pissed him off a bit, I reckon.'

Sanna watched Carl take a long swig of his beer. Even if Ryan wasn't the best presser around, Carl would never say a bad word or dump him for someone else. Carl stood by all his workers. They could all do worse than to emulate him.

Ronnie returned to the table carrying a large pavlova, setting it down alongside a bowl of fruit. 'Happy birthday, Bull!' she exclaimed, as she lit the sole candle adorning the centre of the pav.

'Choice!' exclaimed Crystal.

Sanna agreed. The meringue stood tall and proud, finished off in a mouth-watering bronze glaze.

'You kept that well hidden,' said Carl.

Ronnie led the singing of a tuneless version of 'Happy Birthday'.

'Well, that was piss weak,' laughed Bull.

'How old are you?' asked Crystal.

'Never you mind,' he snapped back.

Ronnie passed Bull a knife and he found the middle of the pav with it.

'Close your eyes and make a wish,' said Lacey, excitedly.

Bull closed his eyes and drew the knife down, making the first cut. 'Done.'

'Now, let's sink some piss!' shouted Pete.

'Just a small piece for me, please,' said Crystal.

'Go on, tell us, Bull. What did you wish for?' asked Sanna.

There was a sudden silence, like she'd just asked a forbidden question.

'If he told you, he'd have to kill you,' said Pete.

Twenty minutes later, Sanna pushed the woolshed door open and heard its familiar creak.

'I thought you weren't coming.' Ryan sounded a little anxious.

'I'm sorry. You're right, we do need to talk.'

They sat on the fadges, the place where they always sat, the place where their baby had been conceived. Once they got down to it, there wasn't actually a lot to say. The facts were the facts, she was definitely pregnant.

She felt Ryan puff his chest out, about to say something.

'Ryan, before you start . . . don't take this the wrong way, but I don't want you thinking that you're making the decisions about this.'

'What does that mean? It's my baby too.'

'Of course. But . . .'

They sat in silence for a few moments, allowing the dark to consume the shed.

'Do you want a baby?' she asked.

'No. I just assumed –'

'Don't. Don't assume anything.'

Ryan took that in. 'So, do you want a baby?'

'No.'

Another pause.

'What about any religious objection?' she asked. 'You know, if I was to have an abortion?'

'Sanna, you know I'm not churchy.'

'Okay. I just needed to ask.'

'I mean, if that's what you decide to do, obviously I'll pay for it.'

Ryan's chivalry was admirable, but he was missing the point. 'It's not about money,' she said.

'Of course.' He held her hand. 'I guess we'd need to go to Auckland. I'd have to find out, but I suppose there are places there. I'll drive you.'

'It's too soon. Then you'll be back at university. And I'll be back home.'

Ryan winced. She guessed the idea of her carrying his baby all the way to Finland didn't sit well.

'Are you going to tell your family?' he probed.

'I don't think so. Maybe Emilia, one day.' She tucked her head onto the top of his inviting shoulder. 'Ryan, just so you know . . . please don't think I wouldn't want to have your baby. You'd make a wonderful father.'

'You sound like my mother now.'

'You know what I mean. It's only that we're too young.'

They kissed, gently. Not to spark something, but to underline the conversation.

'Here, I've got you something,' said Ryan, fumbling in his pocket.

Sanna carefully unfolded the wrapping, to reveal a carved greenstone pendant.

'Something to remember me by,' he said.

Sanna hugged him, then hung the pendant, attached to a black, waxed string band, around her neck.

'It's called Pikorua,' explained Ryan. 'So, these are two pikopiko fern fronds, and their twisting together represents an eternal bond between people and cultures.'

'It's perfect,' she said, through moist eyes. 'So, now I will make a wish.'

Delighted with himself, Ryan admired the pendant. Her body still and eyes closed, it hung beautifully on her.

'You know,' she said, 'we will move on, and maybe some time in the future, there will be babies and everything that comes with that. But we will always know this feeling in the back of our minds, that there once was something else.'

'I think you're going to make a great mother one day,' he said.

'Now you sound like *my* mother,' she laughed.

'So, are you going to tell me what you wished for?'

Sanna smiled and put her forefinger to his lips. 'If I told you, I'd have to kill you.'

42
Tom

'You *what?*' Tom Harten shouted so fiercely the whole police station shook on its foundations.

'But it's not like he's someone off the street. He's training to be a lawyer,' Peterson stammered.

'*Training!* Just like you're training to be a policeman. With fuck-all chance of becoming one, the rate you're going. For fuck's sake!' Froth foamed out of Tom's mouth as if he'd swallowed a dozen Wizz Fizz in one hit. 'Lawyer? He's not a lawyer's arsehole, he's a fucking wool presser. And from what I hear, not a very good one. Not that I'd expect you to know the difference.'

Peterson stood rooted to the spot, regretting he'd ever mentioned Ryan's project to his boss.

'You know what else he is? He's a fucking nobody. He's a snooping little nobody, and you're a fucknuckle. What are you?'

'Sir?'

'*What are you?*'

'A fucknuckle, sir.'

Tom took a sharp, curt breath. His anger was three-fold. He hadn't held much hope for the hapless young constable when he first arrived, but there had been a few green shoots emerging in recent weeks that had raised expectations. But this – giving a civilian access to police murder files? He didn't like his judgement being proven wrong.

Next, he hated it when somebody – anybody – second-guessed his investigation.

Third, it meant that he now had to drive all the way out to Neville Hanigan's farm, down that interminably winding river road, wasting a couple of hours of his time, for no useful purpose other than telling a young upstart to pull his head in and keep his nose out of police business.

'How many patrol vehicles are in the yard at the moment?' barked Tom.

'I believe three, sir.'

'Wash the lot of them. Plus mine. I want them all sparkling, understand? Hopkins will cover the counter.'

'Sir.'

'I'll let your senior know. Just on the off chance he might have thought you'd be doing useful police work.'

'Sir.'

Tom sat at his desk, irritated. To be fair, he was always irritated in court week. He was a working cop, one who enjoyed getting grime under his fingernails, not the detail and tying up of loose ends that followed. All for a circuit judge who was odds on to be half-pissed from the night before. Or fresh from some fancy seminar where a bunch of do-gooders with multiple university degrees – none of them in life experience – had convinced him that overcrowding in prisons meant custodial sentences were detrimental to the welfare and mental wellbeing of the offender, and didn't reflect today's values in society.

To hell they did. Snorkel Titmus was on tomorrow's court list. He was pleading guilty to theft of $45,000 from the Workingmen's Club; the actual amount stolen over time was well north of that. People in the community didn't want to give him a hug and ask him how he was feeling. They wanted him to do hard time in Waikeria Prison. To not be let out until he understood what he'd done and was properly remorseful for it. And to give him a couple in the kidneys for good measure.

Tom was also pissed off for having just wasted two weeks of his annual leave. Scheduled to go on his yearly deep-sea fishing trip to the Bay of Islands with a couple of his old mates from his early days in the force, the skipper of their charter boat had been in a serious car accident the week before. Too late to book another boat and too late to cancel his leave, Tom then stupidly agreed to go to Auckland for a few days with his wife, to visit her parents; as she put it, for them both to 'recharge their batteries'.

Wasn't that what living in the country was for? All they ended up doing was niggling and fighting. Him complaining about how much money she was wasting on clothes and shoes, her complaining about how abrupt he was with her mother. Back and forth, a veritable Punch and Judy show. He supposed he had loved his wife, once, before they were married. In the years since, she had turned into a real battle-axe, resentful not just of his career and the odd working hours, but because it took them to far-flung locations she cared little for. 'I should never have left Auckland,' she told him, at every opportunity.

She was right, she should never have left, and he was a fool for dragging her along with him. She'd since offered Tauranga as a compromise, but positions there were hotly contested, and, after his failure to get a result with the disappearance of the hitchhiker, he'd been pushed well down the list.

As for Wanda, well, that was all down to his wife. He wasn't about to confess to the affair, but at the same time, if he was found out, despite the short-term pain, it would probably be what they both needed. A circuit-breaker that would allow them both to start again, somewhere else, before it was too late.

One phone call established that the Stensness gang was working at Clarindale farms; not as far out of town as the Hanigan farm. At least that was something, he supposed, as he reached for his car key and went outside to check that the bumbling constable had finished.

Once the tarseal gave way to dusty gravel, Peterson's work with the sponge was immediately rendered useless. Tom smiled a wry smile; the hopeless prick could clean it again when he got back.

He walked into the woolshed at ten minutes before noon. Carl noticed him immediately, but Tom shot a wave to assure him that the matter wasn't urgent. He quickly spotted the presser, working on his own at the back of the shed, labelling bales. It would have been a good opportunity to grab him right there and then, but courtesy dictated he speak with Carl first.

'Good timing,' said Ronnie. 'You staying for some kai?'

'Why not?' said Tom. 'A cup of tea and a sandwich will be great, thanks.'

Ronnie grabbed a plate, but Tom stopped her. 'Happy to wait until the workers have got their lunch first,' he said. 'How's your mum?'

'Yeah, she's good, thanks. I've been talking to her and Dad about her giving up the warden work, but you know how much she enjoys it.'

'She's a great asset for the town. And a big help to us. Nothing like nipping trouble in the bud before it happens.'

'It's harder for her now,' said Ronnie. 'The gangs have changed things. With the younger ones, it's like she's competing for their attention. The Mob are in their other ear selling the gang life. And the parents don't seem to be as interested anymore.'

'It's a challenge, that's for sure,' said Tom. He nearly got started up again on the judicial system but, for both their sakes, thought better of it. Instead, he watched on as the gang washed up and took their lunch.

'So, to what do we owe the honour?' asked Carl.

'No major concern,' Tom replied. 'I just need to talk with one of your crew on a matter.'

Suzie stood up. 'You didn't need to drive all the way out here. I would have come in.' She stepped towards him, hands outstretched, as if to give herself up for cuffing. 'Whatever that bitch said about me, she threw the first punch. She deserved a good hiding.'

'Interesting,' said Tom. 'But actually, I'm here to speak to Ryan.'

They took their business outside. Ryan sheepishly propped himself against the front of the police car.

'Get your arse off my bonnet or I'll do you for damaging government property.'

'Stick your nose into police business again and I'll have your guts for garters.'

'You're lucky you're not facing a charge of obstructing an investigation.'

'You come back to town with a big head, from university? Eh? That's not how things work around here. You're just the same as everyone else. You get to abide by the rules, you don't make them.'

Ryan cowered under the withering verbal assault, but nothing was slowing Tom down.

'Get this into your thick skull – because of your interference, I've got one of my constables going over those files again, just to check that nothing's missing. You'd better hope like hell that everything is in order. And one more thing . . . If I hear so much as a critical word from anywhere, about my investigation, you'll regret the day you were born. Understand?'

'Yes, sir.'

'I promise you, if you forget to indicate at an intersection, you're dead in the fucking water. How do you think you're going to become a lawyer with a conviction hanging over your head?'

'You can't do that!' said Ryan.

'Just try me.' Tom cleared his throat and hoicked the remnants onto the grass alongside Ryan. If that wasn't enough for the message to get through, he would personally string the little bastard up himself. He raised a final, stern forefinger. 'Don't you think for a second that we didn't give that investigation our all. Don't you dare think I didn't lie in bed awake at night thinking about that poor Atkins woman and what might have happened to her. We did everything we could.'

With that, Tom got back into his car, did a three-point turn, and sped off. He'd never concede it to his wife, but she was right. That was the trouble with places like Nashville – everyone wanted to stick their fingers into his business.

43

Ryan

Ryan's mood was fouler than a rotting, week-old, maggot-infested carcass. Tom Harten's barbs from the day before were still ringing in his ears, his menacing body language branded into the front of his brain. Ryan wished he could brush it off, but his humiliation and embarrassment had been made complete when he saw that Lacey had parked herself at the top of the stairs to the woolshed and had witnessed the whole exchange. Naturally, she'd rushed inside to make sure everybody else got a blow-by-blow account.

Her stand under control, Sanna joined Ryan at the press.

'Just letting you know, I'm going into town at lunchtime. To go to the doctor.'

'Is everything okay?' asked Ryan.

'Yes. But I need to have a proper check-up.'

'Of course. Although I'd rather I took you.'

She frowned. It pissed him off, but he understood.

'Carl is letting Bull finish early today,' she continued. 'Something to do with a land purchase. I'm going in with him.'

'*Bull?* Like hell you are!' Ryan's admonishment was loud enough for Crystal and Lacey to spin their heads. 'I can't let you do that,' he whispered.

'Ryan, I don't want to upset you but it's not your decision.'

'That's not the point. I don't trust him.'

She rushed back to her stand to take the next belly, then returned.

'You and Bull. I get it,' she said. 'But that's your issue.'

'Fuck, Sanna. You saw what he did to that sheep.'

'And you saw what I did back!'

Ryan sighed. He was losing the argument.

'I'm not sleeping with him, Ryan. Or joining his stupid church. I'm getting a ride into town. Ronnie isn't going in today, or I'd have gone with her.'

Ryan was filthy. Filthier again, when at noon the pair of them washed up, jumped into Bull's car, and sped away. No matter her bravado, it just didn't sit right. Sanna wasn't safe with Bull.

44
Bull

Unless it was the day of Nashville's annual country music festival, finding a parking spot in town was never a problem.

'Meet you back here,' Bull grunted to Sanna, before stalking into the bank. He walked past the counter, straight to Philip's desk. 'I've come about my loan.'

'Perhaps we should sit down, Mr Tipene,' said Philip.

'You can drop the Mr Tipene stuff. It's Bull.'

'Yes, I'm sorry.'

Philip looked nervous. Bull didn't like where this was heading.

'We've received a written response back from the regional office,' said Philip. 'Unfortunately, it seems that, at this stage, your application for finance has been declined.'

'Declined? What do you mean, declined?'

'It means that based on your current circumstances, the bank has decided not to lend you money for the land purchase.'

'Why would they do that? I have over half the amount myself. A hundred and fifty thousand. What's the big deal?'

'I'd have to speak to the officer who signed off on the review, but usually, in these cases, a loan application is declined where the bank has concerns about the ability of the lender to meet the monthly repayments.'

'What fucking concerns? I'm a shearer. How do you think I saved the deposit?'

Philip cast an eye towards the customers waiting in line. 'The other reason, and I'm not saying this is the case here, but sometimes the bank doesn't think the client is a good fit. It's no reflection on you.'

'What does that mean?'

'Well, if you want my advice, you're welcome to resubmit. My personal view is that the financials are sound and there's no reason why you shouldn't be successful. But for example, it could be that your suggested land use raised a red flag.'

'Red flag? *It's a fucking church!*'

All heads in the bank spun their way.

'Please, can we keep this down?' said Philip.

'Sorry,' Bull replied, not looking sorry. 'But that's just bullshit. What else?' This wasn't making sense, there had to be more to it.

Philip shuffled uncomfortably in his seat. 'How can I say this . . . have you ever been to court?'

'Are you trying to be funny?'

'No, I didn't mean . . . what I meant was, if you were to attend court you would usually wear a suit, and present as professionally as you can. That way the judge is more inclined to take you seriously.'

Bull, unshowered and unshaven, and still wearing his shearer's singlet, leaned across Philip's desk. Sunlight caught in his glasses, the cracked lens a sparkling mosaic of intimidation. 'We're not in fucking court.' He paused for effect. 'Not yet.'

'I understand that,' said Philip. 'I'm only trying to explain things from the bank's perspective. About how they manage risk.'

'Here's some advice for you to pass on to your regional loans officer, or whatever he calls himself. The only risk to you and your bank is if I don't get this loan approved.'

Philip fidgeted uncomfortably. Bull stood up.

'Isaiah 54:17. No weapon that is fashioned against you shall succeed, and you shall confute every tongue that rises against you in judgement. This is the heritage of the servants of the Lord and their vindication from me, declares the Lord.'

'I'm not . . . I'm not sure what that means,' stammered Philip.

'It means, I've got a church to build. It means, I'll be back in here in a few days, with a suit on or without a fucking suit on, and you'll be lending me the rest of the money.' Bull's stare burned and he held it for effect.

'I'll do my best,' Philip whimpered.

'You will, brother. And the Lord shall reward you for it.'

'So, where exactly is this church?' asked Sanna.

'We'll go there now,' said Bull. Instead of turning towards the river road, he headed the other way. They were travelling east, out of town.

Bull's mood was dirty. He'd been warned by his uncle, when he'd had a home loan turned down, about how the bank liked lending only to 'their kind'. He'd just had that prejudice confirmed. He would give them another opportunity, just like he'd told the desk jockey. But if they didn't come through, they'd better be ready for him. He wasn't in the business of making idle threats.

'I'm sorry about the bank,' Sanna said.

'What do you care?' huffed Bull.

'It's for a church. I'm sure they'll change their mind.'

A few kilometres out of town, Bull turned into East Hills Road. 'It's just along here.'

Bull pulled up beside a timber gate. They clambered over it, into a flat paddock. At the rear of the paddock was a stream, with a small timber bridge, wide enough for a car or tractor. Beyond that, the land rose up a few metres, to a plateau that backed onto steeper hill country.

'This is mine,' he said, pointing out the boundaries. These two lower paddocks, this is where we'll grow crops. The top paddocks are for the accommodation buildings, and the church. It will reign over the whole property.'

'I'll admit,' said Sanna, 'this is a great location, for –'

'Worship and love,' said Bull, arcing his arms in a wide circle.

They crossed the bridge and walked the track up onto the plateau. Bull found a makeshift cross in the ground, one he'd left on a previous visit, crudely cobbled together from sticks and baling twine. This would be the precise position of his pulpit. He turned around to face Sanna. Over her shoulder, the lower paddocks and the East Hills valley unfolded. His promised land. He held his arms aloft once more and closed his eyes.

'For I speak not on my own authority, but the Father who sent me has himself given me a commandment – what to say and what to speak. But I do as the Father has commanded me, so that the world may know that I love the Father.'

He opened his eyes, to check he still had Sanna's attention. 'Do you believe?' he asked her.

'I believe in something. That there is some higher power, sure.'

'Power? There is power among us. There is power that is vested in virgins. In the scripture, do you know it says to utterly destroy every man and every woman who has lain with a man? And there was found among the inhabitants of Jabesh-Gilead 400 young virgins who had not known a man by lying with him, and they were brought to the camp at Shiloh. What do you say . . . do you think I will find 400 virgins?'

'I don't think so,' said Sanna.

'Are you a virgin? Or have you lain with a man out of wedlock?'

'That's private,' said Sanna.

'If you were to lay with me, I would absolve you of that sin.'

'I think I'll take my chances, if that's okay.'

'Do not make light!' Her flippancy annoyed him. 'Do you know what utterly destroy every woman who has laid with a man means?'

'Yes.'

'These matters are at my discretion.'

'Oh, I get it,' said Sanna. 'You're not just a pastor, you really do think you're God.'

'*Do not make light!*' She had angered him. He'd had enough of people not taking him and his church seriously.

'People aren't like sheep, you know,' Sanna argued. 'You can't make them all do what you want, and if they don't, smash them in the head.'

'*Don't tell me what I can and can't do!*' The rage that Bull had felt that day in the woolshed, at the sheep, at her reaction, had returned. He spat forcefully into the ground and growled – a ghastly, deep-throated rumble.

'You're scaring me,' she said, slowly backing off.

'You need to learn,' he said.

Sanna stumbled backwards, then turned, and started to run.

Bull took two paces forward, then let her go. Where was she running to? She would be back soon enough.

It was then he noticed the vehicle – a small, white farm utility – entering the lower paddock. It drove towards them, crossed the bridge and, moments later, pulled up alongside.

'Hello, Bull,' said the driver, a farmer in his fifties, wearing a cowboy hat two sizes too small for his head. 'Everything still on schedule for settlement?'

'It will be.'

'Let's hope so. I wouldn't want you to have to forfeit your deposit,' he laughed.

The farmer had a round, genial face. He smiled at Sanna, who had returned. 'Hello, miss. You a member of Bull's congregation?'

'I wouldn't say that,' she said. 'Actually, we were just about to leave, to drive back to our quarters.'

'Hop on then. I'll give you a ride back down to the car.'

Sanna couldn't jump up on the tray quickly enough.

Reluctantly, Bull hopped in the cab, alongside the farmer.

'She looks like a nice girl,' said the farmer. 'Take good care of her.'

45
Sanna

Sanna woke with a high temperature and another splitting headache. These were becoming commonplace; this one she put down to stress and anxiety. The farmer's intervention had been timely. She shuddered at the thought of what might have happened had he not arrived.

Ryan was right. Bull needed to be managed. Engaging with him needed to be kept to a minimum. He was an awful individual; he had scared her too, physically intimidating her and threatening her. But it was her own misplaced self-confidence that had put her in that position in the first place. She had handled him before, and she assumed she could do so again. She promised herself she would be more careful in future. Limit her interactions purely to what was required to do her job. It was an easy promise to make. She decided not to tell Ryan. His ego didn't need boosting by being proved right about Bull.

Crystal was an angel, fetching water and tablets for her headache, and smoothing things over with Carl. Suzie wasn't around but Crystal insisted that she and Lacey would cover for her, Ryan would step up too, and they would get through the day. That was partly true; they would cope, although she knew they would have to work like Trojans to do so. She felt terrible for letting them down.

*

Sleep came in fits and starts. Once the light of the day took hold, the cotton sheets nailed to the window offered no resistance. Eventually, she conceded and took a shower. At least the water was soothing. Slowly, she could feel the vice that was clamping her head begin to release.

Emerging from the shower, she reached for her towel. There, directly in front of her, stood Neville Hanigan.

She squealed, in fright more than embarrassment, and slung the shower curtain closed.

'I'm sorry, I didn't know there'd be anybody here,' he said.

She knew he was lying. 'Surely you must have heard the water?'

'Well, yes, but I thought one of you had left a tap running. I was just coming to turn it off.'

Bullshit he was. 'Well, it's off.'

'I can see that, yes. You know, we had some water damage in here recently – I don't want to see a repeat.'

Convenient. Sanna clung to the curtain until she heard him leave the bathroom. She peered out to make certain, then grabbed again for her towel. What was he doing wandering around their quarters, anyway? Was this a regular occurrence? She was missing some knickers and had mentioned it to Crystal, but they put it down to one of life's laundry mysteries. Now, she wasn't so sure.

She dressed and found him sitting at the communal table.

'I really am sorry,' he repeated. 'I didn't mean to scare you. It's very unusual for anyone to be around during the day.'

That much was true. 'I wasn't feeling well this morning, so I stayed behind.'

'Here, let me make you a cup of tea,' he said. 'That usually helps settle the nerves.'

At least he hadn't asked if she was a virgin. 'Black, no sugar,' she mumbled.

They sat and took their tea together. One on one he seemed less awkward, less at sea than when eating with the gang. Or perhaps he'd seen what he wanted to see?

'How is your wife?' said Sanna.

'Why do you ask?'

'No reason. Just asking how she is. Does she enjoy it here, farm life?'

'I told you before. I don't talk about my wife.'

'I'm only asking how she is. I'm not passing judgement.'

Her qualification seemed to ease the tension.

'I don't know for sure. Some days she seems brighter than others. But, unless she finds a way to tell me, I really don't have a clue.'

Surely he wasn't trying hard enough? Mute or not, living with someone every day, for so long, there would have to be cues.

'Do you play tennis?' he asked abruptly.

That was a strange question. 'No. It's not so popular in Finland.'

'When you practise at tennis, on your own, you hit the ball against a backboard. A wall made out of concrete. And whether you hit the ball hard or soft, top spin or slice, left hand or right, the ball comes back to you. Every time, the same way. That's what it is like living with my wife. Whatever I give, whatever I try, I get the same response back, every time. Like a tennis ball bouncing off concrete.'

Sanna took their finished mugs back to the kitchen. He was still there when she returned.

'You must have work to do – please don't let me interrupt your day,' she hinted.

He stood up. 'What is your name?'

'Sanna.'

'S-A-N-N-A. You mean like this?' Neville took a piece of paper from his pocket and showed it to her. It was the one she had left for Janet, when she had written her name for her.

Shocked to see it, Sanna didn't know what to say.

'Stay away from my wife. Understand?' His delivery was slow and precise, the tone firm and ice cold.

'Yes, I understand,' she replied.

'Good. I'm glad we've clarified that. Just needed to make sure, that's all.' Instantly, disconcertingly, his tone had switched back to warm and playful.

'You start work here, in my shed, in two days. Will you be staying in the area, after the shear finishes?'

'No, I don't think so. I will meet up with a friend for some more travel, maybe up north, to the Bay of Islands, before my visa expires.'

'And then, when you leave New Zealand, will you travel elsewhere, or return home to Finland?'

He was asking a lot of questions. Too many. 'I will return. I need to get home for something. Now, I'm sorry but –'

'Yes, of course,' he said. 'Good luck with the baby.'

What? Sanna stood rooted to the spot, helpless, as he walked away. Like a desperate junkie's skin might slither and quiver when going cold turkey, hers was crawling all over. Nobody except her and Ryan knew about her pregnancy. Maybe Crystal too – she was smart enough to figure it out. But she was weeks away from showing. It wasn't possible for him to know.

A sharp pain pierced both sides of her temple; it was starting all over again. What was happening to her? It had been a happy, fruitful summer so far. Why was it all falling apart now, so close to the end?

46

Neville

Once he was out of view of the quarters, Neville stopped walking. He took two slow, deep breaths, wiped away the chilled sweat that had formed on his brow, and leaned against a fence. He chided himself for being so careless. What on earth caused him to say something so stupid? To let on to the girl that he knew her most intimate secret?

He had done the right thing, to scare her off from seeing Janet again. He couldn't afford to have her or anybody snooping around in his house, touching things on his desk, lest they discover his plans to leave. And this girl was smart, too smart for her own good.

But he needed to be better too. He started walking again, towards the house. There was a familiar pattern emerging. The most formidable enemy to his best laid plans was his own stupidity. First Janet's accident, now this.

He was meticulous at planning, he prided himself on that. But he needed to be far more clinical at execution. If not, there would be trouble.

47

Ryan

At last, the final shed for the season had arrived. And the final day. Ryan was working the press when Carl arrived, Neville Hanigan in tow.

'We've just done a rough count,' said Carl. 'If we push through the start of lunch, we'll finish bang on 12.30. By the time we're done eating and had a proper clean-up . . . tell the girls I'll have the cash on the bar by three.'

'Sure, boss,' said Ryan.

Ryan listened as Carl invited Neville to join them for drinks.

'Thanks for thinking of me,' Neville replied. 'I have to go into town later, so I'll be around. Let me see how I go.'

Ryan was aghast. What was Carl doing? This was the gang's time. Neville Hanigan shouldn't be anywhere near them.

'Another thing, mate.' Carl leaned into Ryan's space. 'You've been sulking around for days now. I've got the shits with it, everyone's got the shits with it. We're all going for a drink, and we're gonna have a bit of fun to end the season. There's no place for sad arses. Got that?'

'Got it.'

'Good.'

Carl was right about one thing. He was dog tired, there was nothing left in the tank. Physical work, week upon week, had taken a huge toll on his body. He was running on autopilot, and once they'd celebrated their achievements at the pub, he would sleep for two days.

He'd been grumpy at Sanna too, which was hardly fair. It was nothing she'd done, just him feeling down on himself. The battering he'd taken from Tom Harten was brutal, but it was self-inflicted. When she brought it up, he'd snapped at her. Even so, she'd agreed to spend the night with him at his mother's house, after the pub, before she caught the train north. It was more than his behaviour deserved. He would apologise and thank her later. Smooth things over.

'Hey, lawyer-boy!' Bull was at his stand, set up and ready to go. 'Seeing it's the last day, why don't you try something different? Like not fuck things up for a change?' His laughter rang through the shed.

Ryan walked across to Bull's stand. 'Wherever God might be, if he's happy for you to be his messenger, for you to preach by putting people down, then this whole religion thing? Its days are numbered.'

Bull laughed, scornfully. 'You really have got a lot to learn. I believe. I stand for something. What do you stand for?'

'What do you mean, what do I stand for?'

Bull leaned towards him. 'You think you're clever. You mock me behind my back. Because I'm an easy target. But I'll tell you what: I'm a doer. You? You just want people to like you.'

'That's bullshit.'

'Is it? I've seen you – you play both sides, you want everyone to be your friend. But what do you give in return?'

Ryan couldn't find a response.

'James 1:22. But be doers of the word, and not hearers only, deceiving yourselves.'

'I don't even know what you're talking about,' said Ryan.

'That's my point, lawyer-boy. Life isn't about how many university degrees you have. What counts is what you stand for.'

'Righto,' said Carl, interrupting. 'Enough of that. Let's knock this bugger off.' He pushed his gate open, and Pete and Bull followed. The sprint to the finish was underway.

'You look tired, love,' said Ronnie, passing Ryan a slice of toast. 'You'll be glad to get back to university. I'm sure they don't work you so hard down there?'

At university there were days when he barely had any contact hours. It was cushy as. Ryan laughed. 'It's different kind of work. But yeah, it's good for sleep-ins.'

That was partly true. A law degree was no snack – some of the subjects were a grind, and it was highly competitive. If he was being honest, he was proud of the fact that he could cut the mustard in the woolshed one day, then rub shoulders with private-school snobs the next, out-debating them and even having some of them come to him for help with their assignments. He wasn't the first high-school graduate from Nashville to make a success of university, but the others had done Phys Ed, Arts, the kind of fluff that didn't rate in Ryan's book. They were avoiding joining the workforce. He was going to make a real difference to people's lives.

'I'd love to see you back next year,' Ronnie offered. 'Just so you know.'

'Thanks, Ronnie. We'll see if Carl will have me.'

'Well, you haven't exactly been yourself these last few days. But that's okay, I know you've got your heart in the right place. And so does Carl.'

'Cheers.'

'What about you, love?' Sanna had joined them. 'This outfit isn't going to be the same when you leave.'

Sanna acknowledged the compliment. 'Of course, I will miss everybody. But I am so tired. And I miss my family. I'm ready to go home.'

Ryan kept a steady pace through the rest of the shift. Keeping a close eye on the diminishing numbers of sheep in the catching pens, he pressed his final bale and, with insufficient wool for another, helped the girls place the final few fleeces into a loose fadge.

There was a grab for the sandwiches and a race for the showers, but Ryan lagged behind. Somebody had to be last.

'I'll go in with Ronnie,' Sanna said, as Ryan made a final check of the shed.

He motioned down to the floor, where the fadges had been kept. 'Don't want to hang around here for a bit? Just for old times' sake?'

She smiled back at him. Ever since they'd agreed there would be no baby, the dynamic between them had changed. Their friendship remained strong, the sex still pleasurable, but their meetings were fewer. Partly that was tiredness, but he realised that some of it was because they both knew things were coming to a natural end.

'Let's save that for later,' she said, winking.

Ryan was definitely staying awake for that. 'You go on,' he said. 'I'll see you at the pub.'

Being last into the shower came with benefits. Ryan turned the hot water up as high as his skin would accept and, without the pressure of anyone waiting in line for him to finish, he let a whole summer's work leach out of him.

After what seemed like an age, the hot water finally faltered. He reached for the soap but, in his dreamy state, clumsily knocked the soap holder off its fitting. 'Fuck it,' he thought. Hanigan could replace it later.

With the steam dissipating, Ryan noticed on the wall, behind where the soap holder was positioned, a hole, the size of a nail head. Curious, he leaned forward and trained his eye into and through it. He was looking into another shower cubicle. Next door. The female shower cubicle.

An awful, toxic shudder rippled through his body. The dirty fucking prick had been spying on the girls. Immediately, he recalled times, after they'd returned from whatever shed they'd been working at, when Neville Hanigan just happened to be hanging around. Just a couple of weeks back, when the girls showered, the guys had to wait for twenty minutes, while he was in their bathroom doing 'maintenance'. Now it all made sense. The dirty bastard was perving on the girls. Perving on Sanna.

48

Philip

Philip had his routine down pat. At two minutes before four he lowered his pen and fixed eyes on the large clock that hung above the manager's door. At one minute to, he got up out of his chair and moved to the main entrance. Then, the moment the second hand was vertical he snipped the door shut. Had there been an oil-rich Arab sheik bounding up the steps wanting to deposit a billion dollars, it wouldn't have mattered. At precisely 4pm on Friday, the Nashville branch of the New Zealand First Federal Bank was closed for the weekend.

At least it would have been, if not for the phone call.

Philip didn't care greatly for Madeleine Isaacs. To be fair, although the family and the law firm held accounts with the bank, he didn't know her well. Nor she him, or she would have known not to bother him so late in the day.

'I've just popped a written request in the post, but my father thought it best to call you, to give you advance notice,' she said.

'About what?'

'We're looking to finalise the estate of Edith Bradley.'

Ryan's mum. Philip supposed it made sense. It was time. 'Um, can't this wait until Monday?'

'We already know the account details, and the current balance. But my father has some concerns about taxation liability. It's come to our notice that there were regular deposits being made into her account, and we need to establish if they are assessable as income or not, before we request a transfer and finalise the distributions.'

'I can look into that on Monday,' said Philip, casting an eye towards the clock. He hung up. There was nothing unusual about the conversation or the request, but Ryan's mother didn't work, and she didn't, as far as he knew, have other family or business connections. She wasn't the type to have an annuity, and if she did, it would be clear what the incoming payments were for. He looked at the clock again, then at the tellers. They were fifteen minutes from balancing up and finishing. He decided to have a quick look into her records.

Madeleine was right, there were regular incoming monthly payments, for as far back as there was information. The amount had increased over the years until, at her death, it sat at $250 per month. Well, that was curious.

Philip was invested now; he needed to find the source of the payment. He recognised the bank code: NZ First Federal, Hamilton branch. He glanced at the clock again. They would be in a hurry to get out as well, but it was worth a punt. He dialled straight through to the accountant's desk.

'Sorry, I know it's late, but I'd really appreciate a favour. If I give you an account number, can you please tell me the name of the holder?'

Philip held.

It took less than two minutes for the accountant to return. 'It's interesting,' he said. 'The account was set up at our branch, twenty-one years ago, but the holder has a Nashville address. I'm not sure why they wouldn't have just opened it up at your branch?'

Indeed.

'There are no transactions other than a periodic monthly payment into a different account at your branch,' the accountant continued. 'In the name of Edith Bradley.'

'And?'

'Every month for twenty-two years. Like clockwork.'

'Yes?'

'Have you got a pen? The name of the payer is Jack Nash.'

49
Ryan

There was no hiding Ronnie's car. Ryan spotted it from a block away, pulled into the carpark and took the space adjacent to hers. Inside the pub, he found Carl loading up the leaner with fresh bottles, and pulled him aside.

'I discovered something at the quarters before that you need to know about.' Ryan couldn't spit it out fast enough, telling Carl of the hole in the shower wall. 'I knew Hanigan was a bit sus, but this is heaps worse.'

'He's a strange bastard, that's for sure,' said Carl, expressionless.

'Strange? Is that all?' Ryan gestured towards the rousies. 'The prick's been stalking our girls. Perving. He's a fucking pervert.'

Carl nodded slowly. 'You're right. It's a low-life, dog act. Leave it with me, I'll sort it out.'

Ryan looked across at Sanna, sick inside at the thought of Neville Hanigan invading her privacy, watching her shower. How could Carl be so casual about it?

'C'mon,' Carl said. 'Let's not let this spoil the night. Come and have a drink.'

'Good timing, lawyer-boy,' said Bull. 'Some of these girls were a bit worried you weren't going to turn up, but I told them, he'll be here alright. Especially if he wants to see how real men drink piss. Ain't that right, Pete?'

'Right on, brother,' said Pete, resting his guitar up against the leaner.

Carl laughed out loud. 'That Bible of yours missing a few more pages, Bull? The ones about drinking in moderation?'

'The answer, I believe . . . you will find in Ecclesiastes 9. 'Go ahead. Eat your food with joy, and drink your wine with a happy heart, for God approves of this.''

'There's a song in that,' said Pete, winking.

Ryan acknowledged Sanna, received a smile in return, then latched onto Ronnie; not because he was desperate to talk to her, but it took him out of Bull's line of sight.

'So, tell me, if you were to stop working for the gang, what would you be doing with yourself?' he asked her.

'That's easy,' Ronnie laughed. 'Sitting on my arse at home. Doing nothing.'

'Sounds cruisy.'

'Tell you what I would like – I'd like to take my mum away for a couple of weeks. She's getting too old for all this warden work. I mean, she loves it, but I reckon it's someone else's turn now.'

'A lot of people will miss her if she retires.'

'Yeah, sure. But whatever happens, she's gonna stop one day. It shouldn't be up to her to keep the whole town on the straight and narrow.'

Ryan took that in. 'I guess one side of it is her identity becomes tied to that role. Because it's so strong and she's been doing it for so long, everyone in town takes what she does for granted. Like they don't even notice. And of course, she owes Nashville nothing; it's actually the other way around. But because she's given so much, when it's time for her to step down, it comes at a high price for the town.'

Ronnie nodded as Ryan continued.

'That's the upside and the downside of committing to a small town, all in one.' He recognised it as a commitment he could never make.

'I understand what you're saying,' said Ronnie. 'But, you know what? I don't want her shouldering that burden right up until the day she carks it. I want to see her take things easy in her old age. That's all. She's my mum.'

Ryan's beer slid down easily. He recognised it as one of life's great pleasures; after sustained exertion, on the wool press or at sport, the downing of the first beer.

'Hey, Ryan,' barked Lacey, as bossy as ever. 'Get over here!'

It was better to humour her now while she was sober, rather than run the gauntlet later. Besides, Sanna was standing next to her.

'Yeah, what?' he asked.

'Sanna wants to know why you haven't fitted her up with one of your mates?'

"Cos he doesn't fucking have any mates!'

'Mind your own business, Bull!' Lacey snapped.

Bull extended his middle finger. A touch ungodly, thought Ryan.

'So?' Lacey pressed again.

'So, what?'

'Sanna. She wants to know why you haven't found her a boyfriend.'

Sanna wants to know? Ryan doubted that very much. 'Well . . .' He was struggling for an answer. Bull wasn't that far wrong. About his having no mates. 'I wasn't aware that she was looking.'

'Jesus, Ryan, open your fucking eyes. She's obviously not a lezzo! Of course, she could do with a fella.'

'Well, Sanna, I apologise. I'm sorry for not looking after you better.'

Despite being embarrassed for the attention, she managed to sneak a smile back at him.

'Anyway,' said Ryan to Lacey, 'it's a bit too late now, isn't it? I'm sure she'll have more luck when she gets to Auckland.'

'Yeah, well I did mention that,' Lacey conceded. 'Bit of a small pool we're fishing in around these parts. The good ones are already taken, and half of the rest of them are my dumb-arse brothers!'

They all laughed together.

'That's the thing with these small towns,' she continued. 'Eventually you realise that everyone's related to each other.'

50

Philip

Still in a state of shock, Philip managed to herd the bank staff out the side door, into the bays where their cars were parked. He rechecked that the vault was locked tight, then followed behind.

Sitting on the bonnet of his car, waiting for him, was Becky. 'Hello, sweetness,' she said, offering a broad smile and a hug that he didn't care for.

Fuck. That was all he needed. 'What are you doing here?'

'Nothing's wrong. I finished early and thought I'd catch you before you went to the club.'

'And?'

'I've been thinking. And I wanted to run it by you. I know you haven't seen much of Ryan since he's been at university. Why don't we invite him for dinner?'

'What?'

'For dinner. He'll be going back to university soon. It'll be nice to have him over before then.'

'Hang on, how do you know when he's going back?'

'I ran into him, a couple of weeks back. At the dairy.'

'And he thought this was a good idea, did he?'

'No, I haven't actually asked him.'

'Then let's keep it that way, okay.' It was a statement, not a question.

Becky persisted. 'Is there something you're not telling me? Something between you and Ryan I don't know about?'

'Nothing you need bother yourself with,' he said. 'People change. He's changed.'

'And you haven't?'

'No. Well, even if I have, that's not the point. He's from a different world now.'

'He doesn't think so.'

'I thought you said you didn't speak with him?'

'No. Yes. I mean, no. It's obvious he still thinks he belongs here.'

Philip laughed, sarcastically.

'Philip! It's healthy that people are different. And it might be nice for us to have a new conversation across the dinner table?'

'What's that supposed to mean?'

'You know what I mean.'

'No, I don't. Explain yourself. Is my conversation not good enough for you? Is that it?'

Becky frowned. 'What conversation? Tell me, when was the last time we sat together over a meal? Either you eat dinner out of the oven after you get home from the club, or you eat in front of the telly.'

'So bloody what? I work hard, I pay the bills, I'm entitled to a bit of leeway.'

She rolled her eyes back at him.

'You can cut that attitude out right now,' he snapped, pointing a stern finger. 'And another thing – you'd better tell me now what this is going to be like, because if you're going to be one of those wives ... always banging on about every little fucking grievance, without appreciating all the work that gets done around the house ... then we might be better off knocking this on the head right now.'

Becky exploded into tears.

Philip kicked out at a stone before continuing. 'I don't need you managing my life for me, I've already got my father doing that!' Instantly, he regretted mentioning his father. In between her sobbing, he could feel his blood coming to the boil. 'Pull yourself together, Becky. You're embarrassing both of us.'

'Philip, I don't want to change your life, I don't want to break up, I don't want to cause any trouble. I was just asking if you wanted Ryan to come around for dinner. That's all. For old times' sake.'

'For old times' sake? What the fuck does that mean? Let me ask the same question of you. Is there something you're not telling me? Something between you and Ryan I don't know about?'

'What sort of a question is that? You know we went out, to the end-of-year formal. But that was all, it was just the once.'

'We never really talked about that, did we? What do you mean, it was just the once? One what?'

'Philip, please.' She started sobbing again.

'The wholesome vicar's daughter. Who held out for months because that was the *right thing to do*. Because she wanted to *be sure*. Who, when we finally got around to it, wasn't actually a virgin after all. You never did explain that one properly. Eh?'

Becky averted her eyes.

'This had better not be what I think it is.'

'Philip, I don't want to talk about this. Not here.'

He wagged his finger again. 'Nup. You don't get off that lightly. After all the things I've done for you. Because I genuinely cared for you and supported you. The least you can do is tell me what went on. It was him, wasn't it? *Wasn't it?*'

Through her shaking and tears, somehow Becky managed to mumble out a confession. Yes, she had lost her virginity to Ryan, the night of the school formal.

Philip slammed his hand into the side of his car. 'Of all the blokes in this town, it had to be Ryan, didn't it? Well, fuck me.'

He paced a tight circle, then slammed the car again.

'Philip, come on, we can deal with this. It's not the issue you think it is.'

He brushed her aside and flung open the driver's door. 'Don't wait up!' he shouted.

51
Jack

'G'day, son. What are you having?'

'Piss off, Dad. I'm not in the mood.'

Jack rocked back. He'd come to the club to relax, not to fight a family war. 'I'm just offering to buy you a beer. Since when has that been a crime?'

'Surprised you've got enough money left,' muttered Philip, under his breath.

'What's that supposed to mean?'

'Nothing. Just . . . later, okay?'

Philip bought his own beer and found his way to the leaner where Slurps was already in residence.

'I had the same trouble with my boy,' said Abe Lewis, working his regular shift behind the bar. 'It's not until they get kids of their own that they understand what arseholes they've been.'

'That's just it, Abe. He's not a kid anymore. You work your tits off, lay everything out for them, and that's what you get in return.'

Abe took Jack's individually numbered handle from its hook and poured him a beer. 'It's this generation, Jack. They don't value the same things we learned from our folks.'

'Ain't that the truth.'

'A couple of beers into him, he'll come around later.'

'I expect you're right. We all have our bad days at work.'

Jack elbowed his way into a group at the opposite end of the room to Philip. Nobody should have to put up with being spoken to like that, least of all by your own family. He wouldn't be telling Lois, that was certain. She couldn't stand it when there was conflict between them – it made her tremor. Lois was a good woman, she didn't deserve to be burdened. She would only fret, and her doing so wouldn't make a jot of difference.

Jack wasn't exactly sure when things became difficult with Philip. For years they'd been close; what you'd expect with an only child. He wanted more children, but after Lois discovered she was unable to conceive again, they put the disappointment behind them and directed all their energies into Philip, to ensure the Nash family name endured.

As a young lad Philip was never any trouble. Him and his mates, Ryan especially, they used to ride around town like they owned the place. Not in a bad way. The boys knew right from wrong and were never any concern for the police or for the school. At least not until the young lad drowned himself. Terrible business that was, although Philip insisted he'd have never taken a stupid risk like that. Jack remembered once getting a call from a farmer about the boys sneaking onto a property and nicking off with blackberries and apples. If pinching fruit was the worst of it, that surely reflected well on him and Lois.

Once Philip announced that he wasn't planning to go to university, Jack called in a favour with Bill Meadows, manager at the bank, and Philip Nash, trainee teller, was behind the counter within the fortnight. Since then, he'd introduced Philip not only to Rotary, but every businessman in town and every farmer he knew. Perhaps Philip would have got around to meeting them all anyway, through dealings with the bank, or over a beer at the club, but Jack had trimmed months off the task. Then there was the house he found for Philip and Becky. Opportunities like that didn't come around every day, but he'd secured them a sturdy, weatherboard three-bedder in a great location up by the golf course. Becky appreciated it. She was a solid girl, and he saw a lot of Lois in her. He saw a lot of himself in Philip too, even if Philip was taking his time to realise it.

'Everything alright, Jack?' It was Macca McHendry, nudging him with his elbow.

'Sure, mate, why wouldn't it be?'

'No reason,' said Macca. 'You're just a bit quieter than normal. Prostate not playing up, I hope?'

Ever since Macca had received a prostate-cancer diagnosis a couple of years ago, undergone treatment, then announced to the world that he was in full remission, he'd had an unhealthy obsession with everyone else's arsehole. It was almost as if because he'd had to endure a doctor fingering around in his back passage, it was only fair that everyone else suffered likewise. 'No, Macca. It's all good down there, I promise.'

'Listen, I meant to ask about the Bradley house. How's that going? Had any nibbles?'

'You in the market, Macca?' That was the other thing with him. He always wanted to know what houses were going for. He'd never once made an offer on one, and Jack knew for a fact his wife would never move out of their family home, so what was the point? None, except Macca was just one of those people who had to know other people's business. In which case he should have chosen a different profession. If raking solids out of the ponds at the water treatment plant was your career choice, you could hardly complain about not having your finger on the pulse.

'Well?' Macca pressed.

'It's a good house. I'm sure it will sell. But no, nothing yet.'

'I've seen him around town. A bit ahead of himself, I reckon.'

'He's young. Just sorting himself out, Macca, that's all.' Jack looked across at Philip. They both were, the pair of them. Sorting themselves out.

52

Philip

The white cue ball kissed the black, propelling it towards the gaping corner pocket. The angle was a fraction off and the weight too heavy. The black ball shuddered in the jaws and stayed out.

'Off your game tonight, mate?' said Slurps, jumping off his stool, eager to take advantage of the unexpected opportunity.

'Just a few issues at home. Nothing that can't be fixed.'

From the minute he'd arrived at the Workingmen's Club, Philip's mood had been surly. Becky's confession, if he was being honest with himself, wasn't a total surprise, but he was still entitled to be furious. He would make her pay for it, one way or another. And Ryan too. The hide of him, warning him off his girlfriend. And that coming on top of the shock of discovering the payments to Ryan's mother. That could only mean one thing. If Edith Bradley hadn't died, and he didn't work at the bank, nobody would ever have known, and his dad would have got away with his dirty secret.

A couple of hours later, his mood hadn't improved. He offered up some advice to Slurps. 'The next time anyone has a go at you because you don't have a woman, remind them you're the smart one. The rest of us are fucking idiots.'

'Who goes on about me not having a woman?'

'Sorry. Nobody. That's not what I meant.'

'Well, what did you mean, then?'

'Jesus,' Philip muttered, under his breath. 'It's nothing, mate. You know what it's like. People need something to talk about. Nobody's said anything bad.'

'Tell them to mind their own fucking business,' said Slurps. 'I can get myself a woman any time I want. Tonight, if you want me to prove it.'

'Yeah, sure, mate. I believe you,' said Philip sarcastically.

'Don't fucking push me.'

'Listen,' said Philip. 'I've got Becky giving me the shits. I've got my old man giving me the shits. Don't you start too, alright? Just take your shot.'

'Get fucked,' said Slurps, slamming a red into the side cushion. It doubled back and rattled into the centre pocket.

Philip laughed. It was a total fluke. And now the pink was on too, into the opposite centre pocket. 'My round,' he said, moving towards the bar.

Of course people talked about Slurps behind his back. He ate like a pig, cared little for personal grooming and if he ever vacated his house, it would need to be professionally fumigated before it was safe to enter. He had all of the qualities of a cockroach; unlikeable and continually rubbing folk up the wrong way, but tenacious and durable enough to withstand a nuclear holocaust.

There was one more thing. Slurps was a crack shot. Easily the best Philip had ever seen. They had all the venison and wild pork they could ever eat, and bragging rights across the hunting community. Domesticity might not have come naturally to Slurps, but his bushcraft skills were second to none. Handy attributes in a town like Nashville.

'It's a bit quiet in here tonight.' Terrence Pihama placed his beer on the leaner, alongside Philip's.

Philip barely acknowledged him.

'How are you doing?'

Philip ignored the question, stepped over to the snooker table and took his shot.

'Have you heard the rumours about the railway maintenance yard shutting down?' Terrence tried again. 'That's going to be a blow for the town.'

'It's not good, I'll give you that,' conceded Philip. Economic nervousness was the norm for towns this size. There were never quite enough people, nor the scale, to attract and hold businesses for more than a short time. Accordingly, it was almost impossible for assets – farm and house prices – to appreciate. Which only turned more people away, like it was a never-ending circle.

As much as he hated his dad helping him out, getting a leg-up into a house was huge. Others weren't so lucky. For now, stock and wool prices had held up, but Terrence was right, the railways transitioning out of town was no small matter. For so long it had been not just Nashville's employer of choice, but its psyche. Its financial benefactor. That was typical of the way decisions were made, hundreds of miles away in Wellington. 'Downsizing' was the fancy new term for it. It might add up on paper, something for a government minister to justify in a speech, to win nods of approval from economists and investment bankers. But there was a reason the bureaucrats who decided these things never visited the affected towns; lest they get an inkling of how they were ripping the guts out of local communities.

'How's Becky?'

'Sorry?' Philip snapped back.

'She was one of my best students, Philip. I'm just asking after her.'

'She's fine.'

The next minute passed in silence. Philip was in no mood for an examination of his private affairs.

'How's your mate Ryan doing? Have you seen much of him?' Terrence asked.

'Jesus. What the fuck is this? Twenty questions?'

'Settle down. I'm just making conversation.'

'Well, I'm not interested. How would you like it if I start giving you the once-over?'

'What do you mean by that?' said Terrence.

'You know what I mean. We all know the police had you in the frame for that missing hitchhiker, Mary Atkins.'

Terrence raised his hands, passively. 'Righto. And so, what are you implying exactly?'

'People like that, they don't stop at one.'

'People like *that*?'

'People like you, mate. This town's never been the same since it happened. Girls and women around here still aren't safe.'

Before Terrence could reply, Philip continued, 'Do us a favour. My dad's over there. Go and talk your shit to him. Go on.'

53

Neville

Entering town, Neville Hanigan eased his foot off the gas and cruised slowly up the main street. He was later than he'd hoped to be, but the time had flown by. He'd been pottering in his garage, sorting through his bits and pieces, making sure there wasn't something among his possessions he couldn't bear to be without in Subic Bay. There wasn't.

The town was quiet. The shops and petrol station were long closed. It was only the lights of the takeaway shop, and the two big drinking holes, the Workingmen's Club and the pub nearby, that shone out.

It was too late to take up Carl's offer and join the gang for a drink at the pub. Not that he ever really considered it; he wasn't the social type. Besides, they would all be drunk by now, obnoxious some of them, and, in the case of the backpacker rousey, likely to use that Dutch courage to confront him about what he knew about her pregnancy.

He'd do well to avoid the Workingmen's Club too. He'd never really fitted in there, especially after Janet's accident. The only thing worse than people asking after her was people pretending that they cared, when really they were just digging for gossip.

He did a U-turn at the south end of town and crawled back in the opposite direction. For a while now, his plan had been to slip out of town quietly. No fuss or fanfare, nobody knowing about his departure until well after he'd flown the coop. But as the time had drawn nearer, he wasn't so sure. It would be nice to leave behind his mark on the town. To give Nashville something to remember him by.

54

Jack

Each time Jack tried to get alongside Philip and have a quiet word, he found himself pulled aside and drawn into another conversation. Time had got away, it was late and Abe was ushering whoever was left through the side door of the club, into the carpark.

'You want me to drop you off, Jack?' volunteered Slurps.

He'd taken up a similar offer once before, but Slurps' ute was so filthy and foul-smelling he swore he'd never do it again. 'I'm good, thanks. I'll walk. It's only up the street.'

Jack watched Slurps pull out of the carpark, and drive off towards the pub. That was a little strange; his house was in the other direction. He waved goodnight to some of the others before Philip presented himself. 'Feel better now?' he asked.

'Listen, Dad. It's about time you learned to butt out.'

'I didn't know I was butting in.'

'Well, you were. You are.'

'I honestly don't know what's wrong with you, son. It's like you're carrying this huge chip around on your shoulder.'

'That's bullshit. Maybe I'm just sick of everyone telling me who and what I should be. Maybe, Dad, I don't want to be on the fucking Rotary, because you know what? Because that might be what you want, but it gives me the fucking heebie jeebies. Maybe the bank bores me senseless? Maybe I'm sick of hearing about Ryan all the fucking time? Maybe I'm sick of getting home and being asked about fucking wallpaper and carpet samples?'

'You don't have to feel inferior to Ryan. You've taken different paths. One isn't better than the other.'

Philip sneered.

'I can talk to him, if that's what you want?'

'Talk to him? About what exactly? Those monthly payments you made to his mother for years?'

Jack suddenly felt sick to the pit of his stomach.

'Not so quick to tell me what to do now, are you?'

'Listen, whatever you think about –'

'Don't bullshit me, Dad. You've been doing that all my life.'

Jack sucked a sharp breath of the cool night air and immediately sobered up.

'Big skeleton. Big fucking closet.'

'I'm sorry, son.'

'So, when were you going to tell me?'

Whatever Jack was trying to say, it wasn't coming out.

'You can't even say it, can you? That I have a brother.'

'I was going to tell you. I promise.'

'Probably weren't going to tell Mum, though. Right?'

Despite knowing this day would eventually come, Jack found himself hopelessly unprepared in the moment.

'I'm figuring Ryan doesn't know, either. Right?'

'No. Listen, son, it's complicated. Far more than you know.'

'Doesn't seem so complicated to me. You lying to Mum and me for all those years.'

'Philip, you're the only person who knows about this. I'd really like to keep it that way.'

'Wouldn't you just.'

'I know you're upset. But please, you need to keep this between us.'

'Maybe.'

'What do you mean, *maybe*? This isn't your mother's doing. Nor Ryan's.'

'I said maybe. Alright? And just so you know . . . I'll be making the decisions from now on.' Done, Philip walked to his car.

Shellshocked, his darkest secret a secret no longer, there was nothing for Jack to do but shake his head and wander off into the night. Hopefully, by the time he got home, Lois would already be asleep.

55
Philip

Jack's immediate reaction confirmed to Philip what he knew already. Of course there was no other possible explanation. He'd been paying maintenance for years. Guilt money. Ryan was his half-brother. For over twenty years, his father had been living a lie. On a few levels, it kind of made sense. Jack sucked up to everyone in Nashville, that was his thing, but the attention he'd paid Ryan always had something extra attached. Now he knew why. And he felt stupid for not having realised it sooner.

'*I was going to tell you, I promise.*'

Jesus, his dad could be a weak prick at times. He'd intended to go to his grave telling nobody – that was a truth they both knew. But now it was out. And now, things were going to be different.

Having dismissed Jack, Philip started his car. There was no point in talking further – he wasn't interested in listening to limp excuses and pathetic justifications. His father's day of reckoning was coming. But it could wait until Philip was good and ready.

56

Ryan

It had been 7pm when Ryan felt the mood change. For the first couple of hours they'd practically had the bar to themselves, and Pete had entertained them and the handful of other drinkers with a few songs. But like the proverbial frog in boiling water, Ryan hadn't noticed the place fill up until he realised he was bumping shoulders. The gang still had their leaner to themselves, but it was Friday night and there were all sorts crowding in. The place was chockas. With people who had come to party. And others to make trouble.

Carl came good with dinner: a dozen bags of salt and vinegar potato chips. He pulled the gang in close, around the leaner. 'Before I have to shout too much, and before I forget, thanks again everyone for all the great work over the season. I know we've had a few hairy moments, but anyway . . . as you know, I'm not an emotional kind of guy . . . but I just wanted to thank everyone again for your hard work. And if you've got any complaints, don't bother me – write to the local MP.'

They all shared a laugh, and toasted Carl and his generosity.

By 9pm, Ryan had loosened up and forgotten all about Neville Hanigan.

By 10pm, he noticed how he was no longer talking, as much as shouting and slurring. The jukebox was no longer playing songs, but pumping out an indistinguishable mash of beats and noise.

A half hour later Ryan officially declared himself pissed. 'How ya doing?' he said, sidling up to Sanna. 'You okay?'

'Yes,' she laughed. 'This is a fun night.'

He fondled the pendant that was hanging around her neck, the one he'd bought for her. 'It looks great on you.'

'You can take a closer look later, if you like?' she said, invitingly.

'Later? Or soon?'

She smiled suggestively.

'Let's have one more quick drink,' he said. 'Then you can start saying your goodbyes to everyone.'

'I need to get my pack out of Ronnie's car, too.'

'Sure. Let me know when you're ready. Grab her keys and I'll follow you out.'

Ryan left her to it. Crystal seemed keen to talk to him.

'Are you coming back again next summer?' she asked.

'Depends if Carl will have me.'

'But what if your mum's house gets sold? There'd be no reason for you to come back here.'

'This is where I belong. Where else would I go?'

Crystal shrugged her shoulders.

'People around here know me,' said Ryan. 'They respect me for who I am. Someone local who made good. I don't want to have to start that again somewhere else.'

'They *respect* you?' Crystal sniggered. 'You're either very pissed or very stupid. That's not how it works. You think people give a fuck? They don't. Not just about you personally. But anybody other than themselves. If you think you're any different, I'm telling you, you're not.'

Ryan's first instinct was that she was joking. His ego prickled when he realised she wasn't.

'And with this lawyer stuff, you're going to end up starting somewhere else, anyway. So what actually is it that you're trying to hold onto? Why even bother?'

'Why? Because . . . can I tell you something? For real?'

The music, if anything, had got louder, the throbbing of the bass more insistent. 'It feels to me like I'm losing Nashville. My mum, my studies, my friends . . . everything is pushing or pulling me away. When I'm not ready to be pulled away. I just want people to accept that I belong here, just like them.'

'You know,' she said, 'in all the time working with you, I never realised you were so insecure.'

'It's not insecurity. It's who I am.'

Crystal laughed. 'So, you're going to have business cards with lawyer on one side and wool presser on the other?'

Ryan nodded. She had a point.

Crystal quickly scanned the bar. 'Shame you haven't got some cards here now, ready to hand out. I wouldn't be surprised if this all blows up.'

Ryan could see what she meant. The bar was uncomfortably crowded now. The thumping vibrations added a surreal quality. It wouldn't take much more than an accidental bump, or someone to look at someone else the wrong way – 'eye trouble', they called it – for things to take a nasty turn.

Sanna interrupted them, cupping her hands to Ryan's ear. 'I'll go out and get my pack now.' She waved Ronnie's keys at him.

'No worries.' Ryan excused himself from Crystal and followed Sanna out onto the footpath. The hit of fresh, night air was welcome.

'You don't need to come with me, I'm okay,' she said.

'Sure,' he replied. 'But it's nice to grab a moment alone.' He took hold of her by her upper arms, pinned her to him and kissed her with intent. She responded, pressing back firmly on his lips. Despite all of the beer, he immediately felt himself go hard; 'brewer's droop' was either a fallacy or was reserved for men much older.

'Ryan, I just want you to know that whatever happens to us in the future, I will never forget this time with you.'

They kissed again, just as passionately.

'You go back in,' she said. 'I'll swap the bag over and hang outside for a few minutes, to catch some fresh air.'

'Okay,' he said. 'I won't be long.' He squeezed her hand, watched her cross the street, towards the carpark, and turned back inside. Working himself through the throng, he reacquainted himself with his beer.

Crystal nudged him with her elbow. 'You okay with her going back to Finland?'

Ryan did a double take. She knew about the extent of his relationship with Sanna?

'I see things,' she said.

'Sure,' he lied. Or half-lied. Downplaying their relationship like that made him feel bad. Not for lying – it was nobody else's business – but because it underlined how their summer together was at an end.

'No worries,' said Crystal. 'That's one thing about becoming a lawyer. You'll be batting them away, even if it's just your money they're after.'

'I dunno about that,' Ryan laughed.

'So, where will you end up lawyering? Is that how they say it?'

'Practising.'

'Right.'

Ryan shrugged his shoulders.

'Not back here?'

He was drunk, but not so drunk to jump at any bait. 'It's possible. But unlikely.'

'Just go where your gut tells you to go. Not to where you think you'll make other people happy.'

Ryan nodded. He hadn't known Crystal for all that long, but he liked her. A lot.

Ryan couldn't tell if it was the shouting he heard first, or the sound of breaking glass.

'Come here and say that! *Cunt!*'

'Don't call me a cunt, you *cunt*!'

Ryan made out two prospective combatants. Both nasty-looking types.

A woman's voice cut over the top. 'Don't fucking let him get away with that. Give him a fucking hiding!'

Everything unfolded in slow motion. The music . . . thud, thud, thud . . . even louder than before, even more feverish. Ryan took a step back, as everyone did, leaving space in the middle of the bar for the growling pair to circle each other, taking off their shirts as they did so.

'Take it outside,' came a shout from behind the bar.

'Rip his fucking head off!' came another.

It was on, and on for real. Punches rained, kicks flew. It was crude, ungainly and intensely primal. The two men fell to the ground, grappling, fighting for top position, before Ryan watched a patched gang member step forward and tip a whole jug of beer over them both. As they rolled over, still locked together, another man swept his arm along the top of a leaner, sending everything on it – glasses, jugs, bottles – crashing down onto them. That was the signal for others in the bar to join in, the shouting and screaming reaching fever pitch as bottles and glasses teemed down. Then, from near the jukebox, another man, a six-foot-six beast, picked up a bar stool, and hurled it into the men on the ground.

Ryan saw Pete step forward into the carnage; or was he pushed? A man came up from behind him, picked up Pete's guitar and, raising it high above him, smashed it down on his head. Pete lay strewn in amongst the splinters; conscious but bleeding, not fully comprehending his instrument had played its last tune.

Ryan quickly scanned around the bar. He'd expected Carl to jump in and help his brother out, but he was nowhere to be seen. That didn't seem right – he'd been there a few minutes ago. There were more screams, a mix of horror and whooping delight. Suddenly, Crystal was shoved into the melee. Without thinking, Ryan dived in and tried to haul her out, copping a kick to the ribs for his trouble. Looking up from the floor he could see Bull, making a run for the door. He yelled at him, for him to come and help the girls; Bull turned and caught his eye, momentarily, before turning toward the door again and pushing his way outside. The hand of God extended only so far.

Ryan grabbed Ronnie's arm – by now she was hysterical – linked it to Crystal's, and looked again towards the door. It was log-jammed, there was no safe way out.

'There!' he yelled, pointing. 'The toilets. You girls get in there. Lock yourself in and don't come out until after it's all over.'

A dozen men had now joined the fray, not even sure whose side they were on, punching and kicking at anything that moved. Ryan worked his way to the back of the bar, safe enough for now, with an upturned table for protection. There was nothing for it but for them to fight themselves out, and wait for the police to arrive and mop up.

It felt like an age but, eventually, it passed. One of the instigators had been dragged towards the door by his boots, and once his mates had squeezed him out, the heat inside dissipated.

In just ten minutes of mayhem, the bar had been levelled into a war zone. Ryan stepped gingerly over the rubble: blood, glass, broken furniture and moaning bodies. In all of the fervour, he realised that he'd lost track of Sanna. She would be waiting for him at his car. He slipped out the door, brushing past Ronnie's mother, Honey, on the way, reassuring her that the girls were safe, and then walked across the road, away from the milling crowd.

He felt a sense of relief, glad that Sanna had chosen to go outside when she did, to wait in the carpark. For her final memory of Nashville to be a vicious bar-room brawl would have been a dreadful anti-climax.

There was only one problem. When he got to the cars, his and Ronnie's, Sanna was nowhere to be seen.

January 1983

57

Ryan

'Thanks, Ronnie, you're a star,' said Ryan, reaching onto the communal table and grabbing a tin-foil package on the run. It felt comfortingly warm in his hands.

'Drive carefully,' she said. 'And give my love to Emilia.'

'Where's he off to?' asked Bull.

'Never you mind,' said Ronnie. 'None of your business.'

Ryan held the steering wheel with his right hand and fed himself with the left. Choice cuts of warm roast mutton, carved from the shoulder, before Ronnie had filled the serving platter for the others. She'd even drizzled mint sauce across the top – a nice touch.

Forty-five minutes later, he pulled into the driveway, past Jack Nash's *For Sale* sign, and saw that the kitchen light was on. That bulb had hardly been warmed since the last time his mother used it, and in the time since Sanna had gone missing. It had been a long, painful twelve months. He stopped himself there; he hadn't driven all this way to be maudlin.

'Hello,' said Emilia, rising from the kitchen table.

'Looks like you're settling in okay?'

'Yes. Mr Nash was very helpful. I can't thank you enough.'

'No problem. The house is sitting here doing nothing.'

Ryan produced three bottles of beer – two for the fridge, while he poured them both a glass from the third.

'Cheers,' he said, raising his glass.

'*Kippis*,' she said, in return.

'Kippers? That's a fish,' he laughed.

'No. Kip-pis,' she repeated, slowly. 'It's cheers in Finnish.'

'Ah, got it,' he said, only mildly embarrassed. He relaxed into his chair. 'So, tell me, are you making any progress?'

Emilia hardly drew breath. She'd been asking around town: people were very kind and welcoming, and sympathetic. But she hadn't met anybody – not yet – who could shed any more light on Sanna's disappearance. That included the police. DI Harten had humoured her with what she felt was the minimum amount of information to keep her at arm's length, but he was insistent that there was no new information to warrant doing any more than they were doing already. Which was, according to Emilia, nothing at all.

'You know,' she said, 'thinking about it some more, the worst thing was the look in the detective's eye. Like . . . not that it's all over, but he's happy it's all over. It's less work for him if this whole business just goes away.'

Ryan acknowledged her frustration. 'What else?'

'The lady at the farm. Janet. People around town tell me there's something about her.'

'Well . . . yes.'

'I think she knows something.'

'I've only ever met her the once,' said Ryan. 'Freaked me out a bit, I must say.'

'You already told me her husband is weird,' Emilia said.

'Yes, but –'

'Did you ever see him hanging around Sanna?' she asked.

It was a good time to tell her about the peephole in the shower cubicles.

'I can't believe you didn't tell the police! We have to tell them.'

'Maybe.'

'Maybe? *Ryan!*'

'They won't be interested unless there's supporting evidence. More than a hole in a shower. To be truthful . . . the thing is . . . as fucked up as that is, and as weird as the whole thing is between him and his wife . . . I just don't know.'

He could tell he'd pricked her bubble. 'I'm sorry. But if they arrested everybody around these parts just for being a weird fuck, well . . . you couldn't build a jail big enough.'

Into the second bottle, Emilia changed tack. 'So, you are an only child?' She had seen his photo, in a frame on a pile of things on a chair.

'I have a brother, but he's so ugly, my mother didn't keep any of his pictures.'

His face quickly gave him away.

'I'm not sure about New Zealand humour,' she said. 'All this taking of the piss.'

'Taking *of* the piss?' Ryan laughed out loud.

'What?' she said, sensing something wasn't quite right.

He waved her away. 'Don't worry.'

'Your mother. I'm sure she was very proud of you.'

'That's nice of you to say. But really, I haven't done anything to be proud of yet.'

'You will, I'm sure.'

'You know, growing up here in Nashville . . . it's like going to university is a big deal. I remember my mum telling me about one of the Skinner kids, heading off to Auckland University to become a scientist. That was unheard of. The local paper ran a double-page spread about it. Now? Forget the spread, not even a mention. Just a whole lot of people having a crack at me for getting ahead of myself. Like a law degree is nothing to be proud of.'

'Why do you say that?'

Ryan wondered for a moment if he shouldn't have opened that can of worms. 'It's just small-town thinking. It's more honourable to stay and be a staunch member of the community. I get that. No skiting. No thinking you're better than anyone else.'

'Which you don't. I can tell.'

'It doesn't matter what I believe. You know . . . perception is reality.'

'But what's important to you, Ryan? Do you really care what other people think of you?'

'No. Well, yes. Before, it mattered. I hated it that people had the wrong idea.'

'I know exactly what you mean by that,' Emilia replied, explaining what it was like for her and her parents, to read press reports that made false assertions about Sanna. How she put herself at risk. By being careless, by being promiscuous, by mixing in with drug dealers, by basically asking for trouble.

'I'm sorry,' he said. 'I didn't realise it was like that.'

'That's why I'm here. To protect her reputation. To prove those people wrong.'

Ryan was taken aback by the revelation. Sanna was none of those things. She deserved far better. After he'd reported her missing, when it was apparent that she and her backpack couldn't be accounted for, the police swept in and took over, and everything happened in a blur. He had done nothing to help her, other than to feel sorry for himself, play the victim, travel back to university, almost as far away as it was possible to travel and still be in New Zealand, and detach himself from the whole business. And now, to make things worse, Emilia had flown across the world to right those wrongs, and the police weren't taking her seriously.

'You know, if you don't mind me saying so, for someone who has lived here all their life, you don't appear to have many close friends.'

She seemed to have a knack of forcing him into awkward positions. 'It's mostly being away from Nashville studying, and also the farm work that I do. We stay so far out of town, sometimes for weeks on end.'

'So what? That means you have to give up your friends?'

She was right, that sounded ridiculous. He owed her more than he'd given so far. He poured another beer, dropped his guard and reminisced about his upbringing; about how they lorded over the town, him and Philip. Then later as teenagers, how they treated school as an inconvenience to be ticked off. How, after 3.15pm, the world was once again theirs, whether playing sport or just hanging out, listening to Pink Floyd or the Doobie Brothers and talking shit.

'Sounds like fun,' said Emilia.

'It was a great place to grow up,' Ryan admitted.

'But not so great to live as an adult?'

'I never said that.'

'No. But do you not think that if you stop spending time with the people who connect you to the town – your old best friend, other friends, friends of your family – they might reasonably take the view that you have made a decision to move on from them? That you no longer value them?'

Ryan sat in silence.

'Do you see what I mean? Have you ever looked at things from Philip's point of view?'

'But I'm not Philip, I'm me. He's old enough and ugly enough to look after himself.'

'You're missing the point, Ryan. Putting yourself in his shoes helps you. It better informs your position. As an architect, I cannot decide on what I want to build and continue blindly towards realising my vision. I must ask myself, what is it I must not do? How will it affect others? What are the hidden costs if I proceed down a certain path? Not just financial, but the risk of failure, the opportunity cost of missing out on something better, the cost to relationships: clients, workmates, neighbours.'

Ryan nodded. It vaguely made sense.

'I'm not saying that your friend Philip is perfect, or blameless; I don't know. But if you were to approach things differently with him, no more of this billy-goat head-butting, then I think you will find a better space. Both of you.'

Ryan nodded some more.

'I'm sorry, I don't mean to lecture you,' she said.

'No, not at all.' They had both been dickheads, but being magnanimous cost nothing. Maybe he should be the bigger man and smooth things over with Philip? Buy the beer, bury the hatchet, and be blood brothers once again? Maybe.

'Is that all?' he asked.

'Not quite. I need somebody to work with me to find out what happened to Sanna. Will you do that, Ryan?'

She was extremely persuasive. Bull's words rang in his ears. *'What do you stand for?'* He'd spent a year avoiding the question. Now, thanks to Emilia, he was being forced to answer it. Of course he would help her. He recalled the conversation he'd had with Sanna, in his bedroom.

'If I ever go missing, I hope someone cares enough about me to make a folder like this. Promise me you'll keep looking. Okay?'

'Yes, I'll keep looking. I promise.'

Not only would he help Emilia, he would drive things.

He paused. One more step out of line and Tom Harten would kill his legal career in its tracks; he'd made that very clear last year. He wanted to help Emilia. He was desperate to do the right thing for Sanna. But what she was asking for carried huge risk. Too much.

Emilia pressed again. 'Ryan? Will you help me?'

He avoided eye contact. 'No, Emilia, I don't think I can. Sorry.'

58

Emilia

On a trip of many firsts, this was a new one: a hairdresser chewing gum all the way through her appointment. To be fair, Sharon, the salon owner, was a highly proficient gum chewer. Emilia settled back into her chair, confident it wouldn't end up matted in her hair.

Emilia didn't need a cut – she hadn't been away long enough. But with the police feeding her only scraps, and Ryan declining to help, she figured that, to extract any dark secrets or gossip, Champagne Cutz was the place where everyone knew everything and everybody.

'You're not from around here, are you?' said Rachel, the teenaged apprentice, as she massaged shampoo into Emilia's scalp. Not a promising start.

'You're that missing girl's sister, aren't you? I heard you were in town,' said Sharon, picking up her scissors. That was more like it!

'I'm sorry about what happened,' Sharon continued. 'I never met her but I heard her described as a nice girl. Some bastard should be strung up for that. I'm sorry, love, I don't mean . . . I mean, I hope she didn't suffer. I'm sure she didn't, but, you know what I mean.'

'Yes, I know what you mean. Thank you.' Emilia imagined Sharon had once been the prettiest girl in the local school; but now, fifteen or so years on, had succumbed to the kind of tiredness that juggling motherhood and running a small business brought on.

There was a woman in the chair alongside, mid-fifties, elegant, waiting for her streaks to set. Immersed in a glossy magazine, she lifted her gaze for a moment and nodded to Emilia, as if to add her respects.

Emilia found Sharon chatty, if superficial and easily distracted. She constantly needed prompting. 'So, you must have heard a few stories. What do you think happened?' she asked.

'To your sister?'

No, to the dinosaurs. It was all Emilia could do to stay patient. 'Yes, to my sister.'

'Well, we had a lot of the police in here while it was all going on, and . . . well, my husband and I . . . they're not exactly our favourite people, the police, but you'd hear them talking to each other, and on their walkie-talkies and stuff. And you know how the official line was that your sister was picked up by somebody driving through town, just randomly? Like some kind of nationwide serial killer? Well, I don't think many of the police themselves actually believed that.'

'So you think it was someone local?'

'Yeah, I'd say so,' said Sharon. 'Let's face it, there's plenty of fucked-up guys in this town. And it only takes one to go haywire for something like this to happen.'

'Haywire?'

Sharon rolled her eyes in a strange way and looped her forefinger next to her head.

'Ah. But which one, that's the question?' said Emilia, gently prodding.

'Well, there's a few theories on that but, you know, I wouldn't like to be accused of gossiping.'

You're a hairdresser! 'Go on, I won't think any less of you,' Emilia pressed.

Sharon seemed to appreciate the go-ahead. 'There's that freaky guy in her shearing gang – the one who's setting up a church. The talk was that it was some kind of human sacrifice thing. I mean, whether you believe in that creepy devil's work stuff or not, I've seen him . . . he's pōrangi enough to do something like that.'

'Pōrangi?'

'Oh, sorry. That's crazy too. Like I said, the town's full of 'em.'

Based on what Ryan had told her about Bull, he definitely fitted the mould.

'There's some loner types who drink at the club. Teachers, farmers. There's that lawnmower repair guy, I wouldn't trust him as far as I could throw him. He could easily have been driving past at the time she was standing around in that carpark.'

'Repair guy?'

'Gerry Darlow. They call him Slurps. Lost his parents early, raised by a foster mum but something went a bit wonky. He was in my younger sister's class at school. Got caught with his cock out a couple of times, wanking under the desk.'

Nice. Add him to the list.

'Go on, tell her about the teacher.' The lady with the magazine had invited herself into the conversation.

'Terrence Pihama? He was my teacher too, in fifth form. The police really zeroed in on him, like they did for that other missing girl, the hitchhiker. Apparently, he left the Workingmen's Club around the time of your sister's disappearance, driving towards the pub, not the direction of his house. And then it got out that his next-door neighbour made a statement that she never heard him come home, and his car wasn't in the driveway until the next morning.'

'So, if it was him, he had time to pick up Sanna and take her somewhere?' said Emilia, filling in the gaps.

'Well, yes. *If* it was him,' said Sharon.

'You don't think so?'

'A lot of people do,' she said.

'But you? What do you think?'

Sharon hesitated. Magazine lady took up the invitation.

'Don't waste your time – it's not him, love. People know it too. But they still want to see him strung up,' she said, with authority.

'You seem very sure,' said Emilia.

'He's a homosexual.'

'So that means he can't commit a crime?'

'Not this sort of crime, no.'

Emilia turned to Sharon for her opinion.

'Well, he's never had a wife or girlfriend. And at school, I know some girls who tested him out, if you know what I mean. Tits out, skirt pulled right up, that sort of thing. And nothing, not even a nibble.'

'Maybe he was just being professional?' said Emilia. 'Like any teacher should.'

'Don't beat around the bush. He's a homosexual.' The lady was insistent. 'This is a small country town, love. People don't take kindly to having a homo teaching their children. You know, in case he recruits them or infects them.'

'*Infects them?* What is this place?' cried Emilia.

'That's how it works around here,' said the lady. 'Don't take this the wrong way, love, but some people don't really care about your sister as much as they do him getting taken out of circulation.'

Emilia was shocked. Yes, this was a small town. But nobody in Helsinki would ever say such things. 'So, what about him not having an alibi?'

'You should see him trying to shop at the supermarket. People deliberately change aisle if he walks towards them. It's like Moses parting the Red Sea. Where was he that night? Nashville can't handle one homosexual. You think whoever his boyfriend is is going to own up to being the second?'

Sharon starting the blow-dryer killed the conversation. Emilia pounced again at the first opportunity.

'Tell me about the Hanigans. What do you know about them?'

'The Hanigans? From down the river?'

Emilia nodded.

'I used to cut her hair, before the accident.' Sharon popped a fresh stick of gum into her mouth and offered the packet to Emilia. Arrowmint. 'Want some chuddy?'

Emilia shook her head.

'Since then, I haven't seen her,' Sharon continued. 'Dunno who'd be cutting it now. He comes in. Not much of a conversationalist, I must say. But then again, most of the farmers don't talk much. They just want to get in and out, as quick as they can. Like most men around here, if you get my drift.'

Emilia looked across to the magazine lady, to see if she had anything to add.

She raised a subtle finger, suggesting that she did. 'Rachel, love,' she called to the apprentice, 'do us a favour and grab me a pen and a piece of paper.' The woman scribbled down her name and address. When Sharon put the blow-dryer away, she leaned across and handed the paper to Emilia. 'Give us an hour, and if you want to talk, drop in and see me after that. It's just down the street.'

Emilia had noticed the store before, during a walk around the town. One of the smallest shops on the strip, it looked and felt different to all the others. 'Scout' said the sign on the window, a nice play on words given the bric-a-brac and high-quality designer items that filled the display shelves, for shoppers to forage through at their leisure. Which weren't many in number, according to the owner, Wanda Graves.

'It's nice of you to say so, dear,' she said, acknowledging Emilia's compliment. 'But despite me pretending otherwise, Nashville is really a rural service centre. If I had any sense, I'd pack all this stuff into boxes, put it out the back, and fill the shelves with gumboots, Swanndri's and dog tucker.'

Emilia smiled. 'I promise I'll come back and buy something.'

Wanda returned her smile. 'We moved here three years ago, from Auckland. My husband manages the power authority. We thought the shop would be a way to bring in some extra money, plus keep me out of trouble.'

The glint in Wanda's eye hinted she wouldn't be averse to some 'trouble', if that meant spicing up her mundane country life.

Wanda invited Emilia to sit on a stool, while she sat at the desk that also served as a counter. There were no customers to inconvenience them, nor did Wanda look like she was expecting any.

'So, do you like living here? Or do you regret moving?' Emilia asked.

'No beating around the bush with you, is there, love?'

'I'm sorry?'

Wanda smiled. 'Your European directness is very refreshing. You wouldn't believe the lengths some people go to avoid me, all because they say they'll come into the shop then feel embarrassed because they haven't.'

Emilia understood.

'My husband enjoys it here,' Wanda continued. 'Although God knows why. Every week the newspaper is full of letters complaining about how his company extorts locals. People who live in remote communities expect the same services as city people get, for the same price. I mean, who are they kidding? Please don't tell me it's like that in your country.'

'A little,' said Emilia, knowing Wanda wasn't really looking for a reply.

'I'll tell you the things I love about here.' She counted them off on her fingers, like it was something she did often. 'Once you get used to it, it's a lyrical, restful pace of life. There's no traffic. And I've never grown such wonderful tomatoes.'

It wasn't as if Wanda needed prompting, but Emilia obliged anyway. 'But . . .?'

'I miss my social circle. Champagne lunches on the waterfront. The Ellerslie races. Waiheke Island. You're not married, are you, love?'

'No,' Emilia replied.

'You're young. Do you have a career?'

'I'm an architect.'

'Good for you. Take this however you wish to, but don't be afraid to make your own life. This town is full of women living their lives through *Coronation Street* and their husbands. And here am I criticising them, while doing exactly the same thing!' Wanda laughed, more in scorn than humour, before continuing. 'That's really what I was talking about at the salon. These are good people, salt of the earth as the saying goes. It's a strong community. But they're of a type. Some would say a little bit backward thinking. But I disagree. Smart, fiercely loyal, parochial. They look after their own. Maybe I haven't always tried as hard as I should have, but it's difficult to break in.'

Emilia knew what she was talking about. Wanda wasn't looking for sympathy.

'The dumbest thing I did,' Wanda continued, 'was that for the first year we lived here I continued to drive back to Auckland to see my old hairdresser. I didn't even realise I was doing it, I thought it was natural to continue with what I knew, but I was sending the message that people in Nashville are inferior. Once I figured that out and started to do more things locally, the ice began to thaw.'

'Do you have children?' Emilia asked.

'A daughter. Priscilla. Who, as it happens, my dear, is the reason you're here.'

Wanda excused herself for a moment and went to the rear, private section of the shop. She returned holding a photograph.

'This is her. Just turned thirty-three, she lives in Hamilton. We're lucky – it's not too far away so I visit her often.'

'And what does she do?'

'She's a nurse. Not only is she a nurse, she specialises in speech disorder and therapy.'

'So, she helps people to talk?'

'Yes. And so now you know why I asked you here!' Wanda explained how Priscilla travelled around providing specialist services in the regional towns.

'And one of her patients is Janet Hanigan?'

'Was, not is. But yes, exactly right, my dear.'

This was interesting. Somebody who Emilia believed could be at the heart of Sanna's disappearance, even if she yet didn't know how or why. 'When do you think I'd be able to talk to her?' Emilia asked.

'No need, love. We have a very close mother–daughter relationship. She told me everything.'

Emilia listened intently. Priscilla conducted a monthly outpatient clinic at the local hospital. Her patients were mostly children with speech impediments or elderly stroke victims. And then there was Janet. Her case had fascinated Priscilla from the start. Selective mutism in adults was not something she'd had a lot of experience with, thus she found herself digging into the circumstances of Janet's car accident, the trauma that triggered her mutism. Or so it was assumed. But the more Priscilla probed, the more questions were raised rather than answered. First was the physiological effect of the accident. Janet had suffered a heavy concussion, but a neuropsychologist had been unable to pinpoint any long-term brain damage, and link this to her loss of speech. Janet had even been sent to a city hospital to undergo a CT scan, a new technology that allowed doctors to view slices of the brain in fine detail. But diagnosis of the images threw up no conclusive reason as to why Janet had lost her capacity for speech.

'So, what you're suggesting is that she could speak, if she wanted to?'

'Well, I'm no doctor.' Wanda nodded. 'But yes, that's how I understand it. It seems that selective mutism is just that; the person *chooses* not to speak.'

'Why would she do that?'

'Well, that's the interesting part. Priscilla then started delving into the psychological factors. And taking the medical information into account, she said it became evident that Janet isn't suffering brain damage. And, when she sat with her, she saw signs of recognition and understanding. Therefore –'

'So, why wouldn't she communicate by writing?'

'Yes! Exactly!' said Wanda, delighted that Emilia was in tune.

'If she wanted to communicate, she would,' said Emilia.

'Yes.'

Emilia's mind was racing. 'Then, what would make somebody go to such extremes? To decide to stop communicating?'

'According to Priscilla, it's more common in children. Sometimes they suffer a traumatic event, say a bereavement, an accident, or – unfortunately – physical and mental abuse, and they do this as a way of shutting themselves off to the outside world. Because sometimes, they haven't yet developed sufficient coping mechanisms. But adults? Most people are usually capable of working through grief and shock without such an extreme reaction.'

'And what did Priscilla have to say about the accident?'

'Well, they definitely went off the road, in a gorge, and ended up in the river. But she doubts it was an accident. Or at least how the husband said it was.'

'Wow.' Emilia nodded slowly, as Wanda continued.

'He's extremely controlling. And in a very strange way. She has no immediate family, she's never been allowed to keep friends or have neighbours visit, she's basically been cut off from everything. Both before and after the accident. Priscilla has no proof, of course.

But imagine if you were in a situation like that. How traumatic that would be . . .'

Emilia noticed how Wanda deliberately tailed off her comment. 'Imagine how much more traumatic it would be if it was a deliberate act? Like your husband was trying to get rid of you?'

'Exactly,' said Wanda, rapping the desk with her forefinger.

Emilia's heart skipped two beats. If he was capable of that, he was capable of anything. And Sanna's letter to her, about meeting the mysterious woman named Janet, and her being afraid of her husband . . . now it all made sense.

'Did Priscilla say anything about what might trigger her to talk again?'

'Unfortunately, the most likely outcome is that she won't. Certainly not while her husband is around and she feels threatened in any way. And don't discount what they call battered wife syndrome. As scared as she might be of him, she would be petrified of facing life on her own. If he is the source of her trauma, there is no chance of her condition changing for as long as he casts a shadow over her.'

'I understand,' said Emilia. 'What about the police – do they know any of this?'

Wanda smiled. 'Let's just say that I'm well connected to the local police, love. Yes, they know. But do they think it carries any weight? No, I'm sorry, they don't. Whereas you and I might use our intuition, they just bang on about lack of evidence.'

'But what if I was to talk to Janet? I could try to earn her trust and confidence, then gradually introduce Sanna . . . all in a way that kept her husband at arm's length. Then there might be a possibility?'

'Who knows?' said Wanda. 'But there's a saying we use. Don't bet your house on it.'

Emilia fixed a determined gaze back on Wanda. 'I'm an architect. A good one. I only design houses that are winning bets.'

59

Ryan

If nature was such a wonderful thing, why were so many of the fish in the sea so downright ugly? Ryan stared at the poster on the wall of the takeaway shop, a colourful rogues gallery of the species that populated New Zealand's waters, stuck fast to the plasterboard with the airborne grease and residue of years of bubbling, hot-fried tallow. Ugly or attractive, it didn't really count for much, he supposed. Once they'd suffered the filleter's knife and been swathed in batter, all fish were equal.

'What did you order?'

Even though Ryan hadn't seen him for nearly a year, Constable Peterson's voice was unmistakeable.

'You're brave, saying hello to me. Wasn't exactly a winning career move for you last time.'

'No,' said Peterson, smiling ruefully. 'Tell the truth, when I saw it was you, I nearly didn't come in. But, you know, man's gotta eat.'

Ryan let him order.

'So,' said Peterson. 'Here we are.'

'Yeah. Kind of where it all started.' Ryan waved his hand around the fish and chip shop.

'And so nearly finished,' Peterson quickly added.

'If it's any consolation, I got a *Distinction* for my assignment.'

'Really?'

'Really. Just shows I had good material to work with.'

Peterson saw the funny side of it.

'Didn't help your boss solve the Atkins case though, did it?'

'No. Nor the second one.'

Ryan winced.

'I'm sorry,' said Peterson. 'It must still be quite raw for you and your colleagues.'

'Don't apologise, that's not your fault.'

They both suffered the awkward silence.

'I often wonder what it must be like for the families,' Peterson went on. 'Not knowing.'

'It's a double whammy for them,' Ryan agreed. 'First, the event itself, as horrible as that was. Then not getting any closure.'

'Which is why I admire the girl's sister, for coming here like she has. That can't be easy.'

'No.'

They both dwelled on that for a few seconds.

'What do you reckon?' asked Ryan. 'Will there be closure?'

'For the first one? The hitchhiker? Yeah, I mean, it'll never be official or anything, but there was some new evidence come to light about the suspect who topped himself in Auckland. A family member came forward about a long-standing sexual assault of a minor. Seems he'd been touching up his niece.'

'Oh. Sounds nasty.'

'Like I said, there'll never be enough proof, but if I was that family, I reckon I'd rest easier knowing it was him. But the Finnish girl, Sanna? Yeah, I dunno about that. It feels like she's here somewhere. Somewhere close by. That's what I think. What about you?'

Ryan was about to answer but was stopped in his tracks by someone else walking in.

'Ryan,' said Philip.

'Philip,' Ryan nodded, respectfully. 'What are you doing here?'

'What do you think I'm doing here?' he laughed. 'Same as you, I expect.'

'Busy at the club?' Ryan remembered what Emilia had said about trying to be nice, but he knew it was a stupid question, as soon as he asked it. He was glad for Philip ignoring it.

Philip ordered, then made a circle of three.

'You two know each other?' said Ryan, offering to make the introductions.

'Kind of,' said Peterson.

'The bank sponsored the police charity fun run,' Philip clarified.

'Of course.'

'Although there's been a few murmurings about us asking for our money back. You know, on account of lack of performance. The community has some genuine concerns.'

'Are you having a lend?' asked Peterson.

'Maybe,' laughed Philip sarcastically. 'Then again, a hitchhiker goes missing . . . nothing. Then a backpacker working in the district disappears. What do the police come up with?'

'Hey, that's a bit unf–'

'Unfair?' Philip cut Peterson off. 'Is it? Ryan here . . . he's accountable. Too much wool in those bales and it costs the farmer money. If he doesn't get it right, he's out of a job. Me . . . if each of those tellers doesn't balance, every single night, then I'm accountable for those losses. If I don't supervise that properly, I lose my job.'

Ryan didn't like where this was heading.

'You lot . . . you ask a few questions here and there, scare the crap out of a few people, then start feeding the TV crews whatever bullshit you want. It's all just distraction. Distraction from failing at your job.'

'Jesus, mate.'

'C'mon, Ryan. I'm just letting your friend here in on a few facts. They should know that the community isn't happy. Not just unhappy, they're fucking well pissed off about it!'

The server leaned across the counter. She was young but her broad shoulders and meaty biceps suggested she wasn't for messing with. 'Hey! Watch your language.'

'Language? You hear that, Ryan? That's what's happening to this fucking town. You can't even tell a member of the constabulary a few home truths without being warned off.' Philip turned and pointed at the counter. 'Here's some language . . . stick those fucking chips up your fucking arse!'

There was no need for the server to ask him to leave – Philip made for the door himself. One step outside, he stopped, swivelled and came back in. 'In fact, stick them up Ryan's arse instead. That'd be more useful.'

This time he was gone for good.

'Sorry about that,' Ryan offered weakly.

'Not at all,' said Peterson. 'It's just the beer talking. You're not his keeper.'

'I really don't know what's got into him.'

'It's okay. He's not the only one around town taking pot shots at us these last few months. And, between you and me, I'm not exactly sure the DI got everything right with the investigation.'

Ryan's ears pricked up, before they both realised they weren't game enough to head down that path again.

'I guess that's the DI's problem, then?' said Ryan.

'Exactly. That's the DI's problem.'

Ryan took his order and bade Peterson goodnight. Finding out what happened to Sanna might have been DI Harten's problem. But, despite what he'd just told Emilia about not getting involved, despite the threat to his career, as soon as his mind shifted back to Sanna he realised that the honest truth was niggling away at him. He couldn't rely on the police. Or Emilia even, as well intentioned and motivated as she was. Whichever way he looked at it, he couldn't help thinking that finding out what happened to Sanna was always going to be his problem.

60

Neville

Neville Hanigan stood at the large plate-glass window in his house, and gazed down at his woolshed. His last ten months or so had been full of absolute frustration, forced as he was to put his plans on hold after the rousey had gone missing. But it was nearly time to move on.

The chaos that ensued was interminable; all because she'd been staying in the shearers' quarters on his farm. Everyone in the gang became what the police called 'persons of interest', and they were interviewed, then reinterviewed, by different detectives from out of town. The police descended on his farm in numbers, to check out where she had slept, desperate for any little clue. They'd taken samples for forensic purposes. What was he supposed to do? Disappear to the Philippines in the midst of all of that? What would that have looked like? All he could do was push things out another year, the maximum extension the travel agent allowed him on his original ticket, and wait for the fuss to blow over.

He surveyed his woolshed. Only a few weeks to go now and the shearers would again cycle around to his shed, and his flock. Then, after his shear was finished, he would finally be free to leave this place, and everything that had happened, behind him.

He wondered if, when that final moment arrived, he would feel sentimental, or even a little sad. Right now, he felt neither. Today was today, tomorrow would be tomorrow. A little more patience was all he needed. He would keep his head down, stay out of trouble, and not bog himself down in yesterdays. Only then would he be home free.

61
Ryan

In the days since Ryan declined to help Emilia, he'd been in no hurry to return to the house. Part embarrassment, part shame at his predicament and his selfishness, it didn't really matter which. But even if he'd chosen to protect his career, she was his guest and he owed her the courtesy of a visit.

'I should ask you, check with you, that everything is okay? Here and at home?'

She seemed happy enough to see him. 'My job is okay, I have annual leave provision. If you're asking about my personal life, I don't have a regular boyfriend. Too busy getting my career established. Besides, Finnish guys aren't my thing.' She held her hands up, a couple of feet apart. 'Here, on this side, a Finnish guy at work. Sober and serious. And, usually, very boring. Here, on this side, a Finnish guy at a club. Drunk until he falls over. Everyone is this or that. There are so few guys in between.'

'That sounds dispiriting.'

She shrugged her shoulders. 'It's okay, those things will take care of themselves.'

They sat in silence for a few moments.

'I haven't thanked you properly for letting me stay at your house,' she said.

'Yes, you have.'

More silence.

'So, will you come with me to meet Janet Hanigan?'

'I knew you were going to ask me that!' Ryan slapped his thigh in exasperation.

'Will you?'

After he and Emilia first met, and she mentioned that Sanna had written to her about her concern for Janet, Ryan had found himself wondering more about the farmer and his wife. 'Okay, so let's say he's a beast to his wife and therefore he's a threat to all women. And she knows this. Is that rational? On the other hand, what if she really knows nothing and it's just her condition that makes it look like she's harbouring a secret?'

'Everyone has secrets, Ryan. I just want to know what she saw.'

'I know you do. But –'

'We must make him accountable.' Emilia was insistent.

'If we have evidence, yes. But we have nothing.'

'*Nothing yet*. But what if she knows?'

Ryan did a lap of the table, then sat back down. 'Even if she does know something, how's she going to tell us? You know she doesn't speak, don't you?'

'Yes, but Ryan –'

'Jesus, Emilia!'

She kept at him. 'If we go up to the house, we can take somebody with us. From your gang. Then he'll know we're serious.'

Ryan threw his arms up in frustration. Had she lost her senses? 'This shearing run is Carl's livelihood. Everyone's. Nothing gives us the right to mess with that.'

'Sanna gives me the right to mess with anything, if it means finding out the truth! I don't understand why you won't help me. What is wrong with you?'

They were going around in circles. Ryan grasped for a circuit breaker. 'Let's be sensible about this. If there's a confrontation in that house, things aren't going to end well. Not for you, and not for Janet. And we won't be any further along, we'll actually be worse off.'

'We? That's the second time you've said "we".'

'Slip of the tongue. *You* won't be any further along.' He saw that she was listening. 'Let's be strategic here. Wouldn't it be better to separate them? Get her somewhere where she's relaxed and comfortable?'

'Yes.'

'So, let's think about how we go about that. The smart way.'

'You said "we" again.'

Ryan sighed.

Emilia laughed out loud. 'I am to you like that old saying, "a dog hunting a bone". Am I right?'

'Yes, you're right!' he said, seeing the funny side of it.

The next morning flew by. They were at a property called Braeside Farms, one of his favourites. He enjoyed working their press; it was just like in rugby where teams developed an affinity for certain grounds, where they felt comfortable and, as a result, always played well there. Conversely, there were other venues where the dressing sheds felt inhospitable or the playing surface a drag on their legs, and that was reflected in their performance. There was talk around about how some farms were bringing in electric presses – new technology that was supposedly all the rage. Ryan had yet to strike one, but he figured it was inevitable; anything that sped the process up was welcome. At the same time, it didn't quite sit right. It was the physical aspect of the job, the actual pressing, that provided the most satisfaction. Ryan wasn't a golfer, but if he was, he would walk the course, in the way the game was intended to be played. It didn't make any sense to play for exercise, yet drive around in one of those fancy motorised carts.

Lunch done, Ryan ventured outside to take in the fresh air. He found a solid railing to rest his elbows on, on the edge of the yard.

'Mind if I join you?' Crystal didn't usually have a lot to say, but he enjoyed it when she did.

'How are things with Emilia?' she asked.

'She's very determined, I'll give her that.'

Crystal smiled. 'She's nice. Like her sister.'

'She wants to come back down here to meet Janet Hanigan. Thinks she can get her to talk.'

'Wow, that would be something,' said Crystal.

'It would. I'm not sure how realistic it is, though. Probably not at all.'

Crystal pointed to a ewe in the pen in front of them, its back and hind quarters covered in black tar. 'She doesn't look too flash. Poor thing.'

'She's one of the lucky ones,' said Ryan, nodding at the ewe. 'At least they got her in time.' Flystrike was a persistent issue, blowflies nestling in the fleeces, their eggs turning to maggots that ate into the skin and flesh, just like in a horror movie. This sheep had suffered, but as ugly and painful as the treatment looked, she would survive.

'Ryan, do you mind if I tell you something?'

Her tone was new to him. More serious. More personal. 'Of course.'

'I've never said this before, to anyone.' She paused, as if to make sure of herself. 'But . . . you know I roomed with Sanna. I saw things. I couldn't help but notice.'

'Yes . . . ?'

'I know you had a relationship with her.'

'Well, yes, we all did.'

'That's not what I mean. A relationship. I know you were physical together.'

Physical. 'So . . . ?' Ryan didn't like where this was heading.

'You know how the police asked us all sorts of things, including if she had a boyfriend or any fella she might have hooked up with. I never mentioned you and her to them. Or to anybody. Not even you. I didn't think there was any point – it made no difference to anything.'

'That's exactly what I thought too.'

'The other night, when she was here, Emilia started asking me a lot of questions. About Sanna.'

'That's only natural. She knows you shared a room.'

'About you. You and Sanna.'

Ryan felt an uncomfortable lump in his throat.

'I didn't tell her anything,' said Crystal.

'But . . .?'

'She's nice. And she just wants to know about her sister's life here. I don't want to lie to her.'

'Well, you're not exactly lying, are you?'

'Ryan, please.'

He'd upset her, trying to be too cute.

'If she asks again, I don't think I can keep it from her,' Crystal continued.

Ryan quickly processed the consequences. When the investigation started, he'd explained how she wanted some fresh air and how he went outside with her to the cars. Others in the gang corroborated his account, and because he was only outside for a couple of minutes, then was caught inside the bar when the fight started, there was never a concern about the veracity of his story. He simply never volunteered the relationship to the police, because it was nobody's business. And because he knew how investigations like this always started with family members or lovers. He didn't need all that scrutiny. But the longer it went on, the deeper the hole he needed to dig. If that information came out now, it would send DI Harten ballistic. He could forget about ever being a lawyer.

'There's one more thing too.'

Ryan felt Crystal hesitate. 'What?'

'I know Sanna was up the duff. *With your baby.*'

Ryan felt his lunch back up to the top of his throat.

'What if she wants me to tell the police?' Crystal asked. 'What do I do then?'

'How did you find out? Sanna didn't tell anyone.'

'Ryan. Even when women think they have secrets, they never really do.'

Ryan again saw his law career flash before him. He looked down at the ailing sheep, and imagined himself being slowly immersed in black tar.

'Ryan? What should I do?'

Ryan didn't hear her, so engrossed was he in his own strife. What should Crystal do? *What the fuck am I going to do?*

62

Ryan

Even in the height of summer, snow and ice clung stubbornly to the upper reaches of Mount Ruapehu. Tucked in and around rock formations, in pockets shielded from direct sun, lines of white snaked downwards like veins, before melting to form the alpine streams that stretched out across the lower reaches of the volcanic plateau. Although it was only a short drive from the farms and woolsheds he was familiar with, he might as well have been on another planet. At the elevation where the fertile soil turned to volcanic ash, rock and scoria, the only plants that could survive were alpine tussocks and hardy, wiry little shrubs. This was no place for sheep.

With the terrain so rocky and uneven, there were small waterfalls everywhere, and a larger one, Taranaki Falls – a powerful cascade that, according to the weather-beaten timber sign, fell twenty metres from a cliff's edge to a pool below. He'd escaped here before, when things hadn't fallen his way. Philip would say that the cards always fell Ryan's way, but what would he know?

It was cold; perfect for brooding. Cascading water dissipated into spray and mist, catching Ryan on his face when he stepped out onto a viewing area. He licked at his lips like the water was salve for the situation he found himself in. A year ago DI Harten had torn strips off his hide. As humiliating and embarrassing as that was, things were now about to get worse. He hadn't meant to cause trouble accessing files in the Atkins case, but not telling the truth about his relationship with Sanna was another level altogether. This was like impeding a murder investigation.

The chime of a tui snapped Ryan out of his funk. He drank eagerly from the stream, the water pure and sharply cool, then set off again, up the steep pinch through multiple switchbacks to the top of the falls, then across the plateau, back towards the carpark, eventually wandering past the entrance to the Grand Chateau. Vaguely European, it was a place for wealthy, stuffy folk, who felt better for sipping their tea under a chandelier. He kept walking, across the road, straight into the tavern and, at the bar, found a stool with his name on it.

'Are you sure?' The barmaid's voice was a mix of bemusement and concern.

'Of course I'm sure,' said Ryan. 'Another jug.'

'You've had six already.'

'And . . .? Who's counting, anyway? I'm not causing any trouble, am I?' Ryan had been perched on the stool, alone, for over four hours. She was the only person he'd spoken to, the whole time.

'No. But it's my job to stop you before you do.'

Through hazy eyes, Ryan sized her up. Like Sanna, she was a backpacker, but that's where the similarity ended. Her name was Julia. Not Julie, as she'd made clear. She was Canadian, not American – she'd corrected him twice on that one too – twenty-eight years old, with thick-set shoulders and a cavernous cleavage into which, with an increasing degree of certainty, Ryan was sure he would be able to park the wheel of his bike.

He belched, holding most of it in, out of politeness and not wanting to give her a reason to stop serving him. 'You know what the problem is, don't you?'

'What?' Her response was encouragingly playful.

'You're used to Canadian guys. Obviously, they can't hold their piss. Not like us Kiwis, eh?'

'Really?'

'Well, am I right?'

Julia stopped what she was doing and leaned forward. 'You know how many countries I've travelled to? Have a guess.'

'No idea.'

'Thirty-seven. I've worked in a fair few of them too.'

'And?'

'You know how many guys I've seen drinking, or drunk, all around the world?'

'If you'd actually counted them, then I'd be impressed,' mumbled Ryan.

'The one thing in common,' she continued, 'the quiet guys, the good guys, the wankers, the thugs . . . you're all the same. You all think you're a better drinker than the next man. Trust me, you're not.'

Ryan nodded. 'Well, let's just say, even if you're right, and you probably are, at least I'm the best drinker in here. Today.'

'Well, that's true, I'll give you that,' she chuckled as she scanned the bar. One table held a family with three young children near the window, there was an older couple in full tramping kit, poring over a map, and another table containing two guys and a girl, closer to Ryan's age. Who were drinking lemonade.

'Tell you what,' said Ryan, 'just because you're worried about me on the beer, give us a rum. Coruba. Double. Little bit of Coke. One ice.'

'One ice?'

'One ice. Just to take the fizz off.'

Julia laughed. 'Double Coruba and Coke with one ice, it is. But don't let me down, okay?'

Ryan winked. Not a come-on, but to reassure her. 'I won't let you down, Julie.'

'Who the fuck hit me?' The side of Ryan's head hurt like hell, and a touch of his cheek revealed he was bleeding.

'Here, get this onto you.' Julia pressed a wad of paper towels against his cheek to stem the bleeding. She helped Ryan straighten up, back against the bar. The stool on which he'd been sitting was strewn alongside.

'I'm sorry, but he got away,' she laughed.

Ryan's head was spinning as much as it was hurting, but he was beginning to piece it together. There was nobody in the tavern that would have hit him. 'Did I fall off?'

'Yep.'

'On my own?'

'Yes, on your own.' She passed him a tea towel folded around cubes of ice, and leaned in for a closer look. 'You might need a couple of stitches in there.'

'I don't need stitches, I need a lie-down.' Through the haze Ryan could see that others had gathered around, but he waved them away. 'Sorry for interrupting your evening, folks, but we're all good. Show over.'

'You're a stubborn one, aren't you?' said Julia.

Ryan realised he'd said evening. It was dark outside. He was due in Carl's van at 4.15am. Shit!

'You hit your head pretty hard,' she said. 'I think you're concussed.'

'Concussed, pissed, what's the difference?'

She wriggled her hand into the front pocket of his jeans.

'Oh, hello,' he said, grinning. 'Shouldn't we wait until you've finished your shift?'

'Just making sure you don't do anything stupid, that's all.' She brandished his car keys.

'Probably a bit late for that,' he said, slowly closing his eyes.

The rap on the car door was thoughtfully gentle; just enough to wake him. Ryan saw Julia peer inside, before she slipped into the back seat, underneath his feet. As quickly as she closed the door, she reopened it.

'Hey, it's cold!' Ryan complained.

'It stinks in here,' she said.

He screwed his face at her.

'How's your head?'

'How do you think?'

'At least those sticking plasters have held.' She leaned across, probing his face, gently. 'That's a win.'

'What's the time?' he inquired, slowly adjusting to the morning light.

'Seven-thirty.'

'Fuck! I'm dead.'

She jiggled his keys, tantalisingly, in front of his face. 'You might be late for work, but one day you'll reflect on the Canadian barmaid who saved your life.'

Ryan vaguely recalled her helping him into the car, returning from her cabin with a blanket, then sitting with him, talking – he couldn't remember what about – until he must have drifted off to sleep. Maybe lifesaver was overegging it. But she was kind.

'Listen,' she said. 'I have to meet someone for breakfast. You don't look too bad. What say I swap your keys for my blanket?'

Ryan sat up straight, getting his bearings. 'Sounds like a deal,' he said, exiting the car.

She handed over his keys. He handed over the blanket.

'Thanks for everything,' he said.

'You've got issues, Ryan. Lying to the police, the stuff about your girlfriend and the baby . . . I'm really sorry for what's happened to you. But your friend, Philip, you should fix your relationship with him.

And this girl from Finland, who wants your help – *needs* your help – I think you should get yourself sorted out.'

When he had seen she was gone, Ryan gingerly ducked behind a large flax bush and relieved himself. *You've got issues, Ryan.* Jesus, what had he done? Spilled his guts to a total stranger? His head was throbbing enough as it was. There wasn't much he could do about Tom Harten now, he'd fucked that up already. He was hours late for work, he'd fucked that up too.

By the time he reached the edge of the National Park he realised that she was right. It was time to stop all of the bullshit with Philip. He would be the bigger man. He would take responsibility for getting things back to how they used to be. And, as soon as he could, he would contact Emilia and let her know. No more excuses. No more talking about it. It was time for him to keep his promise and find Sanna.

63

Emilia

Emilia didn't know for certain if Neville Hanigan was at home or not but, according to Ryan, he would be unlikely to be sitting around inside. There was always a mountain of things to do on a farm, jobs that didn't take care of themselves. She would do well to avoid lunchtime, he recommended. Hardworking farmers needed to refuel. But outside of that, there would be a good chance she'd find Janet alone in the house.

Emilia was still on a high from Ryan calling her to say that he'd changed his mind and he was now determined to get to the bottom of what happened to Sanna. She didn't know what had triggered his change of attitude, but the reason wasn't important. He'd come to his senses and his offer to drive her back down to the farm again was another bonus.

She stepped carefully along the uneven track, past the woolshed, up to the farmhouse. Eyes peeled, she saw no sign of Neville. She'd been told to look for Janet in the window, and there she was, seated at first, until they made eye contact. Janet stood up, her long hair falling arrow straight, down below her waist. Emilia waved and Janet waved back in an awkward, robotic motion. Emilia smiled, and drew a smile in response. It was a signal to go inside.

They sat at the kitchen table, like old friends catching up after years apart. There was so much to talk about, but with only one of them able to speak, Emilia didn't quite know where to start.

'I'm here to find out what happened to my sister, Sanna.' She watched Janet intently for a reaction; something to tell her what to home in on. She continued. 'The police say that my sister went missing in town, the same night the shearing gang packed up and left your farm. They say that she went in a car with somebody she didn't know, someone from outside this district, but I think something else happened before then. Maybe here at this farm. And that maybe you saw something that might help me find out what that was.' Emilia took a photo from her pocket, and pushed it across the table. 'This is Sanna. This is my sister.'

Janet studied the picture. That was another thing, Emilia realised. What kind of family home didn't have a single photograph on display? Janet was cradling this one like she'd never seen a photograph in her life.

'Do you recognise her? She came here to the house, didn't she? Did she seem worried about anything to you?'

Emilia stopped herself. She was being ridiculous – there were too many questions. She needed to keep her wits about her.

'Can I ask about your husband? Did you ever see Sanna with him?'

This time there was a reaction; it was undeniable. Janet's complexion changed, her cheekbones lowered slightly. The hint of a scowl perhaps? A scowl tinged with sadness. And fear. Emilia felt sad for her, but at the same time, she was excited. She was getting somewhere.

'Janet, I'm going to ask you another question about your husband. Did you –'

The sound of the back door crashing open stopped her in her tracks. Seconds later, Neville Hanigan was towering over the end of the table.

'Who the hell are you?' he growled.

Emilia's pulse raced. 'My name is Emilia. I'm staying with the shearing gang for a couple of days.'

'Nobody cleared that with me. Those quarters are for workers. It's not a holiday hostel.'

Emilia remembered something her father had once told her about dealing with confrontation: 'less is more'. She sat, passively.

'What are you doing inside my house? You can't just walk in here any time you feel like it!'

Emilia didn't like how he was edging closer.

'And don't say *she* invited you!'

There was a short-tempered, nasty side to Neville Hanigan. It was all beginning to make sense.

'Have you been messing with her head?' His cheeks were glowing red.

'No,' said Emilia, calmly.

'Nobody talks to my wife. Got it?'

Emilia stood up and edged towards the door.

'Where are you from? The accent?'

'Finland.'

His complexion changed as she watched him make the connection.

'Yes, I'm Sanna's sister.'

'Listen,' he said, 'I don't know why you're here, why you'd even subject yourself to reliving all of that, but just leave us alone. Leave my wife alone, and leave me alone. We don't want anything to do with you. Do you understand?'

'Yes,' she answered, meaning the opposite.

'You're going to walk out of my house right now, you're going to go back down to the quarters, where I'm going to let you stay until the shearers return. Then tomorrow you're going to go back into town, or to whatever rock you've been hiding under, and neither myself or my wife are ever going to see you again. Do I make myself clear?'

Emilia looked at Janet, who was staring down at the tablecloth, as she had been ever since her husband's return. She hoped that there would be no repercussions for her. Or was that, no more repercussions? The mental scars were already plain to see. 'Yes,' she said.

For the rest of the afternoon, Emilia sat on the porch outside Ryan's room, hoping the carving knife she'd borrowed from the kitchen wouldn't be needed. There was something about Neville that suggested keeping it handy was prudent.

She couldn't wait to talk to Ryan; they had to figure out how to prise Janet from Neville's control, then they would be able to get to the bottom of things. The cold, threatening way he had spoken to her, the disdain he held for his wife, the evil he exuded . . . how could the police have so easily excused him?

It was 3.30pm when Ronnie's car growled up the metal incline, turned off the road and pulled into the parking area behind the kitchen. Emilia had never been so happy to see a giant orange car, and hear Bob Marley pumping out of the speakers.

'Hello, love,' said Ronnie, as Emilia met her in the kitchen. 'Are you okay? You look a bit pale. Like you've seen a ghost.'

'Not a ghost,' Emilia replied. 'The devil.'

64

Ryan

According to Carl, who had been around the traps long enough to know these things, the summer heat had been biting harder and later with each passing season. It was March, he said, that had become 'the banker', the most reliably sunniest and warmest month. In Carl's world, that meant a long, sustained run into the 'second shear', before he and the other shearers could eventually put their feet up.

None of that explained how hot, dry and unrelenting this January had been. Sanna had once told Ryan how much she loved the narrow, twisting valleys, each with their homesteads and family secrets tucked away within, but it was the hills that rose sharply on all sides that kept cooling breezes at bay. Some woolsheds were no more than ovens built from timber and corrugated iron. And, after another long stint without a break, Ryan was just about cooked.

Carl had been remarkably lenient after his no-show. Any other boss would have sacked him on the spot, turning up at the shed like that at morning teatime, worse for wear. For the first few days he wished he had been fired. What was the point of wallowing in all his self-pity if he was too tired to actually enjoy it?

Whatever happened, this would be the end of the road. Once his degree was finished, an intern job would be in order. That's if he still had a law career to pursue. He'd taken Crystal aside. She hadn't yet spoken to anyone; nevertheless, paranoia was nagging away at him. His problem was acute. Do nothing and, one way or another, DI Harten was going to find out about the baby. Keep working with Emilia to find Sanna's killer and he'd be done again for interfering. If those were his choices, why wouldn't he at least go down fighting?

Emilia had recounted her confrontation with Neville Hanigan, before she'd returned to town. She was right to be suspicious of him. The confrontation sounded frightening, and it certainly made him look like he was capable of being the perpetrator. But still, there was nothing concrete to link him to how Sanna disappeared.

'Hey, Ryan. Can I ask you something?' It was Lacey, snapping the moment. 'If you're looking to sell some of the stuff in your mum's house, do you mind if I come and have a look first? Me and Owen are moving into our own place – we need to start getting a few things.'

'Jesus, Lacey, don't be so forward.' Carl rolled his eyes. 'Sometimes I'm downright ashamed to call you my sister.'

'It's okay,' said Ryan. He didn't expect any more or less from her.

Crystal and Ronnie sniggered at each other.

'What?' snapped Lacey. 'You wait until you get married and get your own house. You won't be laughing then.'

'I've got some calls to make,' said Carl. 'Sorry about her. No fucking idea,' he said, softly slapping Ryan on the shoulder.

He didn't need to apologise. She was a ratbag and he was a great guy – that was the beginning and end of it.

'Go on then, go pack a sad,' spat Lacey, at Carl. She appealed again to Ryan. 'It's not like I'm asking to come in and clean the place out. If you want, I'll pay something.'

Ronnie reached out to Lacey. 'Listen, love, I don't think money's the issue. Maybe just let Ryan deal with things in his own way, that's all.'

A deep monotone rumbled from the end of the table. 'Then he said to them, watch out, be on your guard against all kinds of greed; life does not consist in an abundance of possessions. Luke 12:15.'

It made Ryan feel uneasy, Bull taking his side.

'Bull, you can sit there and spout that clap-trap night after night, for as long as you like,' said Lacey. 'But you're not fooling anyone.'

Then again, it made Ryan feel just as uneasy, agreeing with Lacey.

The thunder came from nowhere, jolting Ryan out of his sleep, sitting him bolt upright in bed. His tired muscles soon dragged him down again, but the weather gods were insistent; flashing, white lightning, followed by the loudest cracks of thunder Ryan had ever heard.

And then it came. A few sprinkles at first, a gentle prelude, then the main event, water hammering so hard into the iron roof, it felt that any minute the whole structure would collapse down upon him.

Ryan tossed and turned, but sleep was impossible. He checked his watch – it was 2.30am. He didn't think it possible, but the rain became even more insistent, belting down with absolute, terrifying ferocity. By now, the noise was intolerable; the sound of a thousand machine-guns spraying their magazines into the tin roof. Ryan got up. Remarkably, the structure was holding and there were no leaks through the ceiling, but he couldn't be sure for how long.

Timidly, he opened his door. There were lights on all around the quarters, and shouting from the common area.

'Quick, get that stuff up on the bench!' It was Carl, taking control, above Ronnie's shrieking.

He could make out Lacey too. Squealing. 'Help me! There's water flowing right through my room!'

Ryan glanced next door. He saw Pete on his doorstep; like him, sizing up the situation. The rain was monsoonal, unheard of for these parts, and there was trouble over in the kitchen area and female quarters. Ryan watched as Pete made a dash for it, up the dirt path and steps that were cut into the sloping earth. But he was running against the elements, water rushing down towards him, shin deep, with such power it took Pete's legs from out beneath him. He fell to the ground and was swept metres, down to where the path levelled out.

'Jesus fucking Christ,' muttered Ryan, under his breath. Instinctively, he made his way across to where Pete had now picked himself up. He was sore but unable to properly check himself for injury because of the intensity of the rain.

'I'm okay,' he said. 'We need to help the others.'

Ryan looked back up towards the kitchen. The path was impassable – they would have to try another route. He motioned for Pete to follow him, and they made their way across the flow of the water, back to their building, then around behind Ryan's room, the route he'd used on his covert visits to the woolshed. They stuck close together, slipping in the dark and in their bare feet, taking turns helping each other up. It took an almighty effort, but within minutes, they had made it to the others, albeit drenched to their bones.

Chaos reigned. There was screaming and shouting, and a torrent of water streaming through the women's rooms.

In the confusion, Ryan caught hold of Crystal's arm. 'Are you okay?' he asked.

'Yes. We have all our stuff up on top.'

'Up top' was Sanna's old bunk. Carl's urgent voice snapped him out of wherever his mind was headed. 'Ryan, give us a hand here, will you?'

They were trying to get boxes off the floor, but had run out of bench space, and now Carl had found his way to the fuse box. 'Listen, everybody, I'm going to have to shut off the power, otherwise these appliances might kill us.'

Together, they huddled in tightly, in a corner of the small kitchen, water slapping at the ankles. Just as another flash of lightning lit up the compound, Carl flipped the mains switch and it all went dark.

Very dark.

'Everyone okay?' asked Carl.

'We're all good, aren't we, girls?' said Pete, trying to reassure them.

Minutes passed in silence.

'Where's Bull?' said Crystal.

'Good question,' said Carl.

'Having a word to his master about stopping the rain,' Lacey quipped.

Barely had she uttered those words when the rain suddenly eased off. In an instant, the veil of fear had been lifted. Rain was still falling, but it was normal rain. The threat of the ceiling caving in now gone, Ryan felt spirits rise. He opened the door, and he and Carl peered outside. Already, in less than a minute, the flow of water had begun to subside.

Carl tapped Ryan on the elbow and pointed down towards the men's bedrooms. Bull was sitting on his porch, torchlight pointing upwards, illuminating his face from below his jaw. It projected an eerie silhouette onto the wall behind him. They watched on, dumbstruck, as he began chanting.

'Behold, I, even I am bringing the flood of water upon the earth, to destroy all flesh in which is the breath of life, from under heaven; everything that is on the earth shall perish.'

'One day,' said Carl, 'we're going to wake to news of a mass suicide, a cult leader gone haywire, in the midst of an armed showdown with authorities. And we're going to know exactly who's at the centre of it.'

As Carl spoke, Ryan noticed something else in the glow of Bull's torchlight. In Bull's eyeline, standing in front of his porch was a figure. Barefoot. Still. Her white nightgown was streaked in mud, her long blonde hair flattened by the rain, her arms extended to the sides, in the shape of a cross. Janet Hanigan. What on earth was she doing there?

Ryan carefully made his way down to Bull's porch. Desperate to look into her eyes, he couldn't find the right angle. She was like an optical puzzle; wherever he moved to, despite her head and body not moving, her eyes never seemed to line up with his. He wanted to reach out and touch her skin, just to prove to himself that she was real and not some kind of illusion.

'She is sent here. By God.' Bull's voice was unusually soft, almost conversational.

Ryan still couldn't figure what to make of it all.

'It is a sign.'

'A sign?' asked Ryan.

'She has submitted herself, here before me, in the face of the deluge, to God. She will be saved. And if you submit, she will save you.'

'What do you mean?'

'You're a slow learner, lawyer-boy. The missing girl. I've seen you with her sister. You want to save her soul?'

Ryan wasn't sure what he meant. 'I just want to know what happened to her.'

'It is not enough simply to wish for something. Don't you see?' He nodded again towards Janet. 'Like this woman, submit before me, to God.'

If that's what Janet Hanigan was doing, that was her business. Ryan wasn't taking that path. 'Or, what?'

'You know the answer. All you can do is stand up for what you truly believe.'

Ryan looked Janet up and down again. She hadn't twitched a muscle in the time she'd been there. The juxtaposition was incredibly powerful. Soaked to the skin, virtually naked, she appeared as fragile as an ancient Ming vase. Yet that same vulnerability belied an immense strength. It was now vividly clear. This wasn't about Janet turning to God. She was asserting herself. Reclaiming her identity. Neville had suppressed her for who knows how long. She might not be able to speak, but now this was her time to shine. Her rebirth. The position he was in with Sanna's case, this wasn't about Emilia, or the police. It wasn't about Neville Hanigan, or anyone else in town. If he wanted Sanna to be set free – and he did, more than anything – he needed to draw, not on Janet's supposed newfound faith, but her strength.

65
Emilia

The steps leading into the police station were now familiar to Emilia. So was the welcome.

'Hello, Ms Sovernen. I could lie and say I'm delighted to see you again.'

Emilia ignored his sledge.

'Sleep through the storm okay last night? Was pretty heavy – there's a few roads cut around the district.'

'Can I please have a word, Detective Inspector Harten?' She was straight down to business. 'There is new information which I'd like to discuss.'

'You know the way,' said Tom, unlocking the door adjacent to the counter, waving her into a vacant interview room.

'You've got ten minutes,' he said on return, dropping a mug of tea onto the interview desk.

'I stayed with the shearing gang, at the farm of Neville Hanigan. I believe his wife, Janet . . . I am certain that she has information about Sanna.'

'Really?' said Tom, more sarcastically than was polite. 'And what would you like me to do about that?'

'Question her, of course. Bring her in.'

'You're an intelligent lady, Ms Sovernen. I'm sure you've noticed already that Mrs Hanigan doesn't speak. She's mute.'

'Yes, well, of course. But that doesn't mean you can't communicate with her. If it's handled sensitively.'

Tom didn't care for the insult. 'Listen, I'm actually going to cut this off right now. You think I'm going to drive out to the farm, bring Neville Hanigan in, and then, without any evidence at all linking him to the disappearance of your sister, arrest him for that crime?'

'That's not what I said,' she qualified.

'Oh. So you want me to bring him in because he's a bad husband? Funnily enough, even though that's not a crime, at least not here in New Zealand, I've actually got more chance of making that one stick.'

'No need to be sarcastic,' sighed Emilia. 'I'm trying to help. Did you know he spies on the females in the shearing gang? In their shower?'

'Listen, Ms Sovernen. You're a nice young lady. You're smart. Smart enough to know that, if that's all you have, a gut feel that a woman who can't talk has some secret she'd like to tell the world but can't blurt it out, and a red-blooded husband who might sneak the odd perve here and there, then – and don't take this the wrong way – you probably should start thinking about buying a ticket back home.'

Emilia stood up. She was less angry at his smug, condescending demeanour than she was at herself for thinking that she might make headway with him. 'Thank you for the advice, Detective Inspector.'

The short walk to the bank wasn't enough time for Emilia to properly clear her head. There had to be a way to break the impasse, to get to the bottom of what secret she was sure Janet was harbouring. Ryan was right about her needing to be smarter. People in country towns didn't like being bulldozed. Being told what to do by outsiders.

She requested the withdrawal of fifty dollars. It wasn't that she was spending a lot of money; what was there to spend it on in Nashville? All the same, she felt better for having something in her purse.

The man she'd seen sitting at his desk stepped out to open the door for her.

'Thank you,' she said.

'You're welcome, Ms Sovernen.'

'Oh, you know my name?'

'It's a small town,' he smiled.

'Well, thank you again, Philip.'

'Oh. And you know mine too!'

She nodded towards his name badge.

'Oh, of course.'

As he smiled again, she came to a realisation. This was *Philip*. Ryan's old school friend.

'How are things going for you on your visit? Are you happy with our service? Is there anything else we can help you with?'

She thought for a second. 'You know, I really need to relax for a little while. And meet some local people. How you Kiwis say, "wind down". Where is the best place for that?'

'Well, there's the pub, a couple of blocks down. But I wouldn't feel comfortable sending you there. Tell you what, I have to rush over to my father's office for half an hour or so, then I'll be back to close up. I can sign you in to our Workingmen's Club. I was heading down there, anyway.'

'That's very generous of you, thank you.'

'You can have a wander around town if you like, or you can wait here.'

She'd wandered enough. It was a good opportunity to start on a letter to home. 'If you don't mind giving me a pen and a sheet of paper, I'll sit down, thanks.'

66
Tom

DI Tom Harten strode from his car, a man on a mission.

'And to what do I owe this honour?' said Jack Nash, inviting him into his office.

'You might want to close the door,' said Tom.

Jack sat at his desk expectantly, like a primary-school kid anticipating a gold star.

'Is Philip coming?' asked Tom.

He'd barely finished the question when Philip tapped on the door and entered. He seemed surprised to find his father had company.

'Oh. What's this about?' said Philip.

Tom straightened his back. 'I'll get straight to the point. Some information has come to light. We probably should be doing this at the station, but I'd prefer we go about this without making a fuss. I want you to cast your mind back to –'

'We already told you everything,' said Philip, jumping in. 'After the club closed, a group of us left at the same time, Dad walked home on his own and I drove straight to my place.'

'I'm not here about that. I'm talking further back, two years ago.' Tom was going to have to spell it all out. 'Jack, early that year, in 1980, you were involved in the sale of a house. The property owned by Rita Sigsworth, up near the golf course.'

'Yes.'

'Mrs Sigsworth passed away, not long afterwards.'

'Yes, I recall.' Jack nodded. 'Very sad. Although she'd had a pretty good innings. In her nineties, I believe.'

'Are you able to tell me, was her house ever advertised for sale?'

'I'd have to check the records, but yes, I'm sure it would have been.'

'You certain about that?'

'Well, yes. All our houses are advertised in the local paper, and in our window, here behind you.'

'All except this one.'

'Let me check the records,' Jack said, standing up.

'Don't bother.' Tom directed him to sit back down. 'I won't beat around the bush. We've been contacted by one of her grandchildren. Concerned that the house was sold for just thirty-five thousand dollars, when it should have been worth more than double that.'

'Well . . . Tom, mate . . . you should have just said. Is *that* what the issue is?' Jack faked a wide smile and opened his arms to match. He'd just failed Body Language 101. 'That may well be their opinion. But this is real estate, Tom. It's an imprecise business. Properties are worth what a buyer is prepared to pay for them, on a given day.'

'You're not sounding too convincing, Jack.'

'That summer was a strange one. Prices were very fickle. And, after Mary Atkins went missing, the arse dropped right out of the market. There was no demand at all. You didn't exactly make life easy for me, you know, Tom. Not catching whoever did it.'

Tom rolled his eyes. Of course, it was all his doing.

'Never seen such a tough market. Couldn't find buyers for love nor money.'

'You found one for Rita's place, though, didn't you?'

'Listen, I think I know what you're getting at, but let me tell you, Rita was happy with the price. She just wanted to sell, in a hurry.'

'In such a hurry that you never advertised the property, never showed it to any prospective buyer; in fact, never breathed a word of it to anyone. Except Philip here.'

'Hang on a minute, I paid good money for that house!' said Philip.

'Strictly,' said Jack, 'it's not just Philip's name on the title. He's a joint owner.'

It was Jack's last defence. A weak one. 'You mean, along with Becky Armstrong, the vicar's daughter?'

'Yes.'

Tom screwed his face up. 'Nashville's a good town, Jack. But that's not such a good look, is it? For the church or the bank. Or the real-estate industry.'

'Tell you what, Tom, it'll be a sad day when a man can't do something to give his son a leg-up,' he said, indignantly. 'No harm in that, is there? He puts in plenty for this town. We both do.'

'Fuck, Dad.' Philip had turned a sickly shade of white.

Tom let Jack run.

'I understand where you're heading with this. And maybe, to an outsider, it doesn't look so good.' Jack leaned forward, over the top of his desk. 'But I've been in real estate a long time. I know cases like this are notoriously hard to prove.'

Tom leaned forward too, until their foreheads were almost touching. 'I've been in policing a long time. I know cases like this are worth having a crack at.'

They both sat back. Advantage Tom.

'I have a constable sitting outside in the car. You're not being charged with anything at this stage, however I do have to caution you that we have a warrant which entitles us to search your records for details on this transaction, and any other transaction which we deem to be suspicious. Do you understand?'

'Oh, fucking hell,' exclaimed Philip. 'Jesus, Dad. What is it with you? It's just one big fucked-up surprise after another.'

'Settle down, Philip,' said Tom.

'It's the Nash way. We're nothing better than a family of bastards and criminals!'

Tom stood. 'Looks like you two have got a bit to sort out.'

Jack shook his head, defeatedly. 'So, what are you saying? That this might be a good time to call a lawyer?'

'That's up to you, Jack. Although I don't expect that will be easy, knowing how highly you speak of the Jewish fraternity.'

'C'mon, Tom, that's just club talk. You know what it's like.'

'Yes, mate. I know what it's like.'

Tom shuffled paperwork at his desk, his heart not really in the rest of his shift. It was always difficult pinching locals, especially blokes from his drinking circle at the club. And with Jack Nash being such a prominent person in town, a Nash in Nashville . . . well, you didn't get more iconic than that. But the job was the job. There were some matters he could have a quiet chat about, to get things back on the straight and narrow without creating a drama, and there were other things he could turn a blind eye to. But pilfering thirty-five or forty grand off an old lady and her estate, all so a family member could get a half-priced house? If Jack's lawyer did his job properly, he probably wasn't going to go to prison. But he would cop a hefty fine and a community order, and that was exactly as it should be. Philip and Becky would lose their house, but they were young enough to start over again.

His phone rang.

'Sorry, boss,' said Peterson, patching the call through.

It was one of his superiors, Mick Evers from regional command. This was either good news or bad news. With the brass, it was never in between.

'Tom, apologies for ringing so late in the day but I've got a decision back from the board about your transfer request.'

'And?'

'You've been unsuccessful with Tauranga, I'm sorry to say.'

Tom cursed under his breath. 'That's disappointing. But thanks for letting me know. Are you able to explain the reasoning?'

'Not in detail, no. But I expect you'll be able to work it out.'

Tom knew.

'Listen, Tom. I know how hard you worked those two cases. But in the end we're all judged on our results.'

Tom cursed the day Sanna Sovernen ever arrived in town. 'And every result, before and since, that all counts for nothing, does it?'

'Don't push me, Tom.'

Tom teetered on the edge of hanging up.

'There's another option that's sprung up, if you're interested. Not quite Tauranga but if you feel things have run their course in the King Country, it might be worth a look.'

'And where's that?'

'Ruatoria.'

'Don't fucking insult me, Mick.'

'Listen, hear me out. There've been increasingly sophisticated drug operations move into that east coast area. Which, as you know, introduces a range of criminal activity. It's an important role.'

'C'mon, don't give me the Selwyn Toogood treatment! Trying to talk me into taking the bag when it's got a booby prize in it!'

'Have a think about it. Make a couple of calls. You never know, the change might do you some good.'

Tom politely said goodbye and hung up. He was insulted alright – Ruatoria was on the other side of the earth. There was no way of painting a transfer there as a promotion. On the other hand, some of what Mick said resonated. *You never know, the change might do you some good.* Perhaps it might.

There was also the matter of his wife. No way would she countenance a move to a town where people still rode horses up the main street. If he took the job they would be done, nothing surer. He chewed things over. That was hardly a fate worse than death. He would see how he slept and make those phone calls in the morning.

There was another option too, buzzing around the back of his consciousness, like an annoying blowfly. He could deliver the culprit in the Sovernen case. In this game, it was never too late to be a hero. It was really that simple: get a result and his career would be back on track. Then it would be him making the play, not being jemmied across the back blocks to where no-one else would go.

'Peterson,' he called out. 'Can you bring me the Sovernen files?'

'Sir?'

'The ones containing the local suspects. Every single one of those pricks who was at the club the night she disappeared.'

67

Emilia

Emilia had been sitting for almost an hour when Philip returned to the bank. There was another man in tow, a rough, unkempt individual who she could tell, even from a distance, carried a stale, unpleasant odour.

'How was your meeting?' she inquired, politely.

'Don't ask.' His mood had changed from eager and open, to curt and surly.

'This is Slurps. He's coming to the club with us.'

Of course. Slurps was just as Ryan had described him. Definitely not the type to be hanging out with.

'Actually, I decided I'm going to leave now,' she said. 'Thanks for inviting me, but –'

'Oh, come on,' said Philip. 'I've had a really bad day. The least you can do is help cheer me up.'

'Thank you, but no, I changed my mind.'

'Then at least let me give you a ride to wherever you're staying,' Philip insisted.

'Yeah,' said Slurps, throwing his weight in. 'You can never be too sure around here. A year ago a girl went missing, from just up the street. Vanished into thin air.'

Philip tried to catch Slurps' attention, but it was too late.

'Really?' said Emilia.

'I don't think we need to talk about that right now,' said Philip.

'So, what do you think happened to this girl?' Emilia pressed.

'Well, no-one really knows. I reckon she tried it on with a couple of blokes. Probably picked someone up outside the pub, then the sex all went wrong.'

'And this girl was loose with men? You happen to know this?'

'Seems like it,' said Slurps.

Emilia stepped forward and slapped his face. Hard.

Slurps reeled backwards. 'Hey, fuck off!'

Philip jumped in between them.

'You should learn to watch your tongue,' said Emilia, spinning on her heels and storming out, not hearing the rest of their conversation.

Slurps nodded to Philip. 'Jeez. Got a feisty one there, mate.'

'Yeah,' Philip muttered under his breath.

'I like 'em when they're more of a challenge,' said Slurps.

68

Ryan

Ryan got up, dressed quickly and bounded up to Hanigan's woolshed. In the week since the flood, the track had dried out nicely. Final shear in the final shed or not, the catching pens still needed to be full at 5am on the button. Pushing open the main door, hearing its familiar squeak, he paused to reflect on how that sound had been a prelude to hours of pleasure. Momentarily, he tried to imagine Sanna, her shape, her hair hanging loosely, wafting back and forth, gently teasing his face, her twisting and contorting in her moment of release. Instead, he felt nothing. Wherever Sanna was, she was no longer in this shed.

'Morning, Ryan.'

'Morning, boss.'

Carl unwrapped the stained, years-old khaki towel that contained his cutting gear. There was no such thing as easing into it with him. First day or last day, 5am or 5pm, Carl never gave less than one hundred per cent. If this really was to be his final job with the gang, Ryan would miss him. He entered Carl's catching pen, opened the rear gate and began the backfilling process. By the time he was back on the floor, the rousies had arrived, the radio had taken over, and it was down to business.

Ryan eased gently into his work. The start of a new shed was always prime thinking time: no backlog, no undue concentration or exertion required.

He kept coming back to his short list. What was in there that he was missing? Hanigan had spied on Sanna in the shower, that much he knew. And Sanna had told him that somehow he'd found out she was pregnant. And Emilia kept insisting his wife knew something. Which, in some kind of weird way, tied to what Bull had said the night of the flood, about her having the power to save him. He supposed it was possible. What was there to have stopped Hanigan driving into town at night, without anyone knowing? To have been driving past, or waiting in the carpark when Sanna came out of the pub? Nothing, that's what.

And Bull? Ryan had seen Bull sneak out of the bar while the fight was on. And after that, nothing. In all of the mass confusion, the aftermath of the fight, the panic around Sanna not being there, nobody could remember him being around.

What of the group of men who were known to have been at the Workingmen's Club, who left there when it closed, at or around the time Sanna went missing? They had been gathered just a couple of blocks away. Why hadn't the police made more of this? Which one of them was harbouring a horrible, evil secret? Over and over, he ran the names through his head. The same two men kept rising to the top. He remembered what he'd told himself about the police investigation; why they had it all wrong. They were running theoretical formulas and using profiling implanted from who knows where. That was all well and good, but it wasn't a patch on using one's gut. Drawing from local knowledge.

From the group at the club, two names. Terrence Pihama. Gerry 'Slurps' Darlow. Both men were of a different breed. This was the crime of someone out of the ordinary. An innocent girl, a bother to no-one, plucked away without her doing anything to warrant it. Unsuspecting and unafraid, Sanna would have offered not resistance to an approach, but a welcoming smile. That alone made this the act of someone shamefully twisted.

Pihama. Darlow. Both men without female partners. One because he was thought to be a closet homosexual, the other because he was someone no woman with the barest skerrick of self-respect would go near. Neither was a crime, even in Nashville. Both men probably had secrets intertwined with their kinks. Things that might, in normal circumstances, be dismissed as 'it's just their way'. But these weren't normal circumstances. A young woman had been taken. 'Their way' was no longer something to ridicule or joke about. 'Their way' potentially put one of them at the centre of this whole affair.

Above the whirr of the electric motors, Ryan heard the tell-tale squeak of the door. He watched Neville Hanigan make his way past Bull's stand, over to greet Carl.

Pihama. Darlow. Hanigan. Bull. Different breeds. This town was full of people who were off the straight and narrow.

Ryan took a swig of water and tried to gather his thoughts. He had to hone it down. The answer, when it came to him, was blindingly obvious. He would call Philip and take him into his confidence; after all, he knew all of these men. Philip would have a view, and he would be able to help. The fact that it would reunite them as friends was a bonus.

69

Neville

Neville Hanigan watched Carl deliver the final blow and push the last of his flock down the porthole.

'Good bloody riddance,' said Carl, straightening his thirty-three-year-old back. 'Maybe I'm getting old, but I'm telling you, this never gets any easier.'

'We're all getting old,' said Neville. 'At least you're still young enough to do something about it.'

'And you're not?' laughed Carl.

'Well . . .' Neville had an answer, but this wasn't the time.

The two men stepped out of the shed and went down to release the newly shorn sheep from the counting pens; Bull's first, then Pete's, then finally Carl's.

Neville held the gate open just enough for two or three sheep at a time to squeeze out. Embracing their freedom, they bolted and buck-jumped into an open paddock.

'Fifty-seven,' said Carl.

'I made fifty-six,' Neville replied. Carl was an expert sheep counter, as good as there was in the whole of the King Country. 'Fifty-seven, it is. Let's go back up and square it off.'

While the rest of the gang tidied up the last of the wool, Carl produced his invoice book, wrote out his final account, tore the page from its serration and handed it to Neville.

'All good,' said Neville, taking a chequebook from his back pocket and settling things on the spot.

'So, we're square for the shear, less the rent for the quarters?' Carl checked.

'Yes. And thank you again, Carl, it's been another top job.'

'Sweet,' said Carl. 'We're good to go again next year?'

'Next year?' Neville had lost the thread of the conversation for a moment. 'Sure. Next year.'

'Righto then,' said Carl. 'We'll leave you to it. This gang's got some drinking to do and they're expecting me to pay for it!'

The shed bulged with finished bales, although it wouldn't be that way for long: Neville had arranged for them to be collected next week. The wool cheque, when it came, would be useful for Janet; guilt money, he supposed. Hers to keep, to pass on to whoever it was that would have to care for her. The farm would have to be sold, of course. She was incapable of running it, and he'd left precise instructions with the lawyer from Hamilton he'd engaged as to how to proceed. He just wanted to be done with it all.

Janet was in her usual spot in the living-room. He made her tea – milk with two sugars, with two Chocolate Wheaten biscuits on the side. He was in no hurry: he wanted to be sure that all of the shearing gang left before he did. With a 7.30am flight connecting through Singapore, he'd contemplated sitting the night out in the car, but it didn't seem worthy to begin his new life by sleeping rough. The airport motel was cheap, but said to be clean and comfortable. More important was that he remember to post his car key back to the lawyer, so it could be collected before the accumulated parking fee became higher than the value of the vehicle.

He showered, leisurely at first, before grabbing hold of a nail brush and determinedly scrubbing away all of the farm, all of Janet, all of his shame from his body. It hurt, as he knew it would, and looking at himself in the mirror as he patted himself dry, he saw that he was fire-engine red, in some places close to raw. But beyond the pain, he felt a soothing calm. He dressed slowly. Even though his shirt and trousers were old, his body felt different. New.

All that was left for him to do was to pack a small carry bag. His suitcase was already in the boot of the car; he'd packed last night after Janet had gone to bed. The climate in Subic Bay lent itself to thin cotton shirts and shorts. Whatever else he needed, he would buy locally. He threw in a few towels, more to fill the space than anything, and slipped in his favourite book, *Colin Meads: All Black*. He'd met the great man on a couple of occasions, once at a stock sale, and another time over a beer at the wake of a farmer they both knew. This would be his one link to the King Country.

Finally, when it was time, he quietly peered back into his living-room and saw Janet from behind. He preferred it that way; there was no need to see her face again. He slipped out the back door, closing it gently, tossed the carry bag on the passenger's seat, and drove off.

Nineteen years of sweat and grind he'd put into this farm. Neville knew that when news broke, people would say all sorts of nasty things about him: 'gutless', 'uncaring', 'selfish'. And worse. His would be a crime judged more heinous than a backpacker being abducted; he was one of them, doing the dirty. Well, fuck them. Fuck their know-it-all, 'I told you so,' post-mortems at the golf club. Fuck their gossipy chit-chat, at the church hall 'Housie' nights. Half of the town would be shocked and disgusted; the other half would be secretly wishing that they themselves had the gumption to pull off something like this.

It took guts to turn your back on two decades of hard work, to let somebody else come in behind and reap the benefits of that. It took guts to start again somewhere completely new, to start again from the bottom. His life wasn't a popularity contest. They could say what they liked. Janet would be looked after, better than if it was left to him. That was one thing everyone would agree on.

Making good time along the river road, Neville felt at peace with himself and his decision. He wouldn't think about it anymore, what was done was done. By tomorrow night he would be in a new country, starting a new chapter.

70

Philip

Philip heard his father's car pull into his driveway and bolted outside to meet him. He didn't want him inside, involving Becky in any of this.

'You've got a fucking cheek, turning up here,' he said, cutting Jack off as he got out of the car.

'Steady on, son.'

'Whatever it is you've come to say, I don't want to hear it.'

Since the meeting with DI Harten, Philip had been spitting chips. Jack was going to be charged, and he and Becky would lose the house. What could Jack say or do to mitigate that?

'I've come to apologise, son. You should at least hear me out.'

'Listen, Dad. I'm sure you're sorry. Sorry for getting caught. But that doesn't change anything – the damage is done.'

'You know I'll probably lose my trading licence over this?'

'So you fucking should! I really don't give a shit about your licence. Or that old lady's family. Or you doing the dirty on Mum. It's my life you've fucked up.'

'I understand that. But surely you know it was only because I was doing what was best for you?'

Philip grimaced. It was always what his father decided was best for him. It had always been that way and it always would be. Right now, it was the outcome that counted, and the last thing he needed was to be losing his house or having the police sniffing around.

'What did Mum say?'

Jack averted his gaze.

'Another thing you haven't told her, no doubt?'

Jack's silence confirmed it.

'For fuck's sake, Dad. You've always been an interfering, manipulative bastard, but until now, I never realised how gutless you are!'

Jack stammered. 'I'm going to tell her tonight, over dinner. She deserves to know the truth.'

'I'm sure she figured you out years ago. But yeah, if you're gonna be hanging around the house, without a job or a business, then it might be an idea to let her know.'

Jack frowned. 'I didn't come up here to be insulted, son. I came to apologise and talk.'

'Mission accomplished, then,' said Philip, indicating the conversation was over.

'What about Becky? I want to make sure she's alright.'

'She'll be fine, don't worry about her.'

Jack opened his arms. 'Listen, I've been thinking . . . because obviously I don't want you to be struggling, starting off again from the bottom of the ladder. There's another place coming up for listing. Only two bedrooms, but it's solidly built and it's on a good street. I'm sure I could –'

'Dad! Stop it. We're done with all of that. With you sticking your grubby fingers into every little thing we do. It's over.'

'We're family, Philip. Nash blood. More than ever, we need to stick together.'

Philip laughed. 'Maybe you should have thought about that a bit earlier. You can't see it, Dad, but you're the one who's broken this family apart. You've never given me room to breathe. I just never called you out for it. Until now.'

Jack winced, and got back into his car. 'I'll come back again, when you've had time to cool down. In the meantime, don't do anything stupid.'

Philip shook his head. 'You have absolutely no idea who I am, do you? What you've made.'

'Philip . . .'

'Whatever happens, however this turns out, this is all on *you*.'

Philip waved him off and went back inside the house, running into Becky at the front door.

'Was that your father?'

'Yes.'

'Why didn't you invite him in?'

'Because . . .' Philip searched for the right answer. 'Because that would have been stupid.'

'Oh, Philip! One day you're going to have to get over this thing with your father.'

'Don't hold your breath.'

'I wanted to show him the sample bathroom tiles I picked up.'

Philip looked at Becky. He pitied her; she really had no idea. To be fair, that was as much his fault as hers, or his father's. Their relationship was just another stupid thing he'd done with his life.

71

Jack

Being the height of summer, the river was running low. Jack hopstepped across rocks that today were sunning their bellies, when they normally would have been submerged. Finding one of the few freerunning channels, he parked himself on a large rock and dipped a hand into the water. It rushed through his fingers, as effortlessly as the years of work he'd put into Nashville were now flowing from his grasp.

He hadn't expected Philip to receive him well. But that hadn't stopped him hoping for better. It would make Philip angry, but next time he would go straight to Becky. She was more forgiving, and if he could get her to understand his good intent, then perhaps some of that would rub off on Philip.

He'd have to find the right moment to tell Lois; news would be around her women's group soon enough. But not today – he didn't have the right words ready yet. Perhaps tomorrow.

He'd cocked things up, good and proper. His time in Nashville was done; he'd known that from the moment Tom Harten stepped into his office and mentioned Rita Sigsworth. If that was his only concern, he supposed he could cope with it. He and Lois would start somewhere else, living a much quieter life, and perhaps that wouldn't be such a bad thing. It was time to let someone else take hold of the reins.

Which was the heart of his problem. Philip was his flesh and blood. He would continue to love him as any father would love his son, but entrusting him with custodianship of Nashville? That was quite a different proposition.

There were other concerns. What Philip had said earlier, outside his house, that wasn't a Nash talking. *You have absolutely no idea who I am, do you? What you've made.* Philip was deeply troubled. And that troubled Jack.

What was non-negotiable was that Jack might turn his back on the town without there being a transition. As there had been from his father to him, and his grandfather and great-grandfather before that.

He felt for the water again. It was cool but it was clear. Just like his plan needed to be. To ensure the Nash family name lived on.

It was delicate, but it was doable. He would find the right moment to talk to Ryan. Turn the dirty secret he'd hid for years to his advantage. This wasn't all about Philip. After all, he had *two* sons.

72

Neville

Approaching Blind Man's Bluff for the final time, Neville looked up at a lone goat standing atop the cliff face and allowed his mind to wander ahead. Everything he'd seen and heard of Filipino girls told him they were beautiful and willing to please. Natural and innocent, firm and soft in all the right places. How he had wasted his life. If he hadn't messed up with the car accident, if things had gone according to plan, he would have been revelling in sins of the flesh long before now. There was lost ground to make up, although he told himself he wasn't going to be greedy. A nice, relaxed lifestyle, with two or three girls on demand, for whenever he felt the urge: that would be ample.

Dislodged by the goat's hind hoof, the rock slid off the top of the cliff face without any warning. It wasn't huge, the size of a rugby ball, but by the time it reached the bottom of the bluff it had gathered startling momentum. Neville, eyes fixed on the road straight ahead, never even saw it. The rock careered off the vertical face, onto a mound of papa, then sprung into the air, as if propelled from a mini-trampoline, across the verge, straight through Neville's windscreen. The force of the impact immediately jagged his car sharply to the right, and with no guard rail in place, Neville and his car sailed over the edge, and somersaulted metres down into the river below.

WHEN THE DEEP, DARK BUSH SWALLOWS YOU WHOLE

The sudden, deafening tumult gave way to eerie silence. The rock had smashed into the side of Neville's head; he knew he was gravely wounded, but that it wasn't enough to kill him. There was terrible pain charging to all points of his body, but he felt a rush of strength that came from knowing how hurtling off a cliff's edge and smashing into the river rocks below was also not enough to kill him. Surprisingly, in the midst of this tangled, hopeless situation, he felt a sense of pride. He was made of sterner stuff than he'd imagined. But as he lay pinned in his car, upside down, the side of his face sheared away, he realised that pride alone would not be enough. It would be the river that would kill him.

Never before in his life had he prayed, but this was the time. He asked for the end to come quickly. He gathered every last shred of strength, and used it to fight, to keep looking ahead. Desperate, he begged for his final, dying thought not to be of Janet or the farm. Mercifully, when the end came, the water that filled his lungs was the warm, gently rolling tide of Subic Bay.

73
Ryan

Arriving at the pub, Ryan was relieved to find the rest of the gang at a different leaner than last year. Being the anniversary was hard enough, without everyone standing in the same spot, re-enacting it all. They were further away from the pool tables too, which seemed prudent. By all accounts there had been less trouble in recent times. The new publican was a hard nut – an ex-pro boxer from Wellington, the story went – and between him and the police they'd taken to barring the worst offenders. Ryan called bullshit on the boxing; he didn't have the deltoids of a pug, or even a wool presser for that matter. It was the reputation that counted. There was no harm in having people think you were handy.

'Hey, lawyer-boy!' Bull barked across the leaner.

Here we go again, thought Ryan.

'Are you coming back next year?'

'I don't know,' Ryan replied. 'I haven't –'

Bull didn't wait for him to finish. 'You can have my stand. I just heard. The builder starts next month. This time next year, I will be leading the congregation at my church.'

'Good for you,' said Ronnie.

'Pressing's a kids' job. Earn yourself some real money shearing.'

'What's the name of that church going to be again, Bull?' asked Carl.

'The Church of the Oracle.'

'The church of the orifice?' Lacey spat her beer out, delighted at her own joke.

'That's perfect,' said Carl. 'There's only one orifice your sermons are coming out of, Bull.'

They all laughed together, but Bull was immovable. 'Mock all you like, brothers and sisters. I will still pray for your souls.'

'You're tempting fate, bringing that in here.' DI Harten had wandered in and noticed Pete's guitar resting against the leaner.

'I do miss my old faithful,' said Pete.

'We're not expecting any more brawls,' said Lacey. 'Not now you're here to keep the peace.'

'If you're interested, I'm on stage tomorrow. 1.30pm. Be there or be square,' nodded Pete to Tom.

With every year, Nashville's annual country music festival was becoming more popular.

'Country music's not really my go,' said Tom.

Ryan had already made a mental note to be nowhere near the festival stage tomorrow. He felt a gentle tug on his shirt.

'Got a moment?' It was the detective inspector.

'Sure,' he said, stepping to the side.

'The Sovernen girl, Emilia. Is she still at your house?'

'Yes.'

'I've been very patient with her. For her benefit, she should start thinking about going home.'

For *her* benefit?

'I've encouraged her, but the message doesn't appear to have got through. She's been hanging around for a few weeks now, but it's over. We're not putting any more resources into it, and I've got a mountain of other work to go on with. And Emilia should go home and get on with her work too. She's become a pest.'

'A pest? And you want me to tell her this?'

'There's more chance of her listening to you.'

Ryan thought it unlikely.

'Listen, son,' Tom continued. 'I asked you to keep your nose out of things. And you've been sensible enough to listen and not to jeopardise your legal career. Think of this as finishing the job off.'

That was the first thing Tom had said that Ryan agreed with. He needed to finish the job off.

At a suitable time, just before it got dark, Ryan sidled up to Carl. 'I'm actually going to sneak away in a minute. Hope you don't mind?'

'No, mate. You do what you need to do. I overheard what Tom said; you've got a job on your hands.'

Ryan laughed a wry laugh. 'So, what do you think happened to Sanna?' He'd never asked Carl before, not like this. It surprised him, spurting the question out of the blue.

Carl took a moment. 'If I were you, I'd be following Tom's advice.'

'If I did that, I'd be letting Sanna down.'

Carl nodded. 'I see why the spotlight was on some of the locals. The teacher. Slurps Darlow. I get it. But the fact is, the police came up with nothing on them. Zilch. I dunno, with these things, it's often the person you least suspect. What's that saying?' Carl looked at Ryan. 'About hiding in plain sight?'

Ryan paused. *The person you least suspect. Hiding in plain sight.* Was that it? Had he and Emilia been looking in the wrong places?

'Ryan!' Emilia thumped the table so hard the vase of garden flowers she'd made up toppled over.

He laughed at her, which only made her all the more frustrated.

'Why aren't you listening to me?' she tried again.

'I am. Let me finish my dinner first.' Ryan had brought home fish and chips. He hated it when they were allowed to go cold.

Emilia reached for the plastic sauce bottle; shaped like a tomato, with a fat red belly and fake green leaves around the spout. 'You know I think little for New Zealand design and architecture. But whoever designed this is a genius.'

Ryan hoovered up the food like a thoroughbred racehorse refuelling after trackwork. Emilia merely pecked at a few chips. And now she had it in for Slurps.

'I thought you were convinced it was Neville Hanigan?' said Ryan, wiping the grease from his hands and mouth with the butcher's paper wrapping.

'Him too, yes.'

'Well, no, that's not how it works, Emilia. You can't just line up all the guys you don't like and accuse them of being a kidnapper or a murderer.'

'Ryan, you said you would work with me!'

'I am. You just don't see it.'

Emilia went over her meeting with Philip and Slurps at the bank. 'Slurps is a shooter too. They talked about going shooting. He would know exactly where to go in the bush to hide somebody.'

'Everyone around here is a shooter. Deer, pigs, rabbits. It's what you do.'

'Not you. You don't have a gun.'

'Everyone around here except me, then.' He realised it was another thing that set him apart from the locals.

'You told me yourself. He's always been strange. A misfit. And mean. And the hairdresser too, she said she wouldn't be surprised if it was him.'

'Stealing other kids' lunch money and tipping worms down the back of Judith Trengove's blouse? That doesn't make you a murderer.'

There he was again, leading with logic. If he could tap into some of her fire, and combine the two, they'd be unstoppable. 'Let me tell you what I decided. I'm going to talk to Philip. Take him into our confidence. Let him talk to Slurps and see if he lets any small detail slip.'

'Really?'

'Yes.'

'Let's do it then,' she said. 'Call him.'

'It's Friday night. He'll be at the Workingmen's Club. I'll track him down in the morning.'

Emilia leaned towards him. 'The trouble with all of what has happened, with the police, with all of the theories . . . we have this person within our grasp, and we all talk about this and that, but that's all we do. There will never be an outcome if nobody takes the initiative. Nobody puts these suspects under pressure. Nobody makes them feel uncomfortable or forces them into a mistake. As long as everybody sits back at a respectable distance, because that's "the process" or however you want to describe it, then that's as good as sanctioning what happened.'

'This process you mention? It's the law, Emilia.'

'Yes. The same law that has failed Sanna.'

Ryan tidied up the table and washed his mouth again, this time at the kitchen sink. She was right. Nobody local had been put in the frame for the crime because there was insufficient evidence. But there was insufficient evidence because nobody had been put in the frame. That would be his task, to make that happen. So far, they'd just been pissing in the wind; cannon fodder for Tom Harten. But working together, they actually had something. That's why so many of those TV cops were duos. Yin and yang.

'I'll move this along in the morning. I promise.'

'Thank you, Ryan,' she said, grasping his hand. 'You're very sensible.'

'You think so?'

'I'm glad I got to meet you.'

For a fleeting second, Ryan felt Sanna through her sister's fingers. It was welcome and discomforting all at once. He withdrew his hand. 'There's one more thing we need to talk about. Actually, two.'

Ryan explained what Tom Harten had asked him to do, and they shared a dismissive laugh. She would wear the label 'pest' as a badge of honour.

'And the other thing?'

Ryan drew a deep, nervous breath and sat down. 'It's about Sanna. About her having a boyfriend.'

74
Ryan

Festival day dawned bright and sunny, but Ryan had other, more important business to attend to. He ran his finger across the phone directory, stopping when he settled on the number. He lifted the handset and dialled.

'Hello?'

'Becky. It's Ryan here.'

'Oh, hello, Ryan. How are you?'

He hated how her voice changed when she knew it was him. 'Good, thanks. Is Philip home?'

'No, sorry. Well, kind of. He's next door, helping Mrs Thomas start her car with the jumper leads. Do you want me to ask him to call you?'

'Yes, please. Or you can tell him to drop in to my mum's place if you like. I need to talk to him about Sanna Sovernen.'

'The Finnish girl?'

'Yes.'

'But why? What's he got to do with that?'

'Well, nothing. But I'd rather not go into it here, Becky.' He sighed, not wanting to go into anything with her.

'Ryan . . . we're okay, aren't we?'

'What do you mean, *we're okay?*'

'It's just that, with all that's happened between us in the past – all those memories – I just don't want there to be any awkwardness between us.'

A deep and meaningful on the phone on a Saturday morning? With someone he hardly knew? Really?

'Ryan?'

'Becky, listen. I'm hoping I can patch things up with Philip. Our friendship, it goes back too far for us to be arguing or fighting. It's too important.'

'Yes.'

'So, I just need . . . I need you to back off a bit, just relax and let things happen naturally, and all of us will be okay. Understand?'

'I think so.'

'Good.' It had to be said. If he was to repair things with Philip, the last thing any of them needed was her overdramatising everything.

'Ryan?'

He felt her tone shift. More fragile.

'He's not the same person you grew up with.'

'That's okay. None of us are. We all grow up.'

'No, it's more than that. Over the last year, he's changed. All the fighting with his father. There's . . . he just gets so angry about things.'

Ryan felt her vulnerability and chose his words carefully. 'Are you okay?'

'Yes. But . . . I just want things back to normal. That's all.'

Ryan hung up. Everyone knew Philip could be hot-headed. But he'd handled him all his life. Today wouldn't be any different.

75

Philip

Philip bustled through the back door, to find Becky folding towels at the dining table. 'That's the third time I've had to charge her battery in the last month. I think she's waiting for me to buy her a new one.'

'She's eighty-five, Philip. Give her a break!'

'That's either too old to be driving, or young enough to get a new battery fitted. One or the other.'

'Be charitable. When you're that age, you'll appreciate somebody helping you out.'

He grunted, opened the fridge door and guzzled down half a pint of milk, straight from the bottle.

'Philip, whatever it is that's been troubling you, I really hope you get over it soon.'

'What's that supposed to mean?' They were due for dinner at his parents' place on Sunday night. Jack could explain himself then.

'Never mind,' she said. 'Oh, while you were out, Ryan called. For you.'

'Ryan? He rang here?'

'Yes.'

'What did he want?'

'He said he wants you to go to his mother's house. This morning.'

'Really? Did he say why?'

'He said he wants to talk to you about the Finnish girl who went missing.'

'He *what?*'

'Philip? What's that all about?'

'How would I know?' Now they were both confused. 'Listen,' he said, 'just don't start all that shit again. Please.'

'Start what?'

'You know what I'm talking about. We got over that business last time, about Ryan. I don't want to go through all of that again, okay?'

'I'm not starting anything.'

'Good.' On that, at least, they were agreed.

'So?' she said.

'So, what?'

'Are you going to call in and see Ryan or not?'

'No!' Philip stormed into the bedroom, kicked off his jandals and put on a pair of socks and work boots, before grabbing a tracksuit top and heading out the back door.

'Where are you going?' Becky asked, running after him.

'Nowhere,' he shouted, not bothering to turn back to look at her.

76
Emilia

Emilia had slept fitfully, the weight of Ryan's confession tugging her mind in all directions. Knowing the real truth was better than not knowing at all, and that should have made the news more palatable. Sanna had indeed been seeing someone – of course, she had – but she and Ryan managed to keep it a secret before her disappearance, and he, afterwards. The fact he only did so by lying to her didn't sit well. And now, here she was sleeping in Ryan's old bed, probably the same place he had been with Sanna. It made her feel uncomfortable.

Learning of Sanna's pregnancy was a shock. A sad one. Not because she would have had the baby; almost certainly, she wouldn't have. If that was the case, it probably would have remained a secret. Forever, or perhaps until some future event, like the funeral wake of one of their parents, where the siblings would have inflicted drunken confessions on each other.

What really saddened her was that the person responsible had not taken one life, but two. The second had remained unborn, but that was not his decision to make. It was Sanna's, and he had denied her that choice.

She heard a soft rap on the door. Ryan opened it gently, peering in from the doorway.

'How are you doing?' he asked. 'Sorry if that wasn't the night you were expecting.'

'I'm okay. Angry with you, yes, but also pleased to know the truth.' She sensed his relief at her response. 'So, what happens now?'

Ryan rummaged in his bag for a fresh shirt. 'I'm just going to pick up a few things in town, before they start shutting things down for the festival. But I'll be back shortly. I already phoned Philip; his fiancée said she'll get him to drop in this morning.'

That perked her up. She stretched straight back in Ryan's bed, as much as the bowed bedsprings would allow. 'See you soon,' she said.

77

Ryan

With both him and Emilia now at the house, Ryan needed to stock up on food and a few basics. In hindsight, with all sorts of festival activity in town, folk hustling around before the main street was shut down for the day, this wasn't the right time to go shopping. He wanted to be certain of being home when Philip arrived.

Crawling up the main drag, his car ground to a stop near the town square, stuck behind a truck laden with hay bales, the driver in no hurry to reverse and manoeuvre his tray into the optimal position. Ryan spied Jack at the front of the temporary stage, fixing one of his blue and red signs to the structure. Just like everything else in town, the Nashville Country Music Festival had Jack's hand all over it.

Jack noticed him in return, and strolled over. 'Come down to give us a hand?'

'Not exactly,' laughed Ryan. 'Can you give this bloke the hurry up?'

'Actually, if you have got a few spare minutes, we could do with some help unloading this hay.'

He didn't have a few spare minutes, but before he could answer, Jack was directing him to a parking space.

'Jump in there. Promise I won't keep you long.'

With a couple of other locals pitching in, it took fifteen minutes to empty the load and position the bales around the edges of the stage.

Jack wiped his brow and thanked Ryan. 'I'm getting too old to do all this myself now. If you're gonna bow out, you want the last one to be a good one.'

Ryan did a double take. 'Last one? I don't think so.'

'Well, let's just say there's a few changes in the wind.'

Ryan didn't believe what he was hearing. The only way Jack was being dragged out of Nashville was in a coffin. And he was looking as fit as a prize bull. 'Something you want to tell me, Jack?'

Jack paused, like there was. 'No, mate, it's all good.'

Ryan wasn't convinced.

'Take a good look around,' said Jack. 'This will all be yours, one day.'

Ryan laughed. 'I doubt it!' There was something in Jack's tone that was strange, but it would have to wait for now. 'I need to push on,' he said, making for his car.

Jack grabbed for his arm. 'There is something else.'

'What?'

'When's the last time you saw Philip?'

'Why do you ask?'

'So you haven't spoken?'

'No. Why?'

'We've been having a few issues . . . let's just say –'

'C'mon, spit it out. I'm in a hurry.'

'When you see him next . . . um, you'll figure it out.'

'You're not making any sense, Jack. And I really do have to go.'

Ryan scanned across three checkout queues, made his selection, and immediately cursed his horrid decision. He was world class at picking the slowest line. When he finally reached the counter, the elderly lady in front shot him a stink-eye, upset at him crowding her space, trying to cut short what was very probably her only interaction with another human for the weekend.

Over the lady's shoulder, through the large display window, Ryan saw a car go by. Philip. His heart skipped two beats. Was he on his way to the house? The meeting with Philip was his idea, but now, with Jack talking in riddles, the sooner he got home so that he and Emilia could talk with him together, the better.

'When you're finished, love, I'd like to put five dollars into my Christmas club.'

The checkout operator smiled and nodded back at the old lady.

Jesus! Another few minutes down the drain. And for what? Christmas was ten months away. If she made it that far.

The lady fumbled with the clasp of her purse, and paid cash for her groceries, counting out the exact change in coins. Then, from a small plastic bag, she took out a five-dollar note and handed that over, along with a small booklet. The operator took an exercise book from a shelf under the till, recorded the payment, then stamped the lady's booklet.

'There you go, Mrs Winterbottom. Going down the street later to watch the festival parade?'

'No, that's not my thing. All that twangy music.'

Hiding in plain sight.

Ryan transferred his weight from one foot to the other.

'I'm looking forward to getting home to a nice, hot cup of tea and a Girl Guide biscuit. They're my favourite.'

The person you least expect.

Ryan felt his sphincter twitch. Uncomfortably.

'I like to listen to Burl Ives on a Saturday. Or sometimes Perry Como.'

She would never get into a car with someone she didn't know.

Of all the people leaving the club that night, who might have driven past the pub carpark, Philip was the only one that Sanna knew.

'No worries. You have a nice weekend,' said the checkout operator.

'Weekend? I know you mean well, dear, but once you get to my age, you don't know if you're Arthur or Martha. Every day's the same.'

Please! Ryan was beside himself. He shooed the lady away with his hands and quickly paid for his items, shoving the change into his jeans pocket.

'Aren't you going to count it?' said the old lady, lingering unperturbed.

'No.'

'You should.'

It was all Ryan could do not to drop his shoulder into her and clear a path to his car.

'If you want my advice, young man, don't be in such a hurry. It's not a matter of life or death, you know.'

78

Emilia

After she showered, Emilia found an old baggy tee-shirt of Ryan's, barely long enough to provide her with modesty, then took an apple and sat on the front porch to let her hair dry in the morning sun. She had got used to the languid pace of the town; cars sporadically passing by in ones and twos, with only the occasional bike rider or school-kid in between. Apple almost eaten, she supposed she should dress properly, but a car arrived and pulled into the driveway. It was Philip.

'Hello,' she said. 'We were expecting you, but not quite so soon. Ryan is doing some things in town.'

'Oh, is he?' said Philip, walking up onto the porch.

Emilia invited him inside. 'Would you like some tea? I was thinking of making some for myself.'

Philip nodded and sat himself down. Kettle on, she sat opposite.

'So, what is it he wants to talk about?' he asked.

'It's about my sister, actually.'

'Yes?'

'Over the last few weeks we've been looking closely at what happened, we've looked at the police files, spoken to some people and so on, and we believe that we've narrowed things down considerably.'

'Really? You mean like you're conducting some kind of investigation?'

'Well, not officially. But if you put it like that, yes. And it comes down to this. We believe the person responsible is a local.'

'Yes, that was one of the theories,' he said, edging forward.

'And not only that, but on the night, he was drinking at your Workingmen's Club.'

'Really?'

'And that when your club closed, he drove up past the pub, saw Sanna, and somehow enticed her into his car.'

In her earnestness, Emilia failed to notice Philip becoming fidgety.

'And when –'

'I'm sorry,' he interrupted. 'How do you know all of this, exactly?'

She paused. She knew she should be waiting for Ryan, but she couldn't help herself. 'Well, we don't know everything. That's why we're talking to you, because we think you have the answer.'

'Me?'

'Yes. We think so.'

'We?'

'Me and Ryan. We wanted to talk to you first, before we go to the police.'

'The police?' Philip glanced towards the door. 'How long did you say Ryan will be?'

'I'm not certain.' She shrugged. 'Maybe another twenty minutes?'

The kettle started to whistle. Philip held up an arm. 'Stay there, I'll get it.'

Emilia could hear him rustling around in the kitchen. 'Black for me, please. No milk, no sugar.' She sat quietly, staring down at the tablecloth. Ryan's mother had quite a collection of them; every colour and design under the sun. Not her style – she preferred something simple and elegant – but it would have been disrespectful not to keep using them. Philip, she found interesting. He seemed oddly defensive, but he had come here freely, so she was optimistic. With luck, he'd be prepared to talk more about the night, and about his friend Slurps.

She would need to slow things down, though. Make small talk over their tea. Find another topic to soak up time until Ryan returned. Hopefully he wouldn't be too much longer, or be upset with her for starting without him. That was her final thought, at the precise moment she took the blow, unseen, a vicious, single crack to the back of her head. Unconscious before she hit the ground, she never heard the large, heavy, cast-iron frypan fall to the floor alongside her.

79

Philip

Philip took in the scenery on the river road, and afforded himself a moment's respite. It was some time since he'd been down this way, a year he supposed, since the business that night with Sanna. There'd been a few awkward moments since, Slurps taking some persuading that they should try out different forests, elsewhere in the district, for their hunting escapades. The chances were slim, but why risk having him stumble across something he shouldn't?

Glad to be done with his father, Philip drove towards the pub, pulling up at the stop sign. He peered across the road, on the diagonal, and his heart jumped. She was there on the footpath outside the main entrance: the pretty Finnish girl. Pretty seemed inadequate; he'd do her in a heartbeat. Pretty, with a spiteful interior. She'd humiliated him in front of his staff. In a strange way, that only made her more desirable. He noticed she wasn't alone. Someone had followed her out of the bar. He was now embracing her, toying with her hair, kissing her. Of course, it was. Ryan.

Philip proceeded through the intersection, then another two blocks, before he was forced to make a turning decision. His head spun and whirred like a roulette wheel. He could go back to the pub and confront them; that would throw a spanner in the works. Left and he would be on the road home. He tugged down on the steering wheel, his car swung to the right, and instantly he was circling around the block, back towards the pub. This would be a good time to tell Ryan his secret – humiliate him and his dad, to get in before they had an opportunity to talk through the discovery. He also wanted to see Sanna again, to cut her down a peg or two, but it was more than that. Her taut body stirred something inside of him, something that Becky, no matter how hard she tried, had never done.

Finding out he and Ryan were brothers had been surreal; almost too much to deal with. The business with Becky was bad enough. It was humiliating to learn that Ryan had been there before him and, the way she would no doubt describe it, had a place in her heart that she would hold forever. How was he supposed to deal with that? It had been that way all through school. Captain of the rugby team? Lead in the school play? Four boys mucking up in the girls' toilets, fixing Glad Wrap across the bowl – three of them given six of the best with the cane in front of the school assembly, just one let off with a warning. Ryan, of course. Always Ryan. And now, here he was again. The only girl in town worth a second glance, someone he had unfinished business with, and Ryan had muscled in on her too.

If he was being honest, Philip found Neville Hanigan a pitiable man. Nobody with a spine ran out on his wife like that. Especially when she required care. On the other hand, Philip felt honoured that he was the only person in town that Hanigan had confided in, about his plan to walk off his farm and decamp to the Philippines. His instructions were clear. He was to wait to receive Hanigan's telex on Monday, with details of a new bank account set up upon his arrival in Subic Bay, into which Philip was to deposit a sum of money.

The morals were rancid – Philip knew that – but as far as the bank was concerned, the state of the Hanigans' marriage was not their business. No bank played ethical and moral arbiter on how money was divided in a relationship. Neville was sole signatory of the account and that was that.

Crossing Blind Man's Bluff, Philip considered his good fortune in knowing Hanigan's whereabouts. He had left his farm yesterday afternoon, after the shear was completed, and driven all of the way through to Auckland. Philip checked his watch. Hanigan would be in the air right now, somewhere over the top of Australia.

'Fuck!' Philip was jolted by a powerful kick into the back of his seat. Taken by surprise, he momentarily lost his grip on the steering wheel and the car veered sharply across the centre line. He corrected it quickly.

'Shut the fuck up!' he shouted over his shoulder.

A second kick smacked into his seat. He pulled over to the verge, opened the rear door, and spat fire. 'Listen to me. Don't make me knock you out again. *Keep still or I'll do what I did to your sister!*'

She was tightly bound, legs tied together at the ankles and wrists, which he'd set behind her back. The tea towel he'd taken from the kitchen bench was tied into her mouth, stopping her from shouting out or talking. She was going nowhere, but now that she'd regained consciousness, she was annoying the tripe out of him. He needed to get to the farm as quickly as he could. His tyres spun in the gravel as he booted it away from the bluff, not noticing, down below, half of a wheel of an upturned, submerged car, protruding forlornly from the water.

Returning from the other direction, Philip again looked towards the pub doorway. This time there was nobody there. He shifted his gaze across the road. His heart jumped again. She was there, alone this time, standing in the carpark, alongside Ryan's car. He waited for a few seconds; watching, contemplating, role playing. She didn't seem to be in any hurry to do anything, she was just waiting. Waiting for him. He scanned around – there was nobody else in sight, everyone was inside the pub. It was time to balance the ledger.

He rolled his car quietly into the carpark and wound down his window. 'Hello there!' he said. 'Nice to see you again.'

'Oh, hello,' Sanna replied. 'How's business at the bank?'

'A bit quiet, to be honest. Money transfers to Finland have dried right up.'

She laughed at his joke. A good sign.

'On reflection, I might have been a bit short with you,' said Sanna. 'I apologise.'

'All good,' Philip replied. 'Actually, Ryan asked me to drop you off at his place.'

'Really? But –'

'I just saw him inside. We had a quick chat. We're like brothers, you know.'

She nodded. 'Okay. But I've still got Ronnie's car key.'

'No problem, I'll run it straight back down. He just said to look after you, get you home and he'll be there soon.'

Philip hopped out, opened the back door and helped her place her pack across the seat. There was no objection. He glanced around quickly; there was still nobody there to see them. His heart was now pumping double time.

'I suppose I should say, this is an unexpected surprise,' said Sanna, climbing into the passenger's seat.

Philip smiled, to reassure her further. As they started off, he could hear a commotion rising in the background.

'What's all that noise?' she asked.

'Dunno.' He stepped down a bit harder on the gas. 'Maybe a fight? It happens.'

'A fight?'

He saw her concern and tapped her gently on the thigh. A calming gesture. 'Don't worry, you're out of harm's way.'

'But Ryan is in there. What about him?'

'Ryan? He'll be alright. Things always work out for him, don't they?'

80
Ryan

At a half-jog, Ryan lugged the shopping bags in through the open front door. 'Sorry I'm late back,' he called out. 'Picked a really bad day to go out.'

In the moment he realised the house was empty, he felt a quiver ripple across the back of his neck; an eerie, knowing feeling. The moment of realisation his house guest had vanished without good reason. The elderly woman's words rang out in his head, as loud as church bells. *Don't be in such a hurry.* How wrong could somebody be?

He tried to think rationally, but every instinct was telling him something was askew, and it had everything to do with Philip. Emilia could have taken a short stroll, but if she'd walked to town he would have seen her from the car. He ran outside and checked the shed. Then her room; his old bedroom. The bed was unmade, her jeans were draped across the top of her pack, and next to that were her black boots. Emilia never went anywhere unless it was in those jeans and black boots.

Ryan was close to panic. This whole mess was his fault. Philip was different now – he wasn't the same person he grew up with. He didn't know him anymore. He should never have trusted him to be alone with Emilia. The living-room looked normal; there was nothing out of place. So did the kitchen. No, on second thoughts that wasn't normal. Two teacups, with teabags sitting inside. Unmade. Would Emilia have had those ready for when he returned? Unlikely.

He dashed outside to the front verandah and scanned across the street and beyond. It was quiet; no neighbours out in their yards, nobody walking the footpaths. He circled the house again, not knowing what he was looking for, other than something out of the ordinary. Nothing.

Coming from around the rear of the house, past the back door, he stepped under the carport roof. There was something, near where the pebbled driveway gave way to the concrete pad. The pebbles had been disturbed. Noticeably. It was as if something had been dragged across it. Ryan needed to be certain. Was this something he or Emilia had done inadvertently? No, that was impossible. He would have noticed it this morning, when he went to his car.

Ryan ducked inside for his car keys and raced to the police station, running the stop sign at the intersection with the main street, zig-zagging through the steadily building festival traffic. Peterson was manning the counter.

'I'm still not supposed to be talking to you,' Peterson said. He leaned forward and whispered, 'Although I did have a wee word to your house guest the other day.'

'Forget all that. Emilia Sovernen. She's gone missing. Been taken.'

Peterson low whistled. 'Are you sure? I mean . . . like I said, I saw her up the street, earlier in the week.'

'This morning.'

'This morning? Maybe she's gone for a walk somewhere?'

'No, I'm sure,' said Ryan, tersely. 'And I know who's taken her.' Even in his panic, Ryan registered what a shock that was; his old school friend a kidnapper and killer.

'Jesus, that's huge, but I wouldn't want to be ringing the DI unless it's absolutely certain.'

'That's a risk I'm prepared to take,' said Ryan. 'If I'm wrong, you'll never hear from me again, I promise.'

'That might be a risk you're prepared to take, but this is my career we're talking about. I'm on a final warning.'

Ryan looked forlorn. And convincing.

'C'mon then, you'd better tell me what's going on,' said Peterson, taking out his pen and notebook.

Ryan spat the facts as quickly as he could. It didn't sound half as persuasive out loud as it did in his mind, but at least Peterson now knew what was going on.

'Philip Nash from the bank? From the fish and chip shop? Your friend?'

Peterson was only half onboard – Ryan needed something more to tip him over to his side. 'Tell you what. Don't go anywhere. I'll get you some evidence, then I'll come straight back. That okay?'

'I need to have something more solid before I call DI Harten, just so you know.'

Ryan understood. He raced to his car again and hit the gas, his tyres squealing as he accelerated out of a sharp U-turn.

'Ryan!' shrieked Becky, as he blew straight past her into her living-room.

'Sorry for bursting in, but I need to ask you a couple of things.'

'Yes?' she said, more in expectation than fear.

'Philip. Do you know where he is?'

'No, I –'

'This morning. Did you tell him to come to my mother's house?'

'Yes. More or less straight after we spoke.'

'And do you know if he did? Or said he was going to?'

'Well, he said he wouldn't, but I didn't believe him.' She hesitated. 'At least, I don't know for certain. We had a fight and he huffed off in one of his moods.'

'A fight? What about?'

'Um . . .'

'Becky, it's *important*.'

'You. It was about you.' She started crying. 'I don't know why, but it's like he gets really aggressive towards you. What did you do to upset him?' She was trembling, her composure lost. 'Ryan, what's going on? You mentioned it was about the girl who went missing. Is everything okay?'

He levelled with her. 'I honestly don't know. We thought he might know a few things that could help us. That's all.'

'Are you saying he didn't come to your house?'

'Not while I was there, no.'

Becky looked puzzled. Ryan pushed harder.

'Is there anywhere, if you had to guess, that he might go to? The bank? Any place where you think he might be?'

'No. I mean . . . I don't know!' She was too agitated to think straight. 'Obviously, he goes hunting.' Becky dashed into one of the rooms and came straight back out. 'He didn't have his hunting gear with him. And his rifle is locked up in its cabinet.'

'Slurps? Would he go to his place?'

'I doubt it,' she said. 'Not unless he wanted to catch cholera.'

Ryan stopped agitating. He was wasting his time – she didn't know anything.

'Ryan? You're scaring me. You have to tell me what's going on.'

He looked her squarely in the eye. 'Truth is, Becky, I don't know.'

That wasn't exactly true, he realised, making for the door. The sudden ringing of the phone stopped him. He watched on as Becky answered, and saw her face turn stark white.

'Yes,' she said, subserviently. Nervously, she extended the handset towards him. 'It's for you.'

81

Philip

Oblivious to the tall, gently swaying poplars framing the driveway, Philip pulled in close to the entrance to Hanigan's woolshed. Dragging Emilia up the few steps into the shed proved harder than moving her from the house. The ties held fast, so there was no danger of her escaping, but she was a determined wriggler. Not unlike her sister.

Eventually, he lumped her into the shed, and caught his breath. He spied the phone mounted on the wall near the sink, and called home. The fragility in Becky's 'Hello?' told him all he needed to know.

'Is Ryan there?'

'Yes,' she mumbled.

'Put him on.'

Philip manoeuvred Emilia over towards the wool press. She was wearing little of substance: one of Ryan's tee-shirts, no bra underneath. In the act of moving her, he felt the rush that came with his hand brushing her breasts. Momentarily, he considered taking things further. She was there for the taking. Hanigan was gone, his wife would be stuck inside the house, there was no-one within cooee to stop him. But he pulled back; he would wait for Ryan to arrive.

Philip took a fadge from the pile and fixed it inside the box of the press. Then, using a rusted Stanley knife he found near the grinding wheel, he sliced open one of the finished bales, so that wool spewed out onto the floor. He was no expert presser, not like Ryan would consider himself to be, although when was he ever as good as Ryan at anything? He half-filled the fadge with wool, then did the same for the other box. It wouldn't be long now.

82

Janet

Janet sat in her usual chair, although this wasn't a usual day. Neville had driven off last night, without notice; not uncommon in itself, but he had always returned. She'd slept lightly. There was no chance of him having come home late and left again. He always returned home: the dogs needed feeding, and no matter what contempt he held for her, it wasn't like him to let them go hungry. Until now. She recalled the phone call from a year ago, to the lady from the travel agency. This was it. This was the time. Finally.

It made her feel exactly as she had known it would. Strong. And warm. The trauma from the accident was real and it had taken her a long time to come to terms with it. Even now, she didn't quite know where her body and mind were taking her and how full her recovery might be. What she did know was that she had found inner strength. Like on the night of the storm. Whatever force it was that had willed her from her bed and taken her to the shearers' quarters; even if she couldn't quite define it now, she felt confident that this would propel her forward. With or without Neville.

Despite having spent countless hours at the window, she never tired of the view. A benign country landscape, framed by the stand of bush to one side, offset by the peeling white of the woolshed in the centre. It was on days like this when the farm looked at its best – warm sun, gentle not baking, a light fluttering through the poplars, and newly shorn sheep, enjoying their freedom.

It was time to put the kettle on, but as she stood up, she noticed a car approaching the woolshed. It wasn't a vehicle she recognised; not one from the shearing gang, she knew all of those. Curiosity pricked, she watched a man get out, then open the back door. He was pulling and dragging something off the back seat. She couldn't be certain at first: a roll of carpet perhaps, although why would Neville have ordered something like that for the woolshed? Whatever it was, she saw it flip and move, like a fish on a boat deck, in its final, gasping moments before death. That startled her. It was a person! She peeled her eyes and trained them in. The man from the car hooked his arms under the person's armpits and dragged them up the stairs into the shed. Just before they disappeared out of view, it came to her. The hair was familiar. Female. Someone she had seen before. The girl who had walked past her house, then visited her. The girl who was looking for her sister. She was in danger and needed help.

Janet stood over the phone and lifted the handset. She trembled; it was years since she'd spoken on a phone. Since she'd spoken to anyone. Would she be able to speak now? She paused and thought again of Neville, and how ironic the situation was. His leaving would engender much sympathy. Her rock of support gone, how on earth would she be able to survive?

Perfectly well, as it happened. The warm feeling returned and she felt it gently flush to all the extremities of her body. Strength. She dialled the number for the police.

A constable answered. 'Nashville police. Constable Peterson speaking,' he said.

She steadied her diaphragm, drew breath and forced the words out. 'My name is Janet Hanigan.'

'Yes?' said the voice on the other end.

WHEN THE DEEP, DARK BUSH SWALLOWS YOU WHOLE

Tears welled in Janet's eyes. It was nothing short of a miracle. The constable had heard her. She had spoken, and he had heard her.

'A woman is in trouble. Please. You have to come.'

83
Ryan

Ryan had driven the river road hundreds of times, but never as quickly. Like most young men his age, he considered himself a better driver than he actually was; for the most part compliant and safe, but not shy to put the hammer down when it was needed. Like now.

Eyes peeled for oncoming traffic, the white centre line was an irrelevance. Ryan found the apex of every corner, cutting precious seconds off the journey. Knowing he would need to reduce speed once he turned onto the gravel road, there wasn't a moment to waste. Emilia's life was depending on it.

'No police!' Philip had insisted. Emilia would suffer if the police were called. He sounded like he meant it. They would sort things out between the two of them.

What exactly were they sorting out? Clearly, Philip resented how their paths had diverged. Like Ryan had some kind of silver spoon while Philip was a victim? That was nonsense. Perhaps Becky had told Philip about them? Yes, that was just the kind of thing she would do. Thinking she was bringing everyone closer together, happy families and all that.

'Hanigan's woolshed' was the other instruction that Philip barked. Ryan didn't have the time or foresight to ask why. It didn't make a lot of sense – there was no link between Hanigan and Philip that he was aware of. Then again, there were so many things he didn't understand. The choice of location was personal. It was weird but slowly it was coming together. Philip was targeting the sisters, hurting them. But really, he was trying to hurt him.

84
Emilia

Emilia tried desperately to loosen the ties around her wrists, but they were too tight and strong. It was the same with the tea towel; working her jaw up and down had opened the slightest of gaps through which it was easier to breathe, but it wasn't enough for her to be able to talk or scream.

If she was going to die at Philip's hand, like Sanna had died, she'd at least like to know why. What it was that had led this madman to target them. They had done nothing to hurt him, nothing to deserve this. Whatever was troubling him . . . why couldn't he take that out on whoever was the cause of his distress?

'Ryan won't be long now.' Philip's voice filled the woolshed. 'Then we'll see how much he really cares for you and your sister.'

What did that mean? Why couldn't he loosen the mouth tie, just for a few seconds, only so she could ask? Whatever was about to transpire, whatever might happen to her, there was just one thing she wanted. To know what had happened to Sanna.

She didn't need Ryan to rescue her; if she got half a chance she'd fight back against Philip. Surprise and shock him with her will to live. She only needed Ryan so she could speak with him. So that after he arrived, they could talk to Philip and help each other discover that truth.

85

Peterson

It had been a funny morning for a Saturday. Peterson took two pieces of raisin bread from the toaster and slapped a wad of butter onto each. His partner was out and about, following up a couple of break and enters, and he'd done little more than answer an innocuous phone call, swear a statutory declaration and polish his boots. People, it seemed, were too busy preparing for the music festival to bother the police. He'd wander down there later in uniform, for a bit of a squiz, but there wouldn't be any trouble – these kinds of days were always cruisy. Well, that was until Ryan Bradley had come charging in and out, in a flap over the Sovernen girl. He hadn't returned when he said he would, however. Peterson wasn't disappointed. Having it come to nothing was best for everyone.

The phone call cutting into his brunch annoyed him. Until it shook him out of his boots. A conversation with a woman whose only claim to fame was that she didn't talk? That didn't happen every day. And now he was going to have to sell that to the DI.

Peterson chomped into the bread, dribbling butter out both sides of his mouth. He'd used raisin toast before, for inspiration. He didn't know what magical or scientific properties it held, only that it was good thinking food. Except he didn't have much time for thinking. A woman had just made an emergency call. He'd never met Janet Hanigan, only heard about her, like everyone else. He couldn't know for certain if it was her. Did she sound like someone who hadn't spoken for years? How the hell would he know what that sounded like?

Of course, she sounded real. Terrified, in fact. A woman's life was in danger. He couldn't afford to wait any longer.

He punched in DI Harten's number.

The voice on the other end was, not unexpectedly, gruff. 'What is it, Peterson? This had better be good.'

86
Ryan

Ryan pulled off the metal road and drove straight through an open gate. Farm gates were *always* left closed. He crawled past the quarters. It all looked as quiet as it had yesterday, when the gang had left. Up ahead, the woolshed presented itself. He was expecting to see Philip's car, but even so, the sight of it chilled him.

Tiptoeing up the stairs to the shed, he was acutely aware that he had no idea what he might be walking into. Going inside was risky. Dangerous, foolish. But he had no hand. He had to take his chances.

He pushed the door half open with his foot, ignoring its familiar sound.

'Come in, Ryan. Don't be shy.'

The voice came from deeper within the shed, over by the press. He continued on.

'That's enough. No further.'

Ryan stopped, as instructed. He didn't know if Philip was armed, or what state Emilia was in. What he did see was a steely, disturbing look in Philip's eyes.

'Here's what's going to happen,' said Philip, pointing towards Carl's stand. 'You're going to walk over there, to that stand. Go on.'

Again, he followed orders.

'On the timber post, next to the gate, there's a plastic tie, hooked around the pole. You're going to place your right hand inside the circle, okay? Go on, let's see that . . . then with your left hand you're going to yank it tight with one hard tug.'

'Where's Emilia?' Ryan asked.

'Just do it, then we'll talk,' came the reply.

Ryan heard a sound from inside the wool press. Then another, a kick against the timber box.

'You prick. What's she ever done to you?'

'Listen to me, Ryan. Do as you're told, or I can end this for her, now.'

Ryan needed to buy time. That was his and Emilia's best chance, maybe their only chance. If he could get Philip talking, he could figure a way through it. Or perhaps Neville Hanigan would appear? He pulled on the tie and felt it jag into his wrist as it tightened against the pole. Philip gestured to try to pull his hand away; Ryan tried but he was stuck fast.

'Bet you didn't think you'd be seeing this shed again so soon, did you?'

Ryan nodded.

'*DID YOU?*'

'No.'

'Some nice-looking bales,' said Philip, gesturing to the stack that filled three-quarters of the shed. 'Sorry I had to mess one of them up. Maybe you can tidy that wool up after I've finished pressing my bale.'

Philip released the ratchet, took the weight on the handle and swung down on it a couple of times. Ryan watched as the lid dropped a couple of inches, squeezing wool from the upper box, into the bottom.

'You bastard.'

'I forgot to ask your friend what she weighed. But what do you reckon . . . sixty kilos? Fifty-five?'

Ryan was in shock at what he was seeing.

'*What do you reckon? Give me a number!*'

'Fifty-five,' said Ryan. Where the fuck was Neville Hanigan when he needed him?

'Fifty-five, righto. Now Neville, I reckon he's a one-thirty kilo man, which means – and you'll have to trust my maths on this, Ryan – but I'd say that's seventy-five kilos of wool to go in, and then we'll have the perfect bale. Agree?'

'What's this about, Philip?'

'You're the smart lawyer here, I'm sure you can figure it out.'

'I'm not sure I can.'

'*TRY!*' Philip barked, taking the handle again and pumping the lid down another couple of inches.

Ryan heard Emilia's muffled scream.

'Tell me, Ryan, champion wool presser. How many more pumps on this handle before a person's vertebrae crumple and their ribs start popping?'

'What do you want from me?' Ryan pleaded. 'I'll help you. You don't need to hurt her.'

'An apology, Ryan. All my fucking life I've had to listen to my parents, to teachers, even my fucking fiancée . . . All of them telling me, "Why can't you be like Ryan?" Well, I'm fucking tired of it! You've had them all on a string. Becky . . . You know what that does to somebody? No, of course you fucking don't, because you're too busy getting yourself off. Sanna, and now this one . . . all of them, fawning over you like you're some kind of fucking god, when all you do is swan back into town whenever it suits, skiting your head off, looking down your nose at good people, slagging them off. Well, you can shit over other people, I don't give a fuck, but I'm done with you walking all over me.'

Ryan stood there, stunned by the tirade, knowing he was running out of time. 'Philip, whatever I've done, I never did anything because it was to hurt you. We were just being kids. And really, we're still growing up. I only told you the other day, I really want us to try to put all this bullshit behind us. That's what I want, that's what your father wants. I know it's my fault, I've been caught up in my own life. Too caught up in my career. I turned my back on what I had already. And I'm sorry for that.' As he spoke, he caught a glint of metal out of the corner of his eye. Sitting on the shelf was a cutting comb. Carl must have left it there.

'Ah yes, my father. You want to know something about my father, Ryan? I was too ashamed to say anything, but have you ever thought about how you're like the perfect pair, you and him? Him trying to control every little thing I do, squeezing the life out of me, and you, too fucking self-absorbed to even notice.'

'I'm sorry, Philip. I really am.'

'And now, he's gonna get his way. Because I'm not going to play his stupid game and carry the Nash name on like he wanted me to. Because he has someone else to do it.'

'What are you talking about?'

'You, Ryan. Nashville. It's all yours.'

'I don't understa–'

'You're a Nash. All these years and we didn't even know it. You and me. We're brothers.'

'Bullshit.' Ryan tried to take it in. Philip was crazed, he would say anything. That couldn't be true.

'Don't believe me? Ask the old man why he looked after your mother so well, all those years.'

'What?'

'Just ask him, Ryan. Ask him why he's lied to everyone for all our lives. He'll tell you. You and him deserve each other.'

'Philip, whatever the truth of this is, we can sort it out. Just don't do anything silly.'

'I don't care what happens to me. My life's fucked, anyway. I just want you to watch this and, one day, when it's all over and you're the keeper of this stupid fucking town, remember it for the rest of your life.'

Ryan quickly assessed the situation. He needed to get to Emilia.

'That's the funny thing,' Philip continued. 'You think I called you here to kill you. Because you always think it's about you. No. Your punishment will be living under your father's control. I've had my turn, now you can suffer.'

It was now or never. Philip grabbed for the press handle again. As he did so, Ryan took the cutting comb in his left hand, jagged the sharp edge straight into the tie and started sawing at the plastic with everything he had. He didn't dare look up at the press. If Emilia was tucked in a tight ball, she probably had another ten or dozen pumps before it would become too much. They were racing each other now.

Ryan winced with the pain – he was taking as much skin off his wrist as he was plastic. The comb wasn't made for this, and the blood was making things difficult, but there was no time to be delicate. He could sense Philip faltering, not used to the hard, physical work. Ryan was nearly through, but then the comb slipped out of his grasp and clattered onto the floor. He looked across in panic. Philip was hunched over the handle, sucking in big breaths, readying himself for a final effort. The comb was in reach of Ryan's foot. He hooked it across the floor, picked it up and started cutting again.

Finally, it came free. Ryan launched himself across the floor towards the press, but Philip saw him coming, dropped the handle and pulled a grappling hook out of a bale. Ryan stood off and they circled each other like Olympic wrestlers probing for an opening. Ryan needed to be precise – the hook could rip an eye out or tear an artery if he got things wrong. He feigned an attack. Philip swooshed with the hook; left, then right.

Ryan focused on staying nimble, waiting to choose his moment.

'How does it feel to have Sanna's death on your conscience? Eh, Ryan? That was all down to you too, you know that?'

Ryan ignored the taunt. He feinted again and Philip swung once more with the hook, but this time he was slower on the return. Ryan lunged forward and, with the best rugby tackle of his life, took Philip out with a powerful, driving shoulder, pinning him to the floor, sending the hook spinning away out of reach.

Philip bucked and fought in fervent desperation, but Ryan was too well positioned and too well conditioned. Philip threshed some more, but no matter how desperately he fought, Ryan used the strength in his chest and arms to keep him pinned to the floor.

Ryan's concern was Emilia. He couldn't hear her; if her neck wasn't broken she would be close to suffocating by now. He felt for Philip's carotid artery. If he could hold him steady enough to apply direct pressure, he could put him to sleep. He wriggled a little, found the position, then went for it, jamming his forearm down into Philip's neck. At precisely the moment the door to the shed burst open.

He'd never been so delighted to see a policeman. 'In the press!' he shouted, instinctively. 'Get her out!'

Peterson looked quizzically at the press, then threw himself onto Philip instead. 'I've got him, you do it,' he said.

Ryan grabbed for the handle, released the pressure and threw off the wire rope. Tom Harten was alongside him now, and Ryan could see that another constable had joined Peterson. Together they were handcuffing Philip.

'Get him outside!' yelled Tom.

'Stand back!' Ryan cried as he spun the top box out of the way, then feverishly began to pull wool out of the bottom. Throwing his arms back into the box again, he felt not wool this time, but something hard. Emilia's head. Mercifully, it moved. She was alive.

Ryan rushed to remove more of the wool then reached in to untie the cloth that was tightly wedged between her teeth. Emilia let go a huge breath, then began to cough, uncontrollably. And weep. Tears of pain, of horror, of relief; of realisation that she was safe.

'Hang on,' he said, to reassure her. He unlocked the side of the box, pulled Emilia out, then he and set to work on untying her hands and feet.

Finally, they were done. For a few moments the shed fell starkly quiet, Ryan and Emilia slumped back against the wool press, hunched tight together, Tom standing over them. Blood was still seeping from Ryan's wrist.

'Stay there, I'll get a bandage from the car.' The detective returned, seconds later, surveying the scene. 'Jesus, what a fucking shitshow.'

'Just like your investigation?' said Ryan.

Emilia squeezed his good hand, in appreciation.

'Nice tee-shirt,' he said, gently squeezing back.

87
Janet

Janet noticed the policemen first. Soon after, Emilia was brought from the shed and she sat down on the grass outside. Watching her, now safe, Janet tingled with satisfaction and pride; a feeling she had long been unfamiliar with. A quiet personal joy she didn't know she was capable of experiencing.

She wondered if she should walk down there, to help comfort her; after all, she had endured a terrifying experience. But the other men were there – more police – and besides, it was already too much for one day. Being free of the farm, free of Neville, it was a lot to take in. Conversing with other people, that would all come, but it would happen in good time – when she eventually felt strong enough and had support around her. So long in isolation, so long repressed, you didn't just open your arms, embrace the world and dive back in as if it was an everyday, natural thing to do.

She went to the kitchen and filled the kettle. The police would be up at the house soon enough. She would make them a nice, hot cup of tea for their trouble.

Perhaps they would want to know when Neville would be arriving home? She smiled to herself. Everything inside her told her that she'd never see her husband again. Perhaps she wouldn't mention the Philippines to the police, at least not today. It looked like they already had a lot on their plate.

88

Ryan

Ryan lifted Emilia's pack out of the back of his car and set it down on the footpath.

'Town's quiet for a weekday,' he said.

Emilia laughed. 'This is *every* day.'

He would be back here tomorrow, to catch the train to Wellington, and from there, a flight south. He was already a few weeks late for the start of the semester, although the police had helped out by contacting the faculty to explain his absence. As far as excuses went – the terrible business with Philip – it was a pretty good one. Philip's arrest had been all over the national news, but Ryan had made it clear he wanted no part of any fifteen minutes of fame. Getting back to his studies and rugby training would do him just fine.

They walked up the rise onto the platform. Save for the old man in his blue New Zealand Railways uniform, it was empty.

'Hello, miss,' said the man. 'Have a safe trip home.'

'Thank you,' said Emilia.

'Auckland train is on time. Five minutes,' he said.

Ryan was glad for them having done their talking already. He and Emilia were bonded through Sanna and through their own shared experience. They had worked through everything together with the police and, over the last two weeks, for hours on end, on their own.

They were as one, but they also had their lives to get on with. Ryan admired Emilia for all she had done, and told her so.

She was returning home without Sanna, but with certainty that the person responsible would be held to account. There were moments when she had marked herself down, but that was nonsense. Her visit and intervention was a triumph. In the days since his arrest, Philip had been unco-operative, and Ryan had cautioned Emilia that, being the type of person he was, the frame of mind he was in, he was unlikely to ever divulge where Sanna was and what he'd done to her. That mustn't be allowed to diminish what they had achieved. Sanna was now at peace, that was all that mattered.

Ryan had battled his own demons too. In his desperation on the woolshed floor, Philip had tried to pin Sanna's death on him. That would haunt him forever if he let it. Emilia helped him through that, as he had helped her. It was cruel and untrue, she said, Philip was merely trying to avoid taking responsibility for his own actions. Messing with his head. Emilia made Ryan promise not to think that way again. He said he would do his best.

'It's ironic, isn't it?' she explained. 'Your friendship was never worth saving in the first place. But because you tried, you saved me, and we found justice for Sanna.'

She was right. Those chapters were closed.

'Look,' said Emilia, pointing down to the street.

Ryan turned to see Ronnie's huge beast, the orange Valiant Charger, pull in. Ronnie made her way up the ramp, carrying a small parcel, wrapped in tin foil.

'I made some fresh scones for the train,' she said. 'There's date, and cheese and bacon. With some creamy New Zealand butter.'

'Thank you,' said Emilia, smiling warmly as she accepted them.

'Did you slip a few slices of roast mutton in there?' joked Ryan.

'I'm done with sheep for a while,' said Emilia.

They all laughed, before the old man approached them again.

'I see you've met my dad,' said Ronnie.

The sound of the train arriving cut short the conviviality.

'Carriage three,' said Emilia, counting the cars out and walking to the spot. Ryan followed a step behind, with her pack. It was all over. There was time for one final embrace, and he felt himself beginning to choke up. This was the farewell he should have had with Sanna; the goodbye that Philip denied them. Emilia boarded, he heard the sound of a whistle, and moments later he was waving to her in the window, and then, as the train picked up speed, he was waving to a steel blur, and then to nobody.

Ryan turned towards his car and took a moment to look up and down the main street. Across the road, next to the cinema, he saw two workmen on a ladder, dismantling the 'Jack Nash Real Estate' signage from atop the awning. Jack had taken things badly. Coming on top of his own arrest for fraud, it was unthinkable he could remain in town. Through Emilia, Ryan had a sense of the horror faced by parents who have a child murdered. He imagined the only thing that might come close was to be the parent of a murderer.

Parent of a murderer . . . it was out of respect to Lois that Ryan chose not to confront Jack about his parentage. With everything that had happened, why make her life any more miserable than it already was? Ryan didn't know where the Nashes were headed, but as long as there was a kitchen, Lois would keep both of them well fed.

Ryan thought again of his mother. She had told him no good would come of him finding his father, and she was right. He'd been numb for days. About Philip and what he did to Sanna, and about Jack's dirty secret. Perhaps one day he would want to talk it through with Jack. Somewhere into the future. There was a time once when he thought it important he know who his father was. Now that he knew, it didn't seem to matter.

Ryan scanned up and down the main street again. The Nashville he'd grown up in was laid out in front of his eyes. He knew every shop, every lamppost, every crack in every footpath. The town had an atmosphere that clung to his body; familiar and intimate. It was a feeling unlike any from anywhere else he'd ever been. And now, to top it all off, he was a descendant of Thomas Nash. Indisputably, Nashville was his town.

He walked to his car. Tomorrow it would be his turn to take the train, heading the opposite way. Nashville was no longer his town.

The sign caught Ryan's eye again: 'Jack Nash Real Estate'. Nothing ever happened in Nashville without Jack's fingerprints being all over it. *Nashville was no longer his town?* Who was he kidding? As always, Jack had seen to things. With him and Philip now out of the picture, he had Ryan just where he wanted him. He was a Nash. There was nothing else for it. Whatever happened from here, Nashville would always be his town.

November 1983

89
Slurps

The undergrowth was heavy, thick with thousand-year-old ferns and masses of tree roots, spearing in all directions, twisted and intertwined as if a playful kitten had been let loose on a skein of wool. Even so, for a skilled, natural-born hunter like Gerry 'Slurps' Darlow, there was no impediment. This was his terrain, and he glided across the floor of the bush like an Olympic skater on ice.

His one disappointment was that, today, there were no deer to be found. He shrugged it off. Hunting was an optimist's pursuit; he would have better luck next time.

In a small clearing, he paused to catch breath and took a swig of water. Hunting solo wasn't everyone's cup of tea, but he'd come to prefer it. Since Philip's trial and conviction, he'd put a quiet word around the club for anyone who might be looking for a new hunting partner, but he'd received no nibbles. He didn't take it personally, just as he didn't care about being asked to 'un-volunteer' from the fire brigade. Most everything else he did in life was on his own, and that suited him fine.

Philip had been a decent mate, the only proper friend he'd ever had, truth be told. But his arrest, the whole story coming out at the trial . . . it just went to show, you could never really know what went on inside another man's head.

Slurps peered up through a gap in the foliage, to get a gauge on the weather. A blanket of grey cloud had enveloped the canopy, and now that he'd stopped, a cool nip on his neck told him the temperature had dropped by a couple of degrees. He would call it quits for the day. This bush wasn't going anywhere and he would be back around soon enough for another crack.

He leaned on a beech tree with his left hand, supporting himself while he tugged at his sock with his right. It was only a short walk to his ute from here; he might even call in to the club for a couple of beers on the way home.

It was a nondescript, medium-sized beech, just like hundreds of others in this reserve, dotted in amongst grander, taller native species. Slurps pushed away from the tree and started off in the direction of his utility. On the other side of the trunk, just inches away from where his hand had been resting, draped over a spur, was a black, waxed string band. From it, hung a greenstone pendant. Pikorua.